Domesticated Bachelors
and Femininity
in Victorian Novels

# Domesticated Bachelors and Femininity in Victorian Novels

JENNIFER BEAUVAIS

McFarland & Company, Inc., Publishers
*Jefferson, North Carolina*

LIBRARY OF CONGRESS CATALOGUING-IN-PUBLICATION DATA

Names: Beauvais, Jennifer, author.
Title: Domesticated gentlemen and femininity in Victorian novels /
Jennifer Beauvais.
Description: Jefferson : McFarland & Company, Inc.,
Publishers, 2020. | Includes bibliographical references and index.
Identifiers: LCCN 2020024590 |
ISBN 9780786460366 (paperback : acid free paper) ∞
ISBN 9781476639628 (ebook)
Subjects: LCSH: English fiction—19th century—History and criticism. |
Bachelors in literature. | Masculinity in literature. | Dandies in literature.
Classification: LCC PR878.B34 B43 2020 | DDC 823/.809353—dc23
LC record available at https://lccn.loc.gov/2020024590

BRITISH LIBRARY CATALOGUING DATA ARE AVAILABLE

ISBN (print) 978-0-7864-6036-6
ISBN (ebook) 978-1-4766-3962-8

Front cover image © 2020 Shutterstock

Printed in the United States of America

McFarland & Company, Inc., Publishers
Box 611, Jefferson, North Carolina 28640
www.mcfarlandpub.com

# Acknowledgments

This book is based on research inspired during my master's and doctoral studies. I am grateful to my English literature professors at both Concordia University and the University of Montreal for their encouragement and for introducing me to the wild world of the Victorians. This book could not have been completed without the insight and careful editing of Prof. Michael Eberle-Sinatra, Prof. Jason Camlot, and Prof. Dennis Denisoff. I am appreciative of the generous funding from SSHRC, the Faculté des Études Superieures, and the Département d'études anglaises. I am also grateful for the patience and feedback from the editors at McFarland.

I am fortunate to have been inspired by the enduring friendship of strong, intelligent, and thoughtful women as I worked on this book. I wish to thank Dr. Stephanie King, Dr. Anna Lepine, and the rest of the Victorian Reading Group, as well as friends and colleagues whose conversations provided motivation and insight over the years. I owe profound gratitude to my parents, Beverly DeCarlo and Ronald Beauvais, who have instilled in me their passion for learning, respect for education, and love of reading, which I hope to pass on to my son, Felix. I would especially like to thank my husband, Jason Taylor, who bravely witnessed firsthand the entire writing process, for his unwavering support, positive outlook, and infinite patience especially in the final stages.

# List of Abbreviations

DG      *The Picture of Dorian Gray* by Oscar Wilde

J&H     *The Strange Case of Dr. Jekyll and Mr. Hyde* by Robert Louis
        Stevenson

WH      *Wuthering Heights* by Emily Brontë

LAS     *Lady Audley's Secret* by Mary Elizabeth Braddon

DD      *Daniel Deronda* by George Eliot

# Table of Contents

# Introduction:
# The Domesticated Bachelor

> The bachelor again is perfectly free: he can go to a friend's house, or to the play with an oyster to follow, or to his club, and he has no haunting dread of black looks and angry word reproaching him with his selfish excess. A latch-key is his open sesame [...] and he turns into bed with the pleasing consciousness of having injured nobody by his pleasures. Poor Brown, who shared his evening, will have a different story to tell. His latch-key was useless, but the noise he made in trying it brought out Mrs. Brown [...] clad in spectral white, shawled, nightcapped, and ghastly ["Marriage Versus Celibacy" 291].

The nineteenth-century bachelor holds the key to open most doors, which allows him to move freely within society while also stepping outside of it in order to provide criticism. This 1868 excerpt from "Marriage and Celibacy" is an ideal example of the stereotypical view of the bachelor's life as full of excess, pleasure, and freedom from domestic responsibilities. While many Victorian novelists and contemporary literary critics remain attached to this image of the bachelor, it is imperative that the bachelor be acknowledged for his ability to move stealthily between the gendered private and public spheres and define his own domestic space devoid of the "spectral" and "ghastly" female presence.

The nineteenth century eventually came to acknowledge women's participation outside of the private sphere, but little attention has been paid to the domesticated bachelor who sought to fill the space they left behind. The Victorian gentleman's appeal towards inhabiting the domestic is a reaction to the anxiety created by the shifting and elusive definition of nineteenth-century masculinity. His early attempts to "fit into" the domestic involve the performance of femininity—the type of femininity Victorian women were striving to move beyond, as evidenced by such social

1

movements as the Infant Custody Acts of 1839 and 1886, the Matrimonial Causes Act of 1878, and the "Woman Question" of the 1880s and 1890s. The pairing of the masculinized female and feminized bachelor are requisite for experimenting with gender performance that allows for the fluid movement between the spheres. While the masculinized woman stretches her reach beyond the private sphere, the domesticated bachelor has access to her boudoir and begins to play her part. By the *fin-de-siècle*, the New Woman[1] was secure in her critique of patriarchal privileges leaving the domestic arena abandoned. At the same time, the domesticated bachelor achieves his own form of liberation by creating a domestic space that does not require the female presence. The "angel in the house" exemplifies the ideal of femininity which was impossible to attain. Over again, the bachelor seeks out these ideal qualities in the women around him, but is disappointed. Instead, as we see in *Daniel Deronda* and *Lady Audley's Secret*, he tries to reenact or perform this role himself. The term is problematic here since he is not held up on a pedestal for worship by anyone, but his attempt to perform these qualities must not be overlooked. As a result, the bachelor creates this new space, and goes beyond simply performing and mirroring aspects of the private sphere; instead, he recreates it by combining the homosocial with the domestic. In the reconfigured sphere, the domesticated bachelor is both "angel in the house," through his use of feminine discourse, and "man about town," maintaining his gentlemanly status.

The domesticated bachelor expands the concept of Victorian masculinity to include men who are not married, but experience the domestic by, at first, experimenting with performing femininity, and eventually redefining the domestic sphere. By the end of the nineteenth century, the bachelor has challenged the Victorian definition of masculinity, which requires that he marry, procreate, and support his family. In *Shirley, Lady Audley's Secret, Daniel Deronda, The Strange Case of Dr. Jekyll and Mr. Hyde*, and *The Picture of Dorian Gray* the domesticated bachelor is represented by his dual natures, gentlemanly status, ability to perform, and his reconfiguring of the private sphere. The domesticated bachelor surrounds himself with elements of the domestic, including comfort, security, virtue, values, femininity, and family. Although performing femininity, it is important to acknowledge the bachelor's success at achieving a new type of domesticity and not simply mirroring the traditional Victorian domestic space. He achieves this by creating a space where the bachelor can achieve his full masculinity without the typical Victorian familial elements. The figure of the domesticated bachelor requires a re-examination of the nineteenth-century concepts of masculinity, the separation of the spheres, and performance.

The evolution of the bachelor is reflected in the literary genres of the novels chosen for this study. Charlotte Brontë's use of industrial and the domestic novel genres in *Shirley* are effective in introducing the domesticated bachelor. The novel awkwardly shifts between these two genres, which the characters mirror with their jarring movements between the public and private spheres, in an early attempt to address the confusion and reimagining of masculine and feminine spaces. George Eliot also attempts to combine a love plot and realism in *Daniel Deronda*. Critics, including Leavis, found the combination of these two genres awkward and considered separating them into two sections. As in *Shirley*, the bachelor moves between these two genres, but in Daniel Deronda's case, he becomes the racial Other. The sensation genre presents the bachelor as suspicious and the Gothic considers him a social threat. The sensation genre and particularly Braddon's *Lady Audley's Secret* exposes the gruesome details of the gender power struggle occurring during the mid–nineteenth century. The gothic genre presents the domesticated bachelor as the criminal Other as we see in *The Strange Case of Dr. Jekyll and Mr. Hyde* and *The Picture of Dorian Gray*. By the *fin-de-siècle*, the bachelor's inclination to move freely between the spheres is problematized and considered monstrous behavior. As a result, Robert Louis Stevenson's all-male community in *The Strange Case of Dr. Jekyll and Mr. Hyde* allows the bachelor to create his own space without female intervention. As is characteristic of the Gothic, rather than a battle of the sexes, power struggles are internalized within the bachelors themselves. Moving from realism and the domestic novel, to sensation and the gothic, the domesticated bachelor evolves towards his own space. At first, he awkwardly moves between realism and the marriage plot through his performance of femininity; he then does battle with the New Woman[2] in the sensation genre demonstrating his desire to rid himself of the female presence; finally, as the Gothic Other he is considered a threat to social order and succeeds in creating a space of his own that calls into question the Victorian concept of masculinity and domestic space.

The pairing of masculinized female characters and domesticated male characters in *Shirley*, *Lady Audley's Secret*, and *Daniel Deronda* explores how both genders experience the pressures of social expectations resulting in a form of role reversal. Similar to the Victorian woman, who is expected to acquire an education only to improve her position as "helpmate" to her husband, the gentleman must secure a balance by controlling his masculinity in favor of sensibility when the situation arises. Selecting the appropriate time in which to repress his masculinity or exert more aggressive behavior is also an important aspect of the Victorian gentleman. Domestic bachelors struggle to maintain a balance in their performance of feminine discourse; the failure to do so results in effeminacy. The definition of the gentleman involves moral responsibilities, like the angel in the house. The main difference between these two socially prescribed paragons of femininity and masculinity is that the gentleman appears to be excused from his failure to become the ideal because of the debate about whether the nature of the gentleman was a natural or learned behavior, which suggests a double standard. Karen Volland Waters notes how men who admitted failure were encouraged simply to attempt to acquire characteristics of the gentleman, "insofar as possible, through imitation of his superiours" (29). Whether through performance or an innate condition, the sexes were presumed to conform to these societal expectations. By the mid–Victorian period, legislation, as well as literary genres, openly reflected the changing attitudes towards gender roles and the rising criticism of the patriarchal system in England.

The bachelor has proven himself resilient and unique in his ability to maintain the crucial balance between the public and private spheres. The bachelor gains access to the domestic sphere of women and marriage while being worshipped by men as representing the ideal of masculinity, and yet he remains elusive to both. This fluid and usually unhindered movement from the private sphere gendered female and the public sphere of men and masculinity makes the bachelor an interesting figure for successfully maintaining this crucial balance. The bachelor's movements between the spheres brings into question the concept of masculinity and a new understanding of manhood. Simultaneously living inside and outside the social circle gives the bachelor a unique perspective on society, especially its social mores; as Katherine V. Snyder states, the bachelor "confound[s] these ordering binarisms of masculine, bourgeois, and domestic life, at once demarcating and crossing the lines that mark the boundaries of these realms" (54). Crossing borders is what defines the bachelor and allows him to remain an ambiguous and fluid figure throughout literary history. His extreme counterpart, the dandy, clearly discards any semblance of masculinity in his attempts to cross the boundaries and is marked as a symbol of ridicule for nineteenth-century readers.[3] The masculinity that the bachelor maintains has the appearance of society's concept of maleness, but he also carries with him more feminine qualities, which in his

4

earlier incarnations allowed the bachelor to enjoy the company of women without risking their reputation.

The dandy reappears in the *fin-de-siècle* embracing his sexual ambiguity and reveling in the freedoms associated with separating himself from social conventions and indulging in an all-male community. Dennis Denisoff provides insight into the complex nature of the dandy-aesthete in *Aestheticism and Sexual Parody 1840–1940*:

> Dandies were people—primarily men—interested in fashioning themselves as art, with the process of artistic commodification leading to a major accord between presenting oneself as art and presenting oneself as valuable [...]. In the eyes of most of the public, they could pass as "ladies' men." And yet, the aura of sexual mystery that surrounded the dandy-aesthete also encouraged them to sustain some representation of what they saw as a crucial difference. Sexual ambiguity became inscribed upon the persona as a characteristic hyper-awareness of performed and assumedly actual identities [7–8].

While his sexual ambiguity, skillful performances, and ability to "pass as a ladies' man" are also appropriate characteristics of the domestic bachelor, this book chooses to exclude the figure of the homosexual for the reason that he falls into another category entirely. There is an interest in the qualities that define the domesticated bachelor and while his sexuality is uncertain at times, whether or not he is clearly homosexual is not the focus here.

Donald G. Mitchell's *Reveries of a Bachelor* (1849) emphasizes the luxurious freedom of the bachelor life, which includes the domestic space of the home. Mitchell's emphasis is on the lack of the feminine with its deception and manipulation in contrast with the truth and boldness of the bachelor:

> But what a happy, careless life belongs to this Bachelorhood, in which you may strike out boldly right and left! Your heart is not bound to another which may be full of only sickly vapors of feeling; nor is it frozen to a cold, man's heart under a silk bodice—knowing nothing of tenderness but the name, to prate of; and nothing of soul confidence, but clumsy confession [54].

Bachelorhood, as described by Mitchell's narrator, involves complete freedom, both physical and emotional. Not only is the bachelor free to "strike out boldly," which Mitchell's narrator demonstrates through his mistreatment of his house, but he is also free emotionally by not being "bound" to another, who carries with them the possibility of misery, pain, and disappointment. The bachelor in *Reveries* possesses a vivid imagination, which allows him to safely explore his life as husband without

5

leaving the comfort of his fireside armchair and cigar. The bachelor's ability to remain on the outside looking in, gives him a sense of superiority and power. Mitchell's bachelor believes he can simply imagine his future as a husband, and save himself from committing such a crucial error before it is too late. The home is a sanctified space where the bachelor revels in his freedom without the presence of the feminine. His tone expresses his sense of good fortune as he boasts of his unique ability to avoid marriage. The exclusively male domestic space present in Mitchell's *Reveries*, and Stevenson's *Dr. Jekyll and Mr. Hyde*, requires that the bachelor substitute for the lack of a feminine presence through his incorporation of both masculine and feminine characteristics.

For this reason the bachelor figure is considered a threat to nineteenth-century bourgeois society. His delay or refusal to marry exasperates the problem of "redundant women," and in some cases he may even practice celibacy. Francis Power Cobbe observes in her 1862 article, "What Shall We Do with Our Old Maids?" how,

> we cannot but add a few words to express our amused surprise at the way in which the writers on this subject constantly concern themselves with the question of *female* celibacy, deplore it, abuse it, prose amazing remedies for it, but take little or no notice of the twenty-five percent old bachelor (or thereabouts) who needs must exist to match the thirty per cent old maids. Their moral condition seems to excite no alarm, their lonely old age no foreboding compassion, their action on the community no reprobation [...]. But of the two, which of the parties is the chief delinquent? [91].

Cobbe addresses society's unequal treatment of female celibates in comparison to male bachelors and how marriage is no longer a woman's only pursuit in life. Anxieties surrounding the spinster are similarly raised in reference to the bachelor, except an important difference is his ability to contribute to the economy and society through the public sphere. Yet, as an 1886 article "London Bachelors and Their Mode of Living" reveals, the bachelor still suffered social ostracism concerning his refusal to marry:

> bachelors, it cannot be denied, have an ill name. If marriage is a warfare [...] a good many of the shots from matrimonial guns are directed against those who remain single. It is suggested that the bachelor lives for happiness, whilst the married man is animated by the thoughts of duty, that the one has an eye only for self, whilst the other sacrifices himself for wife, children, and the world in general. There is no reason, however, why a man should not live a bachelor from wise and creditable motives [240].

Without domestic responsibilities, the bachelor is described as a figure of luxury, excess, and self-indulgence, and according to the nineteenth-century concept of masculinity, the bachelor is an incomplete figure who indulges in excess (Tosh, *Manliness* 38, 71). What is interesting is how bachelors, who through "wise and creditable motives," succeed in achieving their full masculinity as participants in both the public and private spheres. Victorian society did not acknowledge the domesticated bachelor since he refused to follow gender expectations, threatened sexual excess,[4] and destabilized established definitions of masculinity. The possibility of sexual transgressions is evident since there is no way to monitor their activities. Vincent J. Bertolini refers to "the transgressive triple threat" of masturbation, whoremongering, and homosexuality (708), which surround the unmarried, solitary adult male. Brontë, Braddon, Eliot, Stevenson, and Wilde use the bachelor as representative of an alternative to conventional gender roles, and like his female counterparts, the spinster and New Woman, the nineteenth-century bachelor was considered a threat to social order.

There are dangers for a man living alone for years without a womanly influence. In 1868, the Royal Commission on the Law of Marriage compiled statistics over a two-year period comparing the proportion between the death-rates of married and of unmarried men in Scotland. The table below illustrates their findings per thousand of married and unmarried men.

| Ages | Husbands & Widowers | Unmarried |
|---|---|---|
| 20 to 25 | 6.26 | 12.01 |
| 25 to 30 | 8.23 | 14.94 |
| 30 to 35 | 8.65 | 15.94 |
| 35 to 40 | 11.67 | 16.02 |
| 40 to 45 | 14.07 | 18.35 |
| 45 to 50 | 17.04 | 21.18 |
| 50 to 55 | 19.54 | 26.34 |
| 55 to 60 | 26.14 | 28.54 |
| 60 to 65 | 35.63 | 44.54 |
| 65 to 70 | 52.93 | 60.21 |
| 70 to 75 | 81.56 | 102.71 |
| 75 to 80 | 117.85 | 143.94 |
| 80 to 85 | 173.18 | 195.40 |

# Introduction

These numbers reveal the discrepancy between the deaths of married men and their bachelor counterparts, especially between the ages twenty to thirty-five years when the numbers almost double. Dr. Stark, Registrar-General for Scotland, is credited as being one of the first to raise concerns around these statistics. He concludes, based on the results above, "that bachelorhood is more destructive to life than the most unwholesome trades, or than residence in an unwholesome house or district where there has never been the most distant attempt at sanitary improvement of any kind" ("The Ladies' Column" 11). The application of this type of moral discourse to compare the bachelor's lifestyle to that of an indecent lower class serves to place these usually distinct social positions on equal terms. The choice of bachelorhood is compared to choosing an immoral and base lifestyle. The mortality statistics and Dr. Stark's comments insist on associating the bachelor with the most dangerous, corrupt, and unhealthy circumstances. In addition to the dangers of an early death and sexual transgressions, the bachelor's mental health is also at risk.

Loneliness is credited as the instigator for many of the bachelor's dangerous pursuits, as well as the flourishing of eccentricities. A lack of companionship can drive the bachelor to seek the comfort of a prostitute. "Good principles and common sense" ("London Bachelor" 487) are necessary for the bachelor to avoid this dangerous lifestyle, but loneliness also breeds strange behaviors. The bachelor, who has lived alone, can develop eccentricities, such as instances of paranoia, obsessive compulsive disorders, hoarding, and other less serious quirks. One of the cases involved a man whose paranoia forced him to seal up his portmanteau, drawers, and cupboards when he left. Another bachelor never destroyed anything, and obsessed over having a place for everything. The next bachelor's "mania" was to encourage mice, while another collected ancient skulls. Then there is the bachelor who claimed he would take a lodging for years, but never stayed more than one week in any one place ("London Bachelors" 488). The author of "London Bachelors" goes on to describe other examples of odd behavior which he claims results from a solitary life: "men whose peculiarities might perhaps have thriven anywhere, but never certainly to such an extent as on the fertile soil of an isolated life" (488). Companionship puts these eccentricities in check, while the bachelor's ultimate freedom from restraint allows these "manias" to thrive. Masturbation was also considered a physical and psychological danger for the nineteenth-century bachelor. Diane Mason credits the Victorian period as "the era which not only consolidated masturbation's status as a condition of grave scientific and medical importance but during which the paranoia about the practice was at its height" (4). The Victorian masturbator is described as egotistical, insensible to the feelings of others, without moral nature, and lacking of mental and physical energy (Skultans 86); he is a figure of "public scorn, derision, pity, fear" (Laqueur 64). He has an absence of manliness in appearance, no desire for "natural intercourse," and is sure to break off an engagement in marriage (Skultans 87, 90). This description of the insane masturbator demonstrates a complete refusal to adhere to social conventions, which demand an active lifestyle, career, and a desire to marry and procreate. The patients described in nineteenth-century masturbation case studies are usually about eighteen years of age and simply rebelling against impending social responsibilities. There is little mention of the mental health of bachelors in connection with masturbation, although this issue is obviously present in the rejection of the bachelor lifestyle. Diane Mason in *The Secret Vice* states that "monomania [...] is a feature of masturbatory pathology in nineteenth-century medical discourse (109). This is discussed further in Chapter Three concerning Robert Audley's obsessions and sexuality. It is clear that the evolution of the domesticated bachelor is impeded by Victorian society's strong feelings of unease, which is evident in the authors' decisions to force their bachelor figures into questionable marriages and in one instance, suicide. Anti-bachelor rhetoric reveals nineteenth-century society's anxiety towards a figure who refuses to remain in his proper sphere.

Jürgen Habermas' *The Structural Transformation of the Public Sphere* provides insight into the significance of the spheres to nineteenth-century bourgeois society and provides a theoretical foundation for this study's examination of the domesticated bachelor's ability to move between them. Increasing interest in the private and public spheres has resulted in an awareness of the fragility of these gender boundaries by literary critics and scholars. The movement of male characters from the "masculine" public sphere to the supposedly feminine world of the domestic sphere challenges the common reading of these spheres in terms of feminist literary theory and history.

Habermas' public sphere was supposed to be universal and bring people together despite differences in status, religion, and occupation. In reality, nineteenth-century society's definition of the public citizen excluded a number of groups resulting in requirements that only the middle-class male could meet, for example being capable of "rational, disinterested argument, whose mental processes were autonomous and free"

(Hurd 77). Habermas' public sphere was thus gendered masculine, but also required a middle-class appearance so that even working-class men were excluded.[5] Habermas cites 1750 as the beginning of the dissociation of the bourgeois public sphere from aristocratic society especially based on an increase in the reading population (43). The patriarchal conjugal family and its division into separate spheres derived from changes in seventeenth-century architectural style, which Habermas terms the "process of privatization" (44–5). Gender and the spheres are closely linked indicating how the façade of the public sphere remained gendered masculine and the private realm retained its identity as the woman's domain until weaknesses in these barriers were exposed.

Spaces including boudoirs, apartments, counting-houses, parlors, and laboratories are extensions of the gendered public and private spheres in these four novels. Habermas traces the withdrawal of the family back upon itself, as the family distanced itself from the "functional complex of social labor in general" (154). The conjugal bourgeois family had become even more private as it "ceased to be a community of production" (154). This "cutting off" from the public isolates the home and the family even further. The home itself became the woman's domain. Victorians paid particular attention to the natural states of being for men and women, while it was commonly suggested that "women are by nature emotional and passive, to the dogma that men are by nature rational and assertive" (Rosenberg xiv). Women's reproductive role also supported her being restricted to the private domain where the mysteries of birth and death presided. The body defines the person, and consequently the sphere to which it belongs.

According to Habermas, the separation of society from state resulted in public meaning "state-related," and no longer referred to the court (18). The authority of the feudal lord became the police, and the private individuals formed the public. The private sphere includes the private man, who functions as the owner of commodities, head of the family, and property owner, as well the intimate sphere included private relationships so that the private encapsulated the realm of "commodity exchange and social labour" and the "conjugal family's internal space" (Habermas 30). The public sphere existed in the political realm, as well as in the world of letters including clubs, lecture halls, and the press. The division between the state and society contributed to the separation between the public sphere and the private domain. The private sphere was strictly gendered feminine, which Habermas traces through a change in architecture and an increase in the late eighteenth-century reading audience. The creation of gendered public and private spheres appears to be fixed and static, but as current critical studies have shown,[6] the spheres are revealed to be more flexible and permeable than Habermas had considered.

Gestures, mannerisms, and appearances, Judith Butler argues in *Gender Trouble,* are "performative in the sense that the essence or identity that they otherwise purport to express are fabrications manufactured and sustained through corporeal signs and discursive means" (136). Within the public sphere, the female body was considered sexual, while the male body reflected its own rational tendencies as sexually neutral. Thus, simply the presence of the female body would transform the rational, masculine discourse associated with the public sphere, into a more feminized dandyism. Robin Gilmour describes the changing definition of the gentleman in *The Idea of the Gentleman in the Victorian Novel:*

> In both periods [early-eighteenth century and first generation Victorians] the idea
> of the gentleman becomes an essentially reforming concept, a middle-class call
> to seriousness which challenged the frivolity of fashionable life and reminded the
> aristocracy of the responsibilities inherent in their privileges [11].

James Eli Adams' *Dandies and Desert Saints: Styles of Victorian Manhood* describes the dandy as "a fundamentally theatrical being, abjectly dependent on the recognition of the audience he professes to disdain" (22). Women discovered a way in which they could use biology to reinforce their desire to be present within the public sphere. They claimed that men's lust and sexual aggressiveness were more destructive to the public sphere as compared to the female role of mother and nurturer. On June 6, 1866, the "Ladies' Petition" with 1,499 signatures was presented to the House of Commons asking that the vote be granted to "all householders, without distinction of sex, who possess such property or rental qualification as your Honourable House may determine" (Wingerden 2). The suffragette movement also served to challenge the traditional view of women as "docile and dependent" (Rover 37); after the "militant campaign it was no longer possible to look upon women as spiritless creatures, dependent on men for every idea and action" (Rover 37). Mary Wollstonecraft's *A Vindication of the Rights of Woman* (1792) was an early harbinger for the women's rights movements to come. Biology served the nineteenth-century suffragettes[7] by removing the middle-class man from the "abstract sphere of rational-critical debate" (Hurd 102), and from his place as head of the family, and placing him solidly within a sexualized male body. Brontë, Braddon, Eliot, Stevenson and Wilde incorporate aspects of performance in their bachelor figures. While women were excluded from the public sphere based on biology, men, even from the working class, could gain access through performance. This social threat of affected privilege makes the domesticated bachelor such a unique figure in the discussion of the spheres. By performing femininity, he seeks access to the domestic sphere once again confirming the power of performance in redefining nineteenth-century masculinity.

The term "bachelor" requires the female presence in order to define himself in opposition. The early examples of the bachelor involve moving between both the feminine and masculine realms, but in the late–nineteenth century the bachelor is no longer defined by his rejection of marriage, but for his preference for the exclusively male community. H. Rider Haggard's *King Solomon's Mines* (1885), Rudyard Kipling's "The Man Who Would Be King" (1888), and Joseph Conrad's *Heart of Darkness* (1899) are some examples of adventure fiction that are male-centric and take place in exotic locations. The adventure genre is appealing for a discussion of male relations for its isolated settings, high tension, and lack of enforced social regulations, which one might speculate could lead to experimentation with mirroring the domestic abroad and relaxed gender identity, but this is not the case for the domesticated bachelor. By omitting works from the adventure genre, which requires the bachelor to distance himself in order to re-evaluate his identity, my interest remains invested in how the bachelor maneuvers within the constructs of the private and public spheres, and how he is able to remain part of society while creating his own domestic space. In addition, domestic poetry by such poets as Felicia Hemans, Eliza Cook, Alfred, Lord Tennyson, and Coventry Patmore, has been excluded since this genre focuses on not only endorsing attributes of the ideal of domestic life, but also constructing them. Domestic poetry provides a foundation for examples of the domestic ideology that the masculinized female characters attempt to escape and the domesticated bachelor strives to recreate. After its peak in the 1850s, domestic poetry was considered a restricting genre that did not allow for the type of subversion evident in the domestic novel.

In order to identify the domesticated bachelor we can begin by observing their female counterparts. Dacre's *Zofloya* and Brontë's *Wuthering Heights* are two gothic romances that pair female characters who fail at the ideal of femininity with male characters who attempt to "teach" them through their own feminized performances how to fit into the private sphere. Berenza in *Zofloya* and Edgar Linton in *Wuthering Heights* are on a quest to domesticate the female demon. With their teachings Victoria and Catherine are able to perform their femininity while maintaining their rebellious masculinized dual nature. These two novels male "Others" are linked with female characters who fail to "fit in." Victoria learns from Berenza how to affect femininity which allows her to enter into the realm of domesticity where she unleashes her demonic self. Catherine is also taught how to gain access to domestic bliss through Linton's modeling. Her performance is weakened by her interactions with Heathcliff, who rejects her domestic role. The gothic genre allows for the exploration of the demonic female selves and their inability to remain contained inside the domestic arena that they are introduced into by their feminized counterparts. In addition to the gothic genre, in *Shirley*, the domestic novel also attempts to transgress the limits of genre, gender, and class.

Charlotte Brontë's *Shirley* (1849) pairs masculine female characters and feminized men, which breaks down gender boundaries and provides a space for the expansion of the concepts of femininity and masculinity. In *Shirley*, male characters fantasize about inhabiting the feminine space and it is usually because of some weakness that they begin to acknowledge their dual natures. Performance, in this early example, allows characters the ability to temporarily play the role of their opposing sex, but Brontë's double marriage conclusion abruptly places her ambiguous characters back into their proper spaces. The curates and old maids stand in as irritating and grotesque alternatives of a type of third sex that must be rejected. Brontë pairs the plight of the working class and the struggle for women's education when she sets her novel during the Luddite Movement of 1811–12. The relationship between the working-class men and bourgeois women illustrates the threat of performance in gaining access to Habermas' public sphere. Brontë's blend of social justice and a love plot forces the use of industrial discourse to describe the romantic, leading to an interesting fluidity between traditionally masculine and feminine discourse. Brontë's structuring of the novel mirrors the tendencies of the characters in *Shirley* to shift awkwardly between the spheres. While performance in Brontë's novel involves the playful imaginings of restless young women and an escape for confused professional men, Braddon's *Lady Audley's Secret* leaves no doubt about the potential of performance.

The "sensation novel" provides the ideal outlet for reactions to the Divorce and Matrimonial Causes Act of 1857.[8] In the late nineteenth-century periodicals were inundated with articles on the Woman Question, marriage and divorce, and the reform of gender roles by such authors as

# Introduction

Mona Caird, Olive Schreiner, Havelock Ellis, Eleanor Marx, and Elizabeth Chapman. By this time, these topics had become national concerns and journals like the *Westminster Review* kept readers, "keenly attuned to the issues, eagerly anticipating the next riposte, the following counter-thrust and the subsequent parry, the very stuff of serial publication" (Rosenberg 134–5). It appears that the thrill of the sensation genre was passed on to the serial publications of gender debates. For more on the role of the *Westminster Review* in pushing the debate of marriage and divorce forward, see Sheila Rosenberg's chapter "Dialogues on Marriage and Divorce in the *Westminster*" in *Encounters in the Victorian Press*. Although the Divorce Act allowed women to divorce their husbands, it clearly demonstrated a lack of equality since men could divorce their wives on grounds of adultery, but wives needed a husband's adultery "to be compounded by additional harm: bigamy, incest, cruelty, or bestiality" (Chase 186). While the Divorce Act was passed as law in 1857, other legislation, including a reform to the married women's property law, failed. Other domestic debates had arisen earlier in 1839 and the 1840s concerning the Infant Custody Act and the deceased wife's sister debates. Issues of the family and the home had begun moving from the realm of the private to the public space of Parliament and newspapers. Surprisingly, the Divorce Act of 1857 grew from a society that was putting increased emphasis on the idealization of the home. The 1850s feared that with every marriage was the new possibility of divorce. While separations were rare, "even rarer was the only other possibility: to gain a divorce by parliamentary statute. Roughly ten such statutes were enacted each year, only a handful of which over the centuries had even been secured at the behest of a woman. Such a process was inordinately lengthy and inexpensive. To all intents and purposes, divorce was impossible for married women" (Ward 157). According to the 1868 report of the Royal Commission on the Laws of Marriage, 884 cases of bigamy were tried between 1853 and 1863 (Gill 75). As noted in Warren's *Women, Money, and the Law*, in the New York Supreme Court from 1845 to 1875, 23 percent of the cases involving women were divorce cases. In most of the cases, the woman filed the suit. Seventy percent of the divorce cases had a woman as the plaintiff; in only 30 percent was a man the plaintiff. Women were forced to sue for other reasons than adultery since it allowed them to gain monetary support. The social stigma surrounding divorce had women filing for divorce as a last resort. This increased the horror associated with divorce and though it did not become a popular option, the disruptive impact on the Victorian family was immense.

## The Domesticated Bachelor

Braddon's *Lady Audley's Secret* (1862), like Brontë's *Shirley*, pairs a masculine female character, Lucy Audley, with a feminized male character, Robert Audley. The relationship between these two characters is a battle for space, as they attempt to extend into each other's traditional spheres. In the back and forth movement between Lucy and Robert, it becomes evident that Robert is a domestic defender whose main interest is to protect the sanctity of the private sphere from the ambitious, calculating, precursor to the vilified New Woman. In a scene that evokes the blissful domesticity associated with the Victorian home, Robert nurses his friend George back to health in his bachelor apartment. This crucial moment demonstrates how the domesticated gentleman has succeeded in creating his own domestic sphere without a wife. Lucy's fluidity is linked with her ability to act, a skill that is associated with insincerity and superficiality.

The theatricality of Eliza Lynn Linton's "girl of the period" demonstrates the female spectacle at her best. As Nina Auerbach explains, "reverent Victorians shunned theatricality as the ultimate, deceitful mobility. It connotes not lies, but fluidity of character that decomposes the uniform integrity of the self" (*Private* 4). It is the "girl of the period's" ability to move beyond her restricted space that makes her so dangerous. In Linton's words, she is "acting against nature [...] a poor copy" of an unattainable original. Her exaggerated beauty and excess go beyond attracting an audience and instead have the opposite affect. Similar to James Eli Adams' description of the dandy as being fundamentally theatrical, "abjectly dependent on the recognition of the audience he professes to disdain" (22), "the girl of the period" exhibits a similar complex relationship with her audience. While Braddon's Lucy possesses some of these theatrical qualities, George Eliot's Gwendolen Harleth provides a clear example of Linton's "modern English girl," in the way she revels in excess and distances herself from her audience.

George Eliot pushes the boundaries of performance by introducing the male actress in her novel *Daniel Deronda* (1876). Eliot pairs him with female performers, who attempt to act their way out of the domestic sphere, while the domesticated bachelor occupies the space they leave behind. As a result, these gentleman actresses proceed to instruct their female partners on how to act the part of Victorian domesticity. Grandcourt is problematic as the gentleman actress since he, like Gwendolen, suffers from over-acting and becomes the equivalent of the female spectacle. Deronda's performance is more successful at representing feminine qualities that exist outside the domestic sphere. This type of "domesticated

15

theatricality" reflects an inconsistency between acting and action, as D.A. Miller explains, "once a power of social control has been virtually raised to the status of ontology, action becomes so intimidating that it is effectively discouraged" (31). Although performance allows female characters moments of release, their actions remain unacted and blurred between sensationalism and reality. The fluidity of the shifting roles between male and female, and spectator and spectacle challenges the role of theatricality and gender within the domestic sphere.

This is not the case in the exclusively male community of Stevenson's *The Strange Case of Dr. Jekyll and Mr. Hyde* (1886). The feminine characteristics Hyde possesses suggest a redefinition of *fin-de-siècle* masculinity and the possibility of indulging in the private sphere without encountering its female inhabitants. Herbert Sussman observes the transformation of masculinity during the Aesthetic movement by commenting on Walter Pater's description of the expectation of the Victorian male:

> the normative Victorian masculinities—of reserve [...] of manliness as the [...] difficult discipline of desire; of the [...] disciplined male self as analogue of the controlled flame of the steam engine and the forge[9]; of psychic control as "success in life" similar to the mental discipline needed for victory within the commercial competitiveness of the male arena [202].

The bachelor does not promote this type of restrictive masculinity and it is exactly this type of repression and "psychic control" that Dr. Jekyll seeks to escape through the creation of Hyde. The bachelor possesses an amount of feminine qualities that allows him to move freely into the feminized private space, which is dark, mysterious, and seductive while at the same time he maintains the masculine appearance of a gentleman. This double consciousness is found in all of the domesticated bachelors, and it is their inclination to seek out the domestic and "fit into" this space that makes them so remarkable. During a time when masculinity and concerns for the bachelors' increasing tendency to delay marriage,[10] indicated a degeneration in nationhood, the new bachelor finds comfort in a domestic setting surrounded by his male companions. He appears to benefit from the *fin-de-siècle*'s "masculinity in crisis" by expanding his boundaries and pushing himself into the realm of the domestic. Whereas Stephen D. Arata argues that the bachelor sought to escape the isolation and repression of Victorian domesticity ("Sedulous Ape" 243), *Dr. Jekyll and Mr. Hyde* reveals that the bachelor brings to the private sphere aspects of the homosocial, broadening ideas of masculinity and its role in the domestic. Are Stevenson's bachelors simply masquerading as men since, according to the Victorians, they are never completely masculine? This is how the *fin-de-siècle* bachelor blurs the boundaries and pushes beyond the constraints of the spheres and gender by introducing a new type of masculinity.

The evolution of the bachelor extends into the *fin-de-siècle* where the emphasis is on his ambiguous sexuality. The result of an exclusively male community is the creation of the reconfigured sphere. As the bachelor becomes more intent on creating space rather than "fitting in," he is more commonly characterized as the Other. Eliot's Deronda is eventually considered as the racial Other, Hyde is the criminal Other, and finally, like the bachelors in Oscar Wilde's novel, he becomes the sexual Other. The gothic genre used by Stevenson and Wilde, plays a significant role in portraying the bachelor as monster, since he can be ostracized and alienated for his criminal and homosexual tendencies.

The argument here is not the unique ability for men to engage in both spaces, as Tosh confirms, "it is now widely recognized that constant emphasis on the 'separation of spheres' is misleading, partly because men's privileged ability to pass freely between the public and private was integral to the social order" (*Manliness* 39). During the nineteenth century, a man's business and family often shared the same physical space in the home. A husband's impact within the private and a woman's contribution to the public eliminated the idea that the spheres did not allow for movement. Male characters continued to cross between public and private, but what is significant is that the private is no longer the traditional Victorian home consisting of a wife, children, and servants. Tosh argues that the bachelor's lack of a "proper" domestic space excludes him from "exercising [his] full masculinity" (*Manliness* 38). While Tosh grants the bachelor's movements between the spheres, he restricts him by denying his masculinity. As men begin to choose to marry later, at age thirty by the 1880s, it is debatable to suggest that these bachelors have not achieved masculinity. Although it is a man's "privilege" to move between the spheres, it appears that there is little freedom within the constraints of Victorian masculinity and the public and private spheres themselves, to the point whereby engaging in one, you are denied a claim to the other.

# ONE

# Male Models

*Performance and Transformation
in Charlotte Dacre's* Zofloya
*and Emily Brontë's* Wuthering Heights

In early examples of Gothic fiction produced in the eighteenth century, female demons were easily discernible by their grotesque appearances, physical deformities, and power over the supernatural. From the evil sorceress Carathis, the Caliph's mother in Beckford's *Vathek*, in her sinister laboratory with her company of mutes and mummies, to the demon Matilda in Lewis' *The Monk* with her knowledge of witchcraft, the female monster clearly opposes eighteenth century ideals of femininity. The representation of the female changes as the Gothic genre is "rewritten" by emerging women gothic writers beginning with Radcliffe. The distinction between horror writing or the male gothic, and terror writing introduced by Radcliffe and other women writers, becomes rapidly obvious. The Female Gothic is a response from an increasing number of women writers and readers of Gothic novels in the 1790s (Clemens 41). Women reacted to the excessive violence in Gothic novels by men and began to write their own by borrowing and adding to the genre. Clemens argues that women used the Gothic novel as an escape through imagination, to explore female sexuality, and to express their feelings towards their roles in society (Clemens 47).

Fear is another factor that contributes to the gendering of the Gothic genre. The readers' reactions to fear are influenced by their gender, as Kari J. Winter explains, "male writers of Gothic fiction appear to fear the suppressed power of the 'other' ... and delight in graphic descriptions of torture ... and murder of women" (91). Female demons in the Male Gothic are often directly associated with the underworld and represent a deformed and grotesque image of the female body. The concept of the female demon in the early eighteenth century requires that her deranged mind be reflected on her physical form. The plots of the Female Gothic focus on "expos[ing] the terrors of patriarchy from the victims' point of view" (Winter 92). It is important to note that women writers at this time were not seeking to remove themselves from society, instead they adhered to society's regulations and in consequence were able to reveal the many flaws within that patriarchal system.

During this early period of the Female Gothic women writers incorporate two genres: on the one hand while they borrow from the traditional Gothic they are also incorporating elements from the "novel of sentiment" (Clemens 42). The middle class associated with this type of "moral elite" and the cult of sensibility as opposed to the excesses of the aristocracy or the brutality of the lower class. Middle class women were placed on top of this "moral hierarchy" (Clemens 43) because of society's belief that women, especially mothers, are inclined towards moral purity, which leads to an eventual "desexualizing of women's image" (Clemens 44) in the eighteenth century. Women, through their chastity, guard property by securing inheritances. The Female Gothic examines these notions of female sexuality, but also suggests that the "public version of reality is incomplete" (Clemens 49), and that there exists another world below the surface. Eve Kosofsky Sedgwick insists that female sexuality can be found on the surfaces within Gothic fiction through images of the veil: "[g]eneration, sex, and class indeed preside over that circulation, but often in unexpected terms" (266). Her suggestion is that critics have spent too much time looking at Gothic novels in depth and have been unable to analyze the significance of surfaces in the genre. Although the Female Gothic changes the face of gothic heroines and their foils, Valdine Clemens notes how "[t]here is no overt questioning of the validity of the social system that serves women's needs so poorly" (50). The conclusions to Female Gothic novels reinforce women's place in society and their devotion to domesticity, and Clemens is wise to suggest the term "Sentimental Female Gothic" (50) to distinguish these earlier works from more radical examples of the Female Gothic. These two genres maintain their presence in later works, but are often used by authors in parody. Gothic novels from Lewis to Radcliffe incorporate this dialogue between the sexes, as male Gothic writers respond to the Female Gothic by adding more violence against women in their novels, as Winter notes, "the Gothic genre was produced by a dynamic process of action, reaction, and counterreaction, a perpetual writing and rewriting" (93). The flexibility of the Gothic genre provides its readers with a variety of perspectives on the Gothic heroine, as well as her demonic counterpart, both of which undergo a number of changes from the traditional Gothic to the Sentimental Female Gothic, and finally to a particular type of Female Gothic that incorporates the excess and violence of the Male Gothic with issues of the domestic.

Charlotte Dacre uses the violence associated with the genre of the Male Gothic, while addressing issues of domesticity and female sexuality. Radcliffe's *The Italian* responds to Lewis' *The Monk* through the creation of a new genre which incorporates sensibility and the Gothic; Dacre's *Zofloya* is more like a "female version" (Miles 179) of *The Monk* with Victoria as Ambrosio. Dacre reverts to the Lewis brand of writing but adds her own "'feminist' perspective" (Miles 179), which provides a combination of violence and domesticity. Her use of violence usually found in abundance in the more traditional forms of the Gothic, may have convinced readers that the author of *Zofloya* was a male writer had Dacre published anonymously or with a male pseudonym as Emily Brontë did with her novel, *Wuthering Heights* (Craciun 13). Sexual desire and the female obsession with love is victimizing in Dacre's *Zofloya*, which is more than any previous female Gothic writer had attempted (Haggerty 174). Through the excessive nature of the genre and her focus on issues of femininity, Dacre is able to supply her readers with a new concept of the female demon, one who should be feared not because of her physical deformity, but for her ability to conceal her true identity. Dacre's new concept of female sexuality and desire, as well as her use of typically "male" violence, and her ability to add a "feminist" perspective by exploring the role of women in society including issues of love and marriage, place her novel *Zofloya* in a position in which it can be examined alongside later nineteenth-century Female Gothic novels.

The second wave of the Female Gothic includes Emily Brontë's *Wuthering Heights* and demonstrates a new combination of Gothic tropes and elements of nineteenth-century Realism. The Gothic genre changes to include the fears and anxieties that women face in the reality of the everyday lives like their "confinement within the domestic space, their place within the family, the loss of their self identity and the threat of male sexual energies" (Avery 122). These become the "real" dangers explored by nineteenth-century Female Gothic writers, which replaces most supernatural phenomena found in the traditional Gothic genre. Similar to Dacre, Emily Brontë molds existing genres in order to present new perspectives on domestic issues and femininity. The cult of sensibility taking place in the eighteenth century put emphasis on moral codes and as Diane Hoeveler argues in *Gothic Feminism*, Dacre, along with Austen and Shelley were "attempting to codify in their works appropriately gendered behaviour for each of the sexes" (125). This code is what the middle class embraced in order to differentiate themselves from the aristocracy and the lower class. Brontë, in her analysis of women's role in society is also criticizing "the whole notion of what is supposedly 'civilised'" (Avery 127). This serves to reinforce the continuous writing and rewriting of the Gothic genre as it passes from generation to generation. Brontë's combination of the Female Gothic with some Romantic and Realist elements allows for the emergence of a different type of Gothic heroine, and varying perceptions of the ideal of femininity.

Through the examination of the movement of the Gothic genre from the traditional Male Gothic to the Sentimental Female Gothic and later the Female Gothic of Dacre and Emily Brontë, the fluidity and instability of the genre embraced by these female writers allows for a variety of representations of the ideal of femininity, and attempts to explore the boundaries of female sexuality by pushing beyond these social constraints. The female demon transforms and redefines herself along with the Gothic genre. Her evolution is traced back to the early eighteenth century where she appears as physically repulsive and closely linked with supernatural powers. The new concept of the female demon materializes in Dacre's *Zofloya* through the protagonist Victoria and in Emily Brontë's *Wuthering Heights* through Catherine Earnshaw. The term "demonic," like Mary Russo's definition of the grotesque expands to include any "deviation from the social norm" (11), and it is significant that in this case the "female is always defined against the male norm" (12). Dacre and Brontë's female demons are no longer physically grotesque, instead both authors emphasize the ability of the new female demon to "shape-shift" in order to conceal their true "demonic" selves, and roam freely within the domestic sphere. Furthermore, Dacre and Brontë suggest how these female demons may have avoided creating these dual natures had it not been for the interception of particular male characters, such as Berenza in *Zofloya* and Edgar Linton in *Wuthering Heights* who insist on domesticating the female demon and instructing her on how to achieve their perception of the ideal of femininity. It is during this attempt at transformation that the female demons demonstrate an incredible ability to "shape-shift" and perform according to the expectations of society and their male instructors. This newly acquired skill for performance and affectation allows Victoria and Catherine

Earnshaw to deceive as they attempt to conceal their true natures in order to find their place among the inhabitants of domestic sphere. Eventually, Dacre and Brontë demonstrate how the perfection of this performance leads to a loss of self and both female characters reject their domestic identities only to revert back to their demonic selves, which is once again reinforced by their associations with other male characters in the form of their demonic doubles—the Moor in *Zofloya* and Heathcliff in *Wuthering Heights*. Although Victoria and Catherine Earnshaw do not adhere to traditional Gothic perceptions of the female demon, Dacre and Brontë insist that their ability to affect and deceive justify their inclusion in this category.

The typical female demon from early Gothic works is unable to conceal her disturbed and criminal mind because her appearance reflects her unnatural behavior. The female grotesque represents what is "unnatural, frivolous and irrational" (Russo 3). Demonic women are physically represented as "crone, witch [or] vampire" (Russo 1), and emphasis is placed on their bodily functions like "blood, [and] tears (Russo 1). This is the early female demon with her grotesque physicality exposing her ambitious and unnatural mind. The definition of the grotesque as explored by Mary Russo expands to include any female who "emerges as a deviation from the norm" (11). Excess in its many forms including "over-exposure" (Russo 53), spectacle, and risk are components of the female grotesque. Female characters' expressions of sexual desire are "equally central to the damnation of the individual" (Haggerty 173). These examples of excess apply to both Victoria and Catherine Earnshaw, as Dacre and Brontë move away from traditional representations of the female demon. Russo describes the female grotesque as "multiple and changing" (8), while the classical body is statuesque, "static, self-contained, symmetrical, and sleek" (8). The movement of the female demons like Victoria and Catherine towards shape-shifting and dual natures continues to define them as grotesque, while characters like Lilla from *Zofloya* and Isabella in *Wuthering Heights* are closely linked with the ideal of femininity and the classical body that is unchanging.

Judith Butler explores the permeability of the body and the constructs of gender and how the unstable definition of femininity allows for conflicting notions of the female body and women's place in society. Not only does the physical body dictate different degrees of femininity, it is also responsible for placing women within their social roles, as Madeleine Hurd explains, "The sight of one's body affects how one will be addressed" (93). The two groups who are excluded from Jürgen Habermas' bourgeois public sphere are women and the working class. It is important to note that the female demons and their male counterparts from Dacre and Brontë's novel share this link, since both Zofloya and Heathcliff are introduced as originating from the lower classes. The working class and women had no place within the masculinized middle class public sphere and in consequence both appear as outsiders attempting to make their way towards social acceptance. Heathcliff mysteriously returns after years of absence as a self-made gentleman, while Zofloya reveals his superiority through his supernatural powers and transforming his appearance. The body and physical appearances are essential in locating the individual in society. Royalty was rarely thought of in terms of their physical bodies demonstrating their ability to appear to deny their bodily needs, a particular self-discipline thought impossible for the lower classes and women. While the members of the public sphere remained "abstract, [and] disembodied" (Hurd 101), the outsiders, through their physical behavior and appearance, proved to be unable to separate themselves from their bodies. Similar to Russo's image of the female grotesque, women's behavior as well as appearance excluded her from the public sphere; "women are by nature emotional and passive, to the dogma that men are by nature rational and assertive" (Rosenberg xiv). Women's reproductive role also supported her place within the private domain where the mysteries of birth and death presided.

The eighteenth century saw the creation of the public and private spheres through the society's separation from the state. This separation allowed for public opinion and the forum in which to discuss public matters became Habermas' public sphere. Qualifying as a member of the public sphere lead to an emphasis on "being" and "seeming" in order to distinguish the nobleman, who has a right to *seem*, and the burgher, who has nothing and is compelled to *be* (Habermas 13). Performance and appearance become crucial and result in the exclusion of women and the working class from the public sphere. The private sphere includes the private man who functions as the owner of commodities, head of the family, and property owner, as well the intimate sphere included private relationships so that the private encapsulated the realm of "commodity exchange and social labour" (Habermas 30) and the "conjugal family's internal space" (Habermas 30). The private sphere soon becomes gendered feminine, which Habermas traces through an increase in the reading audience.

Women represent the reading audience beginning in the eighteenth century and they embrace the Gothic genre as both readers and writers. The woman writer plays an interesting role as she is balances between the public and private spheres based on her profession, but women are excluded from Habermas' concept of the public sphere and instead are positioned within the private realm of domesticity where they act as naturally emotional and irrational beings according to society's expectations. The role that women's bodies plays in their exclusion from the public is explored further by Judith Butler, while Patricia McKee focuses on women's knowledge as a defining factor. According to McKee it is the "degree of knowledge" which distinguishes positions of upper and lower social classes of women and working class men. Within the private realm women's experiences become inaccessible to public knowledge, which lead women to come to exist within an "unknowable realm" (McKee 4), similar to the Caliph's witch-mother's secret laboratory in her tower. Women fit into a space separate from public knowledge and order, but a place that "assumes characteristics of realms of obscurity discovered, or produced, by disciplines of knowledge" (McKee 5). Victoria and Catherine begin to inhabit the unruly and mysterious realm of nature, as they are excluded from the domestic sphere. Women's incapability for rational thought naturally excludes them from the public realm, but simultaneously shrouds them in a veil of mystery within the private domain that Habermas considers transitory and obscure (Habermas 3).

The mind becomes the focus of fear and anxiety in the late eighteenth and early nineteenth-century Gothic fiction. Ghosts and other supernatural entities are internalized within the mind which becomes a "phantom-zone—given over ... to spectral presences and haunting obsessions (Castle 144). The mind became the space reserved for the supernatural, and there was no longer a ghostly realm outside the mind. Victoria represents this new type of female demon whose powers lie in her mind and her ability to conceal her true identity through affectation. The young Victoria's place within the realm of the domestic is not stable, since Dacre describes Victoria's "corrupt nature" (490) as a child. Victoria's mother abandons the domestic sphere through her excessive sexual desire for Ardolph, but then attempts to return as a promise to her dying husband. It is Ardolph who reminds Laurina in a letter that "[y]our present residence is no place for you" (Dacre 55); her place within the domestic has been "forfeited" (Dacre 55) by her excessive behavior. Similarly, Victoria experiences problems identifying her "proper place" within society. Dacre describes Victoria's natural tendency towards evil as a combination of a powerful spirit and physical beauty: "Victoria ... beautiful and accomplished as an angel, was proud, haughty, and self-sufficient—of a wild, ardent, and irrepressible spirit, indifferent to reproof, careless of censure—of an implacable, revengeful, and cruel nature, and bent upon gaining the ascendancy in whatever she engaged" (Dacre 40). Her beauty opposes traditional concepts of the female demon, yet her nature and behavior deviate from the norm (Russo 11). Like the Female Gothic genre itself, Victoria is unique in that she does not have the appearance of the female demon, yet her nature is ambitious and proud. Victoria's first attempt at affectation occurs when she reveals too much of her demonic self to Berenza. Although curious at first, Berenza is soon "visibly shocked by her preserving and remorseless cruelty to a mother" (Dacre 62). Victoria crosses the line into excess and has lost the interest of Berenza. She reacts immediately: "alarmed at the remotest idea of becoming indifferent to him, she instantly determined on regaining his esteem" (Dacre 62). This scene marks the beginning of many opportunities for Victoria to perfect her skills of affectation in order to meet with Berenza's expectations.

Victoria employs artifice in order to appeal to Berenza's concept of the ideal of femininity, but she also uses her skill of deception to escape confinement. Laurina abandons her daughter a second time when she leaves Victoria in the care of the shrewd and harsh Signora di Modena. The Signora, like Berenza, has expectations for Victoria, as the bitter old-maid exclaims, "I will break that proud spirit, and make her submit afterwards" (Dacre 74). Victoria shape-shifts and becomes "placid, cool and unembarrassed" (Dacre 75), in order to convince the Signora that her punishments are successful. This artifice in turn provides Victoria with freedom to walk in the garden, and finally to escape with the help of Catau. The performances required of Victoria force her to conceal and control her true emotions moving her away from the grotesque and closer to Russo's description of the classical model of femininity (Russo 8). The ability to exert self-control brings Victoria closer to the feminine ideal enforced by both Berenza and the Signora. Dacre draws her readers' attention to this newly acquired skill of deception and Victoria's perfection of this performance: [t]hus, too, did she learn the most refined artifice, which, by practice, became imbued into the mass of her other evil qualities" (75). More than once Victoria struggles to conceal her anger and hatred, and her ability to do so marks her success at truly becoming a new form of the female demon. Her time with Catau also teaches Victoria not to trust appearances.

Victoria's prejudices against the lower class are shaken when Catau proves to be "not so stupid as she was supposed" (Dacre 77). Similar to Victoria the servant Catau practices concealment demanded of her by her occupation and low class status. Catau's hidden abilities are virtues, as opposed to Victoria: she was "possessed of a certain shrewdness, and power of combining ideas, which, hid beneath an habitual silence and placidity of disposition, had drawn upon her the mistaken imputation of heaviness and insensibility.... Catau could think; and what was more, she could *feel*" (Dacre 77). Dacre draws attention to the differences between Victoria and Catau's concealments and how Victoria's are spurred by selfish motives. Dacre immediately follows this description of the hidden nature of Catau by abruptly turning the readers' attention to Victoria, who decides to attach herself to the unsuspecting servant in order to secure her escape (77). The contrasts between Catau and Victoria demonstrate how class is not a signifier of virtue or moral superiority. Catau is able to conceal her true nature by acting cold and distant towards Victoria in order to please her employer, but eventually she defies the Signora, as Dacre describes, "[Catau] had become weary of this assumed character, and returned to the kind, gentle, and respectful conduct, more consonant to her feelings" (80). Although the kind-hearted servant's true nature is in direct opposition to Victoria's she still functions as example of the doubling, which occurs throughout *Zofloya*. Victoria's experiences lead to confrontations with other female characters whose affectations Victoria mirrors but with varying results.

While mistress to Berenza, Victoria masters her performance in order to maintain her relationship and the protection it provides. Victoria confirms her feelings that she does not love Berenza (Dacre 97), but she uses her powers of deception to convince him otherwise, making it her primary duty to keep him under this "delusion" (Dacre 99): "well did she support the character she had assumed; and the tender refined Berenza became convinced, that he possessed the first pure and genuine affections of an innocent and lovely girl!" (Dacre 99). Victoria maintains her performance as she moves from being Berenza's mistress to wife, and finally his murderer. Dacre provides her readers with other examples of deceitful women through the characters of Signora Zappi and Megalena Strozzi. Victoria repeats the errors of Signora Zappi, when she cannot conquer her passion and confronts her brother-in-law, Henriquez, with her true feelings for him. The result of Signora Zappi revealing her feelings of love for Leonardo is rejection and disgrace. She achieves her revenge by putting on an intricately planned performance placing herself as a rape victim and Leonardo the aggressor (Dacre 109). Zappi and Victoria's inability to control their passionate emotions emphasizes their roles as demonical females. These female characters fall under Russo's definition of the grotesque since they are unable to contain and refine themselves (8), and their male victims react with loathsome disgust. From all these examples of the female demon, Megalena Strozzi appears as the most successful. Megalena succeeds where Victoria fails since she secures the admiration of Leonardo and also rids him of his previous affections for the innocent Amamia: "[Megalena] had awakened his soul to new existence; the image of the delicate Amamia faded from his mind, and a more wild, a more unbounded passion took possession of it, in the form of Megalena" (Dacre 123). Dacre explores a variety of ways in which women conceal their true natures through affectation and performance. Catau's hidden personality provides an example of affectation without selfish motives. While Victoria's repeats the errors of Signora Zappi's by losing control of her passions, and Megalena succeeds by maintaining her artifice and concealing her true emotions. Although Victoria's reasons for using artifice are motivated by selfish reasons, her need to affect is also to find a place within the domestic. It is the female demon's ability to mask her true nature and enter into the realm of the domestic which instigates fear and anxiety in readers.

Catherine Earnshaw in Emily Brontë's *Wuthering Heights* discovers her ability to shape-shift and secure a space within Thrushcross Grange, an ideal representation of the domesticity and civility. Similar to Dacre's novel, Brontë focuses on the childhood of her heroine in order to emphasize her true nature. As a child Catherine is mischievous and tests the patience of her parents and Nelly: "[h]er spirits were always at high-water mark, her tongue always going—singing, laughing, and plaguing everybody who would not do the same ... a wild wick slip she was—but she had the bonniest eye, and sweetest smile" (Brontë 40). Like Victoria, Catherine's behavior is excessive, her behavior is child-like, but to the extreme. Her choice of a whip as a gift (Brontë 34) "carries associations of domination and the outdoors" (Ellis 210), which suggests more than just childish play. Nelly describes Catherine as "act[ing] the little mistress" (Brontë 40) towards herself and Heathcliff. Mr. Earnshaw rejects his daughter's unnatural behavior by claiming not to love her (Brontë 41). Similar to Victoria's abandonment by her mother on two occasions, Catherine must cope with her father's disappointment towards her true nature. Nelly realizes that eventually "being repulsed continually hardened her, and she laughed if I told her to say sorry for her faults" (Brontë 41). Catherine, like Victoria, learns to embrace her true identity in the face of her father whom she no longer respects. Catherine loses her father to Heathcliff, and so she makes Heathcliff her own, but she soon realizes that "she cannot have her father's power and his love at the same time" (Ellis 212). Catherine chooses power over her father's approval. Her final words to her father demonstrate her awareness of his faults, and when he asks her to behave like a proper girl, she responds, "Why cannot you always be a good man, father?" (Brontë 41). As a child, Catherine's true nature runs wild among the moors, a "world untouched by man made gender divisions" (Ellis 213), but her need to dominate suggests that she will strive to become something far beyond herself.

Brontë presents Catherine Earnshaw as mutable and fluid and like the traditional Gothic ghost she transforms from Catherine Earnshaw to Catherine Heathcliff and Catherine Linton (Brontë 17). Lockwood discovers these three names in the wood cabinet, and the names themselves appear mutable since they are written in "all kinds of characters, large and small" (Brontë 17). As Lockwood drifts into sleep the names, like the ghostly Catherine, begin to appear as "vivid as spectres—the air swarmed with Catherines" (Brontë 17). Catherine, like Victoria is a shape-shifter, who eludes Lockwood's attempt to place her within a specific social context. When Lockwood is finally able to grasp Catherine, he releases his frustration deriving from his inability to correctly label the inhabitants of Wuthering Heights, and the confusion caused by Catherine's ability to elude him: "I pulled its wrist on to the broken pane, and rubbed it to and fro till the blood ran down and soaked the bed-clothes: still it wailed" (Brontë 23). The result of being "caught" is violence, and this scene demonstrates the reason why Catherine seeks to remain elusive and untouchable. The female grotesque is evoked by the stream of blood, and Catherine's inability to contain herself. Her blood loss, and in consequence her association with the grotesque is caused by a male character—Lockwood. The many names of Catherine demonstrate her different personas, and as she moves away from childhood she is introduced to Thrushcross Grange and undergoes a transformation linking her with more closely with the domestic and the ideal of femininity. Her need to dominate requires that she shape-shift in order to secure her place within this new realm. Thrushcross Grange is in direct opposition to Wuthering Heights with its warmth and wealth, as Heathcliff observes, "ah! it was beautiful—a splendid place carpeted with crimson, and crimson-covered chairs and tables, and a pure white ceiling bordered by gold, a shower of glass-drops hanging in silver chains from the centre, and shimmering with little soft tapers" (Brontë 46). Heathcliff and Catherine believe they would be in heaven in this setting, but they become disgusted by Edgar and Isabella's ideas of amusement by "yelling, and sobbing, and rolling on the ground" (Brontë 47). It takes the firm grasp of Skulker, the Linton's bull-dog, to drag Catherine into this new domestic domain. Catherine's transformation begins immediately inside Thrushcross Grange, as the Lintons and their servants wait on her and nurse her back to health during her five-week stay.

Catherine's return to Wuthering Heights demonstrates the success of her transformation from the "wild, hatless little savage jumping around the house" (Brontë 51), to the "very dignified person, with brown ringlets ... and a long cloth habit which she was obliged to hold up with both hands that she might sail in" (Brontë 51). The shape-shifting complete, Catherine attempts to exert her new persona on the inhabitants of Wuthering Heights, including Heathcliff who feels the pressure to transform himself, as he tells Nelly, "I wish I had light hair and a fair skin, and was dressed and behaved as well, and had a chance of being as rich as [Edgar] will be" (Brontë 55). Heathcliff feels the pressure to match Catherine's new persona, by wishing to change his own. He is unable to change his dark looks, but he does succeed by leaving Wuthering Heights and returning a gentleman. These transformations have elements of the supernatural, because the reader does not question them "for in the world of the novel there are not rites of passage available to men or to women" (Yaeger 227). Their transformations are swift and mysterious. Nelly recognizes Catherine's "double character" (Brontë 66), since Catherine refrains from lady-like manners in Wuthering Heights, but never allows the Lintons to observe her true nature. Similar to Victoria's error of revealing too much of her true self to Berenza while berating her mother with cruel comments, Catherine also frightens the more sensitive Edgar Linton with her cruelty towards Nelly and Little Hareton, and eventually himself when she hits him in her frenzy (Brontë 71). Edgar's repulsion signals to Catherine, as it did to Victoria in *Zofloya*, that she has been excessive. Nelly's exclamation for Edgar "[t]o take warning and begone! It's a kindness to let you have a glimpse of her genuine disposition" (Brontë 71), reveals Catherine as the female demon whose ability to affect and perform allows her to disguise her true nature. Catherine realizes her error, and like Victoria is quick to make amends. She appeals to Edgar's sensibility by threatening to make herself sick (Brontë 72), which is a tactic she uses again when her plans to unite Heathcliff and Edgar are ruined. Catherine's decision to marry Edgar requires that she embrace her affected character, and let her true self perish, instead Catherine finds herself unable to continue as Mrs. Linton and suffers from madness where she is unable to recognize herself. Catherine cannot identify herself in the mirror, as Nelly tells her, "It was *yourself*, Mrs. Linton" (Brontë 124). Catherine denies her true nature until her death, as the frustrated Heathcliff demands, "[y]ou teach me now how cruel you've been—cruel and false. *Why* did you betray your own heart, Cathy? ... You have killed yourself.... You loved me—then what *right* had you to leave me?" (Brontë 161). Catherine's denial of her true nature results in her separation from Heathcliff and madness. This form of hysteria falls under Russo's definition of "over-acting" (68) as representative of the female grotesque. Catherine's mutability results in her loss of identity and the destruction of Heathcliff. Her daughter maintains the flexible nature of the persona of Catherine by adding yet another dimension, as Linton Heathcliff's wife—Catherine Heathcliff, who moves from Thrushcross Grange back to Wuthering Heights. The doubling of the female self onto male characters is common in both *Zofloya* and *Wuthering Heights*. It is because of these male characters that Victoria and Catherine deny their true natures and as a result enter into the domestic, a space that cannot contain them for very long.

Dacre and Emily Brontë begin their novels by introducing readers to the natural disposition of their heroines during childhood. Victoria and Catherine embrace their tendency to deviate from society's norms despite the disappointment of their parents. During their childhood there is no need to affect or use artifice since none are ashamed of their wild behavior. It is only when they are confronted with a rejection from the domestic realm that the female demons redirect their energies into the creation of dual natures. In both novels, the female demons are lead into the civilized and refined society through the insistence of male characters like Berenza in *Zofloya* and Edgar Linton from Brontë's *Wuthering Heights*. Berenza and Linton are the main motivations for the female demons' denial of the self and the use of artifice to gain access into the civilized world in which they belong. The cult of sensibility in the eighteenth century involves sensitizing consciousness "in order to be more acutely responsive to signals from the outside environment and from inside the body" (Barker-Benfield xvii). A moral code was also required so that the middle-class could differentiate themselves from the aristocracy and lower classes. The female demons in these two novels are not familiar with this moral code as young girls, but are encouraged to enter into the realm of sensibility by following the example of these male characters. The culture of sensibility takes for its basis the increase of women writers and readers (Barker-Benfield xix), resulting in a gendering of sensibility. The concept of sensibility being gendered female, and the fact that Dacre and Brontë choose the male characters of Berenza and Edgar Linton as guides for the novels' heroines into the culture of sensibility provides a unique example of gender reversal, another trope of the Gothic genre. Instead of the female heroine using her natural sensibility to come to the aid of a male character in need of moral salvation, Dacre and Emily Brontë present the exact opposite.

The eighteenth century involves a significant amount of changes in concepts of masculinity (Weed 216). Sex, economics, manners, and nationality play important roles in the construction of masculinity during this period. Similar to the cult of sensibility, masculinity requires that one follow strict guidelines and codes that encourage a delicate balance between excess and refinement. Dacre immediately identifies Berenza as an aristocrat and a "man of peculiar sentiments" (58). His purpose for socializing is purely for analytical purposes in order to "increase his knowledge of the human heart" (Brontë 58). His interest lies in examining human relations and also in increasing his understanding of human emotions, but purely as an observer. Berenza sees in Victoria an opportunity to exercise "the power he believe[s] himself to possess over the human mind for modelling her afterwards" (Dacre 58–59). His class status and his refined nature provide Berenza with the freedom to take Victoria as his mistress, and not his wife (Dacre 60). Berenza's decision to remove Victoria from the company of her mother and Ardolph is based on his need to "*save* her from seduction" (Dacre 61). Berenza "seizes" (Dacre 60) the hand of Victoria and begins his quest to reshape her into the ideal of femininity and sentiment. Berenza's ability see through Victoria's beauty and clearly identify her faults allows him to imagine the changes he will have to make: "[h]er wild and imperious character he would have essayed to render noble, firm, and dignified; her *fierté* he would have softened, and her boldness checked" (Dacre 59). Although Berenza appears to have authority over Victoria, Dacre makes it clear that unlike the typical Gothic heroine, Victoria is "beneath his roof, *voluntarily* in his power" (Dacre 90). Victoria is learning from Berenza how to shape-shift and gain entry to this exclusive realm of sensibility and femininity. He is providing her with instruction and an example of how to refine and civilize her behavior, which deems useful. Judith Butler examines gender construction and the place of the female body in society. The concept of matter, according to the Latin or Greek definition is not a "referant or blank slate, but it is temporalized" (Butler *Bodies* 31). Women contribute to matter, while men to form through reproduction, but Butler moves away from the more modern empirical meanings of this term and discusses matter as containing the capacity for creation, intelligibility, and rationality (*Bodies* 30). Butler seeks to problematize the body's meaning and discuss new way for bodies to matter. Berenza is responsible for the creation of her dual natures, but it is in Victoria's power to continue using affectation as a disguise.

Dacre describes Berenza's rationality and ability to avoid romantic notions, yet he is unable to see through Victoria's performance and his plans to reform her are quite idealistic: "the mind of Berenza, ever aiming at perfection, felt, that ere he could avow himself the latter, he must himself new model the object" (Dacre 91). The qualities associated with sensibility are gendered female, and as a result Berenza appears effeminate. Within the public sphere the female body was considered sexual, while the male body reflected its own rational tendencies as sexually neutral, thus simply the presence of the female body would transform the rational, masculine discourse associated with the public sphere, to a more feminized dandyism. Berenza's mismanagement of his mistresses, like Megalena Strozzi, is also revealing since effeminacy may include qualities associated with women like "softness...[and] unmanly delicacy" (Cohen 7), but it also involves being "addicted to women" (Cohen 7). Berenza, like many of Dacre's male characters, "tend to desire only what is thoroughly mediated by cultural norms, particularly regarding feminine attractiveness and virtue" (Dunn 318). Victoria's eventual rejection of Berenza is also representative of her rejection of society's expectations concerning femininity. Although Victoria may be in control of her decision to continue deceiving through affectation, it is Berenza who leads Victoria to create her dual natures as he attempts to reshape her into the ideal of femininity.

Edgar Linton does not make Catherine's reform a personal conquest, but he does have expectations for an ideal of femininity that Catherine feels she must attempt to fulfill in order to gain access to the refined and civilized realm of Thrushcross Grange. Catherine's choice of a husband is similar to Victoria's since both women marry the feminized male, as Diane Hoeveler explains, this choice is unlike the typical fate of a wild-spirited young girl whose lover eventually leaves her to marry a virgin (191). Catherine and Victoria choose a "safe" marriage by associating themselves with the "safely feminized man" (Hoeveler 191). Since Edgar Linton is not up to the task of forcing Catherine into the world of Thrushcross Grange, Skulker, the Linton's bull-dog, "drags Catherine kicking and screaming, into the other, proper world, with its other, proper husband" (Hoeveler 192). Catherine's entry into the realm of the Lintons demands that she transform. Catherine's familiarity with shape-shifting and performance, make this task an easy one for the family. Similar to Berenza's need to reform Victoria, the Lintons treat Catherine as a "fetish..., a new object that they can shape into social conformity" (Hoeveler 193). Edgar's bourgeois status requires Catherine to repress her sexual nature, refine her manners, and civilize her appearance. The realm that Thrushcross Grange represents is in direct opposition to Wuthering Heights. In a rare moment Catherine defends her friendship with the Lintons, and her need to become like them, when she tells Heathcliff, "[a]nd should I always be sitting with you.... What do you talk about? You might be dumb or a baby for anything you say to amuse me, or for anything you do.... It is no company at all, when people know nothing and say nothing" (Brontë 69). Catherine is calling upon her high-class status to distinguish herself from Heathcliff, and identify more with the Lintons. Although she shape-shifts enough to enter into a marriage with Edgar, her ability to perform begins to disintegrate upon Heathcliff's return.

Victoria and Catherine lose their ability to shape-shift and must revert back to their true "demonic" natures. Berenza's revealing that he felt Victoria was "unworthy to become his wife" (Dacre 138) seals his fate and Victoria's begins to seek her revenge and in doing so loses control of her reformed façade. Catherine is unable to continue in her marriage upon Heathcliff's return. Her failure in uniting Heathcliff and Edgar as friends results in her illness, and her alienation from all that Thrushcross Grange represents. The male characters who welcomed Catherine and Victoria into the realm of sensibility and refinement are now replaced by other men who embrace their true identities. Zofloya and Heathcliff have always recognized the nature of their female counterparts, and because of this Victoria and Catherine return to them, and the freedom they represent. The rejection of the domestic occurs because of pride and in Catherine's case a loss of self. The similarities between The Moor and Heathcliff can be found in their lower class status, and the freedom they represent as outcasts of society. Although Victoria and Catherine find it difficult at first to associate with their lower class male doubles, they eventually confide and share intimate bonds with them.

Heathcliff's uncertain background, dark skin and gypsy-like appearance (Brontë 34–35) "insists on a kind of radical indeterminacy for the foundling" (Stevenson 67), which links him racially with the mysterious dark Moor in *Zofloya*. Heathcliff and Zofloya both disappear and return transformed. After hearing Catherine reject him as a possible husband, Heathcliff leaves Wuthering Heights only to return transformed into a gentleman. His "rebirth" (Stevenson 68) is as mysterious as his first appearance, except he has climbed the social ladder. Heathcliff's new image as the "self-made man" (Stevenson 69), makes him more attuned to Catherine's taste, and puts him closer to exacting revenge on Hindley. Gestures, mannerisms, and appearances, Butler argues, are "performative in the sense that the essence or identity that they otherwise purport to express fabrications manufactured and sustained through corporeal signs and discursive means" (*Gender Trouble* 136). A different type of masculinity separated working class men from the middle class men of the public sphere. Male workers began to mimic middle class respectability in their appearance and mannerisms. The workingman's *performance* echoes Butler's argument concerning the construction of identity. This new masculinity had a direct impact on women's status in society, and their contributions to the public sphere could not be overlooked. The working class man has the ability to transform his body to appeal to the requirements of the public sphere, an impossible task for the women who also seek public recognition. Heathcliff's transformation suggests that the movement from his suspicious background to an established member of society is an easier task for men than women.

Zofloya's disappearance is shrouded in mystery, since he is thought to have been killed (Dacre 149), but upon his miraculous return Victoria is keen to notice some changes: "it occurred to her that the figure of the Moor possessed a grace and majesty which she had never before remarked; his face too seemed animated with charms ... and his very dress to have acquired a more splendid, tasteful, and elegant appearance" (Dacre 153). Zofloya's new image seeks to appease Victoria's discomfort concerning his status as a servant. His new majestic appearance appeals to Victoria and allows her to be less apprehensive about sharing her deepest secrets with the Moor, as she can not help thinking that "Zofloya, before his sudden disappearance, and Zofloya, since his return, were widely different of each other" (Dacre 153). Anne K. Mellor focuses on Victoria's sexuality and how the white males in the novel are unable to satisfy her sexual needs. Whether it is Count de Loredani, Count Berenza, or Henriquez they are all sexually ineffective as demonstrated within "the figural discourse of this text, white male bodies literally become smaller, weaker, less potent" (Mellor 172). As Mellor points out, the bodies of Victoria and Zofloya grow in size, as does Victoria's sexual desire for him. This sexual desire between the "empowered white woman for a black man" (Mellor 173) represents a "culturally outlawed sexual desire" (Mellor 173), which finds a secure place within the Gothic genre. Along with other cultural faux pas, this taboo sexual relationships between Victoria and the Moor "enabled Dacre's female readers to explore a far wider range of sexual options, a more aggressive libidinal subjectivity, than did the other writing of her day" (Mellor 173). Victoria and Catherine's return to their true natures includes their association with other male characters who encourage their natural tendencies. Zofloya and Heathcliff share similarities in their origins and their transformations, and they function to help guide their female counterparts back into their natural habitats. Zofloya and Heathcliff mirror the shape-shifting abilities of Victoria and Catherine, which link these male characters to the "demonic" and the socially deviant.

The Gothic genre is itself flexible and dynamic, as it moves from the traditional "Male Gothic," to the Sentimental Female Gothic, and finally to the more radical Female Gothic introduced by Charlotte Dacre and rewritten by Emily Brontë. Similar to the mutability of the Gothic genre, the female demon/heroine undergoes a variety of transformations. Traditionally she is the grotesque sorceress whose appearance reflects her inner corruption. In Dacre's *Zofloya* and Brontë's *Wuthering Heights* the female demon no longer reveals herself through her physical form; instead she has the power to "shape-shift" and use affectation to conceal her true nature. Both authors begin their novels by revealing the natural tendencies of their heroines in childhood. As Victoria and Catherine are introduced to the refined and civilized realm of the domestic, they are called upon by the effeminate male characters of Berenza and Edgar Linton, to create an affected self. This "education" or modeling results from Berenza and Linton's desire to construct the female demon into the ideal of femininity in order to stake claim over her. By reforming the female demon, the feminized male characters seek to make her submissive and yet they have only really succeeded in providing her with the tools to access the domestic space which had remained closed to them due to their masculinized behavior. Once inside the feminized space the female demon's dual nature allows her to move freely among the unsuspecting inhabitants of the domestic sphere and claim it as her own. This evokes similar reactions of fear that the traditional Gothic ghost would have instilled in the reader. The female demon cannot contain herself within the domestic realm and is unable to maintain her performance. She eventually returns to her true nature with the aid of her male demonic double On the other hand, Zofloya and Heathcliff are successful in their transformations which allow them to fit into the public sphere. Although Victoria and Catherine strive to find a place within the public sphere which would allow them to keep their masculine traits, they soon discover that they are being pushed back into the private. Heathcliff and the Moor succeed in gaining access to the acceptable public sphere through a mysterious transformation. Their new "acceptable" personas convince their female counterparts to reject the feminized domestic sphere and instead embrace their masculinized wild self. The female demon fails at her own transformation into the ideal of femininity which suggests that the domesticated men make better models for the domestic sphere than some of the female characters themselves. While Heathcliff and Zofloya experience more freedom in the public sphere than in their roles as "Other," Catherine and Victoria do not. The female demons are forced into their domestic roles as they fail in their attempt to be accepted for their masculinized behavior. Victoria and Catherine reclaim their true identity as female demons through the characters of Zofloya and Heathcliff, who share many similarities including their mysterious backgrounds, low class status, and their ability to shape-shift. The female demon/heroine's newly acquired power of performance and transformation allows her to explore the realm of the domestic, but Dacre and Brontë suggest that her wild spirit will remain untamed and her movement back into her proper sphere is inevitable.

# Two

# Between the Spheres

### *"Dual Natures"* Louis and Robert Moore in Charlotte Brontë's Shirley

> You *do* know what I mean, and for the first time I stand before you *myself.* I have flung off the tutor, and beg to introduce you to the man: and, remember, he is a gentleman [Brontë 577].

> "Now," interrupted Shirley, "you want me as a gentleman—the first gentleman in Briarfield, in short, to supply your place, be master of the Rectory, and guardian of your niece and maids while you are away?" [Brontë 326].

Left unprotected except for two pistols, Caroline Helstone and Shirley Keeldar attempt to stand guard against a working class mob (Brontë 331). As newly-appointed "gentleman, [...] master of the Rectory, and guardian of [Caroline] and maids" (Brontë 326), Captain Shirley Keeldar finds herself in a desperate situation when she realizes her complete helplessness against hundreds of angry mill workers. Even the overly confident Shirley is quick to note the inequality of the circumstances between herself and the middle-class men who have gathered to protect their mill. She is transformed into a "make-shift" man, whose task is to protect the more feminine Caroline, the house, and its occupants, but the odds are against her and unlike the middle-class men and the working-class mob, Shirley is alone and unorganized.

Issues of domesticity, love, and marriage are interspersed with those of economics, the working class, and politics throughout *Shirley*. As a result, Brontë's novel has been criticized as "lack[ing] structural unity" (Hook 10), a narrative technique also reflected in the gender confusion among the characters. The women in the novel possess masculine perspectives on marriage. Although Caroline appears as the ideal of femininity, she displays masculine qualities as represented by her hatred of sewing and her longing to participate in the public sphere by having employment. Shirley's alter ego, Captain Keeldar, provides her with the freedom to behave more manly than she would be allowed otherwise. While Shirley possesses masculine characteristics and attempts to engage in the public sphere, some of the male characters, including the curates and Mr. Moore, are feminized through their participation in feminine discourse. The characters in *Shirley* personify Brontë's narrative shifts from the public and private.

Brontë reveals how male and female characters can either intrude forcibly or slip invisibly into their opposing spheres. The tendency for nineteenth-century women to be caught between two different representations of femininity, as well as two different spheres—the public and private, is explained in Judith Butler's study of the permeability of the body and the constructs of gender. Butler problematizes the body's meaning and discusses new ways for bodies to matter. Her focus in *Gender Trouble* is on how gender constructs are fictional, not biological: "They are fictional in the sense that they do not pre-exist the regimes of power/knowledge but are performative products of them. They are performative in the sense that the categories themselves produce the identity they are deemed to be simply representing" (Jagger 17). Butler's theory supports the flexibility of gender, a concept apparent in *Shirley* by the constant shifting between the spheres and gender performances. The status of women and the role that the body plays in defining gender is unstable and difficult to determine leading to conflicting notions of femininity and women's place in society. Perceptions of the future generation concerning the domestic sphere are shown through female characters like Jessy and the Yorke girls. The changes to the public sphere also introduce new definitions of masculinity. Most importantly, Brontë has young male characters, such as Harry, Martin, and the curates, participate in feminine discourse and the domestic sphere. These characters also demonstrate how the uneasy movements between the public and private realms mirrors the way in which issues of industry and economy are discussed side by side with themes of marriage and love.

There is a clear link between the working class and women during the nineteenth century based on their attempts to penetrate the male middle-class public sphere. The body determines one's place in society, as Madeleine Hurd explains, "[t]he sight of one's body affects how one will be addressed" (93). Women and working-class men find themselves excluded from Jürgen Habermas' public sphere based on their inability to adhere physically to the requirements of a middle class man: "[women's bodies] supposedly determined their non-public proclivities" (Hurd 101). In Chapter 19 "A Summer's Night," Mr. Helstone asks Shirley to stay overnight with Caroline (see second epigraph). That night, mill workers riot through the countryside burning down buildings. The barking dog scares off the rioters and Caroline and Shirley escape to the Hollow unharmed. The scene between Shirley and the working-class mob illustrates the association between the working class and women. The higher classes, including royalty, were rarely thought of in terms of their physical bodies. They appeared to deny their own bodily needs, demonstrating a particular self-discipline considered impossible for the lower classes and women to attain. While the members of the public sphere remained "abstract, [and] disembodied" (Hurd 101), the outsiders, through their physical behavior and appearance, proved to be unable to separate themselves from their bodies. Habermas recognizes this distinction as an example of the "principles of abstraction that are essential to the sphere's inclusivity" (Hurd 98). Gwendolyn Audrey Foster in *Troping the Body: Gender, Etiquette, and Performance* examines the link between etiquette texts and performance. As Foster claims, the nineteenth century was "preoccupied with transforming the performing self, and the grotesque desires of the body, into an aestheticized version of the 'natural' self, a gilded body at times indistinguishable from a decorated home" (1). This is reminiscent of the trope of the female ghost, a role assumed by Caroline Helstone, who appears to move invisibly within the house. Athena Vrettos suggests that Caroline's illness and invisibility arise as a result of her repression and silence in the masculine world of her uncle and Robert: "Eventually she becomes [...] a symbol of walking death, haunting Robert as a ghost from the past rather than a living woman" (41). While Foster is more concerned with the consequences of etiquette on the female body, the effects of performing masculinity should not be overlooked. Foster's work demonstrates how etiquette defined gender roles and kept the spheres separate:

> Significantly, gentlemen leave their hats and coats in the front hall. These outer accoutrements are reminders and manifestations of their supremacy in the public sphere. As they enter the private sphere, they shed these symbols of power and submit to the female-dominated sphere [...]. Most etiquette books for women, then, seemingly enforced a code of subjugation over the marginalized and fragmentized male, who is objectified as a performer of tasks within middle-and upper-class homes [13].

Domestic etiquette functions to alienate men, but as *Shirley* and other works studied in subsequent chapters demonstrate, male characters are able to perform and engage in feminine discourse allowing them entry into feminized private sphere.

A different type of masculinity separated working-class men from the middle-class men of the public sphere. Male workers began to mimic middle-class respectability in their appearance and mannerisms. The working class' ability to perform including his "rational use of leisure and acceptable political tools" (Hurd 85) requires society's acknowledgment of him as a member of the bourgeois public sphere. The working man's performance echoes Butler's argument concerning the construction of identity. Although manners and appearance were central, the working-class man also had to improve his status as family father, which he eventually achieved quite well. Robin Gilmour notes how the Victorians struggled with clearly defining the gentleman:

> Thus, while gentlemanly status offered respectability and independence within the traditional social hierarchy, at the same time it challenged the dignity of the work which made the new industrial society possible. It is this conflict, more than anything else, which explains why the early and mid–Victorian period saw such an anxious debate about the idea of the gentleman, and why that debate was so ambiguous and inconclusive, producing so many conflicting images of true gentlemanliness [7].

While the workers attempted to perform according to their knowledge of the definition of the gentleman, the middle-class males were continuing to develop the flexible, inconsistent, and contradictory concept of manliness. As Gilmour suggests, "the Victorians themselves were, if not confused, then at least much more uncertain than their grandfathers had been about what constituted a gentleman, and that this uncertainty, which made definition difficult, as an important part of the appeal which gentlemanly status held for outsiders hoping to attain it" (3). This new type of masculinity had in turn an impact on the wives of workingmen as they took on the role as moral teachers for their families. Women were expected to teach lessons on manners and morality to their working husbands, which required that these women be perceived as contributing to the maintenance of the public sphere. Ideally, women could encourage working men to be moral, sober, and respectable, while the male worker had enough "solid sense to counter the [upper classes'] corrupt language" (Hurd 89). This moral improvement led, in some cases, to a sort of over-acting, to refer back to Butler's theory of performance, like "hyperrespectablility, a demonstrative public display of manly self-discipline" (Hurd 89). As explored in later chapters, performance and spectacle are feminized. The working-class performance of bourgeois masculinity must not be over-performed as it would suggest effeminacy. The working-man's tendency to over-perform in his role as middle-class man suggests the dangerous tendency to become a spectacle.

The working class' ability to perform is described as a public action based on repetition; as Butler states, repetition is a "re-enactment and reexperiencing of a set of meanings already socially established; and it is the mundane and ritualized form of their legitimation" (*Gender Trouble* 140). The working-class man has the ability to transform his body to appeal to the requirements of the public sphere, an impossible task for the women who also seek public recognition. The pairing of women and working-class men attempting to climb the social ladder is evident through such examples as Victoria and Zofloya in Charlotte Dacre's *Zofloya, or The Moor*, Catherine and Heathcliff in Emily Brontë's *Wuthering Heights*, and Lucy and Luke in Braddon's *Lady Audley's Secret*. It is important to note that similar to *Shirley* the female characters and their male counterparts from Charlotte Dacre and Emily Brontë's novels pair women and the working class, since both Zofloya and Heathcliff are introduced as originating from the lower classes. The working class and women had no place within the masculinized middle-class public sphere, and in consequence both appear as outsiders attempting to make their way towards social acceptance. Heathcliff mysteriously returns after years of absence as a self-made gentleman, while Zofloya reveals his superiority through his supernatural powers and physical transformation. Heathcliff's transformation suggests that the movement from his suspicious background to an established member of society is an easier task for men than women. While the women in all three of these novels attempt to attain the social freedom gained by their male counter-parts, they are unable to shed their female form. Through performance the working man acts his way into the public sphere, as Hurd describes, nonverbal signs, symbols, and modes of ritualized behavior are ways in which

> power relationships are mediated and interpreted [...] the dictates of fashion, manners, and taste were once used by aristocracy to denote its superiority to rich commoners [...] middle class males [...] adapted the gracious manners of the aristocrat to the laws of instrumental reason; neo-aristocratic codes of public civility were fused with abstract rationality to produce the new (male middle class) public debater [92].

As the concept of masculinity changed for working-class men, middle-class males made the necessary changes to distinguish themselves from the performances of the lower class, leading to yet another set of complex manners. Like the women who sought credit for their involvement in the public sphere, the sober, respectable, and cultured working-class man, who committed himself to morality and self-discipline, also craved acknowledgment from the public sphere (Hurd 94–95). The only difference in women and working-class men is the latter's ability to transform himself through his appearance and mannerisms to gain access to the bourgeois public sphere. Butler's theory on gender construction can be applied in this case as demonstrating the power of performance in the construction of identity and how biology does not play a role at all as an argument against women's inclusion in the public sphere.

Shirley Keeldar's performance[1] as Captain Keeldar Esquire is entertaining, but falls short once she is faced with a life-threatening situation. Mr. Helstone calls upon Shirley's ability to transform herself into Captain Keeldar in order to protect Caroline and his home, but when confronted with the reality of the working-class mob,[2] Shirley seems bewildered by her inadequacy to perform as a man. The absence of the middle-class men in this scene strikes not only the reader, but the novel's heroine as well. Shirley's helplessness compared to the more organized and capable working-class men demonstrates her failed performance as a man. Although the working-class men in Brontë's novel do not attempt to perform the part of the middle-class men, they do seek to penetrate the bourgeois public sphere. The women, like Shirley, who perform the role of gentleman are unsuccessful and nowhere near the numbers of the working class. Brontë draws attention to women's lack of support for their crusade for acceptance within the public sphere, and when they attempt to mimic middle-class males they are proven ineffectual and helpless. *Shirley* gives readers a sense that whether it is the threat of outsiders, like the working class or women, the public sphere has been left unguarded by middle-class men. These are the same men who spend a good amount of the novel within the feminized private sphere. The walls that surround Habermas' public sphere begin to crumble as subaltern groups like the Woman's Movement and the rise of the working class demand their own space on equal ground with their male middle-class counterparts.

*Shirley* offers readers a unique combination of the tropes associated with the social-justice novel while simultaneously challenging the conventional gender roles familiar to this genre and the early part of the Victorian period. Carolyn Lesjak traces the genealogy of the Victorian novel in *Working Fictions* and comments on some of the difficulties that arise when authors combine labor and literature:

> Despite the fact, for instance, that labor and the working class are the industrial novel's explicit objects of inquiry, even a cursory look at its "classics"—Dickens's *Hard Times*, Disraeli's *Sybil*, Gaskell's *Mary Barton*, Brontë's *Shirley*—reveals a marked *absence* of representations of work or workers working [2].

Brontë is criticized for attempting to combine a love plot with the Luddite movement of 1811–12. Similarly, George Eliot experienced criticism with *Daniel Deronda*, where she blended the plot of Deronda's discovery of his Jewish heritage with a complex love plot involving Gwendolen Harleth. Eliot's critics, like Brontë's, complained of the disjointed narrative structure. As Juliet Barker notes, Brontë "passionately defended the right of women to work" (601); this is clearly one of her themes in *Shirley*. Brontë writes in a letter to Smith Williams 3 July 1849:

> Lonely as I am—how should I be if Providence had never given me courage to adopt a career—perseverance to plead through two long, weary years with publishers till they admitted me?—How should I be with youth past—sisters lost—a resident in a moorland parish where there is not a single educated family? In that case I should have no world at all: the raven, weary of surveying the deluge and without an ark to return to, would be my type. As it is, something like hope and motive sustains me still. I wish all your daughters—I wish every woman in England had also a hope and motive: Alas! There are many old maids who have neither. (Barker, *The Brontës* 601).

Significantly, as Brontë's letters reveal, her motivation was focused on the woman's movement and the call to educate young girls. Brontë's novel further illustrates the flexibility of the private and public spheres through the realization of masculine perceptions in the domestic sphere and in feminine discourse. Patricia McKee examines the creation of the private sphere as a "place designated [...] a sphere separate from public knowledge and public order, [...] a place that moreover assumes characteristics of realms of obscurity discovered, or produced, by disciplines of knowledge" (5). The "obscurity" described by McKee underscores the issues of confusion, instability, and the lack of consistency that are found throughout Brontë's novel. McKee explains social hierarchy based on knowledge, which puts women and the working class below men. She notes, "[w]omen's lives are not separated from realms of public knowledge, they are known to be incompatible with knowledge, order, and regulation [...] lives of persons beyond the reach of knowledge are ordered simply by being 'kept down'" (5). The creation of the private sphere is based on the belief that women are incapable of meeting the requirements of the public sphere.

The many shifts between literary genres in Brontë's *Shirley* have irritated critics beginning with G.H. Lewes, who wrote in the *Edinburgh Review* in 1850, "all unity, in consequence of defective art, is wanting [...]. The authoress never seems distinctly to make up her mind as to what she was to do; whether to describe the habits and manners of Yorkshire [...] or to paint character, or to tell a love story" (160). In addition, Lewes examines the reasons for the novel's disjointedness:

> There is no passionate link; nor is there any artistic fusion, or intergrowth, by which one part evolves itself from another. Hence its falling-off in interest, coherent movement, and life. The book may be laid down at any chapter, and almost any chapter omitted. The various scenes are gathered up into three volumes,—they have not grown into a work. The characters often need a justification for their introduction; as is the case of the three Curates, who are offensive, uninstructive, and unamusing [159].

Hook adds that Brontë's attempt to deal with all issues, "has nothing whatever to do with the degree of unity it may or may not achieve. To say this is not to deny that there may be a problem [...] but it is important that the problem be correctly identified" (10). Lewes points out how Brontë's use of the social problem genre, which requires that she focus on industry and the working class, conflicts with her tendency to revert to romantic descriptions of characters and landscape, as well as tales of love and heartache. This lack of unity includes disjointed descriptions that move abruptly from the public sphere of the working class and their struggles to the private realm of their employer's love life. According to Elizabeth Gaskell, Brontë's response was disappointment, but less in Lewes' criticism than in his ability to detect a "female pen" (Gaskell 306). Barker discusses in "Saintliness, Treason, and Plot" how Gaskell had already formed opinions on Brontë's family before even visiting Haworth or her father (103). Gaskell's accounts of Charlotte's life and her statements are to be used with caution. Gaskell formed a close relationship with Ellen Nussey who had "begun the process of identifying the originals of the characters and places in Charlotte's novels by taking Mrs. Gaskell round 'Shirley Country'" (Barker 106). Deirdre D'Albertis examines Gaskell's biography as a "disguised form of literary competition with Brontë" (2). The motives and questionable methods behind Gaskell's *Life of Charlotte Brontë* invite therefore a careful approach to the text as a biographical source. Brontë took pride in her belief that *Shirley* revealed less of a feminine influence than her previous publication, *Jane Eyre* (Gaskell 306), and reacted strongly in a letter to Lewes: "I wished critics to judge me as an author, not as a woman, you so roughly—I even thought so cruelly—handled the question of sex" (Spark 174). It appears that Brontë had set out with the intention to mask her feminine identity when writing *Shirley*, which may have led to incongruities within the novel. Barker points out how *Shirley*'s critics were unanimous that Currer Bell was a woman (*The Brontës* 610). She approaches writing the novel with a strong refusal not to recreate *Jane Eyre*, as Gaskell recounts, "[Brontë] was anxious to write of things she has known and seen; and among the number was the West Yorkshire characters, for which any tale laid among the Luddites would afford full scope" (Gaskell 298). Eagleton recognizes the similarities between Louis and Shirley and Jane and Rochester: "Louis, like Jane, a private tutor marries above him and will tame his imperious spouse" (59). Although Brontë opens *Shirley* using the romantic writing style readers enjoyed in *Jane Eyre*, she is quick to reprimand them for expecting this novel to be similar to her previous publishing success. She begins with the curates and invites her readers to forget the present which is "dusty, sun-burnt, hot [and] arid" (Brontë 1), in order to slip into the past and "pass the mid-day in slumber, and dream of dawn" (Brontë 1). A strong authorial voice banishes this romantic description and warns readers of the differences between this novel and her previous works. The way in which Brontë invokes the romantic in her description of the curates and the past only to snuff it out is a recurring pattern that leads her to correct her reader's expectations:

> If you think, from this prelude, that anything like a romance is preparing for you, reader, you never were more mistaken. Do you anticipate sentiment, and poetry, and reverie? Do you expect passion, and stimulus, and melodrama? Calm your expectations; reduce them to a lowly standard. Something real, cool, and solid, lies before you; something unromantic as Monday morning, when all who have work wake with the consciousness that they must rise and betake themselves thereto [Brontë 1].

Brontë must use the romantic in order to successfully dismiss it from her work. This passage also demonstrates how Brontë is well aware of the expectations of her readers, making it even more of a refusal to submit to her readership. It appears that Brontë, even before beginning her novel, demands some changes in her writing style. She also feels the need to write what she knows, which she believes will aid in her realistic approach. Brontë's decision to focus on the realistic aspects of *Shirley* may be one reason why she does not succeed. As illustrated in the opening passage of *Shirley*, Brontë feels the need to include romance in order to emphasize how she is replacing it with realism. This technique culminates with Brontë giving equal time to *Shirley*'s love plot along with issues of industry and the working class.

However, problems arise from Brontë's decision to base her fiction on reality: "[p]eople recognized themselves, or were recognized by others, in her graphic descriptions of their personal appearance, and modes of actions and turns of thought" (Gaskell 298). Gaskell links the characters in *Shirley* to some personages living in and around Haworth. For instance, she states, "[t]he three curates were real living men, haunting Haworth [...] they rather enjoyed calling each other by the names she had given them" (298). At the same time, Gaskell includes a letter from Brontë that denies linking real persons to her characters: "You are not to suppose any of the characters in *Shirley* intended as literal portraits. It would not suit the rules of art, nor of my own feelings, to write in that style. We only suffer reality to *suggest*, never to *dictate*" (307). This is evocative of Roland Barthes' idea of "transparent allegory," which Wendy Parkins skillfully refers to in her reading of *Shirley*. Parkins defines Barthes' "transparent allegory" as "where, quite literally, one (fictional) character or place stands for another (real) one" (127). She supports her argument that Brontë's novel functions as allegory by the ways in which *Shirley* is "concerned with political and socio-economic matters and is set in a particular historical period and a real geographic region [...with] a conscious insistence on historic and regional verisimilitude as shown by [...] the Yorkshire-ness of *Shirley*" (130). Gaskell makes links between the characters in the novel and those in Brontë's life; for instance she claims that Shirley Keeldar was "what Emily Brontë would have been, had she been placed in health and prosperity" (299). By fixing on real characters, Brontë imposes upon herself strict guidelines to follow, which may have added to the lack of unity within the novel. *Shirley* as "transparent allegory" is one way for critics to explain the novel's lack of unity, another involves even more biographical evidence. While writing *Shirley*, Brontë witnessed her brother Branwell's death from consumption throughout 1848, followed in the same year by Emily, and in 1849 by Anne. Phyllis Bentley draws explanations for the novel's "defect as a work of art" (101) from these three deaths. Similar to Parkins' argument for *Shirley* as allegory, Bentley turns to biographical reasons for the novel's weaknesses. Her criticism revolves around the novel's lack of story, "tedious dialogue" (101), and the failure of Louis Moore as a character (101). Brontë's intent to focus on the real by creating her novel as an allegory is one explanation for the lack of passion, which is found in abundance in *Jane Eyre*. The strongest explanation for *Shirley*'s marked differences from any other Brontë novel, is made by Gaskell, who paints a picture of a writer whose previous published success plagues her with a sense of duty to her readership, and also to her newly acquired reputation within the literary world. Gaskell describes Brontë's uneasy dealings with her novel:

> Miss Brontë took extreme pains with *Shirley*. She felt that the fame she had acquired imposed on her a double responsibility. She tried to make her novel like a piece of actual life,—feeling sure that, if she but represented the product of personal experience and observations truly, good would come out of it in the long run. She carefully studied the different reviews and criticisms that appeared on *Jane Eyre*, in hopes of extracting precepts and advice from which to profit [299].

Brontë, it appears, felt the pressure to produce yet another success, but she chose not to revert to the romantic formula of *Jane Eyre*, and even went so far as to refuse outright this type of approach for *Shirley* in her prelude. Instead, the author casts her eyes about and chooses to focus on "a piece of actual life" based on "personal experiences and observations." Brontë comments on the unfavorable reception of *Shirley*'s realistic beginning by stating that, "On the whole I am glad a decidedly bad notice has come first—a notice whose inexpressible ignorance first stuns and then stirs me. Are there no such men as the Helstones and Yorkes? Yes, there are. Is the first chapter disgusting or vulgar? It is not, it is *real*" (Spark 170). This adamant denial of the romantic, her attempts to conceal her sex by assuming a more "male" subject and writing style, as well as a determination to accurately present reality[3] become obstacles that are dealt with uneasily as demonstrated through Brontë's awkward movements from the private to the public spheres. Brontë seeks to incorporate "truth" into the novel through two methods: "life-likeness and of personal experience imaginatively transmuted" (Ewbank 165). With these clear intentions, Brontë sets out to write *Shirley*, a novel that strains under self-imposed regulations.

Brontë acknowledges that a social tension exists with men discussing what is usually defined as "traditionally feminine values—love, intuition, beauty, virtue" (Christ 149). Men do not freely or willingly launch into these conversations, but they do ultimately become active participants. An example of this type of social tension is revealed at the beginning of the novel when Mr. Moore states that he was not seeking female society when he visited Whinbury: "it is only to give Sykes or Pearson a call in their counting-house; where our discussions run on other topics than matrimony, and our thoughts are occupied with other things than courtships, establishments and dowries [...] to the tolerably complete exclusion of such figments as love-making, etc." (Brontë 56). Mr. Malone agrees with Moore, but proceeds to do just the opposite by entering into a discussion of marriage when he replies, "I go along with you completely, Moore. If there is one notion I hate more than another, it is that of marriage: I mean marriage in the vulgar weak sense, as a mere matter of sentiment [...]— humbug!" (Brontë 56). This exchange between Moore and Malone is an accurate example of when and how men in the novel discuss what is considered feminine discourse. They deny talking about such trivialities, but then proceed to discuss those very topics in an ironic twist that seems to escape them entirely. Their conversation might result in a negative view of domesticity, but they are nevertheless discussing the feminine subject of marriage.

It becomes clear that the definition of masculinity relies on male participation with the public and private spheres. Habermas demonstrates the dependence of the spheres on each other as the bourgeois male is defined by his participation in the formation of public opinion, as well as his role as head of the family. During the nineteenth century, the private and public spheres separated as a result of a loss of the private and autonomous individual by the state and mass media (McKee 11). The spheres are linked by the ways in which they create the concept of the private individual who gathers to form a public, but the spheres rely on each other for another reason as well: to provide a definition of femininity, masculinity and later on, arguably, homosexuality. The gendering of the spheres resulted in the search for new forms of masculinity; this new definition of maleness was extremely dependent on the status of women in the private sphere. Maleness was defined in similar terms to Habermas' description of the individual members of the public sphere whose position as head of the family included having their wife and children as dependents. As Joan Landes states, "gender difference occurred via a specific bourgeois male discourse that depended on women's domesticity and the silencing of 'public' women, of the aristocracy and popular classes [...] and the collapse of the older patriarchy gave way to a more pervasive gendering of the public sphere" (2). It is important to note this reliance between the public and private spheres and how the existence of one is dependent on the stability of the other. The working-class man frequently failed to keep his wife unemployed and in consequence, the lower classes were unable to keep the public and private as separate entities. Critics have focused on women and the working class,[4] as well as other emerging groups as examples that argue against Habermas' concept of the public sphere as fixed.

Brontë's curates[5] provide an adverse version of the domesticated man, as they are clearly linked with their female counterparts—old maids. Brontë begins the novel with the curates, who are described as "locusts" (Brontë 42) that descend rather rudely into the parlor of Mrs. Gale. In a letter to Mrs. Gaskell after the publication of her *Life of Charlotte Brontë*, Charles Kingsley admitted that he had been so disgusted by the opening of *Shirley* that he "gave up the writer and her books with the notion that she was a person who lived coarseness" (Wise & Symington 4: 222–3). According to Marianne Thormählen despite the bleak image of the curates, Donne and Malone, Brontë is not anti-curate. The Victorians associated effeminacy with homosexuality, which was considered the third sex in the second half of the nineteenth century (Hekma 213). As Gert Hekma suggests effeminacy

> was a forceful social strategy that marginalized homosexual desires and this prevented the development of gay identities. As an impediment it worked well, but it also provoked a powerful strategy of seduction that made sexual border traffic between gay and straight men possible and satisfactory [...]. For a century, men with same-sex desires were pushed into the role of a third gender [239].

Ellen Nussey comments on Brontë's use of her father as a model for the curates, as she notes, "her father materially helped fix her impressions, for he had held more than one curacy in the very neighborhood which she describes in *Shirley*" (Orel 21). Gaskell also calls attention to Brontë's father and later her husband as curates and her particular portrayal of their profession in her novel: "Fancy him [Brontë's husband], an Irish curate, loving her even then, reading that beginning of *Shirley*" (Orel 156). The curates' reasons for this "invasion" (Brontë 43) are explained by Mrs. Gale and other women of the town as, "nought else but to give folk trouble" (Brontë 43). The image of the curates as parasites, who pester their hostesses out of sheer amusement, serves to emphasize their lack of social responsibility; they quite literally feed off the community, as Brontë describes, "The curates had good appetites, and though the beef was 'tough,' they ate a great deal of it. They swallowed, too, a tolerable allowance of the 'flat beer'" (Brontë 42). "Brontë's correspondence shows that she has a great deal of curate frustration to draw on, and to some extent relieve, when writing *Shirley*" (Thormählen 194). After the publication of the novel she claimed in a letter to Miss Wooler on February 14, 1850, that she regretted having been too merciful, "too tenderly and partially veiling the errors of 'the Curates'" (Wise & Symington 3:75). Even their choice of conversation topics are depicted as, "frivolities which seemed empty as bubbles to all save themselves" (Brontë 42).

The impotence of the curates is made clear in their mock duel in the parlor, where Mr. and Mrs. Gale are undisturbed by their rowdiness because "clerical quarrels were as harmless as they were noisy [...] they resulted in nothing" (Brontë 44). The curates' positions in society features them as inhabiting the public sphere, but Brontë presents them as the unproductive, uninvited, and rowdy visitors to the private sphere of the parlor. As John Ruskin explains in *Sesame and Lilies* a woman's proper place is in the home where she provides a sanctuary for her husband to retreat from the public sphere. The parlor, in addition to having middle-class connotations is a strictly private space, as Thad Logan states,

> While the separation of the spheres was fantasy, insofar as homes did not and could not exist as transcendent spaces outside economic and political systems, the sequestration of women in the home was real enough, and compulsory domesticity was the context of life for middle-class women. The doctrine of separate spheres not only dictated that home was a woman's place but asserted explicitly that her sacred duty lay therein [25].

This idea is further supported by Habermas who credits the architecture of the nineteenth-century homes for increased privatization: "The privatized individuals who gathered here [the parlor] to form a public were not reducible to 'society'; they only entered into it, so to speak, out of a private life that had assumed institutional form in the enclosed space of the patriarchal conjugal family" (46). Their lack of productivity is in direct contrast with Victorian definitions of masculinity:

> To be a successful man is to be a productive man and to be a successful society is to have a large (and ever expanding) Gross Domestic Product. The individual male is remade in the image of social production and the imperative to work combines economics and morality. Similarly, industriousness in the Victorian period combined connotations of individual effort and industrial production [Danahay, *Gender* 39].

Brontë illustrates the curates as figuratively and literally forcing themselves into the feminized parlor: "Malone pushed into the parlour before Miss Keeldar" (Brontë 277). It is as if the curates cannot physically fit entirely into the domestic sphere, but they insist on being there, as Brontë describes, "The little parlour was in an uproar; you would have thought a duel must follow such virulent abuse" (Brontë 44). The idea of dueling in a parlor suggests an affected masculinity since the curates prefer the safe haven of Mrs. Gale's parlor. The curates' activity is deemed non-active, futile, and without purpose or end-product, qualities that are in opposition to the concept of Victorian masculinity.

# Domesticated Bachelors and Femininity in Victorian Novels

Brontë's description of the curates makes clear links to the nineteenth-century stereotype of the old maid.[6] Her redundancy, uselessness, and parasitical nature are all reflected in Brontë's curates, right down to the "vacant cackle of their voices" (Brontë 131). Diana Peschier examines the imagery of nuns in *Shirley*, including Brontë's association of nuns and old maids, both present a dreadful fate for Caroline: "Articulating her dread of loneliness, Caroline Helstone, uses the figure of the nun to depict an extreme image of isolation" (133). The curates, although male with an occupation in the public realm, demonstrate similar characteristics traditionally applied to that most inactive and purposeless Victorian persona. This example of blurring the public and private spheres demonstrates how the discourse of economy and business is applied to the curates, which is emphasized by their inability to "produce" anything. According to Thomas Carlyle's theories, "To not work is to leave the category of 'man.' In other words if you are not working you are not masculine" (Danahay, *Gender* 27). Not only did manliness require productivity, it also required that work be of a certain standard, as Martin A. Danahay explains in *Gender at Work in Victorian Culture,*

> Many forms of work were not "manly" and so it was impossible for some men to feel that they were fulfilling their masculine destiny in Carlyle's terms. They therefore felt less than men and in compensation romanticized other forms of labor undertaken by women and the working classes [27].

The old maid, according to Sally Shuttleworth is "figured both as the butt of cruel ridicule and as an object of supreme pathos, being unable to attain the one ordained goal of female life" (194). Similar to caricatures of the old maid, the curates are certainly used by Brontë as comic relief, but they are also a drain on society as illustrated by their insatiable appetites. Shuttleworth further describes the old maid as one who is "placed outside the cycles of both production and reproduction, denied entry into the former, and made redundant in the latter" (184). Brontë's curates do not appear to fit comfortably into one sphere or the other; instead, they seem to move among the private and public spheres without finding a comfortable position in either. Brontë alludes to this constant movement in her description of the curates "rushing backwards and forwards, amongst themselves, to and fro their respective lodgings: not a round— but a triangle of visits, which they keep up all the year through" (Brontë 40). Similar to the old maid, the curates are not welcome in either sphere since they create an "uproar" (Brontë 44) in Mrs. Gale's parlor within the private sphere, and prove ineffectual in their attempts to perform within the public sphere through their neglect of religious duties, their anti-climactic mock duel, and their purposeless discussions. By applying similar economic rhetoric to the curates, which Shuttleworth notes is also used to describe old maids, Brontë is once again blurring the boundaries between the private and public realms. The curates are one example of the ways in which Brontë shifts swiftly from the discourse of economy and business to feminized male characters.

The boys in *Shirley* are already quite confident about their position on marriage and women. Martin, Yorke's boy, possesses a strong view of the domestic sphere as his comment on women makes clear: "I mean always to hate women; they're such dolls: they do nothing but dress themselves finely [...] I'll never marry" (Brontë 175). Ruskin's *Sesame and Lilies* published in 1865 describes women as being the "helpmate of man" (Ruskin 71), and asks how can a wife be of any help if she is a mere "shadow" or "slave." Of course a woman's education should be limited, as Ruskin clarifies, "only so far as may enable her to sympathize in her husband's pleasures and in those of his best friends" (Ruskin 93). Martin realizes early in life that he can find nothing admirable in women who act as dolls. Later in the novel, Martin's masculine ideas of feminine discourse such as marriage and love are revealed as he tries to understand the relationship between Caroline and the recovering Mr. Moore. Martin declares, "I suppose she is, what they call 'in love'" (Brontë 533). Similar to other male characters in the novel, Martin repeatedly engages in the feminine discourse of love and marriage, despite his adamant dislike of such topics. Although it is expected of the female characters to engage in feminine discourse this is not the case with Caroline and Shirley.

Through the characters of Shirley and Caroline, Brontë presents a masculinized women's view of the domestic sphere. Shirley's masculinity is questioned by John Maynard in *Charlotte Brontë and Sexuality* when he emphasizes her less noticeable female traits such as her feminine appearance, her child-like passion and her vulnerability to men (159). Maynard argues that Shirley is "a non-sexual woman [...] in other ways a woman who has hidden or put off all sexual development" (159). This is in direct conflict with Shirley's own claim to masculinity and her desire, as well as Caroline's, to be a man. These female characters do not share Jessy's enthusiasm towards marriage. Caroline admits that she must await marriage to release her from her current state, and that she is "not quite satisfied" (Brontë 98) with the idea of marriage. In fact, Caroline, at times representing the ideal of femininity, would prefer to make money on her own: "I should like an occupation; and if I were a boy, it would not be so difficult to find one" (Brontë 99). Caroline's fantasy involves working along side Robert as his clerk in his counting-house (Brontë 104),—a clear desire for gender equality and partnership. Caroline presents a masculinized view of the relationship between a man and a woman that resembles one shared between men within a homosocial environment like the workplace, rather than heterosexual husband and wife gender roles. Caroline seems to pass between the public and private spheres without being noticed, as Mr. Moore remarks to her, "It appears you walk invisible" (Brontë 257), and again with Boultby: "he did not see her, he never did see her: he hardly knew that such a person existed" (Brontë 297). Unlike the boisterous and awkward curates who violently intrude on the domestic space, Caroline's physical stature and lady-like appearance make her invisible as a possible invading threat to the public sphere. Caroline's invisibility is reminiscent of the gothic trope of the female ghost, whose partial existence mirrors that of the Victorian woman's lack of status within society. Caroline is permitted to think about working, but that is where Brontë draws the line. Instead, Caroline is only allowed to watch Mr. Moore in his counting-house from the outside (Brontë 256).

Caroline is provided with a male counterpart in the character of Harry, who shares her desire to work. Harry, who is disabled, argues "but I am not warlike, Shirley: and yet my mind is so restless, I burn day and night—for what—I can hardly tell—to be—to do—to suffer, I think" (Brontë 438). Caroline needs to occupy herself with a worthwhile task other than sewing, which she describes as being "insufferably tedious" (Brontë 130). Caroline, like Harry, desires, "something absorbing and compulsory to fill my head and hands, and to occupy my thoughts" (Brontë 235). Shirley informs Harry that like her, his mind is captive in his body: "It lies in physical bondage" (Brontë 438). Terry Castle notes how *Shirley*, despite its historical setting reflects Brontë's own loneliness and isolation:

> Both *Jane Eyre* and *Villette* are fraught, claustrophobic first-person narratives: the thematic links with Brontë's own life (exile, loneliness, poverty, sexual longing) are obvious. Yet even the more spacious *Shirley*, set in rural Yorkshire against the backdrop of the Luddite rebellions of 1811–12, seems to allegorize its author's state of mind. In the excruciating rendering of the nearly book-long melancholia of its heroine, Caroline Helstone, Brontë gives one of the more vividly personal accounts of chronic inward sadness since Burton's *Anatomy of Melancholy* or the journals of Cowper. No wonder biographers since Gaskell have fallen under her spell [161].

Harry resembles Shirley and Caroline in that his physical form inhibits his mental powers. Rita Felski in her study of women and the modern through an examination of the gendering of aesthetic concepts, refers back to the eighteenth-century's feminized artist:

> The conception of the male artists as in some sense a feminine figure is already well established in the works of early Romanticism. The Romantic cult of genius celebrated an ideal of transgressive masculinity while simultaneously endowing the male artist with qualities of sensitivity, intuition, and emotional empathy characteristically seen as the province of women [94].

Brontë's solution for Harry is to become an author or poet (Brontë 438),—the feminized artist.

Shirley's masculinity is quite obvious by the fact that her male counterpart is herself, a personality she names Captain Keeldar. Shirley's occupation as mistress of Fieldhead, her role in business, and her adoration of the counting-house (Brontë 215), all provide her with a strong masculine persona in which she takes pride, as evidenced when she states, "I am indeed no longer a girl, but quite a woman and something more [...]. I hold a man's position [...] I feel quite gentleman like" (Brontë 213). Shirley thinks of herself as transcending her female position in society because of her masculine duties and responsibilities. Her masculine aggression links her with the *femme fatale*, as she asks Robert, "You think me a dangerous specimen of my sex" (Brontë 352). Shirley uses her masculinity as a power she holds over men since she is closer to being their equal. Shirley's behavior undermines Ruskin's belief that "the woman is not to guide, nor even to think for herself. The man is always to be the wiser" (Ruskin 81). Shirley goes so far as to command the curate, Mr. Donne to leave her house crying, "Rid me of you instantly—instantly!" (Brontë 287). The characters of Caroline and Shirley also contribute to the novel's confusion of the spheres. Although Shirley appears as the epitome of the masculinized female. Caroline is equally interested in the public sphere of business and economy. The two characters seem very different, but as Diane Long Hoeveler notes, "they end up married to two brothers, essentially functioning as mirrored doubles of each other" (87). Caroline appears as the ideal of femininity, but it is not long before the reader can find similarities between herself and Captain Keeldar. Throughout the novel, imagery associated with the counting-house is repeatedly examined in relation to the parlor.

Caroline makes this comparison herself when she chooses working in Robert's counting-house rather than "sitting with Hortense in the parlour" (Brontë 104). Shirley makes similar comments in her conversation with

Helstone, reflecting, yet again, a confusion of the public with emotions associated with the private when she supports her statement about the "romance" of the mill (Brontë 215). This example reminds the reader of Brontë's confusion of reality and fancy, as Hoeveler and Jadwin argue, "[t]he novel oscillates continually between realism and romance, public and private issues, in a way that has frustrated readers and caused the work to be considered Brontë's least successful published novel" (90). Romanticizing the working class is a symptom, Danahay argues, of men who did not participate in "manly" occupations (*Gender* 27). The feminization of the mill is then followed by a comparison of the two spheres and, like Caroline, Shirley clearly chooses the counting-house over her "bloom-coloured drawing room" (Brontë 215). The freedom and power that Shirley and Caroline enjoy as they move among the spheres is abruptly taken away in the final section of the novel.

The author's message finds its vehicle through the characters of Shirley and Caroline, but Brontë's conclusion is another example of the novel's uncertain destination. Shuttleworth comments on the conclusion of the novel stating that it "does not resolve but merely exacerbates the novel's sense of the shared powerlessness of women and workers within the operations of economic markets" (185). Moore's taming of Shirley is linked to the oppression of the working class. The authorial voice intrudes and addresses the "Men of England!" (Brontë 378), and calls on the fathers of girls to "cultivate them—give them scope and work" (Brontë 379). Brontë's call for the men of England to take responsibility for their daughters' futures, emphasizes the author's concern over the gradual wasting away of girls who have been made useless from lack of work. The conclusion of *Shirley* with Brontë's abrupt change of course and her return to the traditional ending of a double marriage does not reflect these ambitious sentiments. More importantly, she puts an end to Caroline and Shirley's movements between the spheres. As Shuttleworth points out, "Shirley is reduced to a pining captive" (215), and both women lose their identities as they become known as "Mrs. Louis and Mrs. Robert" (218). By putting Shirley and Caroline back into their proper places, Shuttleworth explains how Brontë is suggesting that, "no matter how far the woman tries to escape her allotted role, to enter into male spheres of social activity and control, she will be reduced by the male gaze to an inner core of sexuality" (212).

Mr. Yorke, Louis, and especially Mr. Moore, exercise a form of repression in order to sustain their masculinity. Herbert Sussman's definition of manliness in *Victorian Masculinities* demonstrates the labor associated with maintaining this maleness, as he explains, "[m]anliness is defined not as this essence but as a hard won achievement, a continuous process of maintaining a perilous psychic balance characterized by regulation of this potentially destructive male energy" (25). Male characters use repression as a means of maintaining their obviously "feminine" ideas from entering into their public spheres. These men provide a masculine perspective on feminine discourse including love and marriage. They exist in both the public sphere through their occupations and in the private sphere by their repressed desires and secrets. As Carol Christ elaborates, "men project ideals of woman that effect values they themselves would like in some way to possess or incorporate, then the ideal of the angel in the house should tell us at least as much about Victorian man as the Victorian woman" (147). These feminized second natures found in the male characters are extremely revealing about masculine perspectives on the domestic. The character of Louis Moore inhabits these dual natures through his profession and his more passionate repressed self.

Louis belongs to the public sphere as a tutor; Brontë describes him as stern and that "he never laughed, he seldom smiled; he was uncomplaining" (430). He does appear to have repressed feelings, as the narrator explains, "his faculties seemed walled up in him, and were unmurmuring in their captivity" (Brontë 430). This is Louis' public nature, but Brontë show us his more passionate nature when all of a sudden Louis feels imprisoned in his school-room, where he erupts, "I am sick at heart of this cell" (Brontë 485). He finds relief by wandering through the empty rooms, "from parlour to parlour" (Brontë 486) in Shirley's house. Louis ultimately crosses over into the domestic sphere and pretends to assume Shirley's position: "I may occupy her room; sit opposite her chair; rest my elbow on her table; have her little mementos about me" (Brontë 487). Louis' occupation of the domestic spaces of the house and Shirley's own room suggests a form of masquerade. As Louis moves within the private sphere, he performs Shirley's gestures and mannerisms. This performance of femininity demonstrates the power of the domesticated man to move between the spheres, and once Louis embraces his femininity he is able to admit to his dual natures: "I have flung off the tutor, and beg to introduce you to the man: and remember, he is a gentleman" (Brontë 577). It is only at this point that Shirley feels "powerless" (Brontë 577), since she has her wish of a husband as master, but also one who considers her as an equal in marriage. Maynard explains how Louis "stands forth as a full man before whom the assertive Shirley trembles" (162). Brontë reverts back to traditional gender roles by having Louis demonstrate his potential as a "complete man," and having Captain Keeldar, the soon-to-be tamed Mrs. Louis, react accordingly. Mr. Yorke also indulges in the feminine discourse with his story of unrequited love. Introduced as being bold and harsh, he finds Robert admirable for being a sharp businessman and for his strict attitude. Although Mr. Yorke appears to be a man of reason, Brontë reveals his repressed and tragic love story. She thus presents a unique perspective of a man's feelings after being rejected by a woman, which is an example of discourse usually reserved for female characters. Mr. Yorke keeps his feelings private and a secret from Mr. Helstone, his rival. The abrupt shifts that Brontë makes within *Shirley* include the characters themselves, but also the structure of the novel. Interestingly, the chapter following "The Curates at Tea," reverts to the public realm of Moore and his workers.

Robert Moore embodies Brontë's brisk movements from the public and private by the way he himself moves back and forth from the masculine discourse of Hollow's-Mill and the new machinery, to the more feminine discourse of marriage. The characters begin to double each other, as Shuttleworth notes, "Moore is divided socially into Robert and Gerard, he also requires a double, Louis" (188). The mirroring among the characters is another example of the novel's instability, as Shuttleworth argues, "[m]ultiplicity breaks down the certitude of identity, both of self and other" (188). After engaging in a conversation with Mr. Malone about his lack of interest in women and his disinterest in marriage, Moore appears to awaken from a trance in order to deal with the more masculine subject of the Mill: "the subject seemed to have no interest for him: he did not pursue it. After sitting for some time gazing at the fire with a preoccupied air, he suddenly turned his head. 'Hark!' said he: 'did you hear the wheels?'" (Brontë 56). Moore's thoughts on marriage and love are abruptly ended by the approach of his new machinery for the Mill calling him back to the public sphere and more masculine concerns. His dealings within the private sphere, with Caroline and Shirley, are also subjected to this type of confusion. In an interesting blend of public and private, Moore uses the discourse of industry to describe his passionate emotions: "[t]he machinery of all my nature; the whole enginery of this human mill: the boiler which I take to be the heart, is fit to burst" (Brontë 496). Caroline recognizes his dual natures when she confronts him with his tendency to treat his workers as if they were "machines" (Brontë 100), but she also notes how he behaves differently in his own house (Brontë 100). This uncertainty in Moore's behavior causes Caroline much grief as she tries to keep up with his two different personas. Like the bewildered Caroline, the novel itself is "confused and ineffectively torn between the public and the private" (Hoeveler 87). The narration of the novel also moves from one storyteller to the other like that of Emily Brontë's *Wuthering Heights*, which Hoeveler and Jadwin argue is a narrative strategy that "leaves the reader with various forms of truth, none of which are complete or final" (107). The instability of the novel leads readers to question what is the truth, and what are the author's true intentions. Hoeveler and Jadwin note the "incompatibility of the public and private versions of the truth" (107), as is demonstrated through the novel's various discussions of men on women and vice versa. The uncertainty and ambiguity of the characters mirrors the novel's vacillating structure.

Moore is more direct about his two natures and his activity in the domestic sphere. In fact, he confesses to Caroline, "but I find in myself, Lina, two natures; one for the world and business, and one for home and leisure" (Brontë 258). Caroline becomes well-acquainted with both these personalities, as the narrator explains, "At a glance Caroline perceived that his social hilarity was gone: he had left it behind him [...] what remained now was his dark, quiet, business countenance" (Brontë 311). Sussman explains these two natures by stating that, "the uneasy relation between the male sphere and the domestic sphere [...results from] the opposition of bonds within the all-male world of work to the heterosexual ties of marriage" (2). Moore cannot seem to find a balance between his involvement in the public sphere of men and the domestic sphere of women and marriage. To cope with this problem Moore's personality splits in two. Thais Morgan notes that self-control is an important requirement for the Victorian man, and without both "ethical virility" and "sexual virility," the Victorian man is "considered effeminate" (111). Moore exhibits a great amount of self-control, and represses his "real" emotions, as his consistent refusal to marry indicates. Mr. Moore also indulges in feminine discourse with Mr. Yorke on the subject of marriage. Brontë reveals that the lack of confidence in the institution of marriage found in Caroline and Shirley is also shared by Robert, when he declares, "Marriage! I can not bear the word: it sounds so silly and utopian, I have settled it decidedly that marriage and love are superfluities, intended only for the rich" (Brontë 180). Robert secures his position within the middle-class and locates marriage and love within the higher classes as a consequence of their abundant time spent in leisure. Mr. Moore also provides his opinion on the ideal wife, which he says should satisfy his taste (Brontë 181), despite being rich or poor.

Ironically, the conversation between the two men end in a reassurance of their masculinity, when Robert confirms, "I am not romantic [...] Love for me? Stuff!" (Brontë 181). Although the men have used domestic discourse at length, they feel the need to reaffirm their masculinity by claiming to be superior to such feminine sentiments as love. Robert's brush with death is a crucial event that unites both natures, and it also provides him with a clear understanding of his social responsibilities. John Kucich raises the argument that Moore is led to this transformation through Shirley's manipulations:

When women in Brontë's world do have power over men, it lies in their ability to instruct men in self-negation, to transform the economic and political privileges of a man like Moore into a libidinal equality; that is, by changing the way in which men think about the sources of their own identity. (*Repression* 92–3). Illness plays an integral role in transforming characters: "Robert's time in the sick room is politically more significant than Louis' since it leads Robert to a vision of his own contribution to female illness" (Torgerson 57). Robert seems more comfortable with the domestic sphere when he returns home after his convalescence, as he admits, "This little parlour looks very clean and pleasant: unusually bright, somehow" (Brontë 555). There is an unquestionable difference in Moore who, before his illness, preferred to live in his counting-house.

The two natures of the characters seem to resolve themselves by the end of the novel. Brontë's final fate for Shirley and Caroline is disappointing and inconsistent with their masculinized characters. The conclusion of *Shirley* is considered artificial by Hoeveler and Jadwin; they argue, along with other feminist critics, that the novel "exhibits unresolvable differences between the public world of war, religion, and business represented by the book's heroes, and private world of domesticity and love, represented by the book's heroines" (106). This ending functions as a commentary on the unfulfilling life of the old maid being unsuitable for Caroline and the need to have Shirley's masculine nature tamed by her masterful husband. Kucich notes how Brontë's novels "betray a nagging, almost obsessional fear that harmonious relationship breeds dullness and decay [...] the courtship of Louis Moore and Shirley, [...] both find love not in tranquility but in the novelty of endless combat" (*Repression* 64). Although both women marry, these two realities remain close to them; for instance Mrs. Prior, representative of the old maid, lives with Caroline and Robert. Shirley is described as "conquered by love, and bound with a vow" (Brontë 592), which underscores the image of a tethered wild animal. The young men, Martin and Harry, present their perspectives on the domestic when Martin discusses how he is clearly looking for more than just appearances in a woman and Harry describes sharing the same feelings of repression and imprisonment also expressed by women, as a result of the restraints of their physical forms. Christopher Lane suggests that, "Victorian literature reveals that character's desires can differ widely their identifications" (1). Mr. Yorke, Louis, and Robert Moore move into the domestic sphere and their characters appear to benefit from possessing both masculine natures and typically female characteristics. Male interest in feminine discourse reveals how Victorian women and men shared similar anxieties regarding marriage and love.

The structure of *Shirley*, the characters, and their discourse about public and private issues emphasize the novel's uncertain and indecisive tendencies. *Shirley* demonstrates, as Maynard argues, "the degree of complication and division that Brontë was finding in her attempts to integrate her central vision of sexual awakening into a realistic view of a detailed social world" (163). There is a sense of the author losing control over her ideas and forcing themes of gender and sexuality into a structure, as demonstrated by the conclusion of the novel, which is inconsistent with the rest of the work. Brontë moves roughly from one sphere to the other, causing confusion among readers and the characters themselves. The two components of realism and romantic love do not find a balance in the novel, and instead the reader is rudely awakened and briskly transported from one realm into the other, similar to Robert Moore's abrupt rousing from his contemplations of love and marriage by the sound of the arrival of his new machinery. The movement between the spheres involves an exchange in gender roles as demonstrated by the masculinized Shirley and restless Caroline, and their feminized male counterparts—Louis, who wanders the parlors, and Robert, who acknowledges his dual natures. This pairing of masculinized female characters and feminized male characters allows for an opening within the spheres they typically inhabit and provides an opportunity for exchange.

# THREE

# The Domesticated Gentleman

### Robert Audley in Mary Elizabeth Braddon's Lady Audley's Secret

The term gentleman in its highest acceptation signifies that character which is distinguished by strict honour, self-possession, forbearance, generous as well as refined feelings, and polished deportment—a character to which all meanness, explosive irritableness, and peevish fretfulness are alien; to which, consequently, a generous candour, scrupulous veracity, courage both moral and physical, dignity, self-respect, a studious avoidance of giving offence to others or oppressing them [...]. Its antagonistic characters are the clown, the gossip, the backbiter, the dullard, coward, braggart, fretter, swaggerer, and bully.—Francis Lieber, *The Character of the Gentleman* (1864)

She who makes her husband and her children happy, who reclaims the one from vice and trains up the other to virtue, is a much greater character than ladies described in romances, whose whole occupation is to murder mankind with shafts from their quiver, or their eyes.—Oliver Goldsmith, *The Vicar of Wakefield* (1766) as quoted in *Mrs. Beeton's Book of Household Management* (1857)

The Victorian lady is not without purpose; her mission as described by Coventry Patmore in his poem *The Angel in the House* and Oliver Goldsmith in the epigraph is as spiritual guardian, savior, angel to her easily tempted husband, and an unfaltering model of morality to her children. There exists a fine balance between allowing a woman to educate herself while ensuring that this knowledge is not being used for personal betterment, but for that of the enrichment of her family. In "Of Queen's

Gardens" (1865), John Ruskin addresses this conflict when he suggests, "[l]et her loose in the library, I say, as you do a fawn in a field" (96). His reasons for encouraging reading women relate back to her place by her husband's side, where she must demonstrate her merit. Ruskin's analogy demonstrates his inability to imagine the literate woman as capable of any harm: "[s]he must be enduringly, incorruptibly good; instinctively, infalli-bly wise—wise, not for self-development, but for self-renunciation: wise, not that she may set herself above her husband, but that she may never fail from his side" (86). Maintaining "eternal youth" (Ruskin 89), and the strengthening of her body and mind are some of the marital duties of the early to mid–nineteenth-century woman. She must fulfill her main re-sponsibility as the angel in the house and protector of the private sphere, as Ruskin explains how a husband "guards" (85) his wife from the "rough work of the open world" (84), by placing her in his house. Within the house the Victorian woman provides sanctuary and "guards" her husband from the outside world. In this house, "as ruled by her, unless she herself has sought it, need enter no danger, no temptation, no cause of error or offense" (Ruskin 85). The home containing the angel is a "place of Peace; the shelter," and "wherever a true wife comes, this home is always around her" (Ruskin 85). Critics have remarked on the unrealistic notion of the complete separation of the public and private spheres, although the mid-dle class encouraged this image. The public infiltrates the private through commerce and the economy of servants who serve under the mistress of the house. The image of the secluded, private sphere was reinforced by the mistress keeping household business to herself. The angel provides her husband with an escape from the public sphere,[1] and her position as Mistress of the house is, as Ruskin concludes, "the woman's true place and power" (86). The angel is not alone in her quest to meet with society's ex-pectations; the Victorian gentleman does not escape unscathed.

Indeed, the Victorian man must adhere to a prescribed code of con-duct and manners in order to win the title of gentleman, and since men of all social classes were vying for the same position, the expectations of the gentleman were rigid, and like the angel in the house, most likely un-attainable. As the middle class felt the increasing flexibility between the classes, the demand for conduct books was equally popular for both men and women. In addition to advice books on gentlemanly conduct, there were a number of marriage manuals that arose in France in an attempt to clarify changing marriage laws and customs. Popular marriage manu-als which formed the body of work labeled *literature conjugale* included

## Domesticated Bachelors and Femininity in Victorian Novels

Balzac's *Physiology of Marriage* (1829). These sometimes serious and satirical conduct books examine the nature of marriage, as well as types
of marriages, including, "Marriages of Affection, of Love, for Money, of
Convenience and Parentally Forced Marriages" (Mainardi 48), as well as
suggestions on the ways to behave in each situation. Most of these books,
such as the excerpt from Lieber's *The Character of the Gentleman*, emphasize how "a gentleman is a *condition*, and not a *process*," and acknowledge
a "paradox of accessibility" (Waters 28) to the status of gentleman. Unlike
Patmore's description of the angel in the house, which women were expected to *be*, the concept of the gentleman appears to remind lower-class
men what they *should be*, but can never become. As Karen Volland Waters acknowledges, "if instruction in gentlemanliness is needed, than the
gentleman cannot be a natural state" (28). *Lady Audley's Secret* can be
read as Robert's progress towards becoming a proper gentleman, similar
to Pip's coming-of-age in *Great Expectations*. While Victorian women are
perceived as possessing the ability to transform themselves into the ideal
of femininity, their counter-parts do not have the means to transcend class
and in consequence are excused from the pressures of *becoming* a gentleman. In this case, men are allowed to perform masculinity, while women
are expected to naturally embody the ideal of their gender, which suggests
a historical articulation of the double standard.

Sensation fiction combines elements of the realist, gothic, and detective genres while recording the domestic horrors taking place in the
decade following the Divorce and Matrimonial Causes Act of 1857. This
new type of fiction realized the nightmares of a society whose concept of
the family was undergoing significant restructuring. The Newgate crime
novels of the 1830s were criticized for their dark and dirty plot lines, and
depicted the social priority of the domestic ideal. The "sensation novel"
or bigamy novel of the 1860s responded to the Divorce Act and the close
link between divorce and bigamy. The continuous debate over divorce and
the Victorian family does not result in the creation of divorce novels, but
rather the focus is on bigamy as "the imaginative manifestation of postdi-
vorce culture because it is the preferred 'quiet' alternative to the divorce
pandemonium" (Chase, *Spectacle* 203). As Patrick Brantlinger points out,
"rather than striking forthright blows in favour of divorce law reform and
greater sexual freedom, sensation novels usually tend merely to exploit
public interest in these issues" (6). The bigamy novel, as a sub-genre of
sensation fiction, similarly gained popularity as a reaction to current court
scandals, confusion over marriage laws, and as Jeanne Fahnestock elab-

orates, "its unique ability to satisfy the novel reader's desire to sin and to be forgiven vicariously" (48). The Victorians favored bigamy, or even murder over divorce, which required the inconceivable notion of legally taking a spouse while the other one still lived. Sensation writers did not have to look far for their material, as Elaine Showalter explains, "[w]hile the actual number of women executed for murder in England between 1830 and 1874 was not very great, forty percent of them had indeed killed their husbands" ("Family Secrets" 102). Arsenic, the preferred method for killing husbands, was soon controlled by law in 1868. The trials for these murderesses drew the attention of many prominent and respectable women, the type of women who also formed the intended audience of the sensation writer.

The women attending the trials of murderesses perhaps identified with the frustration of the female criminal, and usually found the judgment too harsh. These female readers also enjoyed being privy to the criminal lives of the "sensation" heroine. Sensation writers, and especially Mary Elizabeth Braddon, avoided punishing their fictional murderers so as not to disappoint their readers (Showalter, "Family Secrets" 107). Karen Chase and Michael Levenson suggest that sensation fiction of the 1860s is a return to the "depravity, corruption, coarseness, and violence" (206) of the 1820s and 30s. The main difference is that these types of horrors are now accessible to the middle class in the 1860s on a larger scale. *The Times'* 1862 review of *Lady Audley's Secret* compares reactions to sensational crimes and their publicity in the newspapers in a way that mirrors the responses from readers of sensation novels: "every little hint or clue is seized with astonishing avidity; countless suggestions are made and theories are started; millions of readers wait impatiently for more and more news; and the police and the newspaper offices are besieged by correspondents eager to propose new lines of inquiry" (4). The sensation genre blurs the boundaries between non-fiction and fiction, newspapers and novels. The real horror evoked by sensation fiction is that safety is no longer guaranteed in a rural setting or within the confines of the privacy of the home. For the more respectable Victorians of the 1860s, they found their murderers in courtrooms, newspapers, and most importantly in the sensation novel.

Braddon's *Lady Audley's Secret* was a bestseller in the 1860s, along with Wilkie Collins' *The Woman in White* and Mrs. Woods' *East Lynne*. Producing sensation novels came easily for women writers like Woods and Braddon, who used their "female psyches, from their own experiences, feelings and grievances" (Showalter, "Family Secrets" 109). Braddon's life reflects her lack of conformity and her passion for writing. She began writing for half penny journals and continued writing from 1862 through the 1880s after having a short-lived experience on stage where she performed minor roles in order to support herself and her mother (Tromp, *Beyond* xxii). For more on Braddon's work in the theater and the theatrical adaptations of her novels which frequently involved erasing any references to the theater, see Ruth Burridge Lindemann's article, "Dramatic Disappearances: Mary Elizabeth Braddon and the Staging of Theatrical Character." Also, see Lynn M. Voskuil's "Feeling Public: Sensation Theater, Commodity Culture, and the Victorian Public Sphere" for an analysis of the paradox of sensation theater in the way it created a version of the English public sphere through the cultivation of "authentic feelings and sensation" (246). Braddon is well known for her ability to produce sensation fiction at an alarming rate, and for her controversial partnership with William Maxwell with whom she had children, but was only able to legally marry once his wife died in an asylum in 1874 (Tromp, *Beyond* xxiii). It is at this point that Braddon is welcomed into the literary circle of London, and between 1875 and 1885, "Braddon became the *grande dame* of her social circle" (Tromp, *Beyond* xxiii), a circle which included Robert Browning, Oscar Wilde, Whistler, the Du Mauriers, Henry Irving, and Bram Stoker. Braddon's ability to cleverly "manipulate the plot in such a way that the erring wife escaped her punishment through some technicality" (Showalter, "Family Secrets" 107), demonstrates her own pathos towards her heroine, but even more significant is Braddon's creation of a "new type of villainess—the frail, fair-haired child-woman with murder and bigamy in her heart" (Hughes 124). Sensation fiction subverts the traditional domestic novel genre, revealing as Langland states, "the dark side of domesticity" (*Telling Tales* 64). One of the most significant changes to the domestic novel genre embraced by sensation fiction concerns marriage, as Elaine Showalter emphasizes in *A Literature of Their Own*, "the very tradition of the domestic novel opposed the heroine's development. It was so widely accepted that marriage would conclude the representation of the fictional heroine, that 'my third volume' became a coy euphemism for this period of women's lives" (181). The sensation genre allows for a possibility of endings, other than the heroine's marriage, although it is common that order be restored at the novel's conclusion, as Bratlinger reminds us, "the unraveling of the plot seems dimly to represent the working out of destiny: everything is put back in order at the end, all questions have been answered"

(25). Emily Allen in *Theater Figures* pursues how the sensation genre's link with the theater resulted in its labeling as a low form of literature and how Braddon works were specifically targeted based on her earlier career as a professional actress. These tendencies suggested the interplay between sensation fiction and issues of morality. In addition, female sensation writers parodied their male counterparts. Braddon, known as the "queen of the 'sensational school'" (Allen, *Theater Figures* 152), uses *Lady Audley's Secret* to parody Collins' *The Woman in White* published two years earlier. One obvious subversion is how, "Braddon's villain is Wilkie Collins' victim" (Showalter, *Literature* 166), while another example is her choice of Robert, an effeminate bachelor and struggling detective, as the hero of her novel. Robert behaves more like Collins' heroines, rather than a detective hero. If Lucy is the demon in the house despite her ability to conform to social expectations, then Robert represents a more authentic model of domesticity, which includes feminine discourse and virtue.

Braddon's introduction of an angelic Victorian female demon is a particularly disturbing example of female duality and a definite twist on Patmore's angel in the house. The duality present in Braddon's heroine can also be traced within the sensation genre itself. The appeal of sensation fiction is that it hides its tendency towards corruption, murder, and bigamy under the veil of an idealized Victorian family. Similar to Braddon's revision of the angel in the house, the sensation genre mystifies its audience by insisting on a portrait of "respectability [while] finding itself appalled (but also thrilled) by the hectic pleasures that its own dullness secretly enjoys" (Chase, *Spectacle* 206). Elizabeth Carolyn Miller examines the New Woman Criminal, who takes her roots from villainesses like Lady Audley:

> The New Woman Criminal tends, however, to threaten public rather than domestic institutions, and is typically motivated by economic or political desires rather than familial or sexual concerns. This marks a turn away from Victorian literary convention, in which female characters—bad or good—convey the national value of home and family [15].

This duality associated with the sensation novel and its heroine is particularly true of Braddon's *Lady Audley's Secret*, where the eponymous character is established as the new sensation villainess, one that is difficult to grasp and contain despite the efforts of the novel's questionable hero, Robert Audley. Gilbert in "Madness and Civilization" analyzes how *Lady Audley's Secret* functions as the anti-detective narrative and how Robert fails as a detective. She argues that Robert opposes the traditional characteristics of the detective, who is usually an objective outsider, and is often a static character who bases his assumptions on fact and reason (225–26). Gilbert reminds us that, "most of Robert's deductions are wrong, his actions yield little knowledge, and in fact, most of what he is able to use comes to him by chance or through intervention of other women [...] in fact, what he is able to deduce is as likely to be false as true" (225). Vicki A. Pallo also questions Braddon's choice of Robert as detective and analyzes how he must undergo a transformation to succeed in this role. She makes the link between Robert's conversion and changes in society's policing; as Pallo states, "[t]hrough [Robert], Braddon mirrors the reformation of society's enforcers from a group of irresolute, ineffective, and lawless 'rogues' to the modern, efficient policing agents they were fast becoming" (470–71).

By the end of the 1860s, the press recognized the New Woman's "flight from maternity" (Showalter, "Family Secrets" 108). At the center of the sensation novel is a critique of the Victorian family with a particular emphasis on women as the instigators of the changes occurring during this period. Patmore's "The Angel in the House" portrays the idealization of women and their spiritual and moral significance in the Victorian family, while at the same time the sensation heroine reflects her other side, representing the New Woman whose goals for financial success make her the new sensation villainess. This selection from Coventry Patmore's *The Angel in the House* (1854–6) represents the ideal qualities of the Victorian wife:

> Man must be pleased; but him to please
> Is Woman's pleasure; down the gulf
> Of his condoled necessities
> She casts her best, she flings herself [...]
> While she, too gentle even to force
> His penitence by kind replies,
> Waits by, expecting his remorse,
> With pardon in her pitying eyes;
> And if he once, by shame oppress'd,
> A comfortable word confers,
> She leans and weeps against his breast,
> And seems to think the sin was hers [lines 775–90].

While Braddon's *Lady Audley* introduces this new duality, it suggests that there is no place in society for a woman who can imitate the angel in the house to perfection, while possessing a cold and calculating intellect. Despite the fact that Lady Audley's attempt to murder her husband fails, she is still threatening because of her ability to move through society, create complex plans, and succeed financially, which are all "signs of mastery as definitive as murder" (Chase, *Spectacle* 203). Lady Audley is the ideal of femininity, devoted to her "generous husband" (Braddon 56), while her childish beauty disarms anyone who meets her.

Behind the veil of the modest and innocent angel in the house lurks the businesswoman, who calculates her movements in order to gain social mobility and financial success. Braddon begins her story with Miss Lucy Graham as Lady Audley already secure in her place within the impenetrable stronghold of Audley Court. She is enjoying her success having transformed from her previous persona as Helen Maldon, who married for money but found herself and her child abandoned, to Miss Lucy Graham, the governess for the Dawsons, who wins the heart of Sir Michael Audley. As Robert declares, "[g]ood heavens! what an actress this woman is. What an arch-trickster—what an all-accomplished deceiver" (Braddon 254). Her movements up the social ladder are not without criticism; her coldness and cruelty as she abandons her only child, and her selfish desire for money and luxury whatever the cost, make Lucy the epitome of the sensation villainess, but not a madwoman. Lucy's multiple selves demonstrates her ability to evolve and perform to improve her social status. Voskuil in "Acts of Madness: Lady Audley and the Meanings of Victorian Femininity" stresses how the fluidity, flexibility and inconstancy associated with performance exposed yet another social anxiety concerning blurring class boundaries and the definitions of gender roles: "[t]heatricality [...] disrupts and disables selfhood, rendering the self multiform rather than uniform, shifting rather than coherent, constructed rather than (at some level) essential" (615). Her ability to simultaneously perform as the angel in the house while gaining social mobility, makes her unique as Braddon's new villainess. She appears grateful for her accomplishments and the reader finds Lucy in what at first appears to be a solid and "noble" fortress (Braddon 8), where she has retreated safely under the protection of the patriarchal figure, Sir Michael Audley. Lucy's ability to manipulate the Victorian patriarchal system to her advantage and then find shelter within it is exactly what makes her the new villainess of sensation fiction. Her downfall comes at the hands of Robert Audley, who is ultimately more like Lucy than he realizes.

The gentleman of the Victorian period was also idealized and, similar to the angel in the house, felt the same pressure to conform to society's expectations or face harsh criticism. The role of the gentleman is discussed in many conduct books of the time and the excerpt from Lieber's

## Domesticated Bachelors and Femininity in Victorian Novels

*Character of the Gentleman* (1892) demonstrates how easily the Victorian man could fall into the realm of the clown or gossip by one simple error. Robert Audley does not "fit" the definition of the gentleman of the period. His inability to behave as other men do clearly shows how Robert does not adhere society's expectation of the proper gentleman. As Ellen Bayuk Rosenman remarks, although *Lady Audley's Secret* was reintroduced by feminist critics who focused on Lucy's portrayal of femininity, the novel has been "increasingly recognized as a trenchant study in masculinity, especially in its treatment of the homoerotic ties between Robert and George, both raised and resolved by its 'between men' structure in which Robert marries Clara, who closely resembles her brother George" (32). Robert shocks readers and himself, to a certain extent, as he is transformed from an indifferent aristocratic bachelor into a "reluctant detective" (Nesmesvari 521), who realizes his social responsibility as an aristocratic barrister and a Victorian gentleman. This change in Robert is significant, but the process of the transformation is also surprising and unclear.

In addition to Lucy's portrayal of femininity, Braddon reveals the performance of masculinity as epitomized by Robert, as she writes, "Robert Audley was supposed to be a barrister. As a barrister was his name inscribed in the Law List; as a barrister, he had chambers in Fig-tree Court; as a barrister he had eaten the allotted number of dinners [...]. If these things can make a man a barrister, Robert Audley decidedly was one" (Braddon 35). Braddon's emphasis on appearances making the man is reminiscent of instruction books suggesting that one simply imitate the ideals of the gentleman if they to not come naturally.[2] Not only is Robert not a barrister, he is not a proper Victorian gentleman. In the first, his performance succeeds, and in the latter, it fails terribly. Robert joins the ranks of such "gentlemen" failures as, Edwin Reardon in *New Grub Street*, Felix Carbury in *The Way We Live Now*, George Vavasor in *Can You Forgive Her?*, and Fred Vincy in *Middlemarch*. Their deficiencies and misfortunes are made public and serve to ostracize them from the masculine world. Despite representing a broad range of vices, including pride, gambling, irresponsibility, and vacillation, they share a common alienation from the upper-middle class public sphere, and what they are "supposed to be." In all these cases, these performers are provided with the opportunity, through class status, wealth, and familial connections to succeed and yet regardless of these advantages they are destined to fail in all aspects, especially in their manhood. One distinguishing difference between these novels and *Lady Audley's Secret* is that most novels chose to follow the downfall of these gentleman as a moral cautionary tale, whereas Braddon's work, from the outset, places many of the male characters outside the accepted masculine realm, as patriarchal misfits. They are fathers, husbands, military men, lawyers, and aristocrats—they are "supposed" to represent the ideals of patriarchal society and yet they fail to live up to these standards. Pamela K. Gilbert succinctly outlines representations of "alienated patriarchy" (220) in *Lady Audley's Secret*:

> Robert Audley, the Temple Bar lawyer who has never submitted a brief; Lieutenant Maldon, who sells his daughter to the highest bidder and drinks the proceeds; Heavy Dragoon George Talboys, who abandons his wife and baby son; and even Sir Michael Audley, whose love "fever" drives him to take a wife who admittedly does not love him ["Madness" 220].

As a result, Robert is forced into becoming the patriarchal example, and it is his "progress" as opposed to his undoing that becomes one of the novel's narrative threads. Gilbert analyzes the two primary narrative structures including the coming-of-age of Robert Audley and the fall of the manipulative female social climber, and suggests a "third rhetorical space" structured by the detection narrative ("Madness" 218). The focus on Robert's masculinization subverts the sensation genre that Braddon is credited with founding, which conventionally puts emphasis on the female Other. By placing Robert in the role of the new Other, he represents a greater disturbance to society than the manipulative demonic female, suggesting that Robert embodies a more imposing threat than Lady Audley herself.

Braddon, through these titled and misguided examples of masculinity, represents the degeneracy and deterioration of the aristocracy. Published three years after Charles Darwin's *On the Origin of the Species*, *Lady Audley's Secret* expresses anxiety concerning individual identity, the splitting of the self, and the possibility of the animal within.[3] In addition to the apprehension surrounding individuality, Braddon also conveys social concerns around the decline of the aristocracy and the vulnerability of the newly installed wealthy middle class whose roots were loosely grounded in economic capital and not in land. Lucy, though, represents a different anxiety, that of a "new type of woman," and the inevitable destruction of social morality, as Jenny Uglow points out:

> Braddon's books were [...] a forecast of the moral collapse which would inevitably accompany the emancipation of women, fulminated *The New Review* in December, for anyone could see that her heroine was a new type of woman "standing alone, carrying out some strong purpose without an ally or confidant, and thus showing

herself independent of mankind and superior to those softer passions to which the sex in general succumbs" [x].

Surely, Braddon was predicting a version of the New Woman through the adaptable, resourceful and ambitious Lucy, whose incorporation of the traditional female role complicates her position as the typified sensation villainess. Braddon blurs class distinctions through Phoebe's suitor, Luke Marks, who, like his wealthier male counterparts, employs blackmail and violence against Lucy. Phoebe herself serves as a lower-class reflection of her mistress. Class boundaries disappear to reveal similar moral corruption and self-interest. Masculinity in crisis is represented by the degeneration of the leisure class.[4] Adams defines the dandy as a "figure of masculine identity under stress" (*Dandies* 24). Max Nordau's *Degeneration* (1892) criticizes what he considers as the *fin-de-siècle*'s moral corruption of the individual and society and the role arts plays in this degeneration. Robert's refusal to conform to these examples of manhood, whether it be the aristocrat, the military man, or the sportsman, results in his alienation from the male community. Aside from his intimate friendship with George, Robert is unable to perform his way into male circles, and eventually he no longer wishes to do so. Rosenman suggests that George "supplies Robert's missing link to masculinity" (34), which aids in his development toward masculinity The comic image of Robert "lying placidly extended on the flat of his back until such time as the bystanders should think fit to pick him up" (Braddon 118), is reminiscent of Lieber's warning in the epigraph to this chapter against the gentleman becoming his antagonist, the clown. This scene solidifies Robert's failed manhood among the athletic country squires. After several failed attempts, Robert embraces an older version of aristocratic masculinity—the dandy. This outdated model is certainly not the ideal of masculinity for the Victorian middle class. His turned-down collars, French novels, laziness, and eccentric behavior are anything but acceptable forms of masculinity. The dandy later experiences a rebirth during the *fin-de-siècle* and early-twentieth century, when he becomes the hero of literary works, including those by Oscar Wilde, Edith Wharton, and Henry James. The dandified disinterested aristocrat has no place as the hero of a mid nineteenth-century novel. Yet, he is chosen as an equal opponent to Lucy and the restorer of social order implicit in sensation fiction.

Robert's need to discover the events that led to the disappearance of his friend George is obsessive and uncharacteristic. He recognizes this strange powerful desire to find George, and also to uncover Lady Audley's past. Robert's self-discovery is clearly linked to his uncovering Lady Audley's secret, but these two characters are linked in other ways as well. Robert is moved into action by two events that appear to happen simultaneously; the first is his meeting and "falling in love" (Braddon 59) with his new and beautiful aunt, Lady Audley, and the second is the mysterious disappearance of his friend, George. Critics like Richard Nemesvari, Lynda Hart, and Simon Petch explore Robert's unusual need to expose Lady Audley, whether it is Robert's desire to stifle Lucy as a threat to his homosocial bonds (Nemesvari 515), or his pursuit of Lucy as a "quest for a professional future" (Petch 1). However, Robert's motivation is unclear to himself and to the reader at first. Using his infatuation with Lady Audley as a veil to conceal his obsession over George, Robert creates a link which provides him with a reason to maintain an intimacy with both characters because by exposing the one, he will find the other. In other words, by overpowering and conquering the ideal of femininity, Lady Audley, he can find solace by submitting to his repressed homosocial desire for George. This is complicated by his relationship with Clara, who serves as replica for George and is a more socially acceptable alternative. Robert's obsession with Lady Audley is that she succeeds where he fails. She has successfully climbed the social ladder by using any means possible while ridding herself of any respectability through her dissembling, scheming, and by abandoning her responsibility as a mother, but still Braddon, quite ironically, locates her as the exemplar of the Victorian ideal.

Lucy manipulates and devises complex plans to shed her previous identity and eventually finds herself securely placed within the aristocratic domestic sphere as wife to Sir Michael and mistress of Audley Court. Robert, like Lucy, is a type of social misfit, but he does not experience any of the success that Braddon showers on Lucy. As a result, Robert's inability to "belong" or "fit in" to a specific sphere, whether it be that of class such as the aristocracy, or socially within the approved masculine public sphere, produces in Robert anxiety, envy, and an obsession towards Lucy and her strange power that allows her to penetrate into the aristocracy and the domestic sphere where she not only finds her place, but becomes the model of the aristocratic feminine ideal. Robert seeks to depose Lady Audley from her position of power, which extends to both class and social status because of his ability to recognize himself in her dissembling and his desire to locate himself within a specific sphere or socially acceptable identity. Robert's suspicions against Lucy stem from his attraction to her, as Pamela Gilbert recognizes, "Robert does not so much love Lady

Audley as he *is like* Lady Audley—even the object of his affection was once the object of Lady Audley's similar care as her first husband" ("Madness" 227). Robert's ability to recognize Lucy's affectation discloses his own tendency to perform and imitate, especially in his professional sphere as barrister and in the realm of Victorian masculinity. Robert, by displacing Lucy, gains a position for himself. Clearly the ties between Lucy and Robert Audley are strong: they are both social misfits accused of bouts of madness, they share an ability for performance, they are "attracted" to each other, and experience intimate relationships with the same sex. The struggle that ensues between Lucy and Robert is a battle for position and power, and demonstrates their desire to "fit into" a social space by any means necessary.

The role of "attraction" in its varying forms is significant between Robert and Lucy, and their desire to adhere to society's expectations. The female demon, prior to the introduction of the sensation genre, was easily discernible by her insatiable sexual desire, and throughout the nineteenth century "female sexuality and criminality are inextricably intertwined" (Morris 88). These two components form the basis for the villainesses in sensation fiction where "women are capable of committing almost any kind of crime to achieve their personal goals" (Morris 88). Yet, the sensation villainess followed her own set of guidelines, as Virginia Morris outlines:

> they do not kill (or try to kill) children or old ladies; instead they kill able-bodied men and women who threaten their plans or their well-being [...] nor despite their overtly aggressive behaviour, are many women in sensation fiction "masculine" [...] rather they are charming and beautiful—and sometimes quite sexy [...] this combination of apparent loveliness and masked threat was the most radical feature of the genre [88–89].

Braddon's villainess Lucy adheres to these rules except in the area of sexuality. Lucy could "charm with a word or intoxicate with a smile" (Braddon 11–12), but instead of brimming with sexuality, lust, and passion, as would the typical female demon, Lucy's beauty is described as childish, and "that very childishness had a charm which few could resist [...] the innocence and candour of an infant beamed in [her] fair face" (Braddon 55). Despite this type of childish beauty, she instills sexual passion in the hearts of men. Through the male gaze of Sir Michael, her innocent beauty is sexualized: "those soft and melting blue eyes; the graceful beauty of that slender throat and drooping head, with its wealth of showering flaxen curls" (Braddon 12). Lucy's childish features endure a sexualized twist, and her body parts are admired for their ability to be *both* innocent and seductive simultaneously. Sir Michael's reaction is full of passion and lust as he reflects on his previous passionless marriage: "[w]hat had been his love for his first wife but a poor, pitiful, smouldering spark, too dull to be extinguished, too feeble to burn [...b]ut this was love—this fever, this longing, this restless, uncertain miserable hesitation" (Braddon 12). In Sir Michael's case, this type of childish beauty produces undeniable lust.[5] It is the male gaze that sexualizes Lucy and not the villainess herself. Her ability to attract men "in her own childish, unthinking way" (Braddon 58), allows her to gain the devotion of Sir Michael, but she also unwittingly captures her nephew's attention.

The attraction between Robert and Lucy is more complex than the enraptured Sir Michael, although it appears that Robert has fallen victim at first sight. Robert's cousin, Alicia, clarifies to the reader the significance of Robert's response to Lucy, as she notes, "[a]s to his ever falling in love [...] the idea is too preposterous" (Braddon 59). Robert's "peculiar temperment" (Braddon 58), and his lack of enthusiasm "upon any subject whatever" (Braddon 59), serves to emphasize Lucy's power over him when, "[b]ut, for once in his life, Robert was almost enthusiastic" (Braddon 59). Not only does Lucy's beauty instill uncharacteristic feelings in Robert, it also reveals Robert's romantic tendencies, as he exclaims, "George Talboys, I feel like the hero of a French novel; I am falling in love with my aunt" (Braddon 59). This reaction is unique because Robert first locates himself in the masculine role as hero, but unmans himself by admitting his inclination towards reading French novels. The attraction that Robert feels towards Lucy is clearly not love, simply because of Braddon's desire to place him within the mock-heroic mode, from which he is reconstructed as "a full-fledged hero who occupies center stage" (Hart 6). Robert, at first, is taken off guard by Lucy's beauty, but he is unsuccessful in his attempts to place himself in the traditionally masculine role of lover. Both characters attempt to place each other in sexually charged roles that adhere to society's expectations.

Although Robert and Lucy are not sexually attracted to each other, they both fabricate sexual situations in order to adhere to a more socially acceptable explanation for their intimacy. If Robert was ever in love with Lucy, he quickly falls out of it upon the disappearance of his friend: "[h]is mind was so full of George Talboys that he only acknowledged [Lucy's] gratitude by a bow" (Braddon 87). Prior to George's disappearance, Robert views the Pre-Raphaelite portrait of Lucy in her private chambers, which provides another explanation for Robert's loss of physical interest in his aunt. The portrait reveals Lucy as a predator and a paradox: "strange sinister light to her deep blue eyes [...and] a hard and wicked look" (Braddon 72). Her crimson dress inspires images of "flames [...] raging furnace [...] the aspect of a beautiful fiend" (Braddon 72), which foreshadows her attempt at murdering Robert. The portrait, as Morris suggests, "stirs subconscious images of Lucy as a predator and helps convince him she is guilty of some horrible if undefined evil" (Braddon 93). At this point, Robert and Lucy remain attracted to each other, but for selfish reasons rather than for love. Lucy follows Robert's every move in order to be one step ahead, and Robert's obsession with Lucy leads to more clues to George's disappearance. The intimacy between Robert and Lucy grows stronger as the novel progresses, but they are not following their expected gender roles: Robert is not the nephew as sexual predator, who falls in love with his beautiful new aunt, nor is Lucy the villainess, who marries the wealthy and elderly uncle only to find sexual release in his youthful nephew. Instead, Lucy manipulates society's expectations to work in her favor when she suggests Robert has been giving her the wrong sort of attention: "my lady was too young and pretty to accept the attentions of a handsome nephew of eight-and-twenty" (Braddon 132). Sir Michael needs no further explanation: "[h]e shall go tonight, Lucy [...] I've been a blind, neglectful fool not to have thought of this before [...] it was scarcely just to Bob to expose the poor lad to your fascinations" (Braddon 132). This strategy gets Robert out of Audley Court with the understanding that he had simply succumbed to his natural male sexuality. On the other hand, Robert uses a similar method on Lucy when he is forced to explain to Alicia the reason Lucy must leave Audley Court.

Robert imposes society's expectations on Lucy by suggesting she has been unfaithful. Even Alicia is quick to jump to the assumption that Lucy has been caught in an affair: [t]his sorrow must surely then have arisen from some sudden discovery; it was, no doubt, a sorrow associated with disgrace [...] Robert Audley understood the meaning of that vivid blush" (Braddon 356). Robert uses sexual indiscretion as a liable excuse for Lucy's sudden departure, and it is accepted without hesitation. Robert may even be implicating himself in the affair by suggesting that he had contributed to Sir Michael's sorrow (Braddon 357). These two examples of Robert and Lucy as sexual predators and prey demonstrate their recognition of the roles they are expected to perform according to society and the sensation genre itself, except Braddon has introduced these two desexualized characters that are engaging in a more intense relationship based on their similarities exempt from any sexual attraction. Robert and Lucy perform and manipulate society's expectations for their own benefit.

Lucy and Robert's use of socially acceptable sexual roles works to place them securely within the heterosexual realm where they do not necessarily belong. Both Robert and Lucy share another similarity in that they find intimacy in same-sex relationships. This type of homosocial desire is not without sexual connotations, but it does not adhere to the predator/prey relationship that Robert finds so distasteful in Lucy. *The Times* 1862 review of *Lady Audley's Secret* makes an analogy between the detective figure in sensation novels, the insatiable appetite of the reader, and the sports-hunter:

> [i]n many cases the hunter has to go across the world for it—to Australia, to America, but he always finds it. The poor hunted beast is driven to bay; the secret is out, and the tale ends. Tell us not that the hunt is an old story, and that one hunt is like another. So it is; but whether over grass or over paper, it comes always new to the keen sportsman, and he who has been at the hunt oftenest enjoys it best [4].

Like the sportsman on the hunt, the detective and sensation reader recognize the conventional blueprint for the genre and yet still experience the thrill of the adventure. Interestingly, by taking on the role of detective, despite his reluctance and questionable triumph, Robert, through this analogy, becomes the ideal of aristocratic masculinity—the sportsman. The predator/prey relationship between Lucy and Robert serves to place each one in their proper gender roles, and Robert, who rejects the lifestyle of the sportsman epitomized by Sir Harry Towers, plays the role of the quintessential example of the hunter in mid-to-late nineteenth-century fiction—the detective. Robert and Lucy find their same-sex relationships less threatening and dangerous than their potential heterosexual partners; Luke Marks, George Talboys and his father, as well as Sir Michael Audley have all abandoned or threatened Lucy at one point in the novel. Although Robert does not have an interest in women, his vehemence against them reveals how he feels threatened by their very existence, of which Lucy is the prime example. Robert even feels he must submit to Clara Talboys, who is his solution for the closest acceptable replacement for George, her brother. The aggressive imagery used by Robert to describe the nature of women reveals his dislike for their inherent need for change and ambitious energy. It is their lack of femininity that Robert criticizes, and even more striking is his description of a passive, complacent, and ineffectual Victorian masculinity that requires the strong hand of women to yield productivity. The struggle between the sexes is physically challenging, with pushing, elbowing, writhing, trampling, prancing, dragging, buffeting (Braddon 207–08), and the end result, as Robert describes, is that "square men in the round holes are pushed by their wives" (Braddon 208). Robert suggests that women are the reason that men are involved in the "machinery of the government" (Braddon 208), where they do not necessarily belong. In a broader sense, the suggestion is that women force men to be men. Robert's bitterness towards the stronger, noisier, more persevering sex (Braddon 208) manifests itself as a jealousy for their freedom to be both masculine and feminine, when he must conform to the strict guidelines of masculinity. Although Robert seeks to rid himself of nuisances like Alicia and Lady Audley, it appears that the hand, which beckons Robert onwards, belongs to Clara. As Braddon writes, "[b]ut amid all, and through all, Clara Talboys, with an imperious gesture, beckoned him onwards to her brother's unknown grave" (251). The hand reappears when Robert experiences feelings of helplessness pushing him forward, and so he is already on the path to becoming one of the square men pushed into round holes. Robert's and Lucy's reluctance to participate in the traditional battle between the sexes makes homosocial relationships much more enticing.

The sensation genre, as did one of its predecessors, the gothic, explores sexual transgressions including homosocial desire, and as Nemesvari notes, "even the sanctified realm of Victorian domesticity provided no real barrier to the 'deviant' criminal/sexual urges that seemed to be waiting to overwhelm it" (516). Lucy's ability to shape-shift and assume different personas allows her to experience different aspects of the feminine. At first she is Helen Maldon, who marries in order to climb the social ladder. Once she is abandoned by her husband, she sheds her previous self, including her only child, by "burying" herself as Matilda, the sickly and weak feminine aspect, and finds rebirth in the industrious governess persona of Lucy Graham. The theme of doubling continues between Lucy and Phoebe, whose name refers to the moon, which functions as a mirror and reflects light. Phoebe serves at best as a reflection of her mistress. She only lacks color, which Lucy explains can be easily remedied by "a bottle of hair dye, such as we see advertised in the papers, and a pot of rouge" (Braddon 60). Lucy suggests that with the help of these "modern" tools, lower-class Phoebe can be transformed into Lady Audley of the aristocracy. Jonathan Loesberg suggests that the sensation novel responds to a "fear of a general loss of social identity as a result of the merging of the classes—a fear that was commonly expressed in the debate over social and parliamentary reform in the late 1850s and 1860s" (117). Lucy embraces the opportunity to be socially mobile and encourages her maid to follow suit by simply learning to use the modern tools of progress. Lucy is aware of the tools of her age, and uses them freely including telegrams and the railway. Phoebe, like her mistress, could transcend her class with the aid of some artificiality and dissembling. Elizabeth Tilley observes how Phoebe doubles as a "sort of working class parody of the fate of the traditional aristocratic Gothic heroine" (200) through her marriage to the brute Luke Marks and her exile to the Castle Inn. Phoebe also functions as the lower class double reminiscent of Shakespeare's plays, whose life mimics that of her aristocratic counterpart. Through Phoebe, Lucy is able to remind herself daily of her former lower-class persona and her new place as mistress of Audley Court.

Phoebe's shadowy pale figure allows Lucy to cast herself onto this blank slate and reflect on her achievements: "Lady Audley smoothed her maid's neutral-tinted hair with her plump, white, and bejeweled hand as she reflected for a few moments" (Braddon 61). By admitting her artificiality to her lady's maid, Phoebe is now aware of the elements that "make-up" a lady. Miller writes in *Framed: The New Woman Criminal in British Culture at the Fin de Siècle*, "[i]n enabling performativity, makeup enhances women's power of parody, mimicry, or masking, but also constrains them to the burden of playing 'beautiful'" (91–2). Lucy passes on the knowledge to Phoebe suggesting that, "a lady's maid knows that being a lady is a performance" (Tromp, *Beyond* 57). By sharing her secrets, Lucy is sharing with her double and with female readers that "women who plan ahead can get ahead" (Tromp, *Beyond* 57). Lucy allows Phoebe to be her apprentice and female readers listen intently to the Lady Audley's conduct book on how to climb the social ladder and successfully invade the realm of aristocracy. Braddon calls attention to the emergence of technologies and tools with which Lucy becomes familiar and leads to her success against Robert. The doubling between Lucy and Phoebe raises issues concerning the role of progress in the merging of the classes. The homosocial desire between Robert and George also explores an alternative to the male-female, predator-prey imagery surrounding the heterosexual relationships in the novel.

The homosocial relationship between George and Robert is significant once Robert admits to the inexplicable and haunting feelings he has towards his friend George. Through his search for George, Robert is able to finally discover his true potential professionally and he admits the important role George plays in his life: "[t]o think [...] that it is possible to care so much for a fellow!" (Braddon 91). This homosocial relationship resembles the one between Lucy and Phoebe, and is based on a less threatening bond as compared to the portrayal of heterosexual relationships in the novel, especially his predator/prey relationship with Lucy. It is within the safety of this relationship that Robert is able to experiment with his role as detective and be haunted by images of George while freely admitting to his strong emotions for his friend. Robert's sanity is called into question when he begins to have haunting visions of George, which he describes as the "nervous fancies of a hypochondriacal bachelor" (Braddon 252). Lucy makes the case that Robert is insane based on his eccentric behavior (Braddon 326), and his being "moody [...] thoughtful, melancholy and absent-minded" (Braddon 326). This is reiterated by Doctor Musgrave, who scrutinizes Robert mistaking him as the patient. Braddon also reveals the "way in which a growing awareness of the homosocial may incite homophobia, as Robert desperately, and at times angrily, struggles to deny the significance of his reactions" (Nemesvari 523). George's disappearance takes immediate effect on Robert, who recognizes the changes in himself as he claims his gentlemanly status and gains confidence in his profession. Emulating Lucy, who shed her previous self after being abandoned by George, Robert begins a new life with Clara Talboys.

Through his relationship with George, Robert experiences a re-creation of the self, and as a result of George's disappearance, desires a place for himself in the masculine public sphere as a barrister, and embraces his moral responsibility as an aristocratic gentleman. Robert's ability to finally "submit" to a woman is made easier by Clara's close relation to George. Becoming an active gentleman gives rise to many issues surrounding gender instability such as "paradoxes of submission and power, control and lack of control, initiative and restraint, selflessness and egoism" (Waters 35). Robert experiences this paradox in his relationship with Lucy whom he seeks to control and contain, and with Clara to whom he succumbs: "[s] o I'd better submit myself to the brown-eyed girl, and do what she tells me, patiently and faithfully" (Braddon 207). Clara allows Robert to continue to evaluate himself and his relationship with George since they both share a love for him. This heterosexual relationship includes a threatening aspect that does not occur in Robert's relationship with George, nor with Phoebe and Lucy. Clara keeps Robert on the path towards discovering George by imprinting her image on his mind and her physical presence in Essex, which "threatens Robert by making him feel that he is under surveillance by the sister of his lost friend" (Petch 9). In this case, Clara pursues Robert, and although Robert decides to submit to Clara and not Alicia or Lucy, he continues to refer to his relationship with her as a battle: "[h]ow unequal the fight must be between us, and how can I ever hope to conquer against the strength of her beauty and her wisdom?" (Braddon 256). Robert's obvious preference is to revert to his "equal" relationship with George when he pleads with Clara to allow him to search for George alone in Australia (Braddon 431). Clara reasserts a socially acceptable alternative by suggesting they go together and "bring back our brother between us" (Braddon 431). Braddon permits Robert some satisfaction by sanctioning the love triangle between Clara, George, and Robert, who, by the novel's conclusion, live together in the fairy cottage. Robert's participation in a same-sex relationship allows him to explore an alternative to marriage, while George's disappearance is alleviated by Robert's relationship with his look-alike, Clara.

As a young bachelor, Robert does not conform to the characteristic behavior as found in Sir Harry Towers, who like most bachelors, keeps his eyes open for a prospective bride. The thought of marriage does not even enter Robert's mind, despite many obvious attempts by his cousin Alicia, as the narrator explains, "unless she [...] walked straight up to him, saying, 'Robert, please will you marry me?' I very much doubt if he would ever have discovered the state of her feelings" (Braddon 63). Robert's anxiety or "stress" (Adams 55) is his inability on all levels to conform to Victorian masculinity. The suggestion of masculine love between Robert and George implies yet more peril to accepted gender roles and structures, as George Haggerty remarks, "[t]wo men having sex threatens no one. Two men in love: that begins to threaten the very foundations of heterosexist culture" (20). While Lucy is diagnosed as a "dangerous woman" by Dr. Musgrave, Robert must also be examined since he transgresses as much as the madwoman, and forces the boundaries on sexuality and domesticity. Having rejected all forms of masculinity depicted in the novel, including the professional gentleman, the husband, the country squire, and the military man, Robert suggests an alternative in which domestic manhood can exist outside the traditional Victorian familial structure.

Robert's feminine nature provides him with a version of domestic bliss without the angel in the house, an impending reality during the mid–nineteenth-century reform of the Marriage Laws. His affection for strays (Braddon 36), and his well-tempered disposition as one, "who would not hurt a worm" (Braddon 36), conflicts with Braddon's other vicious depictions of masculinity. His child-like inability to imagine himself or George married (Braddon 38), reveals a naïve effeminacy that lacks sexual prowess. Tamara S. Wagner's article, "'Overpowering Vitality': Nostalgia and Men of Sensibility in the Fiction of Wilkie Collins," explores Collins' new antihero, who rejects muscular masculinity and harkens back to heroes of the novels of sentiment in the late–eighteenth century. This version of masculinity is yet another commonality shared between Braddon and Collins, since Robert's sensibility and dandyism reveals nostalgia for eighteenth-century representations of masculinity. Robert's attachment to George, as Andrew King mentions, "would have seemed less subversive than old-fashioned" (209). Homosocial/homoerotic relationships, like the one between George and Robert, were common in *The London Journal* between 1849 and 1855 (King 208). Robert's shining moment comes not when he conquers a madwoman at the end of the novel, but when he nurses George back to health after hearing of his wife's death. In Robert's lodging the two men experience the epitome of domesticity. Robert provides a comfortable space with flowers and singing birds, and he exhibits a gentle manner within his house, as "he laid the precious meerschaum tenderly upon the mantel-piece" (Braddon 41). This greatly contrasts with destructive behavior of Donald G. Mitchell's 1850 bachelor, as discussed in the Introduction to this book, who breaks his furniture, leans his old arm-chair against the plastered wall, and kicks out window panes for fresh air (Mitchell 4). Robert's offer of a strong tea is accompanied by compassionate words, as he "gently forced [George] to lie down again" (Braddon 42). Robert manifests a domestic tendency, which thus far he has only been able to exercise on stray dogs. In this scene, Robert succeeds as the bachelor care-giver: "[t]he big dragoon was as helpless as a baby and Robert Audley, the most vacillating and unenergetic of men, found himself called upon to act for another. He rose superior to himself and equal to the occasion" (Braddon 42). Once the conventional domestic spell is broken by Lucy's image in a Pre-Raphaelite painting, the return to male domestic bliss is made seemingly impossible. The painting exposes Lucy's alternate nature which conflicts with her angelic persona. The juxtaposition of her two natures repulses Robert and spares him from her charms. The artificiality of Lucy's exposed performance extends into her marriage to Sir Audley, suggesting that the only truly authentic model of domesticity exists between Robert and George. Robert's domestic nature and his role as care-taker clash with the dandy's disinterested superiority. Robert sheds the outdated image of the dandy and embraces a new type of masculinity. Linda Dowling comments on how the new Victorian liberalism of the mid–nineteenth-century "struggling in the face of the apparent powerlessness of classical republican 'manliness' to rescue Britain from stagnation and future decay, would so far succeed in their polemical work on behalf of Hellenism as quite unexpectedly to persuade the late–Victorian apologists" to embrace Hellenism (36). Robert's search for a new masculinity and his masculine love for George is reminiscent of this new Victorian liberalism's push for Hellenism and eventually the possibility of love between men. By nursing George back to health in his own lodgings during a year of mourning, and becoming guardian to little George Talboys, Robert puts his domestic masculinity into action. In *Bedside Seductions*, Catherine Judd examines the sexualized relationship between patient and nurse, a "particularly crucial rope within the mid–nineteenth-century domestic novel" (7). Although Judd only focuses on the relationship between the male patient and female nurse, it is interesting to note how the concept of the sexualized nurse may expand into the realm of the male nurse and male patient. Braddon is distorting yet another trope from the domestic novel by having the nursing scene between two men. Interestingly, it appears that George, and not Lucy, is responsible for Robert's renewed virility.

This alternate family structure, suggested by Robert and George, comes at a time when the Victorian household is being publicly exposed in the courts. The Marriage Causes Act of 1857 admitted a failed domestic ideology and in consequence exposed the hypocrisy of the angel in the house. This domestic scene between Robert and George represents the only genuinely nurturing relationship in the novel, suggesting the possibility of a bachelor figure, who achieves the ideals of domesticity— comfort, intimacy, beauty, children, without a female presence. From this stems Robert's monomaniacal desire to return to the domestic by finding George and ridding the domestic sphere of the imposter—Lucy. It is this search that exposes Robert to distorted versions of the patriarchal and feminine ideals. The novel's fairy tale ending implies an interesting compromise for domestic masculinity, while the "magical" setting suggests its impossibility.

The exposed hypocrisy of the angel in the house through the passing of the Marriage Act[6] opens up for discussion the redefinition of masculinity and femininity in the mid–nineteenth century. The exposed performance in one gender, leads to instability within the other. If the angel in the house is a myth, then the patriarchal ideal must also be questioned. Braddon does so with her cast of morally weak and violent male characters, perhaps explaining why the novel's "hero" is chosen from outside this male community. Lucy and Robert enact mythical ideals of domesticity. On one hand, Lucy brings to life the angel in the house, while Robert eventually comes to perform his role as a professional, husband, and father. Issues of performance explored in the novel and the passing of the Marriage Act five years earlier reveal mid–nineteenth-century anxieties concerning authenticity, intimacy, and the intrusion of the public within the private. Accompanying this concern around performance are the psychological aspects of the split self and moral insanity. When the Marriage Act exposed the double lives of men and women, insanity became a popular alibi.

By recognizing Lucy's performance, Robert exposes his own propensity for the domestic as opposed to, as some critics suggest, his rejection of femininity and acceptance of the patriarchal ideal. While it is clear that Robert's quest to discover Lucy's secret and remove her from the private sphere results in his own transformation, it is not so apparent that he must reject his own femininity in consequence. The significance of Robert's journey through the narrative has taken precedence over the discovery of the novel's title character's secret in much of current literary criticism. Robert's "coming-of-age" story and Lucy's secret are two interdependent narratives. Gilbert acknowledges how the 1860s critics, "expressed outrage over the portrayal of the alienated woman and missed the much more subversive portrait of alienated patriarchy" ("Madness" 220). Recent critics, such as Gilbert, analyze Robert's transformation in relation to the hero's journey, as illustrated by Braddon's references to *The Odyssey* Gilbert advocates that for Robert, "women are evil when they have masculine ambitions and take on masculine roles; paradoxically, it is precisely because he does not have these characteristics that he finds them hateful" ("Madness" 224). Robert's abhorrence towards ambitious and masculine women does not originate from envy, but from his role as domestic defender. Gilbert suggests that, "contrary to Robert's perception, Lady Audley's story shows that women are most evil when they conform" ("Madness" 224). Although Robert is enraptured by his beautiful young aunt, it is upon viewing her Pre-Raphaelite portrait that he becomes unnerved. Sophia Andres examines how Braddon uses references to Pre-Raphaelite art in *Lady Audley's Secret* and *Aurora Floyd* to "destablize conventional gender constructs and offer alternatives suppressed by the hegemonic discourse" (1).

Braddon's re-drawing of the portrait through her description brings the reality of the art into the fiction of sensation. She questions gender roles through her analysis of the male gaze and female sensuality. The portrait also functions to reveal Lucy's alternate persona, which diminishes Robert's physical attraction to her. Furthermore, his obsession over George's disappearance effectively distracts him from Lucy's charms. Robert is aware of Lucy's duality and the danger she represents having secured a place for herself in Audley Court. He is able to imagine the deceptive quality of Lucy without being influenced by her beauty and innocence. Following Gilbert's argument would give Lucy the upper hand over Robert, when in fact they are evenly matched in their positions as social outcasts and gender performers. If anything, Lucy teaches Robert the benefits of performing according to social expectations, while having the freedom to continue another lifestyle simultaneously. Robert and Lucy battle for reign over the private sphere,[7] which the Marriage Act through the demystification of the angel in the house had left unprotected. While Lucy's strategy requires that she embody this idealized myth, Robert learns that he must conform to the patriarchal ideal in order to take his own place within the accepted domestic sphere. Once secure with the private realm both find the freedom to once again transgress social boundaries—Lucy by committing and attempting murder, and Robert by fulfilling his desire to return to male domestic bliss with George through his marriage to Clara. Robert experiences dual natures as he progresses towards a new personality, which is strikingly similar to Lucy's multiple selves. This duality is apparent in both characters and links them to the issue of madness.

Madness is one of Lady Audley's well-guarded secrets and she uses it as an explanation for her aggressive and calculating nature. In addition to the domestic ideological hypocrisy publicly revealed by the Marriage Act, the debate concerning infanticide and maternal insanity exposed yet another domestic reality masked by the façade of the angel in the house. Jill L. Matus in *Unstable Bodies: Victorian Representations of Sexuality and Maternity* explains how the laws governing infanticide were inconsistent and lenient, and many of the accused cited insanity as their plea (188). The definition of 'mother' came to represent "instinctive care, nurturing, responsibility, and self-sacrifice [...as well as] precarious mental health, derangement, emotional perversity, and murderous destructiveness" (Matus, *Unstable Bodies* 189). Motherhood suffered the same unmasking as the angel in the house. Maternal insanity, Matus describes, "is itself a slippery term that signifies both madness occasioned by becoming a mother (puerperal insanity) as well as madness inherited from the mother (insanity transmitted through the maternal line)" (*Unstable Bodies* 189). Lucy admits that madness has been passed down to her matrilineally and that the act of childbirth sparks these fits. While Braddon hints at courtroom dramas and the popularity of the insanity plea in her novel, she is also commenting on the ways in which femininity is pushing beyond acceptable boundaries. This type of female transgression through madness, Matus notes, "makes the reader think about maternal inheritance in a symbolic way, not as a matter of biological organisation and bodily functioning, but in terms of legal, social and economic position, and psychologically in relation to the formation of subjectivity" (*Unstable Bodies* 191). Lucy becomes a symbol and no longer a woman, as Robert insists, "I look upon you henceforth as the demoniac incarnation of some evil principle" (Braddon 340); this principle can be construed as the maternal inheritance passed down through the generations that is embodied in the transgressive female. Lucy's claim to maternal insanity is a familiar device to sensation readers as an escape from the courts and the public spectacle.

Robert accepts Lucy's self-diagnosis as a way of imprisoning her without the unwanted publicity of a trial, while at the same time her admission sabotages any sentiment of triumph in Robert's victory over her: "You have used your cool, calculating, frigid, luminous intellect to a noble purpose. You have conquered—a MADWOMAN!" (Braddon 340). Showalter discusses the dual natures of female madness as "one of the wrongs of woman [and] madness as the essential feminine nature unveiling itself before scientific male rationality" (*The Female Malady* 3). This climactic scene demonstrates how Lucy reverts to society's expectations as an explanation for her unfeminine violence and aggression and then she adheres to another set of social expectations regarding women and madness. Lucy has simply moved from one feminine ideal to the other; as a sane woman she is the angel in the house, and as a madwoman she is the ideal of insanity, adhering to all the social expectations of the female deviant. As Showalter notes, "even the murderous madwomen do not escape male domination; they escape one specific, intolerable exercise of women's wrongs by assuming an idealized, poetic form of pure femininity as the male culture had construed it: absolutely irrational, absolutely emotional" (*The Female Malady* 17). Braddon confirms that Robert has achieved the pinnacle of success by appearing as the ideal of masculinity—cool, calculating, and rational.

Braddon makes the issue of madness more complex by leaving her reader unsure whether Lucy is insane, since the author describes Lucy as simply achieving the ideal of femininity and assuring that she maintains this status. As Winifred Hughes recognizes, "[t]he feminine ideal, as [Braddon] portrays it, is potentially treacherous, for both the women who conform and the men who worship them; the standard feminine qualities—childishness, self-suppression, the talent for pleasing—inherently contain the seeds of their own destruction" (124). Hughes addresses the mental instability that may occur as a result of attempting to achieve impossibly high social expectations. The entrance of the mad-doctor into Audley Court completes its image as an asylum.[8] According to Joel Peter Eigen in *Witnessing Insanity: Madness and Mad-Doctors*, the image of the mad-doctor as "this new *expert* witness [...] captured most graphically the merging Victorian conception of insane criminality: a will out of control" (7). The appearance of the mad-doctor in the courtroom indicated a change in criminal trials and, as Eigen notes, "ultimately with larger cultural questions concerning human agency" (6). Lucy's madness is never confirmed by Doctor Musgrave, but he agrees with Robert only after he reveals her as a murderer, and without proof she is "buried alive," as the chapter's title underscores, not for being mad, but for being dangerous. Lucy's potent combination of the "cunning of madness, with the prudence of intelligence" (Braddon 372), makes her a candidate for moral insanity and most especially an affront to the stability of femininity. Musgrave states to that affect, "There is latent insanity! Insanity which might never appear; or which might appear only once or twice in a life-time" (Braddon 372). This type of "latent insanity"[9] becomes quite noticeable in Robert through his obsession over Lucy's guilt and George's unburied body. June Sturrock examines the anxiety surrounding the image of the woman as spectacle on trial and how it reflected general concern for an increase of women in public roles and employment. Sturrock explains how confinement in the asylum saves Robert from the nightmare of a public trial: "[m]ale honour—male social status—is vulnerable through the public exposure of female relations. To avoid dishonour—loss of status—Robert Audley must avoid publicity and hence the law" (81). Robert and Lucy have assumed new positions for themselves in society—Lucy now defines herself as the "madwoman" and Robert embraces his role as her judge and jailer (Braddon 375).

Performance, duality, and madness are linked within the novel and between Lucy and Robert. Whereas the question of Lucy's secret of her inherited madness has been analyzed in depth, the investigation of Robert's sanity, brought into doubt in the novel, is not so prevalent. Matus calls attention to the fact that *Lady Audley's Secret* was written after a "period of 'lunacy panic'" in England, which lead to public anxiety concerning being forcibly institutionalized ("Disclosure" 347). Matus reminds us that Braddon was familiar with this topic since Paul Maxwell, with whom she had six children, had a wife in an Irish mental hospital. Male madness was acknowledged and treated during the nineteenth century, but it was female hysteria that took precedence in institutions and asylums. By the late–eighteenth century, the "disturbing image of wild, dark, naked men had been replaced by poetic, artistic, and theatrical image of a youthful, beautiful female insanity" (Showalter, *Female Malady* 10), as depicted by Lucy's mother. Whereas male patients occupied a wing in an institution, women filled the rest of the building. As Showalter notes, "[b]y 1872, out of 58,640 certified lunatics in England and Wales, 21, 822 were women" (*Female Malady* 52). She makes the connection between the domestication of insanity and the institution to its feminization: "gradually, the percentages of women in Victorian asylums increased, and by the 1850s there were more women than men in public institutions" (*Female Malady* 52). For this reason, the image of the brutish madman evolves into that of feminized weakness and impotence by the *fin-de-siècle* and early twentieth century. Shell-shocked soldiers being treated for hysteria were feminized based on their illness. The emotions produced by hysteria were considered effeminate and many World War I male hysterics were ostracized for their cowardly conduct and in some cases accused of homosexuality. Showalter demonstrates how the shell-shocked soldier's hysteria is considered as a refusal to conform to the strict code of masculinity enforced during this period, which is reminiscent of the New Woman hysteric, who was also alienated for her rebellion against social norms (*Female Malady* 172). The feminization of madness can be linked to what Dr. Phillippe Pinel, chief physician of the Hospice de la Salpêtrière, labeled *manie sans délire*, which would eventually evolve into the theory of moral insanity (Robinson 156). Moral insanity dispels the savage wild man for a "type of insanity that spares the intellect and most outward signs of rationality in a person, who, nonetheless, has greatly diminished powers of self-control" (Robinson 156). Without the telltale appearance of insanity, madness becomes an invisible disease except in moments of loss of self-restraint. Sexual excess and the threat of self-abuse were also linked to male madness.

Monomania, used by Lucy as a diagnosis for Robert's obsession with her real identity, is actually an obsession with finding George. James Cowles Prichard defines monomania as a, disorder of the mind in which a single false notion is impressed upon the understanding which is otherwise unclouded, so that the insane person is capable of reasoning correctly on all subjects connected with a particular train of thought, and even on topics connected with his illusion, if erroneous conviction be conceded as truth and matter of fact [Skultans 169].

Lucy's attempt to suggest that Robert suffers from moral insanity begins harmlessly enough when she voices her concern for her young nephew's attentions to Sir Audley. She insinuates the possibility of the influence of Robert's eccentric father on his own mental health; finally, once cornered, Lucy diagnoses Robert with monomania in an attempt to empower herself by using medical discourse. Matus makes the claim that Lucy's attempt to empower herself through medical discourse is futile since it has already been used to rend her powerless ("Disclosure" 350). The narrator also denies this power from Lucy, when she uses the medical term "psychological peculiarity" (Braddon 285), the narrator relates, "[t]he big words sounded strange from my lady's rosy lips" (Braddon 285). Her knowledge is useless while she maintains her child-like beauty.

Robert becomes the ideal of masculinity as he banishes Lucy from society and begins to embrace his moral and social responsibilities, but before he settles into this new position Robert experiences that same "invisible balance upon which the mind is always trembling" (Braddon 396). The narrator intervenes to remind readers of the fragility and delicacy of sanity: "[m]ad to-day and sane to-morrow" (Braddon 396), and asks, "[w]ho has not been, or is not to be, mad in some lonely hour of life? Who is quite safe from the trembling of the balance?" (Braddon 397). Some allegedly mad prisoners who spoke for themselves during their trials used this plea for the universality of bouts of madness as a justifiable defense. According to documents recorded from 1760 to 1843 from the Old Bailey courthouse, 170 out of 331 supposed insane criminals made a statement during their trial (Eigen 165). One statement spoken by prisoner Frances Paar to the jury echoes that of Braddon's narrator, as Paar entreated, "Gentlemen, we are none of us exempt from disease or accident; judge of me [...] as you would wish to be judged yourselves" (Eigen 57). This suggests that madness functioned as a class leveler by putting emphasis on the indiscriminate nature of mental illness Robert, like Lucy, exhibits bouts of madness through his monomania and his obsession over George's dead body: "Robert's obsessive desire to capture, incarcerate, and bury Lady Audley's body covers his other monomaniacal impulse to find and re-immerse himself in the missing body of [...] George" (Tromp 27). It appears that Robert is well aware of people's tendencies to be "mad to-day and sane to-morrow" (Braddon 396), something which he allows himself to experience, but Lucy's tottering on the "invisible line" is considered punishable by social disgrace and life-long confinement. The madness that is shared between Robert and Lucy defines them as social misfits, and emphasizes their similar tendencies to move against social expectations.

In addition to Lucy's belief that madness is passed from mother to daughter, Braddon suggests that solipsism (the view that only the self exists) is a patriarchal disease. The male characters of Sir Michael, Harcourt Talboys, George, and Robert exhibit symptoms of this "male" illness: "the female protagonist's ambiguous inherited feminine madness is bland [...] when compared with the solipsism that is passed on from fathers to sons and from uncles to nephews" (Tromp 26). Braddon suggests that the accusations of madness against Lucy are questionable, while Robert's monomania is present throughout the novel in obvious forms. Robert's desire to gain a space for himself in society requires that he embrace Victorian masculinity, even though, as Herbert Sussman suggests, Robert's new acquisition of manliness may have increased his bouts of hysteria: "[f]or the nineteenth-century men, manhood was conceived as an unstable equilibrium of barely controlled energy that may collapse back into [...] the gender-specific mental pathology that the Victorian saw as male hysteria or male madness" (13). The "invisible balance" becomes an important image surrounding Robert's contemplations about his unstable mental condition. It is the ghostly vision of George's unburied body that haunts Robert as he tries to participate in the aristocratic masculine public sphere: "[h]ow could he sit amongst them, listening to their careless talk of politics and opera, literature and racing, theatres and science, scandal, and theology, and yet carry in his mind the horrible burden of those dark terrors and suspicions that were with him day and night" (Braddon 395). This is reminiscent of the acknowledgment of dual natures as discussed in Brontë's *Shirley* and Stevenson's *The Strange Case of Dr. Jekyll and Mr. Hyde* Robert's homosocial desire for George keeps him from associating with his "old friends" (Braddon 395), and in turn keeps him from securing a place within society.

Robert, as long as George remains undiscovered, still does not "fit in." Robert is well aware of the progress he has made on his journey towards maturity and social responsibility when he states, "Heaven knows I have learnt the business of life since then; and now I must needs fall in love and swell the tragic chorus which is always being sung by the poor addition of my pitiful sighs and groans. Clara Talboys!" (Braddon 394). He is conscious of the masculine formula and his step-by-step movement towards masculinity, yet he remains dissatisfied. Robert's transformation from indifferent and irresponsible bachelor to a professional, moral, and sensible husband requires immediate adjustment. Similar to the 1860s environment and all its new legislations and technologies, Robert must adjust to the New Woman and the discovery of his homosocial desire. As Richard Dellamora indicates, insanity in men "was regarded as a product of the increasing demands that modern progress exacts on the nervous system" (118). Progress and industrialization were blamed for the degeneration of both sexes. The introduction of the New Woman and the destabilization of masculinity are linked with progress and the decadence of the *fin-de-siècle*. Robert's discovery of his true self, which despite his efforts continues to rebel against Victorian masculinity, results in his increasing monomania and eventually "ghost-seeing" (Braddon 397). Similar to Lucy who performs the feminine ideal, Robert questions whether he can maintain the performance of masculinity to a successful end. The novel's conclusion includes a return to the domestic in which Robert can flourish. Living in the fairy cottage exiled from the inner city and social restraints and expectations, Robert finds an ideal balance with *both* sister and brother.

The ideal of femininity and masculinity, as well as the Victorian family undergoes significant reconstruction during the 1860s and finds expression through the sensation genre. The angel in the house and the proper Victorian gentleman represent society's obsession with gender construction and its rigid expectations of men and women. During this period, the Divorce Act becomes law and society reacts by emphasizing the importance of family and marriage. The creation of the angel in the house demonstrates men's need for protection "from the anxieties of modern life and for those values no longer confirmed by religious faith or relevant to modern business" (Christ 146). Braddon's Lady Audley does not provide this protection at Audley Court, instead she is quite familiar with modern technologies and uses them to serve her needs. Lady Audley does however perform as the angel in the house by using her childish beauty and innocence as an effective veil disguising what hides beneath. Robert is also a social misfit, and he is able to see himself in Lucy's performance and dissembling.

Robert plays at being a barrister through his appearance, yet similar to Lucy, Robert desires a position within the domestic. As Robert seeks to displace Lucy, he learns about his own secrets, such as his homosocial desire for George. Robert's bouts with madness are the consequence of his transformation into a "new man," a concept that finds its basis in anti-bachelor rhetoric of the period. The bachelor figure pushes the boundaries of acceptable sexual and moral behavior through the many opportunities presented to him for excess. One concept of the bachelor suggests his ability to create a domestic life equivalent and in some instances, superior to that of the typified Victorian husband and wife. Robert's relationship with George and especially his role as George's care-taker, exemplify the bachelor's potential to provide an authentic domestic space, a compelling notion coming at a time when the Marriage Acts were exposing the hypocrisy of domestic ideology. Robert is yet another example of the bachelor-domestic defender, who rids the private sphere of its artificial and theatrical intruder. The space that Robert is protecting is not the traditional private sphere, but one which does not require marriage or a female presence. Robert's "forced" relationship with Clara is problematized by the novel's conclusion, which clearly shows the existence of the Victorian love triangle. Robert has found his place in the fairy cottage away from society's restraints, unlike Lucy, who is able to place herself securely within aristocratic society. By embracing performance, Robert is able, like his double Lucy, to inhabit the masculine public sphere as a barrister, but also enjoy a flourishing domestic life. His position, though, remains unclear because he has not decided to shed his authentic self completely and instead lives with both George and Clara, an indication that Robert prefers to remain tottering on the "invisible balance" between the spheres. Although married, Robert succeeds in creating the ideal space where he can indulge in his homosocial relationship, while simultaneously conforming to society's expectations of the gentleman, a theatrical strategy employed earlier by the consummate actress, Lucy. In the battle for position within the domestic sphere, the manufactured and degenerate image of the angel in the house is brusquely pushed aside by the domesticated bachelor, who embodies the potential for an authentic model of domesticity. When considering earlier incarnations of the domestic bachelor, such as Robert and Louis Moore in Brontë's *Shirley*, and Robert Audley in Braddon's *Lady Audley's Secret*, it is clear that performance plays an integral role for the bachelor's incorporation of feminine discourse while in George Eliot's *Daniel Deronda* the male actress pushes the boundaries by focusing on the body as a visible sign of performance.

# FOUR

# "Domesticated Theatricality"

## The Gentleman Actress
## in George Eliot's Daniel Deronda

The correct Englishman, drawing himself up from his bow into rigidity, assenting severely, and seeming to be in a state of internal drill, suggests a suppressed vivacity, and may be suspected of letting go with some violence when he is released from parade; but Grandcourt's bearing had no rigidity, it inclined rather to the flaccid. His complexion had a faded fairness resembling that of an actress when bare of the artificial white and red; his long narrow grey eyes expressed nothing but indifference [*DD* 91].

[Deronda] wore an embroidered Holland blouse which set off the rich colouring of his head and throat, and the resistant gravity about his mouth and eyes as he was being smiled upon, made their beauty the more impressive. Every one was admiring him [*DD* 143].

Despite being a novel that criticizes the role of the performer, George Eliot's *Daniel Deronda* is permeated with spectacles, spectators, artists, and blackmailers. While the fate of female actors is clearly linked in Victorian novels with that of the fallen woman,[1] Eliot's novel follows the rise of a new breed of performer—the gentleman actress. His destiny is not necessarily ruined although his ability to perform inevitably links him with effeminacy. Rictor Norton in *Mother Clap's Molly House: The Gay Subculture in England 1700–1830* provides a thorough history of molly houses and the people who frequented them. Apart from providing a space for homosexual activities, molly houses were also a place for performance, as Samuel Stevens, a Reforming constable reported on 14 November 1725:

I found between 40 and 50 Men making Love to one another, as they call'd it. Sometimes they would sit on one another's Laps, kissing in a lewd Manner, and using their Hands indecently. Then they would get up, Dance and make Curtsies, and mimick the voices of Women [88].

While Deronda and Grandcourt are ridiculed for their attempt to mimic their female counterparts in public, molly houses encourage male performance of femininity within the safe confines of the private sphere. Eliot blurs the boundaries of the public and private on two levels: first by introducing her readers to the character of the male actress, who transgresses gender roles associated with the spheres, and then suggesting that his performance is primarily domestic, unlike the more public spectacles of his female counterparts. The male actress' use of the physical body as an artistic canvas is usually associated with the feminine; this quality of female performance reveals a unique amalgamation of the actress and the gentleman. James Eli Adams discusses the tendency for the gentleman to use his body as a visible marker of status, in response to the increasing accessibility of the gentlemanly ideal to the lower classes (*Dandies* 152). In essence, the gentleman embraces the typically feminine qualities of performance, self-decoration, and mannerisms in order to mark himself as an authentic gentleman. While Adams is referring to the link between the earlier dandy and the gentleman, it becomes clear that the mid–Victorian period inherits these aspects in the performance of masculinity. Joseph Lipvak claims that with the rise of the novel came the "fall of the public man—a fall from the theatricality of eighteenth-century culture into the world of domesticity, subjectivity, and psychology" (ix). Yet, the male as spectacle or dandy continues to find his way into mid–Victorian literature, and specifically in Eliot's *Daniel Deronda*. In Lipvak's discussion of the literary battle between female theatricality and male poetry he refers to "domesticated theatricality" (191), and the domination of poetry in the novel. "Domesticated theatricality" includes such female performers as Mirah Lapidoth, Gwendolen Harleth, and Leonora Halm-Eberstein, but also male actresses, such as Henleigh Mallinger Grandcourt, and Daniel Deronda.

The male spectacle embraces "domesticated theatricality" as yet another method for the domesticated bachelor to infiltrate the realm of the feminine. Ironically, the theater is looked to by Gwendolen and less fortunate Victorian women, as one of the rare options for making money and thus becoming truly independent of the patriarchal system, as Walter Donaldson writes in *Fifty Years of Green-room Gossip* (1881):

[acting is] the only position where woman is perfectly independent of man, and where, by her talent and conduct, she obtains the favour of the public. She then enters the theatre emancipated and disenthralled from the fears and heartburning too often felt by those forced into a life of tuition and servitude [qtd. in Beer, *GE* 209].

Once a domain reserved for the feminine, theatricality in Eliot's *Daniel Deronda*, stretches to include the male actress in his attempt to escape the same patriarchal system.

In Eliot's exploration of performance and theatricality, the gaze of the spectator is fixed by the power of a mesmerist, as *Daniel Deronda*'s opening scene reveals. Anthony Trollope's novel *The Way We Live Now*, which Eliot read in 1874 (Haight, *GE* 458), demonstrates the reliance of the young wealthy classes on gambling to secure actual credit, as opposed to the intangible funds of their inheritances and allowances. Gambling moves from the walls of Beargarden into the lives of the characters as money is replaced by the people. While Eliot may have been influenced by reading Trollope's novel as she planned *Daniel Deronda*, earlier novels including Thackeray's *Vanity Fair*, Gaskell's *North and South*, and the Brontë's works are a few that have also addressed issues of gambling. Gambling is effectively put in its place when Eliot describes the "proper" circumstances for gambling being, "in the open air under a southern sky, tossing coppers on a ruined wall, with rags about her limbs," as opposed to the "splendid resorts which the enlightenment of ages has prepared for the same species of pleasure" (*DD* 3), in which we find Gwendolen and other fashionable women. In September 1872, Eliot was deeply affected by watching Miss Leigh aged twenty-six gambling at a roulette table in Homburg, that she wrote, "it made me cry to see her young fresh face among the hags and brutally stupid men around her" (Haight, *GE* 456). Although Gwendolen clearly stands out as a graceful figure at the roulette table, Eliot chooses the character of a young child to create the striking contrast that she witnessed in Homburg. The child was "a melancholy little boy [...] his face turned towards a doorway, and fixing on it the blank gaze of a bedizened child stationed as a masquerading advertisement on the platform of an itinerant show, stood close behind a lady deeply engaged at the roulette-table" (*DD* 4). This image of the child "actor" raises issues of innocence, performance, and exposure; all of which carry through the rest of the novel.

During a time when theories about individual will power and the evolution of the mind flourished, mesmerism and spiritualism were considered by many, including Eliot, as significant topics of the period. The gambling scene solidifies the novel's preoccupation with the power dynamics between the spectator and the spectacle through the gaze. While it appears that Deronda takes the superior position gazing upon the spectacle, which is Gwendolen at the gaming table, her performance is also self-empowering. While the questions Deronda asks himself at the beginning of Chapter One have been analyzed by critics in depth, how these thoughts enter his mind has been given less attention. In one case Joseph Allen Boone in *Tradition Counter Tradition: Love and the Form of Fiction* argues that this opening scene demonstrates the complexity of Deronda's character: "he attempts to suppress the sexual attraction aroused in him by Gwen's disturbing beauty at the gaming table, for instance, by establishing a never quite successful 'objective' evaluation of her character as a disinterested observer" (175). Indeed, Deronda does not succeed in distancing himself as purely an observer, since there is clearly another relationship occurring during this pivotal scene, one which is reminiscent of a hypnotist and her subject. Following an epigraph that raises the conflict between male and female, science and poetry, and the "make-believe of a beginning," the novel begins *in medias reas*, unsure of its origins. The epigraph which opens *Daniel Deronda*'s Chapter One has been the focus of study for many literary critics. Lipvak in *Caught in the Act* mentions how Eliot's inclusion of poetic epigraphs illustrates the "superiority of poetry to prose" (162), a theme initiated in her first epigraph. Beer calls attention to the epigraph's mention of "make-believe beginnings" suggesting a contemplation of origins, and connection between source and development: "instead of the coherence of uniformitarian sequence what is emphasized is faulture and slippage, the difficulty of interpretation, the inevitable incompleteness of knowledge" (Beer, *Darwin's Plots* 192). These issues fueled debate in the 1870s through such authors as Comte, Eddington, Clerk Maxwell, Clausius, Darwin, and Helmholtz. While the questions Deronda asks suggest his aim at a position of moral superiority, it is Gwendolen who penetrates the spectator and, "raise[s] these questions in Daniel Deronda's mind" (*DD* 3). Gwendolen's early influence on Deronda's thoughts is described in terms of a supernatural power usually associated with the female demon; she is a "sylph" (*DD* 5), "Nereid," "serpent," and "Lamia" (*DD* 7). In an interesting transgression of gender conventions, Eliot then situates Deronda in the traditionally feminized role of witch, whose "evil eye" (*DD* 6), results in Gwendolen's loss at the gaming table.

The primitivity of the gambling house recalls Eliot's preoccupation with evolutionary theory and the development of the human mind. Eliot clearly links gambling and the science of cause and effect based on her reading of R. A. Procter's "The Past and Present of Our Earth" published in December 1874, and "Gambling Superstitions" (Beer, *Darwin's Plots* 189). Her early influences included Charles Darwin's *The Descent of Man*, which as Gillian Beer notes lead to *Deronda's* central themes of "descent, development, and race" (*Darwin's Plots* 182).[2] In addition to Eliot's examination of the individual versus the survival of the community, Darwin's views on sexual selection are also present in the novel. The role of the English gentleman in sexual selection is broadened and his impact on heredity, class, and race of the community of the future combine many of Eliot's sociological, astronomical, evolutionary and genetic theories. *Daniel Deronda* explores a wide variety of Eliot's interests in evolutionary theory and mesmerism. Gillian Beer in *Darwin's Plots: Evolutionary Narrative in Darwin, George Eliot and Nineteenth-Century*, elaborates on Eliot's influences including Butler's *Analogy* (1842), Isaac Taylor's *The Physical Theory of Another Life* (1836), and the idea of the future Life as absolute form of fiction, and William Warburton's *The Divine Legation of Moses Demonstrated on the Principles of a Religious Deist, Omission of the Doctrine of a Future State of Rewards and Punishments in the Jewish Dispensation* (1738–41) (183). In relation to evolution of the mind, Beer states, "the action of the will and of sexual selection become major topics in George Eliot's late work" (186). Although Eliot was not convinced by the power of mesmerism she was curious enough in these pseudo-scientific practices to volunteer to be mesmerized (Haight, *GE* 55), as well as visit a phrenologist (Haight, *GE* 51).The roulette table is life's wheel of fortune in *Daniel Deronda*, where chance and change result in bringing characters together, discovering hidden knowledge, sudden death, and the loss and recovery of possessions.[3] Beer explains how Eliot believed in the "chanciness of consequences, the phantasmagoric out-flaring of need and dread into acts which confirm their own predictions" (*Darwin's Plots* 216). Rosemary Ashton supports the idea that the novel expands on the gambling motif as Gwendolen "gambles on happiness in taking financial security in marriage rather than poor spinsterhood" (84). The issue of sexual selection in the novel forces the question, "can fiction restore to the female the power of selection which, Darwin held, men had taken over? And can the woman writing, shape new future stories?" (Beer, *Darwin's Plots* 218). Female characters in the novel attempt to redefine their socially and culturally prescribed paths, and Beer notes how Gwendolen is Eliot's lone success story, Gwendolen is "untransformed by sexual selection [...] she has for the present survived the marriage market where her beauty and resistance to slavery equally made her sought by a man who favoured mastery" (*Darwin's Plots* 218). Beer elaborates on this thought in *George Eliot* adding how Gwendolen escapes the marriage market, while Deronda escapes British culture and British manhood (227). Though Gwendolen's attempts to secure financial independence through other means than the traditional methods of working as a governess or marrying rich, she is persuaded to avoid the alternate paths of a career as an actress or singer. Her youthful beauty is destined for the purpose of marrying up, and her search for another solution to her family's destitution is terminated by patriarchal expectations. In the novel, Eliot repeatedly grants women power and independence, only to eventually reveal how it serves a patriarchal purpose or leads to death or loss.

The gambling motif allows Eliot to put forward questions on evolutionary theory and the classes, performance and spectacle, free will and natural behavior, as Eliot writes, "but while every single player differed markedly from every other, there was a certain uniform negativeness of expression which had the effect of a mask—as if they had all eaten of some root that for the time compelled the brains of each to the same narrow monotony of action" (*DD* 5). This "admission of human equality" (*DD* 4), certainly exists on a primitive level bringing together those who share a similar vice, yet it also suggests the possibility of another alternative to class, space, and gender roles. George Du Maurier's popular novel *Trilby* explores "hypnotic spectatorship," another perspective on the power dynamics of performance. Published in 1894, *Trilby*, reincarnates similar themes found in *Daniel Deronda*, including fear of the Other (both novels deal with issues of anti–Semitism), the role of the female artist/performer, gender roles in spectatorship and performance, and individual will power and the mid-to-late nineteenth-century's widespread fear of psychic control. While Du Maurier's novel has clear inclinations towards the supernatural, in addition to directly addressing hypnotism, it is important to note that in many instances in *Daniel Deronda*, characters like Gwendolen, Deronda, and Mordecai possess the ability to see into the future. As visionaries they have an uncanny skill for prediction and to some extent they practice mind control. While both novels explore the battle for will power, gender dynamics are worked out through such dichotomous relationships as hypnotist and patient, performer and spectator, private and public. Here Gwendolen fantasizes that she could rule these people, as their priestess: "she had begun to believe in her luck, others had begun to believe in it: she had visions of being followed by a *cortège* who would worship her as a goddess of luck and watch her play as a directing augury" (*DD* 6). The freedom Gwendolen experiences through gambling is similar to the lure of the theater for actresses. Adelaide Ristori, an Italian actress who played Lady Macbeth at Covent Garden and the Lyceum, describes feeling empowered on stage:

It was delicious to me [...] to feel that I could move human souls at my will, and excite their gentlest as well as their strongest passion [...] all this intoxicated me, made me feel as through I were endowed with superhuman powers. (qtd. in Powell 9). As a gambling goddess, Gwendolen finds an alternate space where she eagerly questions gender roles and claims "supremacy" for women.

Gwendolen's performances, like Eliza Lynn Linton's "girl of the period," "act against nature" and adhere to the usual negative representations of woman as spectacle. The serpent imagery surrounding Gwendolen in the gambling scene is reminiscent of William Makepeace Thackeray's mermaid, Becky Sharp, and emphasizes the deceptive qualities of the female performer. Gwendolen's appearance in her *"ensemble du serpent"* (*DD* 7) inspires drama, as Mr. Vandernoodt imagines, "how a man might risk hanging for her" (*DD* 7). Her physical appearance forces the question, "do you think her pretty" (*DD* 7), suggesting that her beauty crosses over into monstrosity linking Gwendolen with the female demon, as Mr. Vandernoodt reflects, "woman was tempted by a serpent: why not man?" (*DD* 7). Judith Butler's theories on the permeability of the body, the constructs of gender, and how the unstable definition of femininity allows for conflicting notions of the female body and women's place in society can be applied to the female performers in *Daniel Deronda*. Mary Russo in *The Female Grotesque: Risk, Excess and Modernity*, describes the female grotesque as "multiple and changing" (8), while the classical body is statuesque, "static, self-contained, symmetrical, and sleek" (8). The actress may mimic the classical body, as Gwendolen attempts in her performance of Hermione in the *tableau vivant*, but she is unable to remain fixed and in Gwendolen's case she succumbs to "fits of spiritual dread" (*DD* 52). Gwendolen as the female demon is confirmed early in the novel, through her mannerisms and as the narrator states, "as it were a trace of demon ancestry—which made some beholders hesitate in their admiration of Gwendolen" (*DD* 55). Eliot provides her with a complexity of character when Gwendolen seeks moral enlightenment from Deronda; without his interference, Gwendolen may have continued on the path of many Victorian female demons before her, including, Becky Sharp, Bertha Mason, and Lady Audley. Artifice and performance are the female demons' greatest weapons. Gwendolen initially falls under Russo's definition of the grotesque since she is unable to contain and refine herself. The significance of appearance for the female performers also extends to the male actresses since gestures, mannerisms, and appearances, as Butler argues, are "performative in the sense that the essence or identity that they otherwise purport to express fabrications manufactured and sustained through corporeal signs and discursive means" (*Gender Trouble* 136). Gwendolen questions why she can not expect the same gambling success as men who are worshipped and admired: "such things had been known of male gamblers; why should not a woman have a like supremacy?" (*DD* 6). The gambling arena becomes a space for gender transgressions and the questioning of gender roles, although it is important to recognize how these are thoughts that remain "unacted," since Gwendolen loses at the gambling table and does not turn out to be the *femme fatale* Mr. Vandernoodt imagines. The male gaze dethrones the goddess of luck: "the certainty she had (without looking) of that man still watching her was something like a pressure which begins to be torturing" (*DD* 6). Eventually, Deronda places Gwendolen in her proper place, as the *femme fatale*, witch, sea-nymph, and serpent, destroying her image as a powerful goddess.

*Daniel Deronda* investigates the delicate balance between spectator and sympathizer and the instability of the position of the spectator leads to the transgression of the self and the merging of characters. Deronda finds himself unable to remain simply a spectator and transitions into the role of performer. His heightened sensibility, excessive sympathy, and his own questionable social status and cultural background result in his tendency to take on the role of victim, usually a burden placed on female characters, like Mirah, Gwendolen, and Leonora. Deronda performs as a type of Svengali—a hypnotist of sensibility. Similar to Du Maurier's Svengali, Deronda envisions greatness in his female victims and proceeds to guide them towards their ideal self. Svengali sees the possibility in Trilby, but instead of teaching her how to sing, he uses her "immense" voice to sing with himself. Deronda's "sessions" with his female patients, Eliot reminds us, always tap into his own insecurities and the selfish desire to elevate himself, as Deronda explains, "I suppose our keen feeling for ourselves might end in giving us a keen feeling for others" (*DD* 387). As hypnotist, Deronda places himself in the role of performer, an undesirable position he has avoided since childhood.

The hypnotist, like his vampiric counterpart, plays on Victorian anxieties of the Other, including their ability to infiltrate minds and bodies rendering their victims helpless, deprived of their own free will. Franz Anton Mesmer's theory is based on the "concept of an imponderable fluid permeating the entire universe and infusing both matter and spirit with its vital force" (Tatar 5), which could be activated by the use of magnets. Mesmer based his theory on ancient traditions "that certain individuals are endowed with healing powers which they can turn to account by focusing their gaze on others or by touching them" (Tatar 4). Mesmer's entire practice was based on performance. His clinic was dark, with heavy curtains, mirrors, soft music; as Tatar describes, "everything in Mesmer's clinic seemed designed to foster an aura of mystery and magical enchantment" (14). Mesmer, himself, dressed the part in a "violet robe of embroidered silk and carried with him a magnetized iron wand" (Tatar 15), and he assumed a powerful and masterful persona by "acting as master of ceremonies, he strode majestically through the room" (Tatar 15). Mesmerism works in relation to nineteenth-century anxieties concerning the power of voice and speech and the ability to take over someone's will and control their thoughts and actions. Coleridge's *The Rime of the Ancient Mariner*, and Victorian novels, like Bram Stoker's *Dracula* and George du Maurier's *Trilby* also address this preoccupation with mesmerism by a foreigner. Mesmerism is discussed later in this chapter in relation to the influence of Grandcourt and Deronda on Gwendolen's performance. In his conversations with the desperate Gwendolen, Deronda adopts the discourse of hypnotism, when he commands her, "You will not go on being selfish and ignorant" (*DD* 383). His obsession with saving Gwendolen from herself, paired with Gwendolen's willingness to offer herself to him, "I wish he could know everything about me without my telling him" (*DD* 368), results in the ideal scenario for invading her psyche. As Gwendolen desperately demands of Deronda, "you must tell me then what to think and what to do; else why did you not let me go on doing as I liked, and not minding?" (*DD* 382). In her plea for Deronda to place himself in her situation and tell her what he would do, Gwendolen provides Deronda with material on which to base his performance. Deronda, as a version of Svengali's hypnotist, uses Gwendolen for his performance, and whereas she might appear as the spectacle, Deronda is clearly the one to watch.

Deronda as actress succeeds in his ability to absorb and perform in accordance with each of the female characters. In his incessant desire to achieve heightened sensibility, Deronda becomes another person, as Leona Toker explains, "Daniel Deronda thus effects a *tour de force* of linking sympathy with the metaphor of anthropophagia, of consuming another human being" (569), thus relating back to his role as the vampiric hypnotist. Deronda positions himself in a variety of female roles, as he assumes the emotional and psychological nature of the women he attempts to save. By placing himself in their positions, as an act of sympathy, Deronda becomes them. He is the quintessential actress even surpassing the female performers themselves.

Empathy and human interconnectedness are central to the novel, as Eliot strived to avoid self-repetition after the success of *Middlemarch*. As a writer, Eliot is known to have struggled with *Daniel Deronda* in her quest for producing something unique, meaningful. In a letter to Mrs. Elma Stuart on 10 January 1875, Eliot describes her commitment to avoid at all costs the publication of a frivolous novel: "for our world is already sufficiently afflicted with needless books, and I count it a social offence to add to them" (Haight, *GE Letters* 113). Catherine Gallagher examines Eliot's "anxiety of authorship" (*Body Economic* 118), as she approached writing *Daniel Deronda*. George Henry Lewes took seriously his role as Eliot's protector from negative reviews and commentary on her writing. As proof of Eliot's lack of self-confidence as a writer, refer to George Henry Lewes' letter to John Blackwood, 30 January 1876:

> I write to inform you against any mention of criticisms that may have appeared on *Deronda*—Mrs. Lewes is so easily discouraged and so ready to believe and exaggerate whatever is said against her books that I not only keep reviews from her but do not even talk of them to her. When people sometimes speak indignantly of objections that others have made they little know how it depresses her, and therefore whenever the subject is approached I step in if I can to stop their mouths [Haight, *GE Letters* 218].

Eliot's main concern which supersedes her dislike of "overconsumers," is revealed by Gallagher as a class of readers who, in Eliot's words, knowingly "complain but pay, and *read while they complain*" (*Body Economic* 120). With this difficult readership in mind, it is not surprising that Eliot lacked motivation to write her last novel.[4]

The "Jewish part" of *Daniel Deronda* raised both criticisms and accolades from readers, and Eliot clearly refers to this section as the most important element in the novel. Through her inclusion of Jewish characters and society, Eliot wished to expose what she described in a letter to Harriet Beecher Stowe, as the "intellectual narrowness—in plain English, the stupidity, which is still the average mark of our culture" (Haight, *GE Letters* 302). In the same letter addressed to Harriet Beecher Stowe on 29 October 1876, Eliot writes, "moreover, not only towards the Jews, but towards all oriental people with whom we English come in contact, a spirit of arrogance and contemptuous dictatorialness is observable which has become a national disgrace for us" (Haight, *GE Letters* 301). Clearly, Eliot's criticism of British "stupidity" in relation to their international interactions becomes the defining element of *Daniel Deronda*. While in *Middlemarch* the author positions a microscope onto the lives of some small townspeople, in *Daniel Deronda* Eliot's perspective broadens into a message of tolerance for other races and the uniting force of the human condition. As Eliot writes in a letter to John Blackwood, 3 November 1876, "this is what I wanted to do—to widen the English vision a little in that direction and let in a little conscience and refinement. I expected to excite more resistance of feeling than I have seen the signs of, but I did what I chose to do—not as well as I should have liked to do it, but as well as I could" (Holmstrom 157). Her reaction to critics who divided the novel into Gwendolen's story and the Jewish section reveals her obvious frustration with the misunderstanding of *Daniel Deronda*'s purpose and the necessity of its cohesion for delivering its message.[5] *The Saturday Review*, 16 September 1876 notes how, "the ordinary read ignores these mystic persons, and in family circles Gwendolen has been as much of a heroine—if we may so term the central and most prominent female figure—as if there were no Mirah" (Holmstrom 145). Joseph Jacobs writing for *Macmillan's Magazine*, June 1877 disputes Eliot's claim that the novel be read as whole when he states, "*Daniel Deronda* is made up of two almost unconnected parts, either of which can be read without the other" (Holmstrom 154). F. R. Leavis is known for separating *Daniel Deronda* into the "good half" and the "bad half." He goes so far as titling the good part, *Gwendolen Harleth* and suggesting that, "as for the bad part of *Daniel Deronda*, there *is* nothing to do but cut it away" (Leavis 122). Leavis explains in more detail how he would succeed in saving the novel by removing the "good half" from Deronda's section:

> and to extricate it for separate publication as *Gwendolen Harleth* seems to me the most likely way of getting recognition for it [...]. Deronda would be confined to what was necessary for his role of lay-confessor to Gwendolen, and the final cut would come after the death by drowning, leaving us with a vision of Gwendolen as she painfully emerges from her hallucinated worst conviction of guilt and confronts the daylight fact about Deronda's intentions [Leavis 122].

Eliot responds to letters of praise from Jews and Christians in her letter to Mme Eugène Bodichon on 2 October 1876: "this is better than the laudation of readers who cut the book into scraps and talk of nothing in it but Gwendolen. I meant everything in the book to be related to everything else there" (Haight, *GE Letters* 290). In fact, many reviewers simply concentrated on the character of Gwendolen and ignored the "Jewish part" of the novel. John Blackwood refers to Gwendolen as a "mermaid" and a "witch" in many of his letters to Eliot (Holmstrom 122, 123, 124), and reviewers acknowledge Eliot's skill in her depiction of Gwendolen's depth of character.[6] In an ironic twist, Eliot watched while readers showed more concern for Gwendolen's insolent nature and Grandcourt's violence, rather than raising a discussion on the Jewish Question, as Eliot herself writes, "yes, I expected more aversion than I have found" (Haight, *GE Letters* 302). Indeed, the characters themselves insist on the inseparability of the "two sections" of the novel based on their evident mirroring and the commonality of their stories and heredities.

Performance is another element shared among the characters of *Daniel Deronda*, and yet not all performances are acted out or expressed. Despite class, racial and gender differences, most characters' performances are solitary and remain unexpressed. When considering *Daniel Deronda* as a novel about acting, Beer's statement that "it is a novel about that which does not occur" (*Darwin's Plots* 234), is problematic. In *George Eliot: A Biography*, Gordon S. Haight notes how George Eliot and Lewes discussed "new projects for the *novel and play* Deronda. The possibility of a dramatic form, mentioned several times, was Lewes's idea, not [Eliot's], and was soon abandoned" (471). The idea of *Daniel Deronda* presented in a dramatic form accounts for the essence of theatricality permeating the novel. Yet, the inaction of the characters essentially reflects the artificiality of the theater, in that their performances do not necessarily get "acted out" outside of the theater of the mind or, as Eliot suggests, the equally isolated domestic sphere. The "domestication of theatricality" is not as Lipvak suggests "the fall of the public man [...] from theatricality [...] into domesticity [and] subjectivity" (ix), but is an invention of the domesticated bachelor who seeks to suppress the female spectacle. The male actress is yet another manifestation of the domestic bachelor who navigates between the public and private, a skill which the female actress is denied. Her position in the public sphere is condemned, and yet, as *Daniel Deronda* suggests, the male actress' performance of femininity and his regulation of domestic virtue and feminine values allows him to create a space for himself. In order to discuss the male actress as a unique representation of the domestic bachelor, the female actress and her various depictions must first be examined.

Eliza Lynn Linton provides a thorough description of her impression of the modern English girl, putting emphasis on the value of authenticity and the superficiality and deception of artificiality:

> The girl of the period is a creature who dyes her hair and paints her face, as the first articles of her personal religion; whose sole idea of life is plenty of fun and luxury; and whose dress is the object of such thought and intellect as she possesses [...]. Nothing is too extraordinary and nothing too exaggerated for her vitiated taste [...] she is acting against nature and her own interests when she disregards [men's] advice and offends their taste [...]. Men are afraid of her; and with reason [...]. Besides, after all her efforts, she is only a poor copy of the real thing; and the real thing is far more amusing than the copy, because it is real [172–5].

Henry James disapproved of Eliza Lynn Linton's portrayal of the "modern woman" in "The Girl of the Period." James found it unjust to condemn and set apart "modern women" from "modern men" (*Literary Criticism* 24). In response to Linton's piece, James writes,

> The various tricks of the marriage market are enumerated with a bold, unpitying crudity. It is a very dismal truth that the only hope of most women, at the present moment, for a life worth living, lies in marriage, and marriage with rich men or men likely to become so, and that in their unhappy weakness they often betray an ungraceful anxiety on this point [*Literary Criticism* 22].

James appears to sympathize with Gwendolen, whose feeble attempt at avoiding the marriage market is quashed by Herr Klesmer, which, as one of the characters in James dramatic review of *Daniel Deronda* suggests, is "one of the finest things in the book" (James 265). Another character in the theatrical review sides on Gwendolen's behalf stating how "Gwendolen is the perfect picture of youthfulness" (James 263), while another disagrees pointing out how "Gwendolen is not an interesting girl, and when the author tries to invest her with a deep tragic interest she does so at the expense of consistency" (James 263). Gwendolen fits James' definition of the "girl of the period" who becomes trapped in an inevitable fate, and yet he is unable to grant her too much sympathy since it does not coincide with her character. An anonymous reviewer in *The Examiner* on the 2 September 1876 relates:

> there must be hundreds of girls more or less like Gwendolen among George Eliot's readers, and the exposure of her shallow frivolous aim is meant to make them ashamed of themselves, and to lift them into a higher conception of their duties and destinies [...] perhaps if George Eliot had thought fit to make this lesson to the

**105**

girls of the period more than a gentle hint, she ought to have increased Gwendolen's punishment [qtd. in Holmstrom 137].

This supports Gwendolen as a representation of the modern English
girl and unlike the fallen woman, Gwendolen's fate, as *The Examiner*
recognizes, allows for her myriad possibilities. Although it is unclear if
she will recover from her nervous fits, she is adamant that she will live
and be better (*DD* 692). In some respects, Gwendolen is "the girl of the
period"; her bold behavior at the gambling table, her extravagance and
selfishness, her marrying for money, and her inability to empathize with
others, are all qualities that match Linton's list. Apart from simply being,
as Blackwood describes, "a fascinating witch" (Holmstrom 123), Gwendolen's charm and complexity take over the novel, to Eliot's dismay.[7] Like
Linton, Eliot loses her patience with the frivolity and lack of intellect in
such girls as Gwendolen, as the narrator harshly states,

> could there be a slenderer, more insignificant thread in human history than this
> consciousness of a girl, busy with her life pleasant?—in a time, too, [...] when
> women on the other side of the world would not mourn for the husbands and sons
> who died bravely in a common cause [...] what in the midst of that mighty drama
> are girls and their blind visions? [*DD* 102].

The narrow perspective of "the girl of the period" allows her to ig-
nore life's hardships, including as Eliot notes, the events of the American
Civil War. Although Gwendolen shares these attributes with the "modern
English girl," her mask of independence quickly shatters upon meeting
Deronda, as John Kucich explains, "Gwendolen's story is less a drama of
moral conversion than it is a lesson in overcoming a basic independence
on external relation" (199). Her declaration that she will never be able
to love (*DD* 68), finds an exception in Deronda, who strikes her interest
based on his lack of similarity to other young men (*DD* 9). For a woman
who will not behave as other women do (*DD* 57), a man who does not act
like other men becomes the ideal companion.

Gwendolen's performances range from the gambling goddess, virgin
disciple of Diana, witch, sea-nymph, wood-nymph, ghost, Shakespeare's
Hermione, seductress, the other woman, mistreated wife, hysteric, and
murderess. Her multiplicity is remarked upon by Mrs. Arrowpoint who
states, "this girl is double and satirical. I shall be on my guard against her"
(*DD* 41). Theatricality is part of Gwendolen's nature, and yet as Herr Klesmer recognizes, the soul of the artist is beyond her. Eliot speaks through
Klesmer to reveal her position on female performers versus female artists.
Mirah, Gwendolen, the Meyricks, Mrs. Glasher, and Leonora are all linked

through performance, and yet Eliot draws a clear line between those who are actresses and those who are, as Eliza Lynn Linton recognizes, "the real thing" (172–5). Gwendolen, always the consummate actress, is denied full entry onto the public stage when Klesmer explains, "in sum, you have not been called upon to be anything but a charming young lady, whom it is an impoliteness to find fault with" (*DD* 216). Clearly, Gwendolen's talent is designed for the private sphere and in securing herself in a profitable marriage. When Klesmer is asked to point out the difference between Gwendolen and the artist, his passionate response raises Art out of her reach: "I am not yet worthy, but she—Art, my mistress—is worthy, and I will live to merit her. An honourable life? Yes. But the honour comes from the inward vocation and the hard-won achievement: there is no honour in donning the life as a livery" (*DD* 217). The life of the authentic artist and the skillful deceptions of the "girl of the period" are not to be compared.

Indeed, the comparison between the whore and the actress/performer permeates the novel: Leonora sells her child to preserve her singing career and Mirah's singing performance are interchangeable with prostitution. Gwendolen's ultimate decision to sell herself in marriage as a replacement for Grandcourt's mistress, Mrs. Glasher, also reveals the fine balance between sexual commodity and performance. As Gallagher deduces, "indeed, all three women's stories indicate that art and prostitution are alternatives in women's lives, but alternatives with such similar structures that their very alternativeness calls attention to their interchangeability" ("George Eliot" 54). Yet, the Meyricks present another alternative in that they are involved in commerce through their illustrations and sewing, and yet retain an innocence and respectability denied the more "public" figures of female artists, as Eliot describes, "[they] were all united by a triple bond—family love; admiration for the finest work, the best action; and habitual industry" (*DD* 167). In their miniature row-house, Kate draws for a publisher, while Amy and Mab embroider satin pillows for "the great world" (*DD* 166). Gallagher explores the author as whore in her essay "George Eliot and Daniel Deronda: The Prostitute and the Jewish Question" as a legitimate concern during Eliot's writing career. As Gallagher explains, "when women entered the career of authorship, they did not enter an inappropriately male territory, but a degradingly female one" (40). Unlike the questionable professions of female singers, actors, and authors, the Meyrick women, while contributing to the public sphere, undeniably remain hidden within the restricting confines of their domestic space.[8] Like dolls in a dollhouse, Eliot describes how the Meyrick women, "if they had been wax-work, might have been packed easily in a fashionable lady's travelling trunk" (*DD* 167). This appears to be the only way in which the Meyrick women could suitably experience the outside world. Similarly, Gwendolen experiences feelings of terror when she contemplates the vast existence of the universe and her place within it, as Eliot states, "solitude in any wide scene impressed her with an undefined feeling of immeasurable existence aloof from her, in the midst of which she was helplessly incapable of asserting herself" (*DD* 52). The narrowness of the domestic space provides comfort and protection to the Meyrick women and quells Gwendolen's obsessive need for control, but while these cramped spaces provide female characters with a form of power and independence, these spaces also keep them from moving into the public realm and risk becoming a public spectacle.

According to Oliver Lovesey, the Meyrick household "is one example of constricting female communities" (507), which serves as a demonstration of the patriarchal hold. Marlene Tromp ascribes to Grandcourt's "ghostly army" (*DD* 384), the power to secretly enforce gender boundaries through threats of violence ("Gwendolen" 456); this patriarchal agency sustains social conventions even in Grandcourt's absence. In *Daniel Deronda*, the home is unable to expand into the public, because, as Monica F. Cohen points out, "Eliot makes it clear that the act of making the home public by making it professional is an artistic act. By making the artistry of professionalizing the home overt, Eliot's domesticity must unmask the essential oxymoron at the heart of the professional home" (157). The Meyrick's home illustrates the failure to incorporate professionalized domesticity. Klesmer's visit serves to further emphasize the parodic nature of the Meyrick's domestic production, as Eliot describes Klesmer's entrance into the home, "the rooms shrank into closets, the cottage piano, Mab thought, seemed a ridiculous toy, and the entire family existence as petty and private as an establishment of mice in the Tuileries [...] while his grandiose air was making Mab feel herself a ridiculous toy to match the cottage piano" (*DD* 413). The male intruder breaks the spell of the Meyrick household revealing its insecurity, futility, and impracticality. This brings into question Eliot's initial description of the house as being, "spotlessly free from vulgarity, because poverty has rendered everything like display an impersonal question, and all the grand shows of the world simply a spectacle which rouses no petty rivalry or vain effort after possession" (*DD* 166). Despite their aversion to spectacles, the Meyrick women are easily transformed into amusing playthings in their own drawing room.

# Four. "Domesticated Theatricality"

While Eliot links art and morality through the work of the Meyrick women, they are still only replicating a patriarchal system of production. The difficulty for the female artists in *Daniel Deronda* is navigating between the dichotomous worlds of public spectacle and private playthings. Gwendolen refuses to fade away into the private as a governess and seeks a public life as a performer. Klesmer bars Gwendolen from the respectable sphere of the artist and leaves her to perform within the theatricalized domestic sphere—her "natural" space. By denying Gwendolen her profession as an actress, he seals her fate in one of the Victorian era's most theatrical roles, as a wife in what Mr. Gascoigne terms, "a first-rate marriage" (*DD* 28).

Gwendolen's "career" as an actress publicly begins when she becomes Mrs. Grandcourt. Although Gwendolen is a theatrical character, Grandcourt succeeds in honing her skills by sharing his own acting techniques.[9] Grandcourt is representative of the female actress, as the epigraph to this chapter describes: "his complexion had a faded fairness resembling that of an actress when bare of the artificial white and red; his long narrow grey eyes expressed nothing but indifference" (*DD* 91). As Gwendolen's "acting coach," Grandcourt instructs her on domesticated theatricality, a technique employed in various degrees by other characters including, Leonora, Mirah, Mrs. Glasher, and Deronda. In his role as female actress, Grandcourt educates Gwendolen through a variety of experiments and tests. Similar to the dreaded situation Klesmer depicts of the harsh reality of life on stage, Gwendolen sells herself into the private theater of "domesticated theatricality," where the private is acted out publicly. Gallagher in *The Body Economic* outlines the many ways exchange and commodity play a role in *Daniel Deronda*. Gallagher describes how Gwendolen represents a commodity based on her obvious "self-sale" in marriage, the knowledge that her marriage is love-less, and the clear role of Grandcourt as disinterested consumer purchasing Gwendolen "Harleth," which is suggestive of "harlot" (131).

Under Grandcourt's tutelage, Gwendolen is brought to her knees like a horse in a training arena (*DD* 269). Although she is a theatrical character prior to her marriage, becoming Mrs. Grandcourt allows her to truly hone her performance. Illness figures significantly in Gwendolen's performative nature, as it does in many of mid-to-late nineteenth-century theatrical heroines. Madness or illness can be traced as the cause for a female character's questionable morality or theatrical behavior. Charlotte Brontë's rebellious Shirley suddenly retreats into domesticity after battling a fever; Lucy blames her murderous tendencies on inheriting her mother's madness in Mary Elizabeth Braddon's *Lady Audley's Secret*; Emily Brontë's *Wuthering Heights* explores many representations of madness including Cathy's use of performative madness to escape and redefine her place within the patriarchal system. Gwendolen begins, like the young Cathy, as the pet of the household and possessing a keen sense of superiority. Similar to Cathy's madness, Gwendolen's fits are referred to as a potential explanation for her erratic behavior. The narrator, though, reminds the reader to bear in mind that Gwendolen's behavior is easily found in "very common sort of men" who share a "strong determination to have what was pleasant, with a total fearlessness in making themselves disagreeable or dangerous when they did not get it" (*DD* 33). The desire for ambition at any cost links Gwendolen with her male counterparts, and yet as the narrator comments, "she had the charm [...] the fear and the fondness being perhaps both heightened by what may be called the iridescence of her character—the play of various, nay, contrary tendencies" (*DD* 33). Gwendolen demands respect through her complex blend of charm and intimidation, and it is this intricacy of character which enchanted many of Eliot's readers and resulted in a deluge of unauthorized sequels for those dissatisfied with the novel's ambiguous ending. Leavis's intention to publish the dissected "good half" of *Daniel Deronda*, retitled "Gwendolen Harleth," is one of many attempts to re-write the novel. Picker in his article "George Eliot and the Sequel Question" analyses the use of the sequel as a reproach to Eliot's novel: "in aesthetic and ideological ways, the sequels and related 'variations' on *Deronda* offer critical attacks on Eliot's plot, structure, and characters, but especially her treatment of the Jewish Question" (363). For these reasons and the novel's resistance to closure, there were many unauthorized sequels and remakes of *Daniel Deronda*, which serve to reveal the readers' responses to Eliot's work. Picker cites the *Punch* sequel to *Daniel Deronda*, which appeared at the end of 1876 and uses Jewish stereotyping and attacks the tediousness of the novel (369). There is also Anna Clay Beecher's novel *Gwendolen; or, Reclaimed: A Sequel to Daniel Deronda by George Eliot*, published in Boston in 1878, which allows Deronda to return to England to reclaim Gwendolen. Beecher's sequel has been called perhaps the "most virulent anti–Semitic novel of the American nineteenth century" (Picker 376). Picker also cites Henry James' *The Portrait of a Lady* as inspired by Eliot's analysis of egoism (380).

Gwendolen's mix of female beauty and typically feminine mental sensitivity with masculine determination and purpose is a character flaw which results in her ultimate downfall. Her ability to integrate the public and private aligns her with Deronda, who also struggles to find a space for himself (*DD* 153). Eileen Sypher explains how, "Gwendolen is neither a successful figure of action in a new social work, nor a serene, self-contained figure in an alternative domestic arena" (521). Gwendolen remains unacted in the outside world, as is the case with many of the novel's characters, and within the domestic her actions are theatricalized. As Eliot's narrator reminds the reader, "if only she had kept her inborn energy of egoistic desire, and her power of inspiring fear as to what she might say or do" (*DD* 33), Gwendolen may have proved to be more effective, yet her feminine charm detracts from any possibility of moving outside her domestic empire. Gwendolen's desire to avoid "domestic fetters" (*DD* 30), is complicated by her feminine beauty and charm; she certainly does not suffer the physical effects of her masculine drive, which is a tendency with heroines who deplore marriage and embrace spinsterhood. Such female characters as Rachel Verinder in *The Moonstone*, Marion Halcombe in *The Woman in White* by Wilkie Collins, Shirley Keeldar in Charlotte Brontë's *Shirley*, and countless spinsters in mid-to-late Victorian novels, such as George Gissing's *The Odd Women* and Elizabeth Gaskell's *Cranford*, have been masculinized for their refusal to marry or their resemblance to the New Woman. Yet, Gwendolen is nothing like her unwomanly counterparts; she is an enticing combination of male and female, as Eliot describes how she shares her desire to lead with her male counterparts, "for such passions dwell in feminine breasts also. In Gwendolen's however, they dwelt among strictly feminine furniture, and had no disturbing reference to the advancement of learning or the balance of the constitution; her knowledge being such as with no sort of standing-room or length of lever could have been expected to move the world" (*DD* 31). The space that Gwendolen inhabits allows her to exercise a certain degree of leadership and masculine behavior, yet, she remains securely within a confined, feminine space where her actions remain futile. Gallagher examines Gwendolen as commodity and more specifically her role as Grandcourt's prostitute. Gwendolen is taken out circulation based on her position as a prostitute to a disinterested lover. Gwendolen's value diminishes, rendering her a "redundant item, slipping constantly toward the margins of the disdainful consumer's desire" (*Body* 138). The valueless prostitute and the spinster are linked through their redundancy and figure prominently in Gwendolen's position as both the purchased Mrs. Grandcourt and the perpetual maiden. The exercise of knowledge within the safety of the private sphere is encouraged by John

# Domesticated Bachelors and Femininity in Victorian Novels

Ruskin in "Of Queens' Garden's" where he supports female education, but only for the betterment of her relationship with her husband. The spoiled child's masculine play within a strictly feminine space mirrors the fabricated industry of the doll-like Meyrick women.

The performance of femininity by Mirah, the Meyrick women, Gwendolen, and Leonora suggests a commonality in their latent patriarchal ideologies, redundancy, and theatricality. While there are exceptions such as Miss Arrowpoint, who defies her duties as an heiress in order to marry for love, and young Anna Gascoigne, who is granted a small rebellion in her refusal to participate in society, including choosing her brother over marriage, overall the novel's female characters are restricted in their actions. Through their performances these actresses seek independence and respite from the domestic sphere. Mirah's singing suggests financial security, Gwendolen's acting may have saved her from working as a governess or entering into a marriage for money, and Leonora uses her talent as an excuse to circumvent her responsibilities as a mother. Barbara Hardy acknowledges Leonora as "one of George Eliot's most interesting foreign characters [...] she articulates and represents a woman's problems as no Englishwoman in any of the novels is ever allowed to do" (62–3). Tim Dolin links Leonora and Eliot, as he states, "Eliot is able to explore this dangerous ground—the woman of genius who rejects maternity: a woman somewhat like herself—through an exotic and safely remote figure" (161). In addition to using the profession of acting and singing as a direct method for eluding patriarchal control, these female characters also engage in a domesticated gender performance.

Gwendolen's duplicity is apparent in the men she attracts; her performance wavers between feminine vulnerability which entices the dandy, Rex, who, after the Hermione scene, considers her to be "instinct with all feeling" (*DD* 52), while her bold strong will seduces Grandcourt. Her performances are flexible, mutable, in that she transitions between female spectacle and feminine ideal, making it difficult to discern her "real" self. Prior to becoming Mrs. Grandcourt, Gwendolen experiences "fits of spiritual dread" (*DD* 52), including cruel behavior followed by extreme remorse, and a deep fear of revealing her true self. Deirdre David in *Fictions of Resolutions in Three Victorian Novels* compares Gwendolen's "troubled consciousness and the culture she inhabits" (176). David clearly points out how Gwendolen is a metaphor for her culture and that she shares her psychological conflicts with her nation, including how her "psychological imperialism is analogous to the domestic and foreign imperialism of

British politics; her obsession with performance is paralled by the theatricality of social events; her arrested sexual development [...] is analogous to the arrested and sterile condition of upper-life" (176–7). The tableau scene in which Gwendolen is struck by terror at the sudden opening of a moveable panel revealing a painting of a dead man's face and a fleeing figure, suggests that the audience has caught a glimpse of the genuine Gwendolen, including her fear of "open[ing] things which were meant to be shut up" (*DD* 20). Ironically, in this abrupt moment of truth, Gwendolen is denied her true emotions since they occur during her performance.[10] Tromp compares Gwendolen with the (in)famous Victorian actress, Rachel, who also used the protection of performance to subvert social conventions during her shows ("Gwendolen" 459). Comparisons can be made, as Vrettos notes, between Gwendolen's frozen figure of fear in her tableau scene and the grotesquely exaggerated postures of Charcot's hysterics (64). Jean Martin-Charcot (1825–1893) gave lectures at Salpêtrière with hypnotized women engaging in theatrical fits, where they would act like animals, and were often sexualized. As Elaine Showalter indicates, "Charcot's hospital became an environment in which female hysteria was perpetually presented, represented, and reproduced" (*Female Malady* 149). The photographs taken by Charcot of his patients were fraudulent and he was exposed by his assistant. Comparing Gwendolen to Charcot's troubled female patients also brings into question performance and authenticity. Similar to Gwendolen's fit during her performance, the photographs of Charcot's patients also blurred the boundary between reality and sensationalism. The audience questions whether Gwendolen's revealing of her authentic self was part of the play, an idea which Klesmer encourages so as to protect Gwendolen's fear of exposure: "she liked to accept as belief what was really no more than delicate feigning. [Klesmer] divined that the betrayal into a passion of fear had been mortifying to her, and wished her to understand that he took it for good acting" (*DD* 50). This crucial scene introduces Gwendolen to the freedom and protection of performance. Although Eliot's female characters are able to find an outlet through performance, they must also beware of the delicate boundaries of over-acting. Tromp is keen to recognize how, "Eliot interrogates the ways performance offers women a potentially subversive, if dangerous, alternative to silence" ("Gwendolen" 458). Although a dangerous strategy, Gwendolen, often engages in performance during her tortuous marriage to Grandcourt.

In becoming Mrs. Grandcourt, Gwendolen transitions from theatricalized fits into an absolute characterization. Her intentions entering the marriage are indeed to "act" her way through it, as Eliot writes, "Gwendolen had no awe of unmanageable forces in the state of matrimony, but regarded it as altogether a matter of management, in which she would know how to act" (*DD* 265). While facing such management problems as Lydia Glasher and her own lack of feelings towards her husband, Gwendolen turns to performance as a solution. Her loss of identity and the blurring between reality and fantasy take root when she engages in physical contact with her husband for the first time. In this scene, Gwendolen clearly begins to welcome passivity when she disconnects from herself as if moving from actor into spectator, as Eliot describes, "was not all her hurrying life of the last three months a show, in which her consciousness was a wondering spectator? [...] a numbness had come over her personality" (*DD* 301–2). This slippage from performer to spectator serves to illustrate Gwendolen's feelings of powerlessness and subservience. In these moments Grandcourt, the "retired actress" takes center stage while Gwendolen is forced to simply watch. Her fits of madness including her reaction to Grandcourt's entrance after receiving the necklace,[11] and note from Lydia are her attempts at once again becoming the female spectacle.

In the same way Eliot's female characters share their theatricality, they are also commonly associated with madness. Lydia Glasher's battle with Grandcourt over returning the diamond necklace is a strategic game of wits, not unlike gamblers at a card table, or actors on stage. Glasher's performance during this scene demonstrates the various methods these female characters employ to gain the upper hand in a rather powerless situation. Her courageous resolve transitions into threats of madness, which Grandcourt appears familiar with when he invites Lydia to "play the mad woman" (*DD* 295), if she likes, while he silently considers "how to play his cards" (*DD* 296). Pushed to desperation Lydia resorts to hysterical crying, while simultaneously promising to "be very meek after that" (*DD* 296). This childish state clearly exposes the performative aspect of madness. Gwendolen, in her violent refusal to become a governess, asks her mother, "help me to be quiet" (*DD* 225). In both cases, the performance of the mad woman is accompanied by a desire or promise to act according to conventional ideals of femininity.

The performance, then, is to be understood by their male counterparts, as nothing more than an act, as Tromp remarks, "though clearly not an unequivocally propitious construction of female identity, these characters' excursions into performance allow them a wider range of tolerated behavior. As long as the "madness" is always perceived as sensational performance, they may gain some ground" ("Gwendolen" 458). Eliot's description of Lydia's performance as containing a "strange mixture of acting and reality" (*DD* 296), is reminiscent of Gwendolen's hysterical fit during her tableau performance. Leonora's speech about the obstacles of her past and her passion for singing is described as, "what may be called sincere acting: this woman's nature was one in which all feeling—and all the more when it was tragic as well as real—immediately became matter of conscious representation: experience immediately passed into drama, and she acted her own emotions" (*DD* 539). "Sincere acting," attributed to Leonora, defines the female performance in *Daniel Deronda*, as an acceptable combination of truth and exaggeration, actuality and theatricality.

While the female performers attempt to abandon the domestic sphere through such spectacles as madness, gambling, suicide, and acting professions, they are encouraged back into their domestic roles through the intervention of the male actresses, who not only instruct these women on the ideals of femininity, but act them out. As a "retired actress," Grandcourt continues to take satisfaction in being a spectacle. Like the "indifferent" dandy, Eliot describes how Grandcourt's performance is dependent on an attentive audience: "Grandcourt went about with the sense that he did not care a languid curse for any one's admiration; but this state of not-caring [...] required its related object—namely, a world of admiring or envying spectators: for if you are fond of looking stonily at smiling persons, the persons must be there and they must smile" (*DD* 500). This dependence is reflected in Grandcourt's relationships with Lydia, Gwendolen and Mr. Lush, although Grandcourt seems to discard them at various points, he always returns. Lush holds an interesting position in a world where "no one is entirely immune to the practices of watching and concealment, which are felt as coercion" (Welsh 261). Ashton refers to the novel's apparent male conspiracy of "respecting the secrecy of a man's sexual experience and keeping girls in ignorance of sexual matters" (89) as Eliot's criticism of English society. Lush revels in his knowledge of Grandcourt's sexual history placing himself above the naïve Gwendolen. As the only blackmailer, who cannot be blackmailed himself, Lush embodies the power of silence—the unspoken language of blackmail which permeates the novel. The positioning of the blackmailer within the public and private spheres simultaneously makes him an interesting figure in relation to the domesticated bachelor. This is explored further in the following chapter on R. L. Stevenson's *The Strange Case of Dr. Jekyll and Mr. Hyde.* Adams describes the dandy as, "a figure of masculine identity under stress [...] the failure to realize a life of 'manful action' and the radical failure of autonomy inherent in the dandy's abject appeal to an audience" (*Dandies* 24). This lack of "manful action" echoes the novel's preoccupation with inaction that carries through to Deronda's character, who, based on his class status and mysterious background, is unable to fulfill his social responsibilities. Grandcourt appears to fail in his portrayal of a national masculinity. Eliot's physical description of Grandcourt in the epigraph to this chapter describes him as the epitome of indifference, a faded actress, and a rather vapid version of the proper Englishman gentleman. Grandcourt's deadened appearance is compared to the uselessness of an actress without her make-up, a comparison which takes Grandcourt beyond simple effeminacy into the realm of a profitless prostitute. Grandcourt links to death through the recurrent motif of the dead man's face in the portrait that haunts Gwendolen after the tableau scene, which culminates in Grandcourt's drowning. In addition, Annabel Herzog suggests that Grandcourt's death was inevitable "because [he] is a 'reincarnation' of [Gwendolen's] dead stepfather" (42), while J. Jeffrey Franklin attributes Grandcourt's inanimate demeanor to his representation of the "inherent theatricality of a decaying aristocratic order" (96). Lydia remarks to Gwendolen in her letter, "the man you have married has a withered heart. His best young love was mine; you could not take that from me [...] it is dead; but I am the grave in which your chance of happiness is buried as well as mine" (*DD* 303). Grandcourt is effeminized, physically, emotionally, and even sexually, by the only woman who loves him. Writing for *The Spectator* on 10 June 1876, R. H. Hutton recognizes Grandcourt's performance of femininity as representing "more the insolence of a bad woman, than the insolence of a bad man" (Holmstrom 133). *The Spectator*, 8 April 1876 targets a specific scene between Grandcourt and Mr. Lush as an example of the, "kind and degree of insolence which a proud and selfish woman would show to a dependent, than what a *man* who has at least passed through the public discipline of school and college life, would be likely to show (Haight, *GE Letters* 240). In her defense, Eliot remarks in a letter to John Blackwood dated ten days later that another reviewer had commented, "the very best parts were the scenes between Grandcourt and Lush [...] several men of experience have put their fingers on those scenes as having surprising verisimilitude, and I naturally was peculiarly anxious about such testimony where my construction was grounded on less direct knowledge" (Haight, *GE Letters* 240). Lush's position as "prime minister in all [Grandcourt's] personal affairs" (*DD* 107), Eliot suggests, is a result of Grandcourt's lack of patriarchal guidance since his father's death at an early age. Grandcourt as a male actress uses performance as a means of escaping what Rex, a "reverse of the dandy" (*DD* 55), considers the harsh reality of manhood: "[men] are forced to do hard things, and are often dreadfully bored, and knocked to pieces too" (*DD* 57). Performance serves a common purpose for both sexes who seek to evade gender conventions, and while Grandcourt attempts to impose patriarchal order onto Gwendolen, he simultaneously transgresses typified masculine behavior in his own feminized role as spectacle.

While Grandcourt appears as a failure of masculinity, Deronda's youth and energy combined with his performance of femininity suggest a new type of Victorian domesticated masculinity. Deronda's childhood introduction to theatricality results in his clear abhorrence of spectacle, as Eliot remarks, "in spite of his musical gift, he set himself bitterly against the notion of being dressed up to sing before all those fine people who would not care about him except as a wonderful toy" (*DD* 144). In his desire to pursue the education of a gentleman, Deronda does not leave his skill for performance behind. In addition to inheriting his mother's talent for performance, Deronda feels that his high social standing leaves him emasculated. This is reminiscent of how men in the higher classes romanticized the working class for exercising their full masculinity through physical labor and production as discussed in Chapter One on Brontë's *Shirley*:

> there was no need for him to get an immediate income, or to fit himself in haste for a profession; and his sensibility to the half-known facts of his parentage made him an excuse for lingering longer than others in a state of social neutrality. Other men, he inwardly said, had a more definite place and duties [*DD* 153].

This social neutrality[12] extends into Deronda's gender identity, as he struggles to find a place for himself in the masculine world. Similar to other versions of domesticated men who experience neutrality as they move between the public and private spheres, Deronda, through performance, incorporates characteristics associated with the ideal of femininity.[13]

Deronda's feminization is most apparent in his performance of sympathy. According to Adam Smith "as nature teaches the spectators to assume the circumstances of the person principally concerned, so she teaches this last in some measure to assume those of the spectators" (*Theory* 23). To share in sympathetic understanding one must "assume" the emotions of another, a skill which requires performance, and which Deronda is accused of committing to excess. Ironically, Deronda, who considers the theater as inferior, becomes the novel's most successful actress. As a sympathetic spectator, Deronda performs what Sarah Ellis describes as the "disinterested sympathy of a generous heart" (21), a characteristic representative of the Victorian domestic woman. Franklin explains how "the figure of sympathy can be understood both as a reaction against the Romantic doctrine of feeling and as the culmination of that very discourse within the Victorian context" (120). Certainly, the excess of sympathy and altruism during the mid-to-late nineteenth century necessitated debate over the domestic woman's role outside the home. Charles Dickens' caricature of excessive charity, Mrs. Jellyby in *Bleak House*, presents an exaggerated nightmare of a domestic mother who neglects her own children, husband, and house in favor of her work abroad for the Brotherhood of Humanity in Africa. A mother who neglects her own children and leads them to cry, "I wish Africa was dead!" (Dickens 60), is the epitome of misplaced sympathy and altruism. In Deronda's case, sympathy is theatricalized based on his inability to truly understand and yet his insistence on its authenticity. This type of performative sympathy makes Deronda the most theatrical character in the novel. In his performance of femininity, Deronda suffers the consequence of inaction shared by other female characters like the "miniature" Meyrick women, Gwendolen, and Mirah. As Eliot explains:

> a too reflective and diffusive sympathy was in danger of paralysing in him that indignation against wrong [...] he had become so keenly aware of this that what he most longed for was whether some external event, or some inward light, that would urge him into a definite line of action and compress his wandering energy [*DD* 308].

Deronda is aware of the "meditative numbness" (*DD* 308) taking over his demeanor and seeks to maintain a balance between his feminine and masculine characteristics.

The danger of inaction is reiterated throughout the novel and is associated with the feminization of theatricality. Eliot illustrates an interesting gender reversal in the "angel in the house" scenario when she places Deronda in the position of Gwendolen's conscience:

> he was unique to [Gwendolen] among men, because he had impressed her as being not her admirer but her superior: in some mysterious way he was becoming part of her conscience, as one woman whose nature is an object of reverential belief may become a new conscience to a man [*DD* 355].

Beer in *Darwin's Plots* suggests that the complex relationship between Deronda and Gwendolen is therapeutic, erotic, and passive, making it noticeably unpatriarchal in nature (229). As Beer relates, "Deronda has an almost maternal relation to [Gwendolen]" (*Darwin's* 229). Although Deronda embodies the conflict between femininity and masculinity, he criticizes patriarchy while remaining under its protection, as Leonora is keen to point out. His maternal nature masks his expectations for the ideal of domesticity and femininity, which he imposes on characters like Mirah and Gwendolen. Yet, Deronda fails as angel, priest, and savior when Gwendolen's burden of Grandcourt's death "unmans" him (*DD* 594), and he is unable to remain disinterested in Mirah. Deronda's sympathy is purely performance, as the narrator relates, "that voice, which like his eyes, has the unintentional effect of making his ready sympathy seem more personal and special than it really was" (*DD* 600). His performance of sympathy lacks authenticity and it is his mother, Leonora, who challenges his denial of theatricality. His demeanor upon meeting his mother clearly reflects his performance of femininity, which is apparent to the successful singer-actress. Deronda's blushing like a girl (*DD* 535), and his attempt at sympathizing with his mother, as he did for Mirah and Gwendolen, are not lost on Leonora, who delivers the most profound statement in the novel: "You are not a woman. You may try—but you can never imagine what it is to have a man's force of genius in you and yet suffer the slavery of being a girl" (*DD* 541). This challenge is interpreted by Rachel Hollander as serving to reinforce the many links between Leonora and Gwendolen: "both perform their identities, both rebel against the restrictions society places on women, and both call into question Daniel's ability to understand" (88). With this declaration, Leonora exposes Deronda as female spectacle and criticizes his performance of femininity as being simply theatrical.

In his journey to find a place for himself within society, Deronda becomes savior to many, but he soon realizes that he desires a young man similar to himself as a companion, someone to lean on and confide in, someone who is equal. Debra Gettelman in "Reading Ahead in George Eliot" suggests that "wish-fulfillment is explored in a new way in Eliot's last novel [...] in which the deepest hopes of several characters in fact appear to be achieved outside of themselves" (43). The idea that action and fulfillment take place outside of the characters supports the novel's insistence on inaction. Cynthia Chase elaborates on how the performative act of naming leads to action; for example, she cites how Deronda assumes the identity of Mordecai's imagined companion as a "consequence of Mordecai's act of claiming him" (167). The act takes place outside the self through a performative utterance Mordecai and Deronda fulfill each other's needs, while sharing a love superior to all other representations in the novel. Mordecai's supernatural nature mirrors Deronda's social neutrality as they both inhabit worlds in-between.[14] Their union is flawless and immediate, as Eliot describes, "in ten minutes the two men, with as intense a consciousness as if they had been two undeclared lovers, felt themselves alone in the small gas-lit book-shop and turned face to face" (*DD* 424). This brotherly love is later upheld as ideal by Mirah, who criticizes womanly love based on her own feelings of jealousy. In *Male Love: A Problem in Greek Ethics and Other Writings* John Addington Symonds examines the classics in support of male-male love while looking down upon lust usually associated with loving the opposite sex. Mordecai and Deronda adhere to many of Symond's description of Achilleian love:

> It was a powerful and masculine emotion, in which effeminacy had no part, and which by no means excluded the ordinary sexual feelings. Companionship was the communion [...] not luxury or the delights which feminine attractions offered. The tie was both more spiritual and more energetic than that which bound man to woman [3].

While this male-male relationship is upheld by Mirah for its spiritual basis, Deronda clearly brings feminine qualities into the relationship, including jealousy and lust. The marriage of souls between Mordecai and Deronda is a union of equals overshadowing Deronda's socially acceptable marriage to Mirah, as Press explains, "Deronda's marriage to Mirah, although literal, takes place out of reach of the narrator's eye; in contrast, Deronda's marriage to Mordecai is dramatized, staged repeatedly, and centrally framed as the novel's definitive act of closure" (312). The *ménage-à-trois* between Mirah, Mordecai, and Deronda represents a suitable conclusion for the reconciliation of Deronda's femininity combined with his desire to fit into society. Mirah, becomes an instrument, like other women in the novel, through which Deronda and Mordecai seal their union. The marriage triangle is a popular conclusion, as seen in Brontë's *Shirley* between Robert, Caroline, and Mrs. Pryor, and Braddon's *Lady Audley's Secret* between Robert, Clara, and George Eliot uses Deronda as an example of feminine qualities existing outside of the domestic sphere.

The conflicted performance of femininity by the male and female players in Eliot's novel illustrates the attempt by male actresses to re-establish certain gender conventions, while simultaneously broadening the notion of masculinity. Eliot's actors use performance as a dialogue about gender conventions[15]; in one case performance pushes the boundaries of femininity, while on the other hand, it expands the definition of masculinity. While performance encourages communication between the sexes, silence figures prominently in *Daniel Deronda* as another indicator of the novel's tendency towards inaction and stagnancy. Andrew Dowling in "'The Other Side of Silence': Matrimonial Conflict and the Divorce Court in George Eliot's Fiction," credits silence with two functions: "silence as a literal symptom of oppression [...and] as a rhetorical device that addresses a readership increasingly interested in the 'unspeakable' details of married life" (323). In *Daniel Deronda* silence indicates violence and specifically marital abuse. Dowling interprets silence in the case of the Grandcourt's marriage as a sign of sexual tyranny, as well as a forced concealment of the self ("Other Side" 333). As Dowling reminds us, "the eighteenth-century legal injunction to 'suffer in silence' was being revised and challenged by the mid–nineteenth century" ("Other Side" 335). Through their own performances, male actresses, like Grandcourt and Deronda, exhibit particular feminine traits and engage in feminine discourse while filling the space neglected by the female performers. Eliot, in *Daniel Deronda*, introduces the male actress as a version of the domesticated bachelor, who through performance, assumes a female identity challenging gender boundaries and the empire of domesticity. The most common consequence of male characters moving between the spheres is struggle with dual natures evident through Louis and Robert Moore in Brontë's *Shirley*, effeminacy as demonstrated by Robert in Braddon's *Lady Audley Secret,* and the disgrace of theatricality as evidenced by Deronda and Grandcourt in Eliot's *Daniel Deronda*, but Jekyll's creation is complete in that Hyde can penetrate both the public and private spheres without changing identities.

# FIVE

# Men Gone Wild

### *Male Exclusivity in Robert Louis Stevenson's* The Strange Case of Dr. Jekyll and Mr. Hyde

> Men have before hired bravados to transact their crimes, while their own person and reputation sat under shelter. I was the first that ever did so for his pleasures. I was the first that could plod in the public eye with a load of genial respectability, and in a moment, like a schoolboy, strip off these lendings and spring headlong into the sea of liberty [...]. Think of it—I did not even exist! [...] Whatever he had done, Edward Hyde would pass away like the stain of breath upon a mirror; and there in his stead, quietly at home, trimming the midnight lamp in his study, a man who could afford to laugh at suspicion, would be Henry Jekyll [Stevenson, *J&H* 80–1].

> We were full of the pride of life, and chose, like prostitutes, to live by a pleasure. We should be paid, if we give the pleasure we pretend to give; but why should we be honoured? We are whores, some of us pretty whores, some of us not, but all whores: whores of the mind, selling to the public the amusements of our fireside as the whore sells the pleasures of her bed [Stevenson, *Letters* 171].

As a self-described "sick whore" (Stevenson, *Letters* 171) who would probably be taken off the streets for possessing a "fatted brain and [...] rancid imagination" (Stevenson, *Letters* 171), in the above 1886 letter to Edmund Gosse, Robert Louis Stevenson playfully compares writers to prostitutes. The analogy reveals Stevenson's position on authors and their relationship with "that fatuous rabble of burgesses called 'the public'" (Stevenson, *Letters* 171). As "whores of the mind" writers find themselves choosing a way of life centered around "pretending" to give pleasure for financial gain. In the same letter Stevenson explains, "I do not write for the public; I do write for money, a nobler deity; and most of all for myself, not perhaps any more noble but both more intelligent and nearer home" (Stevenson, *Letters* 171). The writer certainly does not romanticize authorship, but he does make it clear that his devotion is to himself, in the form of money and personal achievement, and not to his public. He succeeds in creating an analogy that is both self-deprecating and empowering. The image of selling fireside pleasures to the public exposes the delicate balance between the public and private spheres, which the writer and prostitute must tread. The separation of the public and private spheres was strongly enforced against female authors and actresses, who were often associated with prostitutes for exposing themselves publicly for financial gain, as discussed further in Chapter Four on Eliot's *Daniel Deronda*. By relating to female prostitutes Stevenson feminizes the writer, and yet he avoids allusions to victimization and passivity. Instead, the public is construed as the senseless, passive consumer who is non-selective and more than willing to sacrifice his money for simple pleasures.

Stevenson conflates these issues in *The Strange Case of Dr. Jekyll and Mr. Hyde* through his emphasis on a male-only community, the absence of female characters, and representations of class and gender, as well as the public and private spheres. The novella's principle characters are all professional men separated from the vacuous public by their class status, intelligence, and morality. Andrew Lang praises Stevenson's choice of an all-male society in his article in the *Saturday Review* dated 9 January 1886: "His heroes (surely *this* is original) are all successful middle-aged professional men [...] we incline to think that Mr. Stevenson always does himself most justice in novels without a heroine" (200–1). The male-only community harkens back to that which Eve Kosofsky Sedgwick notes is the classical Spartan and Athenian models of virilizing male bonds by fully excluding the world of women (207). It is *Dr. Jekyll and Mr. Hyde's* exclusively male community that allows for the exploration of issues of masculinity and the private sphere without the presence of the ideal of the domestic space—women. Through the absence of female characters masculinity appears more fluid and mutable which is enhanced by the fact that these male professionals are all bachelors. Arguably, these men are not in traditional masculine roles since they are not husbands, and yet the position of the bachelor, by the late–nineteenth century, has become an acceptable way of life for higher-class men. The bachelor demands attention for their redefining of masculinity and the remodeling of the domestic sphere.

## Domesticated Bachelors and Femininity in Victorian Novels

The male community in which Stevenson sets his novella allows for the exploration of masculinity, and possibly homosexuality, but it is in combination with the theme of duality and the creation of Hyde that a clearer understanding of the role of the public and private on issues of sexuality develops. In order to explore sexuality and masculinity, Stevenson must create a character that has the ability to introduce what is considered the traditional masculine public into the private, creating a new space where the domestic can exist without a female presence. It is at this point that the late nineteenth-century bachelor separates himself from his earlier incarnations. By placing the bachelor within an exclusively male community he does not lose his ability to move between the public and private, except that these spheres are no longer categorized as the world of men versus women. Instead, the public and private in the male community become strictly masculine. The private and public within the male community do not lose their respective links to femininity and masculinity, but they are discussed in relation to male double consciousness.

Dr. Jekyll is the bachelor in his public life; he is a professional, reputable man, but is unable to participate in the private domain without losing his public identity. In this case, the bachelor of the male community cannot travel unscathed between the public and private spheres, and as a result Hyde is born. Mr. Hyde strips Dr. Jekyll of his profession, and grants him another identity through which he explores the secret world of the male private realm. The suggestion here is not that Jekyll represents the public persona, and Hyde the private; instead, Hyde is both simultaneously. While Jekyll appears unable to explore the private, his friend Mr. Utterson revels in it and finds it impossible to keep business and personal issues separate. The novella provides its readers with a variety of amalgamations of the public and private through the lives of its bachelor characters. In some instances, the private dominates over the public as is the case for the lawyer Utterson, or perhaps as in Dr. Jekyll's experience the public is all-consuming. While Utterson protects the traditional concept of the domestic, Dr. Jekyll creates Mr. Hyde in an attempt to escape the restrictive spheres. Stevenson's Hyde represents the new "bachelor" of the late–nineteenth century, who redefines the domestic sphere within an all-male society by replacing the traditional component of the Victorian family with the homosocial and masculine intimacy.

Dr. Jekyll attempts to describe his unique predicament to the inquisitive Mr. Utterson by explaining, "I am painfully situated, Utterson; my position is a very strange—a very strange one" (Stevenson, *J&H* 45). The bachelor in Stevenson's novella masters the art of contortion and although this ability is "painful" and "strange" at first, he begins to embrace his situation and construct his own space. The bachelor is fluid and mutable, all characteristics associated with the feminine, and he makes the most confining and seemingly impenetrable space his own. This space is redefined from the traditional domestic sphere into one that includes the bachelor. Issues of exclusion and inclusion arise from this dichotomy, but there are no outsiders or outlaws here. The Other is redefined in *Dr. Jekyll and Mr. Hyde*; he finds his place within the public and private without transforming into the typical monster. Nor is he the racial Other, which plagues Deronda as discussed in Chapter Four on Eliot's *Daniel Deronda*. Stevenson's novella champions the new bachelor and places him within a community of men who share similar characteristics. It also attests to the bachelor's evolution throughout the mid-to-late nineteenth century.

The New Woman had been crossing boundaries and knocking down barriers for three decades prior to Stevenson's publication of *Dr. Jekyll and Mr. Hyde*. During the Romantic period, the image of the helpless, young madwoman gained popularity. Eventually, though, this image transformed from the mad virgin into that of the sexually insatiable intelligent New Woman. Showalter links the rise of the New Woman and the increased diagnosis of female hysteria: "[in the] 1850s there were more women than men in public institutions [...] by 1872, out of 58,640 certified lunatics in England and Wales, 21, 822 were women" (*Female Malady* 52). Doctors blamed the changes in women's aspirations, especially those of the New Woman. The relationship between the doctor and his female patient represented the power dynamics between the sexes on issues of physical and mental freedom. Her desire for education doomed her possibility to reproduce and doctors linked hysteria and other nervous diseases to her unconventional lifestyle (Showalter, *Sexual Anarchy* 40). As Showalter explains, "For centuries, hysteria had been the quintessential female malady, the very name of which derived from the Greek hysteron, or womb; but between 1870 and World War I—the 'golden age' of hysteria—it assumed a peculiarly central role in psychiatric discourse, and in definitions of femininity and female sexuality" (*Female Malady* 129). In *fin-de-siècle* literature, hysteria and femininity were commonly linked as representing a vast range of emotions. The female hysteric found herself not only represented in novels, but also performing under Jean Martin-Charcot's (1825–1893) supervision at Salpêtrière hospital, where hypnotized women engaged in theatrical-fits for an audience (*Female Malady* 148). Female hysteria proved a useful excuse for excluding women from the more professional ranks, as Showalter remarks:

> During an era when patriarchal culture felt itself to be under attack by its rebellious daughters, one obvious defense was to label women campaigning for access to universities, the professions, and the vote as mentally disturbed, and of all the nervous disorders of the *fin de siècle*, hysteria was the most strongly identified with the feminist movement [145].

After World War I, the male hysteric (usually a shell-shocked soldier) replaced his female counterpart and is credited with the instigating the medical transition to modern psychiatry (*Female Malady* 18). Male hysteria included anxiety concerning effeminacy, impotence, and homosexuality and brought into question the rigidity associated with masculinity during wartime. Social and sexual deviance form the basis for the diagnosis of hysteria in both males and females. In Stevenson's novella the reader is struck by a different dissident, another bold boundary breaker whose gender, like that of the New Woman, undergoes a refiguring. Mr. Utterson holding the kitchen poker high, ready to break down Jekyll's cabinet door (Stevenson, *J&H* 62), is the epitome of the late nineteenth-century domesticated man. During a time when gender boundaries are becoming blurry, here stands the domesticated gentleman armed with his weapon of choice: "The lawyer took that rude but weighty instrument into his hand, and balanced it. 'Do you know, Poole' [Utterson] said, looking up, 'that you and I are about to place ourselves in a position of some peril?'" (Stevenson, *J&H* 63). Unlike Hyde's ability to cross boundaries with the agility of a ghost, Utterson is less discreet with his symbolic breaking down of the door.

Edward Hyde changes from being inexperienced into full maturity and superiority over his parent, to finally exposing weakness and degenerating by the novella's conclusion. This fluid changeability results in many different interpretations of this character by literary critics. These varying arguments on Hyde's true identity exposes his essence and supports his position as the elusive new bachelor. Stephen Arata argues that Edward Hyde is not "monster" or "villain," but "gentleman" (*Fictions* 38). Basing his argument on F.W.H. Myers' series of letters written shortly after reading the novella, Arata agrees that Hyde may not be an "image of the *upright* bourgeois male, but he is decidedly an image of the bourgeois male" (*Fictions* 38). Hyde as gentleman takes his position on equal ground next to the novella's principle characters, Dr. Lanyon, the lawyer Mr. Utterson, and "well-known man about town" Mr. Enfield (Stevenson, *J&H* 31).

Although Arata suggests that Myers's reading may be exaggerated, he is clearly interested in how easily Hyde is interpreted as representing the very image of "sobriety, and industry, manfully disdainful of the shop window, the art gallery, the concert hall—of anything that might savor of the aesthetic or the frivolous" (*Fictions* 37). Hyde's apparent bourgeois class status and taste allow him to fit in perfectly with the other bachelors. Even his dubious morality is considered acceptable and mimics Enfield's own tendency for secrecy. Hyde transforms himself by the end of the novella when, as Arata notes, he successfully "embod[ies] the very repressions Jekyll struggles to throw off" (*Fictions* 39). Hyde's degeneration is not a downward motion towards the lower classes, nor does he become the dandy-aesthete[1]; instead, he comes to represent middle-class morality—a position abhorred by Stevenson in his 1886 letter to Gosse.

Hyde's embodiment of bourgeois morality and patriarchy is problematic for many critics. Michael Kane explores Hyde's role as representing the "Other" and Jekyll's desire for "difference" outside the masculine bourgeois self (25). This longing for the "Other," Kane interprets, is what leads to Jekyll's discovery of his own "femininity." Hyde, according to Kane, personifies Jekyll's feminine nature through his irrationality, desire for pleasure, and the fluidity of his identity. The ambivalence surrounding Hyde is in direct opposition to Jekyll's stable, rigid, and strict adherence to social expectations. According to Kane, Hyde functions as Jekyll's "unconscious" and his feminine "double" (26), which allows him the freedom to rebel against an already dissipating traditional patriarchy. Kane labels the indefinable nature of Hyde as a feminine characteristic, while Arata claims Hyde's changeability demonstrates his education towards becoming a gentleman. Hyde endures many other literary interpretations including representing the primitive form of human nature,[2] perverse male sexuality,[3] Jekyll's devilish "wife,"[4] the phallus,[5] and Jekyll's homosexual lover.[6] Arata's masculine and patriarchal Hyde versus Kane's feminine "Other" provide examples of the two extremes of Hyde, and calls attention to his ability to cross gender and class boundaries. Based on these two theories, this chapter argues that Hyde, as representative of the "new" *fin-de-siècle* bachelor, epitomizes both aspects of masculinity and femininity providing him with the skill that both Kane and Arata acknowledge that he possesses—his ability to move between the public and private spheres. The *fin-de-siècle* bachelor's conflation of the masculine and feminine within the domestic is a unique symptom of this exclusively male community.

Stevenson introduces his readers to a primitive, devilish, ugly Hyde who has just trampled over a girl. In the scene retold by man-about-town Mr. Enfield, Hyde takes his place as representing the primitive, pleasure-driven criminal aspect of Jekyll, but what follows requires a reassessment of Hyde's social status. Enfield's behavior towards Hyde suggests that they share similar social positions since Enfield quickly decides that the ideal method for dealing with Hyde is to threaten him with something worse than death—scandal (Stevenson, *J&H* 33). It is clear that this threat would not have any impact on a lower class man, and so even though Hyde is described as a Juggernaut, readers quickly recognize that he is a gentleman. Hyde is "the man in the middle" (Stevenson, *J&H* 34) surrounded by the bloodthirsty lower class and the higher-class Enfield, who prefers financial blackmail to physical revenge. Hyde responds to Enfield's threat as if he is quite familiar with blackmail, as Hyde states, "No gentleman but wishes to avoid a scene [...n]ame your figure" (Stevenson, *J&H* 34). The scene culminates with Enfield inviting Hyde, the doctor, and the child's father to stay the night at his house and breakfast in the morning. Enfield's "prisoner" (Stevenson, *J&H* 33) soon becomes a guest and is the first to suggest he stay the night to ensure the check is not a forgery. Hyde's ability to adapt and perform according to his social status as a middle-class gentleman allows him the freedom to move between the private world of the dark and mysterious streets of London and the public world of status and scandal. Unlike Dr. Jekyll, Hyde is able to live in both worlds simultaneously.

Hyde as bourgeois gentleman, articulate, worldly, practical, yet refined continues his education but by the novella's conclusion, Hyde's feminine characteristics become more prominent. Arata argues that Hyde's indoctrination leads him to become more like Jekyll (*Fictions* 39); he begins to feel the pressures of society, and the importance of reputation and repression. The novella suggests that Hyde's instruction leads him towards a nervous breakdown and a complete surrender to his feminine nature. Arata notes how Stevenson not only allows for "middle class anger directed at various forms of the Other" (*Fictions* 39) through the figure of Hyde, but also turns this anger back onto middle-class morality through the failure of the education of the gentleman. Hyde's ideal state is one in which he can continue seeking out pleasure in his private life, while maintaining his bourgeois status and public image. Of course, this was Dr. Jekyll's motivation for the creation of Hyde in the first place, except that for a short period Hyde succeeds in sustaining his dual natures based on the commingling of his feminine and masculine characteristics.

Hyde is as Jekyll declares, "natural and human" (Stevenson, *J&H* 79), and stands in direct opposition to the inhuman expectations of Victorian society. Hyde battles against Victorian standards and simultaneously adheres to them, so that he gains access to both worlds. Hysteria and lust are typically linked with the feminine, but by excluding women in his novella Stevenson can focus on masculinity and hysteria without the disruption of female characters. Hyde's hysteria and typically feminine characteristics of excess and lust demonstrate yet another mixture of the masculine and feminine, as Stephen Heath explains, "[*Dr. Jekyll and Mr. Hyde*] is a male representation, men's story, but it is also women's narrative" (104). The exclusion of women from their own narrative allows for the exploration of male sexuality and the discovery of a new male language, and as Heath argues "the emergence of the hidden male" (104). The changed voice coming from Jekyll's laboratory signals his transformation into Hyde, but Jekyll, in many ways, portrays himself as unmanned when he describes to Utterson the "sufferings and terrors" (Stevenson, *J&H* 56) he has endured. The silence that he demands from his close friend is also a passive reaction to the situation. The person crying behind the door is unrecognizable to Jekyll's butler Poole, perhaps it is the "thing" (Stevenson, *J&H* 65), or Jekyll who is "weeping like a woman or a lost soul" (Stevenson, *J&H* 65), but in Jekyll's final words he reveals that when Hyde returns to dominate him Hyde will sit "shuddering and weeping" (Stevenson, *J&H* 91). By becoming closer to Jekyll, Hyde also embraces the male hysteria experienced by the doctor and thus succumbs completely to his feminine nature. Silence is another typically feminine characteristic employed by Stevenson's male community to ensure discretion. The bachelors' emphasis on the power of the unspoken leads to issues of secrecy and blackmail.

Enfield's reactions to Hyde's trampling of the young girl and his ability to produce one hundred pounds in someone else's name at such an early hour reveal a familiarity with this process of blackmailing. Enfield's comment on Hyde's procuring of another man's check as "business" (Stevenson, *J&H* 34), which he considers unrealistic and "apocryphal" (Stevenson, *J&H* 34), demonstrates that he is aware of the real business which is at hand. The repetition of "my gentleman" and "my man" permeates Enfield's story of the door. When Enfield states, "For my man was a fellow that nobody could have to do with" (Stevenson, *J&H* 34), he clearly links himself with an established outcast of society. Arata believes that this statement demonstrates how Enfield "seems to be describing not a violent criminal but a man who cannot be trusted to respect the club rules"

("Sedulous Ape" 241). Enfield's rules alienate him from Utterson, who is ignorant of them, and from Hyde who does not follow them, yet Enfield still associates with Hyde based on his knowledge of the club despite his disrespect towards the rules. "My gentleman" is then contrasted with "one of [Utterson's] fellows who do what they call good" (Stevenson, *J&H* 34). This creates a barrier between Enfield and his domestic companion. Enfield and Hyde take one side as members of "the club," while Jekyll and Utterson are linked as outsiders.

Enfield's refusal to name names is described as a club "rule" (Stevenson, *J&H* 35). It appears that "delicacy" is an attribute for club members like Enfield: "The more it looks like Queer Street, the less I ask" (Stevenson, *J&H* 35). Although it would appear that the club simply requires that one be a professional male, Utterson's lack of knowledge in this area suggests there is more to it. Silence and discretion are key characteristics of club members, as Enfield states, "I knew what was in his mind, just as he knew what was in mine [...] we could and would make such a scandal out of this as should make his name stink from one end of London to the other" (Stevenson, *J&H* 33). Silence unites Enfield and the doctor on the scene of the trampled girl. Their ability to read each other's minds and agree on the proper method for dealing with Hyde reveals many hidden signals. Not only does Enfield and the doctor identify with each other, they then determine that Hyde is one of them, and finally they agree on the appropriate punishment based on their "club rules," all of which is achieved in silence. Enfield's weapon against Hyde is to break club rules and expose him publicly. Enfield appreciates Utterson's silence: "the pair walked on again for a while in silence; and then 'Enfield,' said Utterson, 'that's a good rule of yours'" (Stevenson, *J&H* 35). Enfield's use of silence differs from Utterson's. While Enfield's is a deliberate decision to keep quiet, Utterson's is a tendency towards effeminate passivity and a deep respect for the private.

Whereas Hyde represents the rebellious intruder of the public and private spheres, Utterson is reminiscent of the typical bachelor who finds himself unable to navigate between the two and suffers the consequence of embracing the one. The consequence of secluding oneself in the domestic traditionally results in a form of feminization. The bachelor is a prime candidate for feminization, but, as John Tosh remarks, the family man is also susceptible: "the danger of domesticity to true manliness applied not just to sons, but to the head of the house himself; the man who spent too much time in the company of wife and daughters might become effeminized, at the expense of his manly vigour and his familial authority" (*Manliness* 70). Although Utterson falls into this category of bachelor, he gains credit by evolving to meet late nineteenth-century expectations. Utterson is not completely domesticated and he makes an interesting figure in contrast to Hyde's violence. Utterson does attempt to balance his role as lawyer and friend, but without becoming both at once. Utterson is so fully in the private that he cannot trespass into the private space of others without feeling like an intruder. He then discovers the freedom of his professional and public self when he enters into the "business" of others. William Veeder notes, "though he can only spy furtively on the domestic door of Jekyll the sleeping patriarch Utterson can break with impunity the professional door of Dr. Jekyll the errant scientist" (135). This leads to Veeder's argument that the entire male community *Dr. Jekyll and Mr. Hyde* uses "profession [as] a screen for the domestic" (135). Although this is indeed the case for the lawyer Utterson, it does not apply to Hyde. This is one of the attributes that differentiates these two types of bachelors. One is so deeply immersed in the domestic as its defender that he is unable to penetrate both spaces, while the other has the power to fully participate in both spaces simultaneously. As protector of the domestic, Utterson cannot bear to intrude on the private space of Jekyll. He does so occasionally, but mostly under the guise of his profession. Utterson, as domestic defender is confronted with Hyde, who does not follow these rules, as Utterson imagines him sneaking into Jekyll's bedchamber and other sleeping houses in the night (Stevenson, *J&H* 39). Why is Utterson interesting if he does not cross over these barriers? One reason is that he is associated with the improper sphere. Unlike previous studies of male characters who engage in domestic/feminine discourse, Stevenson's late nineteenth-century lawyer begins and ends inhabiting the domestic space. There is no question why he is there and whether he belongs; instead his role is simple—to protect the domestic space from intruders like Hyde. Why is Utterson's presence in the domestic sanctified? Based on earlier male characters whose place within the domestic was challenged, by the 1890s, the bachelor's position within the domestic had become acceptable. What is unacceptable is the roving, fluid and shifting figure whose place is nowhere, not within the public or private but within a newly-defined male sphere which excludes the purely domestic bachelor like Utterson. In fact, it would appear that Utterson is the "outcast" (Gaughan 193). Since Enfield hints towards having knowledge of this new space but chooses to no longer linger there, and Lanyon does cross over but is unable to survive the process, it appears that it is only Utterson who, even with a strong curiosity for this new frontier, remains loyal to the traditional domestic space.

The feminizing effects of inhabiting the domestic are evident when Utterson's affections are described like ivy (Stevenson, *J&H* 31), evoking the popular nineteenth-century image of the ivy and the oak used to describe a woman's role in marriage:

> As the vine, which has long twined its graceful foliage about the oak, and been and been lifted by it into sunshine, will, when the hardy plant is rifted by the thunderbolt, cling round it with its caressing tendrils, and bind up its shattered boughs, so is it beautifully ordered by Providence, that woman, who is the mere dependent and ornament of man in his happier hours, should be his stay and solace when smitten with sudden calamity; winding herself into the rugged recesses of his nature, tenderly supporting the drooping head, and binding up the broken heart [Washington Irving selection of "The Wife" in *The Sketch Book of Geoffrey Crayon, Gent.* 1820].

This passage refers to the popular nineteenth-century metaphor of man as oak and woman as vine. Immediately following this reference is a scene reminiscent of a marriage grown old. Utterson and Enfield's walks are permeated with suggestions of the tedious routine of married life: "they said nothing, looked singularly dull and would hail with obvious relief the appearance of a friend" (Stevenson, *J&H* 31). Yet, there is a sense of duty and commitment that is so strong that even "the calls of business [were] resisted" (Stevenson, *J&H* 31). This walk is a domestic duty for both involved, although it appears that Enfield also finds pleasure in other pursuits. His three o'clock stroll on a winter morning coming from "the end of the world" (Stevenson, *J&H* 32) supports Enfield's reputation as a "well-known man about town" (Stevenson, *J&H* 31). When Utterson chooses to retreat to his cozy fireside, Enfield has other plans. His encounter demonstrates how Enfield can relate more to Hyde than Utterson. The incident at the door reveals how in Stevenson's male community it appears that Hyde fits in better than the lawyer Utterson.

Hyde's first intrusion into the domestic is marked by the disturbance in Utterson's nightly regime. After hearing Enfield's description of Hyde, Utterson chooses his office over his bed, where he retrieves Jekyll's private document. Utterson as defender of the domestic is also the passive keeper of Jekyll's Will. The Will, as Utterson states, reveals either Jekyll's "madness" (Stevenson, *J&H* 37), or "how I begin to fear it is [his] disgrace" (Stevenson, *J&H* 37). Jekyll's reputation is in Utterson's safe-keeping. Under the veil of professionalism, Utterson recounts his emotional reaction to

Jekyll's Will, which is made worse with the introduction of Hyde. It is Utterson's sleep or rather his "great dark bed" (Stevenson, *J&H* 38) that confirms the impact of Hyde, as the lawyer "toss[es] to and fro" (Stevenson, *J&H* 38). Utterson's domestic space is no longer a safe haven, which is what he imagines is also the case for Jekyll. Utterson is less concerned about the theft and deceit associated with the business of the Will, and instead puts more anxiety into Jekyll and Hyde's interactions in the bedroom. Utterson imagines how Jekyll's private space has been infiltrated by Hyde when he describes how the "curtains of the bed [were] plucked apart" (Stevenson, *J&H* 39). Interestingly, it is the power dynamics in the bedroom that concern the Lawyer Utterson. His second bedside image of Jekyll and Hyde reveals Utterson's obsession with the protection of Jekyll's domestic space: "It turns me cold to think of this creature stealing like a thief to Harry's bedside; poor Harry, what a wakening!" (Stevenson, *J&H* 43). Utterson is anxious about his friend's abandonment of the domestic in favor of this new space self-designed by the late–nineteenth-century bachelor.

Utterson's rejection of Hyde is strongest when he trespasses into Jekyll's domestic space, especially his bedroom and the "pleasantest room in London" (Stevenson, *J&H* 42)—Jekyll's hall. The description of Jekyll's hall clearly idealizes the domestic: "a large, low-roofed, comfortable hall paved with flags warmed after the fashion of a country house, by a bright, open fire and furnished with costly cabinets of oak" (Stevenson, *J&H* 42). This space favored by both Utterson and Jekyll as a "pet fancy" (Stevenson, *J&H* 42) is chosen by Stevenson to emphasize Hyde's successful penetration of Jekyll's private space. Upon entering the hall Utterson "seemed to read a menace in the flickering of the firelight on the polished cabinets and the uneasy starting of the shadow on the roof" (Stevenson, *J&H* 42). Hyde is "both part of and an intrusion upon a scene" (Gaughan 193). Hyde is without and within simultaneously as spectacle and spectator, female and male.[7] The domestic defender is able to recognize the smallest signs of intrusion and he is able to see beyond the comforting firelight and identify the "menace" within.

As domestic defender, Utterson clings to what is left of the bourgeois gentleman's code of conduct. He struggles to maintain the performance of masculinity among a community of men who question these traditional gender foundations. Andrew Smith insists that Stevenson's male community "represents the bourgeois male in a state of terminal decline" (37). Smith also reveals how he would prefer to move the debate beyond "readings of masculinity as a reactionary response to the women's suffrage movement" (4), and instead suggests that the crisis of masculinity in the *fin-de-siècle* arises from a "male tradition of writings on degeneracy" (4). Although Stevenson's male community represents *fin-de-siècle* masculinity in crisis, it becomes clear that Utterson rejects this movement towards "degeneration." Max Nordau in *Degeneration* (1892) claims that decadence is "based on a model of a dangerous, potentially perverse and possibly infectious version of male effeminacy" (qtd. in Smith, *Victorian Demons* 2). Nordau makes the link between masculinity in crisis and the decline of the nation during the *fin-de-siècle*. Enfield has never completely embraced bourgeois masculinity, and Lanyon's scientific curiosity allows him to explore the possibilities while keeping his distance. Utterson is the only one who appears to completely embrace this brand of masculinity and defend it at all costs.

Utterson is confronted with Hyde's refusal to perform traditional masculinity, as Smith indicates, the "theatricality associated with the performance of the bourgeois gentleman is ostensibly threatened by the feral qualities of Hyde" (*Victorian Demons* 38). While Hyde functions as a disrupting force, Smith points out how, "an alternative case can be made that it is the demands of performance that creates the possibility of this horror" (*Victorian Demons* 38). Although Utterson struggles to maintain the performance of masculinity, he indulges in moments of lapse similar to Jekyll's desire to create Hyde. Strangely, in a domestic scene with Guest, Utterson embraces the role of patriarch seeking advice from a Victorian icon of effeminacy, the clerk, as opposed to placing himself in the role of the effeminate domesticated man. A. James Hammerton examines the phenomena of Pooterism in "Pooterism or Partnership? Marriage and Masculine Identity in the Lower Middle Class, 1870–1920." Pooterism "refers to the dependent weakness and inflated social pretension of white-collar workers" (Hammerton 294). The clerk becomes an emasculated figure for his subordinate position at work, which was assumed to also carry over into the domestic sphere. This is remarkably similar to a husband and wife relationship, where the professional lawyer seeks comfort by soliciting advice from someone he considers inferior. The scene is intentionally planned for Utterson's purpose and Guest plays the role of the Victorian wife fulfilling the patriarchal fantasy. The setting evokes the domestic as the two men sit on each side of the hearth and "midway between, at a nicely calculated distance from the fire, a bottle of a particular old wine" (Stevenson, *J&H* 52). In order to fully participate in this scene, Utterson requires the aid of wine, which is described using a combination of scientific and poetic diction. This draught of fermented acids aged to perfection is equivalent to Jekyll's potion.[8] Jekyll himself compares his dependence on the potion like that of an alcoholic (Stevenson, *J&H* 84). The wine allows the lawyer to melt insensibly (Stevenson, *J&H* 52), while Jekyll uses similar terminology to describe how the potion allows for "moral insensibility" (Stevenson, *J&H* 84). With the effects of the wine, Utterson is able to experience the same freedom as Jekyll with his potion.

Guest is accustomed to these domestic scenes and is the possessor of many of Utterson's secrets, "and he was not always sure that he kept as many as he meant" (Stevenson, *J&H* 52). As head clerk Guest fills the role of employee and confidante. The transition between these two roles is initiated by the staging of domestic accouterments and especially the freeing effects of wine. The significance of this scene is that it calls into question traditional constructs of the bachelor. John Tosh describes the relationship between the bachelor and manliness, suggesting that "the appeal of all-male conviviality is probably greatest among young unmarried men who are temporarily denied the full privileges of masculinity" (*Manliness* 38). Contrary to Tosh's image of the incomplete bachelor, the bachelors in Stevenson's all-male community are clearly exercising their full masculinity by successfully incorporating homosociality into the domestic. Guest needs only drop a remark that Utterson might use to "shape his future course" (Stevenson, *J&H* 53). Like the angel in the house, Guest's advice must remain limited to a brief communication, which in the hands of the "patriarchal" lawyer, will be brought to its fullest potential. Within the comforts of a room made "gay with firelight" (Stevenson, *J&H* 52), these two male professionals engage in a completely domestic scene while exercising every aspect of Victorian masculinity. Although Stevenson practically banishes female characters from his novella, a tendency arguably shared with several other *fin-de-siècle* male writers, the feminine and the domestic are clearly present. As Tosh points out, the "arrival of R. L. Stevenson and H. Rider Haggard on the literary scene in the mid–1880s signaled the rapid rise of a new genre of men-only adventure fiction, in which the prevalent concern of the English novel with marriage and family was quite deliberately cast aside in favour of a bracing masculine fantasy of quest and danger" (*Manliness* 107). The evolution of masculinity and especially the bachelor has created a space where the private no longer requires a feminine presence and a family. Indeed Tosh puts the homosocial in opposition to the home, as belonging to two separate spheres (*Manliness* 40). The homosocial, which has been defined as belonging to the public sphere, becomes a vital component of the *fin-de-siècle* private sphere.

The exclusively male community in Stevenson's novella allows the bachelor to discover a new masculinity, one which is neither completely male nor female. The ambiguity and fluidity of the gender identity of the *fin-de-siècle* bachelor suggests that his sexuality also wavers. Hyde eludes the gaze and remains indescribable, while the narrative attempts appear to fail, the discourse of writing is also employed for a similar purpose, but as M. Kellen Williams observes all attempts whether spoken or written will remain unsuccessful "so long as he eludes the proper name" (421). Williams follows the paper trail which he argues only leads to further discontinuities in the narrative discourse:

> Rather than any definitive depictions of Edward Hyde there are instead stories, handbills, and journal entries which fail to describe him; rather than any hard evidence for the connection between the two title figures, there are mysterious "enclosures," registered letters, "immodest" wills, and arcane notes; rather, in short, than some material, accessible referent there is always at least right up until the last dramatic scene, "nothing but papers, and a closed door" [420].

Although it would appear that the discourse of writing also fails to contain Hyde, it is the language of blackmail that provides the reader with insight into these seemingly disconnected written documents. The "unspoken" language of blackmail and homosexuality reveal that these male characters share a common understanding. Sedgwick identifies the Gothic genre as having "relatively visible links to male homosexuality, at a time when styles of homosexuality, and even its visibility and distinctness, were markers of division and tension between classes as much as between genders" (91). The Gothic tradition is evident in Stevenson's novella including murder, transformations, and potions, but also suggestions of sexual perversions, suicide, and homosexuality.

The language of *Dr. Jekyll and Mr. Hyde* involves secrecy, and unspoken insinuations which function as tropes of the Gothic genre, as Sedgwick outlines, "[s]exuality between men had, throughout the Judaeo-Christian tradition, been famous among those who knew about it at all precisely for having no name—'unspeakable,' 'unmentionable'" (94). Hyde appears to have more in common with Enfield and Utterson, rather than with his own creator, Jekyll. The unspoken words between Enfield and Utterson in the opening scene, and the clear understandings between Hyde, Utterson, and Enfield about scandal and disgrace reveal a secret language among the members of this exclusively male community, and as Sedgwick remarks that the "defining pervasiveness in Gothic novels of language about the unspeakable (94). The unspoken becomes more concrete in the form of blackmail, which Sedgwick classifies as yet another example of a Gothic trope. "Homophobic blackmailability" (Sedgwick 90) finds a forum in the Gothic tradition where issues of homophobia and homosocial bonds can be worked out. Blackmail, secrecy, power, and control surround the male community in *Dr. Jekyll and Mr. Hyde* and suggest yet another variation of the bachelor as androgynous which Michel Foucault cites as an early understanding of homosexuality (43). The bachelor moves between the public and private spaces of the novella while transforming himself from an exemplar of middle class patriarchy, to the model of fluid and elusive femininity, into his final transformation as the "man in the middle"—the homosexual.

Hyde as middle-class gentleman leading a public and private life is not exceptional, and his ability to perform these actions becomes part of the unspoken language between the men in Stevenson's work. Foucault describes the nineteenth-century homosexual in Volume I of *The History of Sexuality*:

[he] became a personage, a past, a case history, and a childhood, in addition to being a type of life, a life form, and a morphology, with an indiscreet anatomy and possibly a mysterious physiology. Nothing that went into his total composition was unaffected by his sexuality. It was everywhere present in him: at the root of all his actions because it was their insidious and indefinitely active principle; written immodestly on his face and body because it was a secret that always gave itself away [43].

The homosexual becomes an identity that is apparent in every aspect of his life, including his physical appearance. The body becomes the surface on which the secret of the homosexual is exposed. Anatomy, physiology, and phrenology were the methods by which Victorians categorized criminals, the insane, and the sexually deviant. Stevenson emphasizes Hyde's physicality and appearance using a unique combination of detail and uncertainty, which triggers Utterson's obsessive desire to see Hyde's face for himself. Hyde's physicality is described as repulsive, but no one is able to explain the reason for their disgust. This suggests that the reaction towards Hyde by the masses and the higher-class professionals is based on the vagueness of Hyde's sexuality and not a distinguishing feature.

The inability to pinpoint specific characteristics about Hyde demonstrates how feelings of disgust are based more on Hyde's entire demeanor, or as Foucault states "his total composition." Enfield's lacking description of Hyde titillates Utterson's interest in seeing Hyde for himself:

> He is not easy to describe. There is something wrong with his appearance; something displeasing, something down-right detestable. I never saw a man I so disliked, and yet I scarce know why. He must be deformed somewhere; he gives a strong feeling of deformity, although I couldn't specify the point. He's an extraordinary looking man, and yet I really can name nothing out of the way. No, sir; I can make no hand of it; I can't describe him. And it's not want of memory; for I declare I can see him this moment [36].

The ambiguity coupled with Enfield's certainty that he experienced feelings of disgust suggests Foucault's description of the nineteenth-century homosexual, and yet Hyde appears to succeed in maintaining some sort of mystery about him. Enfield's obscure picture of Hyde leads Utterson to believe that if he could only see Hyde's face he would know all:

> [i]f he could but once set eyes on him, he thought the mystery would lighten and perhaps roll altogether away, as was the habit of mysterious things when well examined. He might see a reason for his friend's strange preference or bondage [....]. At least it would be a face worth seeing: the face of a man who was without bowels of mercy: a face which had but to show itself to raise up, in the mind of the unimpressionable Enfield, a spirit of enduring hatred [39].

Utterson's assumption that by seeing Hyde's face all will be clear is reminiscent of Foucault's description of the Victorian belief in the power of physical appearances to expose secrets. Utterson also suggests that he would be a better candidate than Enfield for deciphering Hyde's features.

Ronald R. Thomas also recognizes a strong link between Hyde and Utterson and refers to the dream Utterson has about Hyde sneaking into Jekyll's bedchamber. Alongside Utterson's obsession over Hyde's appearance is his fixation on Hyde as "Henry Jekyll's favourite" (Stevenson, *J&H* 48). As Thomas states,

> [t]he images and action of the dream are characterized by power, stealth, and self-censorship. Hyde is as much Utterson's dream as Jekyll's here. His "power" is exercised over both of them. Utterson is "the law" to Jekyll's crime, and his response to the dream demonstrates that he is as subject to its bidding as Jekyll is [240].

Utterson's profession as a lawyer strengthens his belief that he, like Jekyll, is bound to the criminal, Hyde, as Utterson states in his well-known pun, "If he be Mr. Hyde [...] I shall be Mr. Seek" (Stevenson, *J&H* 39). The unspeakable language fails to provide spectators with the appropriate image of Hyde as homosexual/criminal, but succeeds in delivering an overall impression of repulsion and, as it appears in the case of Utterson, attraction. Hyde's shroud of mystery relates back to his status as the *fin-de-siècle* bachelor and his ability to adapt, transform, and evolve to "fit into" a particular space, class, and gender. The language between the men in Stevenson's novella involves a codified structure with a variety of "dialects" including physical appearances, and the more threatening method of blackmail.

Numerous letters, insinuations, and assumptions permeate *Dr. Jekyll and Mr. Hyde* so that one can interpret these as part of the unspoken language within this male-only community. The language of blackmail suggests to Showalter that Stevenson's novella is a "case study of male hysteria, not only that of Henry J., but also of the men in the community around him. It can be most persuasively read as a fable of *fin-de-siècle* homosexual panic, the discovery and resistance of the homosexual self" (*Sexual* 107). Utterson, Sir Danvers Carew, Enfield, Jekyll, and Hyde are all suspect in the art of blackmail by their use of its codified language. Enfield makes the first reference to blackmail when he encounters Hyde after trampling the girl. Hyde and Enfield speak the same language and understand each other plainly when Enfield demands financial retribution or else he will suffer the consequences of a tarnished reputation (Stevenson, *J&H* 34). Enfield understands the language of blackmail and he believes that Jekyll is "an honest man paying through the nose for some of the capers of his youth" (Stevenson, *J&H* 34–5), and refers to Jekyll's abode as "Black Mail House" (Stevenson, *J&H* 35). References to blackmail are immediately followed by the unspeakable when Enfield states, "No sir, I make it a rule of mine: the more it looks like Queer Street, the less I ask" (Stevenson, *J&H* 35). Blackmail as a topic of conversation appears to be more acceptable than what Enfield concludes is at the heart of the "Story of the Door" and reverts to the codified language of the unspoken in order to express his concern. Utterson clearly understands Enfield's silent message and begins to fear for Jekyll's reputation and creates a scheme to blackmail Hyde: "This Master Hyde, if he were studied [...] must have secrets of his own; black secrets, by the look of him; secrets compared to which poor Jekyll's worst would be like sunshine. Things cannot continue as they are. It turns me cold to think of this creature stealing like a thief to Harry's bedside" (Stevenson, *J&H* 43). Utterson reverts to the language of blackmail to shield his close friend, but it requires, on Utterson's part, the knowledge that Hyde must have secrets of his own. The silence between the men in *Dr. Jekyll and Mr. Hyde* is filled with the codified language of an exclusively male community where by saying nothing one is saying something. The ideal example of the unspeakable comes in the form of the letter.

Letters from Jekyll to Utterson, Lanyon to Utterson, Jekyll to Lanyon, and Sir Danvers Carew to Utterson, circulate throughout the novella. Most letters are read openly while some remain a mystery, like the letter Carew was mailing when he was murdered. The state of Carew's body raises suspicion: "[a] purse and gold watch were found upon the victim: but no cards or papers, except a sealed and stamped envelope [...] which bore the name and address of Mr. Utterson" (Stevenson, *J&H* 47). Stevenson ensures readers that Hyde did not murder for money, but his lack of identification and his letter to Utterson remain unsolved. After seeing the letter, Utterson responds using the language of silence: "I shall say nothing" (Stevenson, *J&H* 47), confirming the unspeakable. Without speaking, these letters reveal the unspeakable. Jekyll's written invitation to Utterson for dinner and Hyde's written statement unintentionally reveal Jekyll as a forger for a murderer. On first seeing the letter, Utterson reads on the surface and is pleased to find that the note "put a better colour on the intimacy than he had looked for: and he blamed himself for some of his past suspicions" (Stevenson, *J&H* 51). The letter speaks to Utterson's guilt and doubts, but most important is what the letter does not say, which Guest reveals. The matching handwriting uncovers the unspeakable truth concerning Hyde and Jekyll. Foucault emphasizes the significance of interpreting the discourse of silence as a way of saying things differently to achieve different results: "[t]here is no binary division to be made between what one says and what one does not say; we must try to determine the different ways of not saying things, how those who can and those who cannot speak of them are distributed, which type of discourse is authorized, or which form of discretion is required in either case" (27). Silence, as a codified language flourishes in Stevenson's male community, and knowledge as well as class, play a role in determining who can speak and which type of silence they employ. These marks of silence through letters and written statements participate in the language of the unspeakable in the male community of *Dr. Jekyll and Mr. Hyde*.

Hyde, as the *fin-de-siècle* bachelor, immerses himself in this male community initiating this codified language and instilling, especially in the mind of Utterson, thoughts of duality, bondage, blackmail, and sexuality. Hyde's ability to present himself as a middle-class gentleman, and yet seek out pleasure either reminds male characters like Enfield of their own indiscretions, or as is the case with Utterson, they find that they too live a dual existence. This suggests, just as Thomas argues, that Hyde has equal power over Jekyll and Utterson; the figure of Hyde penetrates into the lives of the male community reminding Jekyll and Utterson of their hypocrisy and seducing them with his boldness. When Lanyon meets Hyde to give him the ingredients he needs, the doctor takes a superior position reminding Hyde to use etiquette and to compose himself (Stevenson, *J&H* 73), but once Hyde gains control of himself and the chemicals, Lanyon is no longer an obstacle. Hyde proceeds to seduce Lanyon with knowledge recalling the image of the snake and Eve in the Garden of Eden. This scene strongly portrays Hyde as devil, and Katherine Bailey Linehan explains that the "language of deviltry" (93) permeates Stevenson's work. Similar to Satan, Hyde seduces Lanyon using his weakness for knowledge and science, as he states, "Will you be wise? Will you be guided? [...] or has the greed of curiosity too much command of you? Think before you answer, for it shall be done as you decide" (Stevenson, *J&H* 74). Knowledge is power in the male community; Lanyon instructs Hyde on the appropriate discourse and in exchange Hyde offers Lanyon the ultimate experience of scientific achievement. While the male community educates Hyde about their codified discourse, he introduces a new language into their closed society. Hyde as Satan seduces Lanyon which leads indirectly to his death, but the balance between crime and pleasure is too thin and eventually Hyde transforms from seducer to murderer.

As stated in the epigraph to this chapter, Hyde is created to seek out pleasure: "Men have before hired bravados to transact their crimes, while their own person and reputation sat under shelter. I was the first that ever did so for his pleasures" (Stevenson, *J&H* 80). Hyde's sole purpose is to indulge in pleasure; however, Stevenson demonstrates how easily Hyde crosses between the world of crime and the aesthetic world of pleasure through his murder of Sir Danvers Carew. Martin A. Danahay explains the confusion over Hyde's murder:

> There is no logical reason why the absolutely selfish Mr. Hyde should commit murder, as it gains him nothing. Stevenson is through murder expressing a fear that the autonomous self is innately inimical to social bonds. Murder is the most extreme antithesis to social behaviour, especially the healing function of a doctor, and is an act that precipitates the confession with which the tale ends [141].

Danahay questions Hyde as murderer and resolves that this act serves to emphasize Hyde as Jekyll's doppelganger and social outcast, but the way in which Carew is murdered reveals that Hyde is indeed performing according to his intended design. Stevenson's motivation for the murder is to put stress on the fine line between pleasure and crime evoking the lifestyle of the nineteenth-century homosexual. The murder of Carew is replete with the sensual, the sexual, and violent images of pleasure, as Jekyll recalls, "With a transport of glee, I mauled the unresisting body, tasting delight from every blow [...I] fled from the scene of these excesses, at once glorying and trembling, my lust for evil gratified and stimulated, my love of life screwed to the topmost peg" (Stevenson, *J&H* 85). The scene employs the language of sensuality and pleasure to described a murder. Hyde's criminality stems from his position as a selfish plea-sure-seeker and not a murderer. The physical body of Carew becomes the feeding ground from which Hyde gratifies and stimulates himself. Hyde's "murder" of Carew symbolizes his transformation into a sexual predator and according to the Labouchère Amendment, otherwise known as the "Blackmailer's Charter" (Showalter, *Sexual* 112), Hyde has also become the Victorians' worst nightmare. The Labouchère Amendment of 1885 regarded acts of "gross indecency between men as 'misdemeanors' made punishable by up to two years' hard labour, and this in effect brought within the scope of the law all forms of male homosexual activity" (Weeks 102). This law was enforced to its maximum penalty on Oscar Wilde when he was found guilty after his trials in 1895. There was some gov-ernment resistance to the Labouchère Amendment since it attempted to control both public and private behavior (Weeks 103). It is significant to note that when such legislation as the Labouchère Amendment, the 1898 Vagrancy Act, the 1912 Criminal Law Amendment Act were enacted they were part of a "general moral restructuring, and were primarily con-cerned with female prostitution" (Weeks 106), since male homosexuality and prostitution were considered as "products of undifferentiated male desire" (Weeks 106). The corruption of youth, especially of young girls into prostitution, was blamed on male homosexuality. Indeed, it was the issue of the corruption of youth, both in Wilde's life and in his novel *The Picture of Dorian Gray*, which was the central concern during Wilde's trial. Prior to 1885 in England the only legislation against homosexuality was limited to sodomy. The 1533 Act of Henry VIII condemned to death anyone participating in buggery of any kind and was technically in effect until 1861. Legislation like the Labouchère Amendment brought into question the identity of the homosexual, which as Jeffrey Weeks notes remained, as late as 1871, "extremely undeveloped both in the Metropol-itan Police and in high medical and legal circles, suggesting the absence of any clear notion of a homosexual category or of any social awareness of what a homosexual identity might consist of" (101). This ambivalence led to confusion concerning the characteristics of the homosexual and the type of behavior punishable by law. In consequence effeminate men risked being unjustly accused of homosexuality and homosexuals were threatened by blackmail at the risk of having to expose themselves publicly. Hyde's space within the male community becomes narrower as he is forced off the streets of London and into the prison of Jekyll's small laboratory.

While Enfield instructs Utterson on the discreet ways of becoming a man-about-town, the novel itself is unable to express exactly where the problem lies with Hyde. The problem certainly exists, but it remains unclassifiable while the narrative discourse is unable to provide an explanation. The language of writing and the ways it empowers the writer is explored by Stevenson's male professionals. Money and economy rely on the written word as evidenced by the first monetary transaction between Hyde and Enfield in the opening chapter. What is later revealed as Jekyll's signature, "a name at least very well known and often printed" (Stevenson, *J&H* 34), is questioned for its validity. Enfield's description of this scene where Hyde enters Jekyll's house and emerges with a signed check in Jekyll's hand combines issues of silence, the written word and exposure. In addition to Enfield's doubt towards the signature on the check, he also must keep the signature a secret: "signed with a name that I can't mention, though it's one of the points of my story" (Stevenson, *J&H* 34). Silence is a requisite in the male community, and something Enfield considers as a rule, which Utterson appears to be still learning. In this case, silence undercuts Enfield's narrative leaving an empty space. The signature also appears to fail or at least is not enough on its own. Variations on and repetition of the term "hand" pervade *Dr. Jekyll and Mr. Hyde*, and can be interpreted in relation to sexuality, class, race, and evolution. References also link to handwriting, imprinting, and reading. There are approximately twenty references in *Dr. Jekyll and Mr. Hyde* to the terms "hand" and "writing," numerous references to the phrase, "bore the stamp/ name," and the terms "blot out," "quills" and "pen." In Enfield's failed attempt to describe Hyde, he remarks, "No, sir; I can make no hand of it" (Stevenson, *J&H* 36). This act of deciphering Hyde as if he was mysterious handwriting is reminiscent of the scene between Utterson and Guest, who reveals Jekyll and Hyde's writing to be one and the same: "the two hands are in many points identical" (Stevenson, *J&H* 53). Jekyll's Will becomes a written document that obsesses Utterson throughout the novella.

Although the written Will is in Utterson's charge, all of Jekyll's "possessions were to pass into the hands of his 'friend and benefactor Edward
Hyde'" (Stevenson, *J&H* 37). The physical Will is held onto by Utterson as
proof of his significance in Jekyll's private affairs, and yet the writing in
the Will puts Hyde in control of everything, once again evoking the term
"hands"; in this case as a method for passing along power and control.
The Will becomes an extension of Hyde's physical deformity, as Utterson
appears disgusted by its contents. It is the "lawyer's eyesore" (Stevenson,
*J&H* 37) and an "obnoxious paper" (Stevenson, *J&H* 37), which can only
lead to "disgrace" (Stevenson, *J&H* 37). The Will's power extends beyond
its function as a legal document, since it also retains the power to offend
Utterson, "both as a lawyer and as a lover of the sane and customary sides
of life" (Stevenson, *J&H* 37). Utterson allows the Will to transcend beyond
a professional matter (the public), into a personal vendetta (the private).
The ultimate power of the written word here is that the Will combines
Hyde's printed name with Jekyll's wish to transfer his funds to this unknown intruder. This written document allows Hyde to move from the
printed page into a physical being. The image of Hyde emerging off the
page is equivalent to a second birth. This time it is Utterson who creates
the being, clothing it, and providing it with a form, as Stevenson writes, "It
was already bad enough when the name was but a name of which he could
learn no more. It was worse when it began to be clothed upon with de-
testable attributes; and out of the shifting, insubstantial mists that had so
long baffled his eye, there leaped up the sudden, definite presentment of a
fiend" (Stevenson, *J&H* 37). The Will and his new knowledge of Hyde allow
Utterson's imagination to provide him with a shape, and yet Hyde himself
remains vague as representative of the demonized Other. The mists part
to reveal Utterson's haunted imagination and his deliberate alienation of
Hyde through the written word.

The written word transcribes what cannot be spoken within the male
community. The knowledge that Jekyll and Hyde's letters are written by
the same person is kept silent, as Utterson instructs his clerk, "I wouldn't
speak of this note, you know" (Stevenson, *J&H* 53). The letter is alive and
dangerous for the secrets it candidly reveals. It is fitting that as Jekyll's
lawyer, Utterson retains control over these "noisy" witnesses: "he locked
up the note into his safe, where it reposed from that time forward" (Stevenson, *J&H* 53–4). Like his carefully stored vintage wines which have
the power to unleash secrets, so too are these writings kept from causing "public injury" (Stevenson, *J&H* 54). Lanyon's letter "brackets" Jekyll's

name (Stevenson, *J&H* 56), constraining and separating him without words. As possessor of Jekyll's Will, Carew's letter, Hyde's note, Lanyon's narrative, and finally Jekyll's full statement, Utterson protects the borders of the public and private spaces from their threatening contents. Like the other written documents, Lanyon's letter "[sleeps] in the inmost corner of [Utterson's] private safe" (Stevenson, *J&H* 56). Their confinement within the private suggests repression and alienation, an enforced silence reminiscent of the codes of Victorian masculinity.

Writing has the power to transfer control and dictate orders, and in Hyde's hands the written word has the power to "simply blot out" Utterson (Stevenson, *J&H* 54). The discourse of writing reveals the unspeakable on the faces of the characters: Hyde has "Satan's signature upon [his] face" (Stevenson, *J&H* 42), and later Lanyon has his "death-warrant written legibly upon his face" (Stevenson, *J&H* 55). Faces are read, decoded, and studied by these professional men as if they were ledgers, texts, or medical documents. What cannot be said is written down, like Lanyon's written account and Jekyll's full statement of the case. Emphasis is on the interpretation of written word under the analytical and professional masculine eye. Lanyon's letter is studied closely by Utterson: "an envelope addressed by the hand and sealed with the seal of his dead friend. PRIVATE: for the hands of G. J. Utterson ALONE, and in the case of his predecease to be destroyed unread" (Stevenson, *J&H* 56). In this case, Stevenson calls attention to both meanings of the term "hand" suggesting a dissection of both the physical body and the letter itself into its component parts. The letter screams out and yet commands silence. The breaking of the seal is reminiscent of Utterson's wine "ready to be set free" (Stevenson, *J&H* 52), and foreshadows breaking into Jekyll's cabinet and the description of the release of Hyde. The moment of release is anticipated, elaborated, and celebrated throughout the novel.

The term "blank silence" (Stevenson, *J&H* 60) is used to describe Jekyll's frightened servants, and divides them from the fullness of the silence experienced by the bourgeois professionals. The servants' silence is empty and cannot be read, unlike the "rich silence" (Stevenson, *J&H* 44) between gentlemen, which contains valuable, readable information. As Foucault remarks, "There is not one but many silences, and they are an integral part of the strategies that underlie and permeate discourses" (27). Class status affects the interpretation of the silent discourse. Hyde's note is treated differently from the other legal documents in Utterson's possession. This note is "crumpled" (Stevenson, *J&H* 62), and handled "like so much dirt" (Stevenson, *J&H* 62). Yet, this note reveals information about the writer under the scrutinizing eye of the professional, as Utterson interprets, "but here with a sudden sputter of the pen, the writer's emotion had broken loose" (Stevenson, *J&H* 62). This note is uncontainable and exudes emotion through its message and the actions of the pen itself. The clashing of the classes allows Stevenson to demonstrate the obsession of the professional for minute details and the unseen, while the servants' frustration is an attempt to draw the professional outwards into reality, as Poole declares, "But what matters hand of write [...] I've seen him" (Stevenson, J&H 62). Utterson's skill for reading is useless amongst the working class; instead it is experience and seeing for oneself which has superiority over reading. Poole reveals the investigative methods used thus far by Utterson to be ineffective when confronted with clear facts. As Poole informs Utterson, "O, I know it's not evidence, Mr. Utterson; I'm book-learned enough for that; but a man has his feelings" (Stevenson, *J&H* 64). In this case, instinct has precedence over professionalism. While it would appear that Poole is revealing a weakness for confusing the personal and the professional, he also acts as a mirror reflecting Utterson's own propensity for fusing the public and private. The type of writing reflects the nature of the writer. Hyde's note and blasphemous scribblings in the margins of his books demonstrate a degeneration in the written form and its author. In Jekyll's Will the pen replaces Hyde with Utterson suggesting an interchangeability between the two men.

Hyde's letter combines the significance of space and writing. The location of where the letter was written affects its interpretation, as Utterson states, "it had been written in the cabinet and if that were so, it must be differently judged, and handled with more caution" (Stevenson, *J&H* 52). The door of the cabinet functions as a barrier between the public and private. Poole and Utterson spend a great deal of time outside the cabinet deciding on the best way to get in. They discuss breaking down the door (Stevenson, *J&H* 64) with tools or with their own bodies, and they listen at the door to distinguish the inhabitant's footfall (Stevenson, *J&H* 65). The red baize door is brought down in a "blow [which] shook the building" (Stevenson, *J&H* 65), and falls "inwards on the carpet" (Stevenson, *J&H* 66). The wrecking of the door is significant and signals the violence associated with intrusion of the public into the private. This act can also be interpreted as an attempt to rescue Jekyll from the increasing sense of imprisonment of the house (Doane & Hodges 69). Indeed, Utterson and Poole believe they are embarking on a dangerous quest for liberation, and yet when faced with the ideal scene of domesticity their forced entrance seems unnecessarily violent. While Janice Doane and Devon Hodges attempt to resolve the conflict of Hyde amidst a domestic scene by comparing him with the New Woman who functions as both angel and demon in the house (70). It is problematic to remove the emphasis from the relationship between domesticity and masculinity. The specter of the New Woman surfaces in the novella as an attempt to discover a discourse for the domesticated man. The reader anticipates the breaking down of the door and is greeted with a scene which contrasts the domestic and the horrific. The intruders' eyes fall onto the domestic scene: "quiet lamp, a good fire glowing and chattering on the hearth, the kettle singing its think strain [...] papers neatly set forth on the business table, and nearer the fire, the things laid out for tea; the quietest room you would have said, and, but for the glazed presses full of chemicals, the most commonplace that night in London" (Stevenson, *J&H* 66). The chattering, singing and eventually the startling noise of the kettle boiling over (Stevenson, *J&H* 66–7) are in contrast to the silence associated with the male community. The room is alive with domestic sounds despite the still "twitching" (Stevenson, *J&H* 66) body in the middle of the floor. The scene is complex since it appears that Hyde was in the process of enjoying domesticity and then suddenly driven towards the violent action of suicide. The intruders into the sanctified space of the cabinet are the sole cause of Hyde's suicide. The cheval-glass which they are unable to penetrate shows them nothing except themselves (Stevenson, *J&H* 67). As if in response to their reflections in the glass, the pair once again mirror each other when Utterson echoes Poole using the same tones (Stevenson, *J&H* 67). The mirror echoes the dichotomy of inside/outside once again since Poole and Utterson are denied entry into its depths. As Alex Clunas states, the "mirror horrifies Poole and Utterson because it is empty and because it is a sign of itself [...]. In the mirror, space is turned back on itself, emptied in infinite reflection" (181). Indeed it is their failure to interpret/read the contents of the mirror which accounts for its refection of "their own pale and fearful countenances" (Stevenson, *J&H* 67). The cabinet is Hyde's/Jekyll's "last earthly refuge" (Stevenson, *J&H* 91); it is a space which clearly incorporates the public and private, and yet it is also an attempt to create a new space within the male community.

In contrast to the cabinet is Hyde's house in Soho, which represents his duality as both gentleman and "criminal." Jekyll's house represents his dual natures by its backdoor connection to Hyde's quarters, which Vladimir Nabokov claims reveals how Jekyll is not separated from his evil side, but instead he is "a mixture of good and bad" (188). Hyde's Soho residence mirrors his own duality through his mixture of "luxury and good taste" (Stevenson, *J&H* 49), and its location in a "dismal quarter of Soho [...] with its muddy ways [...] a district of some city in a nightmare" (Stevenson, *J&H* 48). The woman who greets Utterson at the door is far from feminine when she betrays her master by taking pleasure in his demise, but once inside, the duality of Hyde's residence becomes apparent. At first sight Hyde's gentleman status is reflected in his practicality by only using a couple of rooms, as well as his good taste for wine, silver, and art (Stevenson, *J&H* 49), except this luxurious setting is tainted by the rooms "having been recently and hurriedly ransacked" (Stevenson, *J&H* 49). Hyde's residence reveals his public persona through his good taste, while its state of disarray symbolizes his secret private life that eventually disrupts his public reputation. The bachelor's residence is an interesting space because of the lack of the feminine usually associated with the home. The absence of the female in the bachelor's life and especially in his home is the ultimate male freedom.

The expansion and contraction of spaces comply with the fluidity and elasticity of Hyde as he moves through the streets of London, into the cabinet, hall, and bedchamber of Jekyll's house, Enfield's chambers, Hyde's own apartments and into Jekyll's Will. Although the streets of London seem a fitting place for Hyde to wander, it is his ability to "glide more stealthily through sleeping houses" (Stevenson, *J&H* 39), and particularly "steal [...] like a thief to Harry's bedside" (Stevenson, *J&H* 43). His movements form the primary tension of the novella, as well as fuelling Utterson's obsession. Space, whether in Soho or Jekyll's domestic Hall, communicates what the novel has difficulty expressing through narrative discourse.

Hyde is everywhere and nowhere—he is described as a ghost (Stevenson, *J&H* 39, 49), who transpires and transfigures (Stevenson, *J&H* 42), and yet he can become earthly, animalistic, and quite concrete, as when he tramples a little girl and clubs Sir Danvers Carew. This transformation from swift invisibility to "ape-like" (Stevenson, *J&H* 46) fury and deformity is the essence of Hyde as Other. In between these two extremes there is Hyde—the gentleman with furnished luxurious rooms and a knowledge of London and its customs. Hyde is no longer the traditional Gothic Other; instead, he is a hybrid who pushes the gender boundaries and forces the bourgeois professionals to explore their masculinity. Their stagnancy and failure to meet with the *fin-de-siècle*'s new definition of masculinity results in tragedy. The flexing of space is a silent commentary on the re-engineering of social order and gender roles. Space is controlled by Hyde, whether it be on the streets or within the intimate chambers of Jekyll's home, Hyde conquers all spaces in the novella. Since narrative discourse fails to contain Hyde, the discourse of space and of writing attempt to express the unspeakable.

Hyde's movement between the public and private spaces of *Dr. Jekyll and Mr. Hyde*'s exclusively male community is possible based on his ability to possess both masculine and feminine characteristics. His status as gentleman and defender of middle-class patriarchy, as Arata argues, provides Hyde with a social status that promotes the existence of dual natures and the need to keep secrets. Hyde's middle-class masculinity is the ideal mask to hide behind and allows him to penetrate into the male community. His feminine characteristics provide him with a fluid and elusive identity that cannot be categorized and, as Kane states, this signifies Hyde as the Other and Jekyll's discovery of his own feminine nature (25). Hyde is the ideal bachelor who, like Donald G. Mitchell's bachelor narrator, finds a place within the domestic space through the exclusion of women. The unspoken language used by this male community reveals yet another transformation for the *fin-de-siècle* bachelor. Hyde as homosexual questions the delicate balance between pleasure and crime, sensuality and murder. The unspoken language of blackmail reveals a community familiar with homosexuality, but uncomfortable with the ambiguous and obscure sexual identity of Hyde. This becomes the essence for the *fin-de-siècle* bachelor, who incorporates masculine and feminine characteristics as a tool for moving between public and private spaces. Hyde flourishes in Stevenson's male community by violently questioning Victorian masculinity and creating a new understanding of the nineteenth-century bachelor.

While Stevenson employs the discourse of writing and imprinting in an attempt to "capture" what is left unsaid, he is in essence engaging in a typically patriarchal scientific mode of defining the "feminine"—the ghost, the elusive. This discourse aims to bring a scientific method into the chaos which is *Dr. Jekyll and Mr. Hyde*. Although born from a laboratory potion, the science of Jekyll and Hyde ends there. Rather, the reader spends more time within the characters' parlors, halls, dining rooms, private offices, and bedchambers. The spaces within the novella leave the science fiction genre behind, and although this is a male-only community, it becomes clear that the themes do not stray from such familiar issues of identity, gender, and society associated with the domestic novel genre.

## Domesticated Bachelors and Femininity in Victorian Novels

The spaces in *Dr. Jekyll and Mr. Hyde* contradict its basis as an exploration of the moral issues affiliated with the progress of science at the *fin-de-siècle*. Instead, the exclusively male community and the wide array of private spaces suggest an emphasis on the re-evaluation of masculinity and domesticity.

The tension between male domesticity and homosociality (Tosh, *Manliness* 71) is resolved by the reconfiguring of the domestic space. The bachelor is able to engage in every aspect of masculinity including issues of domesticity without the female presence. Stevenson's use of domestic space demonstrates how the bachelor not only transgresses private and public boundaries, but reshapes the private to assume characteristics of the homosocial. Tosh uses the example of the London journeymen as "living out the dictates of 'separate spheres'" (*Manliness* 71) by being married and yet still acting like bachelors, "according to a fraternal ethos of drunken misogyny" (*Manliness* 71). This is a version of the bachelor as young, promiscuous, drunk and exempt from the domestic. Stevenson's bachelors, on the other hand, perform as if they are married, and indulge in domestic bliss while exercising their claim to masculinity. Instead of being a source of male repression and isolation, Victorian domesticity expands to include the bachelor. Although the new male-only adventure fiction genre of the mid–1880s, as Tosh points out, appears to do away with the marriage novel in favor of "bracing masculine fantasy of quest and danger, a world without petticoats" (*Manliness* 107), it becomes clear that these domestic issues are still present, but have taken on a different and significant form in this *fin-de-siècle* male-centric genre.

Nineteenth-century writers[9] have shown an interest in the bachelor by making him a central character, but it is Stevenson's 1886 novella and Oscar Wilde's *The Picture of Dorian Gray* (1891) that provide the best examples of these exclusively male communities. Katherine V. Snyder discusses how these works "encompass both the imaginary consolidation of charged relations between men within the figure of a single man and the imaginary distribution of a single man's self, driven by conflict, between two male figures" (105). The position of the bachelor as an accepted visitor in both the domestic and public spheres results in the creation of dual natures and double lives, which accentuates the delicate balance which the bachelor must preserve. This duality though has nothing to do with the bachelor's ability to manoeuver between the worlds of women and men; instead, he must define himself in relation to other men. The dualism that arises from the bachelor among men involves questioning homosocial bonds and the possibility of being both bachelor and homosexual simultaneously. Here the bachelor figure defines himself in contrast to the acceptable Victorian status of the unmarried man through his public persona, while privately he is defined solely in relation to the male community no longer as "bachelor," but as "homosexual."

# SIX

# The Reconfigured Sphere

*Dandyism and Decadence*
*in* The Picture of Dorian Gray

> "Of course it is true, Lord Henry. If we women did not
> have you for your defects, where would you all be? Not
> one of you would ever be married. You would be a set of
> unfortunate bachelors. Not, however, that that would alter
> you much. Nowadays all married men live like bachelors,
> and all the bachelors like married men."
> "*Fin de siècle*," murmured Lord Henry.
> "*Fin du globe*," answered his hostess.
> [Wilde, *The Picture of Dorian Gray* 179].

Degeneration and pessimism epitomize the 1880s and 90s, which
for the most part represented not only the end of a century, but also two
decades of sexual scandals, and the crossing of racial and sexual boundaries. As Karl Miller states, "Men became women. Women became men.
Gender and country were put in doubt" (209), and as Lord Henry and
Lady Narborough discuss in the epigraph, the fin de siècle feels like a car-
nivalesque version of the apocalypse. In this sexual and cultural turmoil
and confusion, the Aesthete dandy finds a space for himself. According to
Charles Baudelaire, the dandy "is a sunset; like the declining daystar, it is
glorious, without heat and full of melancholy" (799), indicating how the
dandy's fate is irrevocably bound to the death of the century, although he
persists as representing the century's last survivor of the leveling effects of
democracy. Baudelaire responds to manifestations of the dandy in North
American tribes:

> those tribes that we call "savage" may they not in fact be the *disjecta membra* of
> great extinct civilizations? Dandyism is a sunset [...] But alas, the rising tide of
> democracy, which invades and levels everything, is daily overwhelming these last

representatives of human pride and pouring floods of oblivion upon the footprints of these stupendous warriors" [799].

Baudelaire describes the dandy in comparison to a disappearing civilization emphasizing his temporary state of being; however, the dandy lives on as a literary figure. Oscar Wilde, like Baudelaire, presents the aesthete-dandy in decline in *The Picture of Dorian Gray*, and yet it is within this atmosphere of confusion, this fin-de-siècle decadence that the dandy finds a space for himself. Dennis Denisoff defines the dandy-aesthete in *Aesheticism and Sexual Parody 1840–1940*:

> Dandies were people—primarily men—interested in fashioning themselves as art, with the process of artistic commodification leading to a major accord between presenting oneself as art and presenting oneself as valuable [...]. In the eyes of most of the public, they could pass as "ladies' men." And yet, the aura of sexual mystery that surrounded the dandy-aesthete also encouraged them to sustain some representation of what they saw as a crucial difference. Sexual ambiguity became inscribed upon the persona as a characteristic hyper-awareness of performed and assumedly actual identities [7–8].

The dandy's relationship with society is complex since he delicately maneuvers between social boundaries including the private and public arenas. It is the dandy's ambiguous and flexible sexuality that provide him with the unique ability to move between the public and private spheres. Unlike the domestic men, the dandy-aesthete insists on the creation of a separate, reconfigured sphere, which Wilde in *The Portrait of Dorian Gray* supplies through his depiction of a male-only society where issues of sexuality and gender performance can be played out freely.

The dandy and all his excesses take flight in the age of Decadence, which evolved as an extreme form of the Aesthetic movement. H. G. Cocks states that the 1880s Aesthetic Movement was the first of three waves that began the modern gay movement:

> Its [Aestheticism] key tenets, although not openly homosexual, nevertheless rejected Victorian bourgeois ideals like duty and morality. Instead aestheticism replaced the notion that art should perform some moral function with a love of art for art's sake, a passion for intense feeling and an embrace of classical Greece, including its subtly homoerotic ideals of beauty [...]. By the 1890s, British writers who wished to make a case for the legitimacy of homosexuality had taken up [...] that homosexuality was somehow innate or congenital and was not, as popularly supposed, merely a symptom of moral degradation or wickedness [108].

The domestic man differs from his Aesthetic counterpart by integrating bourgeois ideals into his own space, as opposed to dismissing them completely. In direct opposition to the Romantics who preceded them, the Decadents believed that nature alone did not accurately represent beauty and that it benefited from artificial improvement. The Decadents' desire to improve upon nature leads to the development of the cult of the artificial (McMullen 33). The dandy participates in the cult of the artificial by attempting to mask his sexuality through his use of make-up, costumes, and mannerisms, as Marjorie Garber suggests, the dandy is a major component in the existence of a "third transvestite sex" (10). The third sex, according to Garber, is a "mode of articulation, a way of describing a space of possibility. Three puts into question the idea of one: of identity, self-sufficiency, self-knowledge" (11). Her interest in transvestism derives from its ability to create "*a space of possibility structuring and confounding culture:* the disruptive element that intervenes, not just a category crisis of male and female, but the crisis of category itself" (17). His sexual ambiguity and his artificiality make the dandy an ideal representative of the age of Decadence except that the dandy seeks to avoid conformity by turning his back on the social system in his search for the original self. The Decadents, like the dandy, seek to distance themselves from Victorian standards and in consequence their behavior becomes more extreme including obsessions with perversity and drugs, as well as obsessions with death and the "perception of beauty in corruption and in death" (McMullen 40). Once again, the dandy's complex nature emerges since he can never completely distance himself from society because of his absolute dependence on it to provide him with an audience and with the social values which he will rebel against.

The dandy is always evolving to maintain a distinct status from the masses. The life of the dandy intertwines with beauty and art to the point that the dandy emulates art and seeks to transcend nature by employing artifice, which includes aspects of gender performance. When the aristocratic class resorts to complex and expensive costumes, the dandy distances himself from them by choosing simplicity and originality. On the other hand, when society dresses modestly, the dandy is extravagant. Fashion is one example of the dandy's dependency on society, and although he appears "disinterested" he constructs himself based on society's preferences. Baudelaire describes the effects of the dandy's lack of conformity as a feeling of "joy of astonishing others, and the proud satisfaction of never oneself being astonished" (799). The dandy's ability to shock and not be shocked himself increases his sense of superiority and distance from the crowd. He is a god-like figure who can make an impression on people's lives without enduring any retaliation. This shock defense allows the dandy to appear untouchable while having an emotional impact on the masses.

Elisa Glick points out there are two models of dandyism: one has the dandy celebrating in the aesthetics of commodity, while the second model features the dandy protesting against the "commodification of modern life" (131). Glick proves how these two models bind together with each other and with issues of capital. The dandy's awkward position leaves him, in Glick's words, "straddl[ing] the contradictions of capitalism" (131), just as he straddles the boundaries of gender and the public and private spheres. The contradictions, fluidity, mobility, and gender performances of the dandy place him in an unusual space between the spheres. The dandy is not caught between the spheres, but instead he attempts to create his own realm where he can exist apart from society and yet within his own space. This view of the dandy as participating in commodity and production through his love of the artificial and his simultaneous rejection of capitalism is a contradiction explored by Wilde. Money is not discussed in *The Picture of Dorian Gray* and yet it is a significant requirement for the dandy to maintain his lifestyle. The dandy finds himself in yet another privileged position since he is admitted into the wealthy societies, while he does not associate himself with them. It is because of his ability to penetrate into these restrictive spaces, like aristocratic society and the public sphere, that the dandy becomes an integral figure in any discussion of the permeability of the spheres.

The male community Wilde creates in *The Picture of Dorian Gray* suggests a space reserved for members who possess the ability to travel between the public and private spheres without incurring social consequences. The male characters in Wilde's text live double lives as an artist, a husband, and an innocent youth, while secretly participating in unspeakable acts in opium dens, and cavorting with thieves in Whitechapel. In the 1700s, men considered sodomites were also known as *mollies*, "a term that had first been applied to female prostitutes" (Trumbach 7). Molly Houses in London consisted of transvestite males, who were considered a third gender since they were neither male nor female since they "combined some characteristics from each of what society regarded as the two legitimate genders" (Trumbach 7). While Molly Houses were eventually destroyed, the London Clubland of the 1800s flourished with male-only clubs designed to emphasize "both the sensual and the masculine, celebrating [its] ostentatious virility" (Huggins and Mangan 202). Hyde and Dorian appear to participate in the more secretive aspects of these clubs raising suspicions of criminal activity. Like an evolved version of Dr. Jekyll, Wilde's characters do not need to create another identity to indulge in pleasure, instead the figure of the dandy succeeds in a double life which allows him to hold a prominent position in society while fulfilling secret desires without answering to a conscience or social punishment. There are many similarities between Stevenson's *The Strange Case of Dr. Jekyll and Mr. Hyde* and Wilde's work, including their use of the gothic, their preoccupation with the dual nature of men, and the ways in which these opposite identities can be reconciled. It is a complicated matter for Dr. Jekyll: he must create a potion, endure a disfiguring transformation, and maintain a strict separation between the two selves, while in Wilde's novel the dandy serves as an ideal candidate who can keep his own appearance, participate in secret activities, and still continue to be accepted in society. John Paul Riquelme argues in his essay, "Oscar Wilde's Aesthetic Gothic" that "[Lord Henry] Wotton is an avatar of Victor Frankenstein, who produces an ugly, destructive double of himself" (616). The suggestion that Lord Henry creates Dorian Gray as his monstrous double is problematic since the relationship between the men in Wilde's novel involves a more complex interdependence. Indeed Lord Henry intends to be to Dorian what he is to Basil Hallward. Lord Henry wishes to "dominate" Dorian (Wilde 36), not simply to live a double life through him, but to possess the same degree of power that Dorian holds over Basil. The complexity of the matter is intensified when Basil feels Dorian's power over him, and yet confesses that he put too much of himself in Dorian's painting (Wilde 11). Jeff Nunokawa comments on the interconnectedness of the male characters and suggests that "the expression of homosexual desire cancels, rather than clarifies the definition of the character through whom it is conducted" (313). This argument begins to take shape when the male characters' desires for each other subsume their individual identities so that they are universalized and are nowhere and everywhere at once, which is the ideal state for the dandy (Nunokawa 320). The distribution of power centers around Dorian and yet both Basil and Lord Henry claim him for their own purposes. This interconnectedness and cyclic power relationship remains within the community of men until Dorian begins to seek another type of power outside the male sphere. The gothic motif of doubling does occur in *The Picture of Dorian Gray*, except that with Wilde's choice of the figure of the dandy there is no longer a need for the Jekyll and Hyde personalities since the dandy encompasses both under one identity.

Secrecy is essential in both *Dr. Jekyll and Mr. Hyde* and *The Picture of Dorian Gray*, and yet the dandy does not need to separate public and private and unlike typical Victorian gentlemen, he is *expected* to follow his senses and indulge in pleasure—this is his nature. As Alan Sinfield points out, "The dandy figure serves Wilde's project because he has a secure cross-sex image, yet might anticipate, on occasion [...] an emergent same-sex identity [...] Wilde is exploiting the capacity of the image of the dandy to commute, without explicit commitment, between diverse sexualities" (73). Sinfield emphasizes how the dandy's ability to move between the sexes makes him ideal, but taken a step further Wilde also illustrates how possessing a diverse and ambiguous sexuality functions as a type of "passport" for the dandy allowing him the freedom to travel between the public and private realms. Sexual ambiguity marks the difference between Dr. Jekyll's need to create another identity in Hyde and the dandy's ability to simply be himself in order to have the best of both worlds. Having established that the nature of the dandy allows him to "commute" freely between the sexes and the spheres, it becomes clear that similar to other social spheres, Wilde's male community has its own requirements and expectations.

Dorian Gray's initiation into the male community involves surrendering himself body and soul. The monstrous transformation of Dorian's portrait fits with George E. Haggerty's description of eighteenth-century depictions of the sodomite:

> They were transformed into monsters to the degree that they threatened heteronormative culture with the dark, unknown otherness of sexual transgression [...]. Like hideous monsters, these creatures were constructed as figures of deformity in order to display outwardly the inner depravity their sexual interests were imagined to reflect [...]. The sodomite is a threat that comes from both without and within. He is the excremental non-ego and bloody identity, blended in this image of monstrosity. That is what makes his presence so uncannily tormenting [*Queer Gothic* 47].

Basil's painting captures Dorian's soul and Lord Henry seduces Dorian into accepting an "education" that aims to fulfill physical desires. There is something about Dorian that attracts both Basil and Lord Henry; for Basil it is his recognition of homosexual desire and for Lord Henry it is his need to "dominate" (Wilde 36) and "influence" (Wilde 24). In both cases, Dorian provides the blank slate of youth and beauty onto which Basil and Lord Henry inscribe themselves. John Addington Symonds examines the Dorians in Greek history and their approaches towards male love:

> It would appear that the lover was called Inspirer, at Sparta, while the youth he loved was named Hearer [...]. The lover taught, the hearer learned; and so from

man to man was handed down the tradition of heroism, the particular tone and temper of the state to which, in particular among the Greeks, the Dorians clung with obstinate pertinacity [13].

The Dorians emphasis on the institution of paiderastia is evoked in the novel through the education of Dorian within the male community. Lord Henry notices Dorian's darker quality when he refers to him as the "son of Love and Death" (Wilde 36). After hearing the "strange [...and] modern romance" (Wilde 35) of Dorian's parentage, which includes his mother's pursuit of passion leading to a hideous crime and her death in childbirth, Dorian reaches the pinnacle of attractiveness, as Wilde writes, "it posed the lad, made him more perfect as it were. Behind every exquisite thing that existed, there was something tragic" (Wilde 35).[1] Lord Henry appears enticed by Dorian's passionate history and his contradictory nature. It is Dorian's youthful and innocent beauty that is "perfect" to corrupt; the attraction here is Dorian's ability to represent at once love and death, innocence and crime. Without Lord Henry's "influence" Dorian would never fully represent these contradictory elements. It is with Lord Henry's education that Dorian is able to expand beyond this male community towards a life of crime and corruption.

Dorian's dandy status is taken a step further when he seeks to cross into the shadowy darkness of thieves, drugs, corruption, and blackmail. Eve Kosofsky Sedwick in *The Epistemology of the Closet* draws parallels between drug use in *Dr. Jekyll and Mr. Hyde* and *The Picture of Dorian Gray*: "drug addiction is both camouflage and an expression for the dynamics of same-sex desire and its prohibition: both books begin by looking like stories of erotic tension between men, and end up as cautionary tales of solitary substance abusers" (172). While both men inhabit the criminal world, their tale remains primarily one of an exploration of male-only communities. In both novels, the space filled with drugs and blackmail is a version of a male-centric private space, where private addictions and sexuality are worked out among men. Dorian's movement in the public sphere of the theater demonstrates his confusion of art and reality. Lord Henry represents the dandy in all his excess. Art and reality are made one and the same by Lord Henry, who considers everything in life as fulfilling a desire for pleasure, and he is aware of the constant theatricality of life, and the roles that people play. Dorian falls prey to Henry's corrupted influence and begins to blur the lines between art and life, which becomes most evident in his dealings with Sibyl Vane's suicide, where her life becomes a play and her roles as Ophelia, Juliet, Cordelia, and Desdemona replace her real identity. It is Lord Henry that makes this suggestion to Dorian after her death: "The girl never really lived, and so she has never really died [...]. The moment she touched actual life, she marred it, and it marred her, and so she passed away" (103). Sibyl's death becomes another act in a play, one she performs but does not actually experience. Henry's insistence that life imitates art leaves Dorian to believe that Sibyl's suicide represents the return of her artistic talent, which she lost when her love for Dorian became "real." Dorian worships Sibyl's artistic suicide performance and she regains a place in his heart because of it. The corrupted influence of Lord Henry on Dorian leads him into an underworld of crime, and unspeakable acts. This movement between the public appearance of the dandy seen at social events, concerts, and the theater differs greatly with his dark private world. Once again, the dandy's lifestyle proves to blend the ever-present dichotomy between the pubic and private spheres.

Lord Henry succeeds in dominating Dorian and Wilde's novel through the typical dandy position of being both inside and outside the text. Joseph Bristow in his essay, "Wilde, Dorian Gray, and Gross Indecency," examines how *The Picture of Dorian Gray*

> explores various structures and theories of deviant desire to witness the formation of Dorian's 'Greek' sensibility [...the novel] moves from the same-sexual interests of narcissism implicit in the painting, to Lord Henry's misogyny, and finally to Dorian's outlandish experiments [...] to examine how homosexual desire might be articulated [57].

Lord Henry's "education" of Dorian leaves him in a state between life and death, where he no longer feels but still indulges in his desires, and where he can no longer distinguish life from art. According to Bristow, Lord Henry may represent "the worst of Walter Pater's materialism" (61), but he goes against Greek ethics when he gives Dorian the poisonous book (Wilde 125). This book marks a significant change in Dorian and leads to his downfall. As Kenneth Womack states, the book is "[e]ssentially a handbook for decadent living, the volume—a yellow, paper-covered French novel—influences Dorian's progress toward spiritual and ethical ruin" (176). Lord Henry gives the book to Dorian as part of his "education," but the book seems to have a more powerful effect on the young beauty. Julia Kent explores the connections between the yellow book and J.-K. Huysmans's *À Rebours* in relation to English and French literature:

> Des Esseintes, the hero of the yellow book, and Dorian Gray are enthralled to an exhausting search for new forms of consumption. And throughout the episode

on the yellow book, Dorian is himself turned quite literally into an object, in the sense that he is "poisoned by a book" rather than remaining actively in control of his own self-development. Even while Wilde values the French novel's capacity to challenge models of real desire, then, he also attributes to the French novel some of the most problematic aspects of a self-fashioning based on consumption. In marking the foreign text as distinctly French, Wilde thus also takes distance from the particular problems of self-fashioning that complicate Dorian's power to fashion himself [11].

The yellow book is mostly responsible for Dorian's movement away from the male community of Basil and Lord Henry towards a world of corruption and crime. Although Lord Henry has obviously read the book and yet is not lead towards darkness, Dorian falls prey to its influence. Why does it have this effect on Dorian? As in past scenes, including his affair with Sibyl Vane, Dorian easily confuses life and art and the book provides the ultimate example, as Wilde writes, "And, indeed, the whole book seemed to [Dorian] to contain the story of his own life, written before he lived it" (127). Dorian's life mimics that of the poisonous book making his life a living art. Lord Henry recognizes Dorian as the ideal representative of the fin de siècle, when he says, "You are the type of what the age is searching for, and what it is afraid it has found. I am so glad that you have never done anything, never carved a statue, or painted a picture, or produced anything outside of yourself! Life has been your art" (217). The book provides Dorian with the ability to make his life into an art form, which is the ideal for the Aesthetic movement. Whereas Lord Henry has shaped his student by providing him with an aesthetic education, he does not suffer Dorian's severe fate. Dorian takes this education too far with the help of the yellow book and decides to pursue corruption by leaving the community of Basil and Lord Henry.

Dorian realizes that his new corrupted and dark desires can only be played out in the private sphere and have no place in the public. Expanding beyond the male community of Basil and Lord Henry into the community of corruption results in Dorian losing his dandy status and adopting that of a criminal and murderer. Dorian experiences a loss of freedom when he seeks to penetrate other worlds. Eventually Dorian is excluded from the realm of the public and he loses his dandy status as a result, as Wilde writes,

It was rumoured that [Dorian] had been seen brawling with foreign sailors ... in distant parts of Whitechapel, and that he consorted with thieves and coiners and knew the mysteries of their trade. His extraordinary absences became notorious, and, when he used to reappear again in society, men would whisper to each other

in corners, or pass him with a sneer, or look at him with cold searching eyes, as
though they were determined to discover his secret [141–42].

Dorian adopts the criminal world as his own and sacrifices his position
as dandy in the public sphere. He is on the outside without the dandy's
ability to reenter this male community. His "reappearance" in society
results in his banishment through whispers, and rumors that suggest
that he is no longer trustworthy and that he protects his secrets from
this male community rather than participating in their own shared secret.
Instead, Dorian is forced by the members of this male community to
retreat and live out his mysterious pleasures in the shadowy world of
the private, which is symbolized by the portrait of Dorian that remains
veiled and hidden.

The degeneration of the dandy links him with the monstrous Gothic
Other, since he raises similar anxieties regarding sexuality, space, identity, and race. The dandy's greed and self-commodification is reminiscent
of late nineteenth-century stereotypes and caricatures of the Jewish man.
Dennis Denisoff explains how the Svengali's caricature "was a common one
in late–Victorian England, where an assumed physical difference between
Jews and gentiles made the Jewish man a surrogate for all men considered
to be threateningly abnormal. Du Maurier's novel [...sustains] the common association of Jews with avarice" (*Aestheticism* 84). As Dennis Denisoff states, "the late–Victorian dandy-aesthete and the Jew [are] virtually
interchangeable stereotypes signifying cultural degeneracy" (*Aestheticism*
84). Denisoff calls attention to Du Maurier's drawings of Wildean characters in 1880, one year after Wilde settles in London. The dandy-aesthete
becomes a caricature possessing Wilde's own physical qualities. When Du
Maurier turns to the novel, he caricaturizes Svengali using similar physical
traits: "scraggly, black hair, mischievous, heavy-lidded eyes, svelte body,
and comparatively foppish sartorial inclinations" (Denisoff, *Aestheticism*
89). Indeed, as Denisoff remarks, "this man is Du Maurier's *Punch* dandy-aesthete taken to a derogatory extreme" (*Aestheticism* 89). *Trilby* and
*Daniel Deronda* explore anti–Semitic sentiment and the immigrant artist in comparison with their English counterparts. Svengali, described as
an "incubus" (Du Maurier 93) and "powerful demon" (Du Maurier 92), is
extremely anti–English. His Jewish heritage raises many instances of anti–
Semitism throughout the novel, but there is also the question of Jewish
blood being linked with creativity and art. Svengali's music is praised by
the narrator when he describes, "Svengali and Gecko made music together,
divinely ... these bars of beauty and meaning! ... gypsy dances, Hungarian

love-plaints, things little known out of eastern Europe ... till the Laird and Taffy were almost as wild in their enthusiasm as Little Billee's silent enthusiasm too deep for speech" (Du Maurier12). Throughout *Trilby* there exists a struggle between admiration for the creativity and beauty Svengali is able to create and the stereotypical anti–Semitic references: "[his] Jewish aspect, well-featured but sinister ... [with] thick, heavy, languid, lustreless black hair fell down behind his ears to his shoulders, in a musician-like way that is so offensive to the normal Englishman" (Du Maurier 11). Klesmer in Eliot's *Daniel Deronda* shares a similar description with Svengali as musicians: "his mane of hair floating backward in massive inconsistency with the chimney-pot hat ... his tall thin figure clad in a way which, not being strictly English, was all the worse for its apparent emphasis of intention" (*DD* 88). In both cases, the foreign artists are accepted based on their creative skills, but any attempt to infiltrate the social structures on another basis, such as marriage, is quickly put to an end. As Eliot points out Klesmer's harmless eccentricities transform once he becomes Mrs. Arrowpoint's prospective son-in-law, "while Klesmer was seen in the light of a patronized musician, his peculiarities were picturesque and acceptable; but to see him by a sudden flash in the light of her son-in-law gave her a burning sense of what the world would say" (*DD* 209). Just as Svengali is admired for his music, its Eastern influences are later criticized as evil: "the mysterious East! The poisonous East—birthplace and home of an ill wind that blows nobody good" (Du Maurier 282). Klesmer's mysterious background marks him as Other, as Mrs. Arrowpoint describes him as, "nobody knows what—a gypsy, a Jew, a mere bubble of the earth" (*DD* 210). It would appear that the English characters are able to accept Svengali's foreignness as long as he is creating something beautiful, like music.

Through art and genius, the Other is accepted into English society, but there are strict limitations to their movements and freedoms. *Trilby*'s Little Billee is an example of the right mixture of Jewish and English blood. His "tinge" of Jewish blood makes him the successful artist that he eventually becomes, as the narrator explains this precious gift, "just a tinge of that strong, sturdy, irrepressible, indomitable, indelible blood which is of such a priceless value" (Du Maurier 6–7). Deronda's background demands that he possess the spirit of the performer, according to Eliot's cast of characters, and despite his refusal of the feminized artistic world Sir Hugo introduces to him in childhood, Deronda eventually becomes a performer as discussed in Chapter Three of this book. Deronda's Jewish heritage also seems to account for his performance skills, although he represses it from childhood. Denisoff explains how Du Maurier links the aesthete-dandy with representations of the Other from his cartoons to novel:

in contrast to his earlier cartoons' parodic inscription of ethical deviancy onto a feminized and homosexualized male body, Du Maurier's novel *Trilby* presents such unconventionality as a sign of possible creative genius. The author still denigrates artistic egoism and self-commodification, but in this text he does so through an anti–Semitic depiction of the mesmerizing musician Svengali [*Aestheticism* 83–4].

This tendency to associate the dandy with the Other clearly reveals his descent, like Dorian who is pushed to the fringes of society where he must conduct his business in secrecy. Dorian's portrait, like the art that caricaturizes Wilde and Svengali, is a mingling of artistic ability and degeneration.

By the fin-de-siècle, the bachelor has moved closer to his gothic counterpart–The Other, as depicted through examples like Daniel Deronda, Dr. Jekyll and Mr. Hyde, Dorian Gray, and Svengali. While Svengali's methods of hypnotism are clearly more tortuous and cruel as compared to Deronda's delicate machinations, they both succeed in possessing the female body and instilling their own values, artistic skills, and anxieties. Svengali is able to corrupt and violate Trilby with his language and speech. He distorts her name and her identity, and then proceeds to describe her in fragments as he says, "He would adore you too, for your beautiful bones; he would like to count them one by one ... and ach! what a beautiful skeleton you will make! And very soon, too, because you do not smile on your madly loving Svengali" (Du Maurier 92). His wooing consists of threats and a dissection of her physical self, into bones, a mouth, and essentially a corpse, ready to be his tool for finally gaining the success he has been craving. Deronda, uses a similar technique as he critically observes Gwendolen at the gambling table, asking himself, "was she beautiful or not beautiful?" (*DD* 3). The reader follows his scrutinizing gaze as he traces, "the movements of the figure, of the arms and hands ... return[ing] to the face" (*DD* 5). Gwendolen falls under the impression that, "he was measuring her and looking down on her as an inferior ... examining her as a specimen of a lower order" (*DD* 5–6). Like Mesmer, Svengali and Deronda employ the discourse of the hypnotist. Svengali speaks with confidence, as if he has the ability to know the future. He describes to Trilby nightmarish visions of her future, when he reprimands her for not listening to him, and he describes a slab of brass that she will find herself asleep on and "over the middle of you will be a little leather apron, and over your head a little brass tap, and all day long and all night the cold water shall trickle" (Du

Maurier 75). These elaborate descriptions work to convince Trilby of her ultimate doom, even without being completely under his spell.

In a similar fashion, it does not take Deronda very long to convince Gwendolen that she can no longer trust her own instincts, as Eliot writes, "[Gwendolen's] confidence in herself and her destiny had turned into remorse and dread; she trusted neither herself nor her future" (*DD* 368). Deronda succeeds in making her feel like a child, who is completely dependent on him for her thoughts and actions. In *Trilby*, the Laird sums up the typical nineteenth-century reputation of a mesmerist when he says, "they get you into their power, and just make you do any blessed thing they please—lie, murder, steal—anything! and kill yourself into the bargain when they've done with you!" (Du Maurier 52). Trilby remains under Svengali's control even after being mesmerized: "she was haunted by the memory of Svengali's big eyes ... and his dirty fingertips on her face; and her fear and her repulsion grew together" (Du Maurier 53). Despite Trilby's efforts to fight him off he has entered her mind and "like an incubus she dreamed of him oftener than she dreamed of Taffy, the Laird, or even Little Billee!" (Du Maurier 93). In addition, there exists a sinister quality to Deronda's control over Gwendolen, as Eliot writes, "[Gwendolen's] anger towards Deronda had changed into a superstitious dread—due, perhaps, to the coercion he had exercised over her thought—lest that first interference of his in her life might foreshadow some future influence" (*DD* 278). Although Gwendolen makes it clear that she desires Deronda's advice, she is overwhelmed by his power over her. The struggling, the singing, the mesmerism all have their toll on Trilby as she wastes away after each performance. Like Dorian's Sibyl Vane, Gwendolen and Trilby become the artistic canvas for the dandy-aesthete. By taking control over these female victims, the dandy functions as artist by practicing the aesthetic principle of life imitating art—they take possession of the female body and, like a puppeteer, perform the feminine. In addition to having his own feminine qualities, the fin-de-siècle dandy crosses boundaries by enlisting female characters to perform according to their expectations of femininity. In these cases, female characters are convinced, through a form of hypnotism, that they can no longer rely upon their own feminine instincts and must succumb to the dandy's vision of themselves. The dandy-hypnotist, like his vampiric counterpart, plays on Victorian anxieties of the Other, including their ability to infiltrate minds and bodies rendering their victims helpless and at their mercy.

Although Trilby's voice is admired for its strength, it is only when mesmerized that she is able to create the ideal sound. Trilby is considered a "singing-machine—an organ to play upon—an instrument of music ... a flexible flageolet of flesh and blood—a voice and nothing more—just the unconscious voice that Svengali sang with" (Du Maurier 299). Trilby is used as a tool or medium; she appears as empty like Svengali's flageolet that only makes beautiful music when he blows through it. Nina Auerbach in "Magi and Maidens" suggests that Trilby is not simply empty only to be filled by the male artist, instead the mesmerized woman "reveals a sort of infinitely unfolding magic that is quite different from the formulaic spells of the men" (284). Auerbach's point holds true with Gwendolen; although, she is being used as a method of therapy for Deronda's own insecurities, as Eliot notes, "he was uttering thoughts which he had used for himself in moments of painful meditation" (DD 383), Gwendolen eventually breaks free of Deronda's misguided advice to "turn your fear into your safeguard" (*DD* 388), as she begins to plot her escape through her husband's murder. As is the case throughout *Daniel Deronda*, Gwendolen's thoughts remain unacted and the novel's ending is unclear about the final condition of her psychological state.

   *Dorian Gray* and *Trilby* explore the delicate balance between spectator and sympathizer, as Athena Vrettos explains,

> the choice, as Du Maurier presents it, is either to become a voyeur who participates in Svengali's scopic manipulations of Trilby by watching her performance from a stance of aesthetic distance and sexual desire, or to overidentify with the heroine and become feminized, indeed hypnotized, by her performance into a state of emotional collapse [103].

While Du Maurier suggests that one must choose, the dandy balances between performer and voyeur simultaneously. The dandy's unique position between the spheres carries through into every aspect of his life, including his sexuality, desires, and love of beauty and pleasure. *The Picture of Dorian Gray* contributes to yet another element of the public and private, since it became integral to Wilde's own real-life drama. Wilde's double life puts him in a similar position to that of Dorian, as Susanne Schmid notes, "the literary hide-and-seek is involved when an author creates literary characters resembling him, thereby introducing a new dimension to the game of public vs. private spheres" (84).

   *The Picture of Dorian Gray* was used against Wilde during his trials in 1895 where art and reality, and the public and private were blurred. The cross-examiner read passages from the novel, which focused on Lord Henry's deliberate corruption of Dorian. It was not long before an analogy was made between Lord Henry and Wilde, and Wilde's lover Alfred Douglas and the young Dorian Gray. Ed Cohen describes the significant role the newspapers played in the trials. He notes how the newspapers would omit passages from *The Picture of Dorian Gray* that were read aloud in the trial so that "instead of appearing to refer to the characters in his novel, the references to "the artist" seem to evoke Wilde himself" (162). This omission served to fuel the confusion of spectators who believed the passages from the novel were instead references to Wilde's relationship with Douglas. The use of *The Picture of Dorian Gray* in Wilde's trials ironically serves to maintain the constant intermingling between life and art that is such a prevalent theme in the novel. Wilde ended up in court in order to prosecute his lover's father, the Marquess of Queensbury, for libel. Queensbury had hunted Wilde down after finding his son's love notes. Tracking him to the Albemarle Club in February 1895, Queensbury left a note on which he wrote, "To Oscar Wilde, posing Somdomite" (Cocks 140). Once in court, it became obvious that the tables had turned. Queensbury had gathered an enormous amount of evidence against Wilde's lifestyle, including his novel *The Picture of Dorian Gray*. Queensbury succeeded in bringing down his prosecutor and Wilde was faced with a criminal trial, where he was eventually convicted of gross indecency on 25 May 1895 and sentenced to two years in prison (Cocks 141). In addition to his own writings being used against him, the prosecution brought as evidence Douglas' poem "Two Loves" written in 1891 that mentioned "the love that dare not speak its name." It is Wilde's response to the prosecution's question, "what did it mean?" that became his famous triumph during the trial. As Wilde states:

> It is that deep, spiritual affection that is as pure as it is perfect [...]. There is nothing unnatural about it. It is intellectual, and it repeatedly exists between an elder and a younger man, when the elder man has intellect, and the younger man has all the joy, hope and glamour of life before him. That it should be so the world does not understand. The world mocks at it and sometimes puts one in the pillory for it [Ellmann 435].[2]

The struggle for position within the private and public spheres from the mid-to-late nineteenth century marks a crucial rethinking of the concepts of masculinity and femininity. The recognition of dual natures sparks the domestic man's infiltration of the private sphere. He begins to incorporate the feminized private sphere into his own lifestyle, spaces and relationships. Feminine performance allows the domestic man to mimic his female counterparts. His tendency to perform links him with the dandy. The bachelor eventually creates an exclusively male private sphere that provides him with the advantages of "family life" without a female influence. Finally, the bachelor creates his own space based on the intermingling of private and public, while embracing his ambivalent sexuality.

Art, beauty, the body, gender performance all figure prominently in the nature of the dandy as proven through examples from Wilde's novel. The dandy is a contradiction that problematizes definitions of the public and private spheres; he has no space, but he insists on a multiplicity of spheres, and as such provides a suitable conclusion for this book. As Lady Narborough observes in the epigraph to this chapter, in his fin-de-siècle incarnation, the bachelor behaves as a married man; he has succeeded in achieving his own space without a female companion. In his final manifestation, the domestic man becomes the homosexual, who achieves both public and private spaces among men. The dandy functions as commodity while rejecting conformity, he is the spectator and the performer, and he lives inside and outside the spheres. He seeks out the masses but then he becomes distant, and cold. His dichotomous nature makes the figure of the dandy essential to the study of the spheres, and calls attention to the role of gender performance in his mutability and fluidity as he navigates freely between them.

# Conclusion:
# The Reconfigured Sphere

While the domesticated bachelor has been performing femininity for decades, he remains invested in refashioning the existing conventions, rather than reinventing himself. The dandy-aesthete's sexual ambiguity and his artificiality links him to the domesticated bachelor, except the dandy seeks to avoid conformity by turning his back on the social system in search of his original self. At the same, both the domesticated bachelor and the dandy can never completely distance themselves from society because of their absolute dependence on it to provide them with an audience and with the social values they will subsequently rebel against.

Although this book illustrates moments where the domesticated bachelor can be considered representative of the Other, in terms of race, sexual identity, and violence, this is where the dandy-aesthete departs from his predecessor. The dandy-aesthete's link with homosexuality categorizes him as sexual Other and therefore he removes himself from the definition of the domesticated bachelor, as George E. Haggerty explains in his description of eighteenth-century depictions of the sodomite:

> They were transformed into monsters to the degree that they threatened heteronormative culture with the dark, unknown otherness of sexual transgression [...]. Like hideous monsters, these creatures were constructed as figures of deformity in order to display outwardly the inner depravity their sexual interests were imagined to reflect [...]. The sodomite is a threat that comes from both without and within. He is the excremental non-ego and bloody identity, blended in this image of monstrosity. That is what makes his presence so uncannily tormenting [*Queer Gothic* 47].

The bachelor's movement towards representing the homosexual is most noticeable in Stevenson's *Dr. Jekyll and Mr. Hyde* where Hyde's indescribable deformity is evocative of his association with the homosexual figure of the *fin-de-siècle*. In defining the domesticated bachelor proving homosexuality is not a priority; instead, this book is concerned with his ability to remain sexually ambiguous while avoiding becoming the Other, as Roper and Tosh explain, "[i]n their conscious attempts to change themselves, heterosexual men may have shed more light on the personal constraints of masculinity in the domestic sphere, than on their power in society" (12). The *fin-de-siècle* marks the end of this inconspicuous version of the bachelor. In addition to being ostracized as a homosexual figure, the dandy's greed and self-commodification is reminiscent of late nineteenth-century stereotypes and caricatures of the Jewish man. In his *fin-de-siècle* incarnation, the bachelor behaves as a married man without a female companion.

In domesticated bachelor narratives, conclusions problematize the bachelor's status in society. *Shirley, Lady Audley's Secret,* and *Daniel Deronda* end in complicated marriages that suggest the bachelor must follow social norms that require that he eventually take a wife, except he is not forced to completely abandon his bachelor lifestyle. In *Shirley*, newlyweds Robert and Caroline are joined in domestic bliss by her recently revealed mother. Shirley and Louis's marriage attempts to put the masculinized female character and the domesticated bachelor back into their proper places. In *Lady Audley's Secret*, Robert eventually marries Clara, but they live together in a remote cottage with her brother George, Robert's bachelor obsession. A similar triangle concludes *Daniel Deronda*, where Deronda and Mirah's marriage is shared with Mordecai. Here, Deronda satisfies his desire for the beauty of a woman, while maintaining his idealized "male love" for Mordecai. These narrative conclusions demonstrate the domesticated bachelor's success at maintaining an appearance of social conformity while fulfilling his desire for homosocial bonds. These problematic conclusions beg the question, does the private sphere disappear when the family is not present? In *Dr. Jekyll and Mr. Hyde* the domesticated bachelor begins to reveal himself as the Other by no longer masking his inclination to rid himself entirely of female companionship; as a result, he is severely punished as represented by Hyde's suicide. Within the exclusively male community, the narrative conclusion struggles to find a solution for the bachelor when marrying is not an option.

By proving that the bachelor possesses the "latch-key" allowing him the freedom to move between the public and private spheres and eventually reconfigure the domestic so that he ultimately exiles the ghastly spectacle of the female presence, this book exposes the fragility of the concept

# Conclusion

of gender roles in the nineteenth century. The domesticated bachelor, unlike his socially deviant public image, seeks the solace of the domestic space increasingly neglected by women searching for opportunities in the public sphere. Louis, the tutor, finds relief performing femininity within the private sphere, while Shirley as her alias Captain Keeldar protects the house from the rioting workers. Robert Moore eventually acknowledges his dual natures, while Caroline contemplates working alongside him in his counting-house. Robert Audley's obsession with questioning his aunt's legitimacy as Lady of Audley Court results in his idealizing the domestic and taking George as his companion. While Grandcourt and Deronda are both enthralled by Gwendolen because she is a challenge to domesticate, both men spend most of the novel instructing her on feminine performance revealing their own inclinations towards acting and the domestic. Although there is no female counterpart in Stevenson's all-male community, Hyde is created, who, rather than simply representing Dr. Jekyll's private and therefore feminine persona, is able to move between both spheres with more ease than Jekyll himself. In defining the domesticated bachelor, this book reveals the fluidity between the spheres and nineteenth-century concepts of masculinity and femininity. It is the blatant disregard of the domestic by masculinized female characters that initiates the bachelor's desire to experience the domestic on his own terms, and eventually reconfigure the private sphere into an exclusively male space.

# Chapter Notes

## Introduction

1. The term "New Woman" was coined by British journalist Sarah Grand in an 1894 article for the *North American Review*. Overall, she represented women's rebellion against the stringent norms of the Victorian middle class and especially those of the institution of marriage. Novelists writing in the 1890s, such as Mona Caird, Emma Brooke, Sarah Grand, Olive Schreiner, Grant Allen, George Gissing, and Thomas Hardy explored in particular the New Woman's rejection of marriage for sexual freedom or her preference of intellectual stimulation over physical desires (Caine 136). Although the New Woman broke with conventional female roles, it was only Mona Caird, in *The Daughters of Danaus*, who went so far as to challenge "maternal instinct" (Weeks 166). Elaine Showalter in *Sexual Anarchy: Gender and Culture at the Fin de Siècle* explores male anxiety surrounding the New Woman and the interplay between the sexes on issues of sexual freedom, marriage, and education.

2. For examples of women's writing in the 1890s, see Carolyn Christensen Nelson's anthology *A New Woman Reader: Fiction, Articles, Drama of the 1890s*, and for literary criticism written by women see Solveig C. Robinson's anthology *A Serious Occupation: Literary Criticism by Victorian Women Writers*. Both collections include works by women pushing beyond the boundaries of their proper spheres into the "male" realm of literary criticism and exploring sexuality and the institution of marriage in their fiction. Elaine Showalter in *A Literature of Their Own: British Women Novelists from Brontë to Lessing*

provides a thorough examination of women's literary tradition through the nineteenth century into the early twentieth century, including the brief but momentous interval of New Women's writing.

3. An early example of the emasculated and satirized dandy is "effeminate dandy" and "delicate fop" Witwoud from William Congreve's *The Way of the World* (1700), who fails at his attempts to match the more courtly and witty bachelor, Mirabell.

4. Thomas W. Laqueur in *Solitary Sex: A Cultural History of Masturbation* explains how "Masturbation *is* excess [...]. The onanist is never satisfied but wants to do it more and more; the urge to masturbate always exceeds any natural urge" (237).

5. Brontë's *Shirley* combines the plight of the working class and bourgeois women for recognition within the public sphere.

6. Works that challenge the ideology of separate spheres: Dalton's *Engendering the Republic of Letters: Reconnecting Public and Private Spheres in Eighteenth-Century Europe*; Beach's *Women, Business and Finance in Nineteenth-century Europe: Rethinking Separate Spheres*; Davidson's *No More Separate Spheres!: A Next Wave American Studies Reader*; Kerber's "Beyond Roles, Beyond Spheres: Thinking about Gender in the Early Republic," Klein's "Gender and the Public/Private Distinction in the Eighteenth Century: Some Questions about Evidence and Analytic Procedure"; Vickery's "Golden Age to Separate Spheres?: A Review of the Categories and Chronology of English Women's History"; Boxer's *Connecting Spheres: Women in the Western World, 1500–Present*; Nicholson's *Gender and History: The*

*Limits of Social Theory in the Age of the Family*; Pateman's *The Sexual Contract*.

7. For more on the British women's suffrage movement see: Fletcher's *Women's Suffrage in the British Empire: Citizenship, Nation, and Race*; Ramelson's *The Petticoat Rebellion: A Century of Struggle for Women's Rights*; Pankhurst's *The Suffragette Movement: An Intimate Account of Persons and Ideals*.

8. For more on the serial versus volume-format publications of *Lady Audley's Secret*, as well as the several queries which appeared during its run in the *London Journal* on the law of divorce, separation and legitimacy, see Andrew King's *The London Journal, 1845–83: Periodicals, Production and Gender*.

9. The use of industrial discourse to describe masculine desire is also discussed in Chapter Two on Brontë's *Shirley* when Robert states, "the machinery of all my nature; the whole enginery of this human mill: the boiler which I take to be the heart, is fit to burst" (496), as a means to explain his passionate feelings for Caroline.

10. Grace Moore explains in "Something to Hyde: The 'Strange Preference' of Henry Jekyll," how "with middle-class men often waiting until their thirties to marry, concerns extended to the continence of the bachelor" (150).

## Chapter Two

1. For more on theatricality in *Shirley* see J. Jeffrey Franklin's *Serious Play: The Cultural Form of the Nineteenth-Century Realist Novel*.

2. Brontë's *Shirley* was published one year after the defeat of Chartism, but is back-dated to the Luddite events of 1812, as Terry Eagleton notes, "the contemporary class-struggle was too fraught and precarious an issue to render it an ideal context for such an assured outcome" (45).

3. Brontë's references to the Luddites in *Shirley*, are attributed to her father's memories of the Luddite Riot in 1812 (Bentley 103).

4. Sally Shuttleworth also argues that there is a link to be made between the middle-class women in the novel and the "unemployed worker" (183).

5. For more on the third sex see: Willy's *The Third Sex*.

6. See Peschier's *Nineteenth-Century Anti-Catholic Discourses* for more on Brontë's religious references in her novels.

## Chapter Three

1. For more on the merging of the public and private spheres through the angel in the house, see Elizabeth Langland's "Nobody's Angels: Domestic Ideology and Middle-Class Women in the Victorian Novel."

2. See Water's quote at the beginning of this chapter.

3. For more on the impact of evolutionary theory on popular literary works of the Victorian and Edwardian periods, see Lisa Hopkins' *Giants of the Past: Popular Fictions and the Idea of Evolution*.

4. See James Eli Adams' *Dandies and Desert Saints: Styles of Masculinity* for an in-depth analysis of figures of the dandy and the prophet as differing models of masculinity.

5. In *Disease, Desire, and the Body in Victorian Women's Popular Novels*, Pamela Gilbert examines how love functions as disease and infection in *Lady Audley's Secret*.

6. For more on the effects of Marriage Acts on domestic ideology see Lisa O'Connell's "Marriage Acts: Stages in the Transformation of Modern Nuptial Culture," and Mary Poovey's *Uneven Developments: The Ideological Work of Gender in Mid-Victorian England*.

7. For more on Robert's depiction of women as violent, see Rosenman's article "'Mimic Sorrows': Masochism and the Gendering of Pain in Victorian Melodrama."

8. See Langland's chapter "Gendered Geographies" in *Telling Tales* for more on the effects of the Enclosure Acts of the late-eighteenth and early-nineteenth centuries on the landscape of Victorian England, issues of gender, and class in determining spaces, as well as an analysis of the asylum imagery surrounding

descriptions of Audley Court. For an analysis of setting, including the asylum imagery associated with Audley Court, and the ways in which *Lady Audley's Secret* "may still be struggling with the legacy of the Gothic tradition" (191), see also Chiara Briganti's "Gothic Maidens and Sensation Women: Lady Audley's Journey from the Ruined Mansion to the Madhouse."

9. For more on insanity trials see Ruth Harris' *Murders and Madness: Medicine, Law and Society in the Fin de Siècle*, and for specific cases from the Old Bailey Courthouse from 1760–1843, see Joel Peter Eigen's *Witnessing Insanity: Madness and Mad-Doctors*. See Daniel N. Robinson's *Wild Beast and Idle Humours: The Insanity Defense from Antiquity to the Present*, and Melling and Forsythe's collection on *Insanity, Institutions and Society, 1800–1914: A Social History of Madness in Comparative Perspective* for more on the history of insanity and asylums in the nineteenth century. Frank Mort's *Dangerous Sexualities: Medico-moral Politics in England Since 1830* examines the power dynamics between female sexuality and professional masculinity in the roles of the patient and doctor.

## Chapter Four

1. Some other novels that associate the actress with the fallen woman include Sibyl Vane in Oscar Wilde's *The Picture of Dorian Gray*, Flora in Mary Elizabeth Braddon's *A Lost Eden*, Anne in Wilkie Collins' *Man and Wife*, and Magdalen in *No Name*.

2. For more on Eliot and evolutionary theory see Nancy L. Paxton's *George Eliot and Herbert Spencer: Feminism, Evolutionism, and the Reconstruction of Gender*.

3. See John Plotz's *Portable Property: Victorian Culture on the Move* (2008), for more on the "value" of Victorian possessions and the instability between fungibles and relics, including a chapter on George Eliot.

4. In her chapter "*Daniel Deronda* and Too Much Literature," Gallagher seeks to explain how the "fear of overwriting became an overwritten novel" (*Body Eco-*

*nomic* 120). In addition to citing some of Eliot's personal anxieties, Gallagher also reveals the influence of psychologist Alexander Bain on Eliot's motivation to write *Daniel Deronda*.

5. For more on Leavis and *Daniel Deronda* see John M. Picker's "George Eliot and the Sequel Question," Claudia L. Johnson, "F. R. Leavis: The 'Great Tradition' of the English Novel and the Jewish Part," and Richard Storer's "Leavis and 'Gwendolen Harleth.'"

6. For positive reviews on the character of Gwendolen see *The Academy*, 5 February 1876, which states, "Gwendolen's individuality is established [...] by some personal traits that are not commonly supposed to be associated with the general type of character" (Holmstrom 126). R. H. Hutton writing for *The Spectator*, 29 July 1876, notes how Gwendolen "rises to the dignity of tragedy when she passes into the tragic scenes" (Holmstrom 136). *The Examiner*, 2 September 1876 remarks on Gwendolen's function as an example to young girls to "lift them into a higher conception of their duties and destinies" (Holmstrom 137), and yet as Blackwood confessed, "I shall not be able to help feeling for her" (Haight, *GE Letters* 144–5).

7. See Eliot's letter to Mrs. Harriet Beecher Stowe, 2 October 1876: "this is better than the laudation of readers who cut the book into scraps and talk of nothing but Gwendolen" (Haight, *GE Letters* 290).

8. Monica F. Cohen in *Professional Domesticity in the Victorian Novel: Women, Work and Home* examines how Eliot insists on using the home as a "representation of universality." Cohen elaborates on the increasing tendency for conservative Victorian "feminists" to expand "the female private sphere by collapsing politics into drawing-room sociability" (157), a theory that Eliot considers problematic.

9. In *The Figure of Theater: Shaftesbury, Defoe, Adam Smith, and George Eliot*, David Marshall records Gwendolen's entrance into the theatrical world as the moment she meets Grandcourt (201), and her "public debut" takes place at Sir Hugo's "grand dance" on New Year's Eve (206).

10. For more on female hysteria and

asylums see Showalter's *The Female Mal-ady: Women, Madness, and English Cul-ture, 1830–1980.*

11. Jeff Nunokawa suggests that mate-rial property in the novel represents a certain mastery over its owner, as in the example of Deronda retrieving Gwendo-len's necklace from the pawnshop. This act puts Gwendolen in his debt. As Nunokawa explains, "the alienation of property is an irreversible act, at once the realization and termination of ownership's potence" (85). This is represented in Grandcourt's feel-ings of "imperfect mastery" (*DD* 297) over Lydia Glasher when she refuses to return his diamonds.

12. Jacob Press in "Same-Sex Unions in Modern Europe: *Daniel Deronda, Alt-neuland,* and the Homoerotics of Jewish Nationalism," analyzes the role of the marked body, through Deronda's circum-cision, in relation to societal alienation.

13. For more on the nineteenth-century scientific approaches to gender and the brain see Rachel Malane's *Sex in Mind: The Gendered Brain in Nineteenth-Century Literature and Mental Sciences.* Malane points out how the "gendering of emotion as female and intellect as male became the base of more detailed discussions about the sexes' cerebral function" (23) during the mid–nineteenth century.

14. For more on the relationship be-tween religious mysticism and Victorian identity in the novel, see Sarah Willburn's essay "Possessed Individualism in George Eliot's *Daniel Deronda.*"

15. For more on Victorian marriages and the law see James A. Hammerton's "Victorian Marriage and the Law of Mat-rimonial Cruelty," and Roderick Phillips' *Putting Asunder: A History of Divorce in Western Society.*

## Chapter Five

1. The dandy-aesthete will be discussed further in the Conclusion.

2. See Ed Block, Jr.'s "James Sully, Evo-lutionary Psychology, and Late Victorian Gothic Fiction."

3. See Stephen Heath's "Psychopathia Sexualis: Stevenson's *Strange Case.*"

4. See Katherine Bailey Linehan's "'Closer Than a Wife': The Strange Case of Dr. Jekyll's Significant Other."

5. Mark Kanzer's "The Self-Analytic Literature of Robert Louis Stevenson."

6. See Elaine Showalter's *Sexual Anar-chy: Gender, Culture at the Fin de Siècle.*

7. Traditionally, the female functions as spectacle submitting to the gaze of the male spectator. Judith Butler in *Bodies That Matter* and *Gender Trouble* examines gender performance and the role of the body in gender construction. Mary Russo analyzes the Gothic trope of female as gro-tesque spectacle in *The Female Grotesque: Risk, Excess and Modernity.*

8. Daniel L. Wright in "'The Prison-house of My Disposition': A Study of the Psychology of Addiction in *Dr. Jekyll and Mr. Hyde*" claims that the novella is "not just a quaint experiment in gothic terror but Victorian literature's premiere reve-lation, intended or not, of the etiology of chronic chemical addiction, its character and effects" (263). Wright links Jekyll's drinking of the potion to alcoholism, but he does not analyse Mr. Utterson's drink-ing habits.

9. Nineteenth-century writers that have bachelor protagonists but do not limit themselves to male characters include Thomas Hardy, Anthony Trollope, Charles Dickens, George Gissing, Donald Grant Mitchell, Emily and Charlotte Brontë, George Eliot, Bram Stoker, Henry James, as well as the male adventure writers including Arthur Conan Doyle, Rider Hag-gard, and H.G. Wells.

## Chapter Six

1. For more on the meaning behind the term "pose," which was carefully cho-sen by Queensbury in his note to Wilde, see Dennis Denisoff's "Posing a Threat: Queensbury, Wilde, and the Portrayal of Decadence" and Sylvia Molloy's "The Pol-itics of Posing: Translating Decadence in Fin-de-Siècle Latin America" in *Perennial Decay: On the Aesthetics and Politics of Decadence.*

2. For more on Wilde's trials see: Den-nis Denisoff, "Posing a Threat: Queens-

bury, Wilde, and the Portrayal of Decadence." *Perennial Decay: On the Aesthetics and Politics of Decadence.* Eds. Liz Constable, Dennis Denisoff and Matthew Potolsky. Philadelphia: U Pennsylvania P, 1999. 83–100.; Merlin Holland, *Irish Peacock & Scarlet Marquess: The Real Trial of Oscar Wilde.* London: Fourth Estate, 2004; *The Real Trial of Oscar Wilde: The First Uncensored Transcript of the Trial of Oscar Wilde vs. John Douglas (Marquess of Queensbury), 1895* / Merlin Holland; foreword by John Mortimer.

# Bibliography

Adams, James Eli. *Dandies and Desert Saints: Styles of Victorian Manhood*. Ithaca, NY: Cornell University Press, 1995.

Allen, Emily. *Theater Figures: The Production of the Nineteenth-Century British Novel*. Columbus: Ohio State University Press, 2003.

Andres, Sophia. "Mary Elizabeth Braddon's Ambivalent Pre-Raphaelite Ekphrasis." *Victorian Newsletter* 108 (Fall 2005): 1–6.

Arata, Stephen D. *Fictions of Loss in the Victorian Fin de Siècle*. Cambridge: Cambridge University Press, 1996.

_____. "The Sedulous Ape: Atavism, Professionalism, and Stevenson's *Jekyll and Hyde*." *Criticism: A Quarterly for Literature and the Arts* 37.2 (Spring 1995): 233–59.

Ashton, Rosemary. *George Eliot*. Oxford: Oxford University Press, 1983.

Auerbach, Nina. *Private Theatricals: The Lives of the Victorians*. Cambridge, MA: Harvard University Press, 1990.

Avery, Simon. "'Some Strange and Spectral Dream': The Brontës' Manipulation of the Gothic Mode." *Brontë Society Transactions* 23.2 (1998): 120–135.

Barker, Juliet RV. *The Brontës*. New York: St. Martin's Press, 1994.

_____. "Saintliness, Treason and Plot: The Writing of Mrs. Gaskell's *Life of Charlotte Brontë*." *Brontë Society Transactions* 21.4 (1994): 101–15.

Barker-Benfield, G.J. *The Culture of Sensibility*. Chicago: Chicago University Press, 1992.

Baudelaire, Charles. "From *The Painter of Modern Life*." *The Norton Anthology of Theory and Criticism*. Ed. Vincent B. Leitch. New York: W.W. Norton & Co., 2001. 789–802.

Beach, Robert, Béatrice Craig, and Alastair Owens, Eds. *Women, Business and Finance in Nineteenth-century Europe: Rethinking Separate Spheres*. Oxford: Berg, 2006.

Beer, Gillian. *Darwin's Plots: Evolutionary Narrative in Darwin, George Eliot and Nineteenth-Century Fiction*. London: Ark Paperbacks, 1983.

_____. *George Eliot*. Key Women Writers. Brighton: The Harvester Press, 1986.

Beeton, Isabella. *Mrs. Beeton's Book of Household Management*. 1861. Ed. Nicola Humble. Oxford and New York: Oxford University Press, 2000.

Bentley, Phyllis. *The Brontës*. London: Thames & Hudson Inc., 1997.

Bertolini, Vicent J. "Fireside Chastity: The Erotics of Sentimental Bachelorhood in the 1850s." *American Liteature* 68.4 (Dec 1996): 707–37.

Block, Ed Jr. "James Sully, Evolutionary Psychology, and Late Victorian Gothic Fiction." *Victorian Studies* 25 (1982): 443–467.

Boone, Joseph Allen. *Tradition Counter Tradition: Love and the Form of Fiction*. Chicago: University Chicago Press, 1987.

# Bibliography

Boxer, Marilyn J., and Jean H. Quataert, Eds. *Connecting Spheres: Women in the Western World, 1500-Present.* New York: Oxford University Press, 1987.

Braddon, Mary Elizabeth. *Lady Audley's Secret.* 1862. Ed. Jennie Bourne Taylor. Toronto: Penguin Classics, 1998.

Brantlinger, Patrick. "What Is 'Sensational' About the 'Sensation Novel'?" *Nineteenth-Century Fiction* 37.1 (1982): 1–28.

Briganti, Chiara. "Gothic Maidens and Sensation Women: Lady Audley's Journey from the Ruined Mansion to the Madhouse." *Victorian Literature and Culture* 19 (1991): 189–211.

Bristow, Joseph. "Wilde, *Dorian Gray,* and Gross Indecency." *Sexual Sameness: Textual Differences in Lesbian and Gay Writing.* Ed. Joseph Bristow. London: Routledge, 1992. 44–63.

Brontë, Charlotte. *Shirley.* 1849. Ed. Andrew and Judith Hook. London: Penguin Books, 1985.

Brontë, Emily. *Wuthering Heights.* Ed.Ian Jack. Oxford: Oxford University Press, 998.

Butler, Judith. *Bodies That Matter: On the Discursive Limits of "Sex."* New York: Routledge, 1993.

_____. *Gender Trouble: Feminism and the Subversion of Identity.* New York: Routledge, 1990.

Caine, Barbara. *English Feminism (1780–1980).* Oxford: Oxford University Press, 1997.

Calloway, Stephen. "Wilde and the Dandyism of the Senses." *Cambridge Companion to Oscar Wilde.* Ed. Peter Raby. Cambridge, UK: Cambridge University Press, 1997. 34–54.

Castle, Terry. *Boss Ladies, Watch Out!: Essays on Women, Sex, and Writing.* New York: Routledge, 2002.

_____. *The Female Thermometer: 18th Century Culture and the Invention of the Uncanny.* Oxford: Oxford University Press, 1995.

Chase, Cynthia. *Decomposing Figures: Rhetorical Readings in the Romantic Tradition.* Baltimore: The Johns Hopkins University Press, 1986.

Chase, Karen, and Michael Levenson. *The Spectacle of Intimacy: A Public Life for the Victorian Family.* Princeton: Princeton University Press, 2000.

Christ, Carol. "'Victorian Masculinity and the Angel in the House." *A Widening Sphere: Changing Roles of Victorian Women.* Ed. Martha Vicinus. Bloomington: Indiana University Press, 1977. 146–62.

Clemens, Valdine. "Sentiment versus Horror: Generic Ambivalence in Female Gothic and Ann Radcliffe's A Sicilian Romance." *The Return of the Repressed: Gothic Horror from* The Castle of Otranto *to* Alien. New York: State University of New York Press, 1999. 41–58.

Clunas, Alex. "Comely External Utterance: Reading Space in *The Strange Case of Dr. Jekyll and Mr. Hyde.*" *Journal of Narrative Technique* 24.3 (Fall 1994): 173–89.

Cobbe, Francis Power. "What Shall We Do with Our Old Maids?" *'Criminals, Idiots, Women, and Minors': Victorian Writing by Women on Women.* Ed. Susan Hamilton. Peterborough, Canada: Broadview Press, 1996. 85–107.

Cocks, H. G. "Secrets, Crimes and Diseases, 1800–1914." *A Gay History of Britain: Love and Sex Between Men Since the Middle Ages.* Ed. Matt Cook. Oxford: Greenwood World Publishing, 2007. 107–44.

Cohen, Ed. *Talk on the Wilde Side: Toward a Genealogy of a Discourse on Male Sexualities.* New York: Routledge, 1993.

# Bibliography

Cohen, Michele. *Fashioning Masculinity*. New York: Routledge, 1996.

Cohen, Monica F. *Professional Domesticity in the Victorian Novel: Women, Work and Home*. Cambridge, UK: Cambridge University Press, 1998.

Conger, Syndy McMillen. "The Reconstruction of the Gothic Feminine Ideal in Emily Brontë's *Wuthering Heights*." Ed. Juliann E. Fleenor. *The Female Gothic*. Montreal: Eden Press, 1983. 91–106.

Congreve, William. *The Way of the World*. 1700. New York: Barron's Educational Series, 1958.

Craciun, Adriana. "Introduction." *Zofloya*. Peterborough, Canada: Broadview Press, 1997. 9–32.

Dacre, Charlotte. *Zofloya, or The Moor*. 1806. Ed. Kim Ian Michasiw. Oxford, UK: Oxford University Press, 1997.

D'Albertis, Deirdre. "'Bookmaking Out of the Remains of the Dead': Elizabeth Gaskell's *The Life of Charlotte Brontë*." *Victorian Studies*. 39.1 (1995): 1–31.

Dalton, Susan. *Engendering the Republic of Letters: Reconnecting Public and Private Spheres in Eighteenth-Century Europe*. Montreal: McGill-Queen's University Press, 2003.

Danahay, Martin A. *A Community of One: Masculine Autobiography and Autonomy in Nineteenth-Century Britain*. Albany: State University of New York Press, 1993.

_____. *Gender at Work in Victorian Culture: Literature, Art and Masculinity*. Aldershot, Hampshire: Ashgate, 2005.

David, Deirdre. *Fictions of Resolution in Three Victorian Novels: North and South, Our Mutual Friend, Daniel Deronda*. New York: Columbia University Press, 1981.

Davidson, Cathy N., and Jessamyn Hatcher Eds. *No More Separate Spheres!: A Next Wave American Studies Reader*. Durham: Duke University Press, 2002.

Dellamora, Richard. *Masculine Desire: The Sexual Politics of Victorian Aestheticism*. Chapel Hill: University of North Carolina Press, 1990.

Denisoff, Dennis. *Aestheticism and Sexual Parody 1840–1940*. Cambridge, UK: Cambridge University Press, 2001.

Dickens, Charles. *Bleak House*. 1852. Ed. Nicola Bradbury. Toronto: Penguin Books, 2003.

Doane, Janice, and Devon Hodges. "Demonic Disturbances of Sexual Identity: The Strange Case of Dr. Jekyll and Mr/s Hyde." *Novel: A Forum on Fiction* 23.2 (Fall 1989): 63–74.

Dolin, Tim. *George Eliot: Authors in Context*. Oxford: Oxford University Press, 2005.

Dowling, Andrew. "'The Other Side of Silence': Matrimonial Conflict and the Divorce Court in George Eliot's Fiction." *Nineteenth-Century Literature* 50.3 (1995): 322–36.

Dowling, Linda. *Hellenism and Homosexuality in Victorian Oxford*. Ithaca, NY: Cornell University Press, 1994.

Du Maurier, George. *Trilby*. 1894. Ed. Dennis Denisoff. Oxford: Oxford University Press, 1998.

Dunn, James A. "Charlotte Dacre and the Feminization of Violence." *Nineteenth-Century Literature*. 53.3 (1998): 307–327.

Eagleton, Terry. *Myths of Power: A Marxist Study of the Brontës*. 1975. New York: Palgrave Macmillan, 2005.

Eigen, Joel Peter. *Witnessing Insanity: Madness and Mad-Doctors in the English Court*. New Haven: Yale University Press, 1995.

# Bibliography

Eliot, George. *Daniel Deronda*. 1876. Ed. Graham Handley. Oxford and New York: Oxford University Press, 1998.

Ellis, Kate Ferguson. "Emily Bronte and the Technology of the Self." *The Contested Castle: Gothic Novels and the Subversion of Domestic Ideology*. Chicago: University of Illinois Press, 1989. 207–222.

Ellis, Sarah. *Women of England: Their Social Duties and Domestic Habits*. New York: Appleton, 1843.

Ewbank, Inga-Stina. *Their Proper Sphere: A Study of the Brontë Sisters as Early-Victorian Female Novelists*. London: Edward Arnold Publishers Ltd., 1966.

Fahnestock, Jeanne. "Bigamy: The Rise and Fall of a Convention." *Nineteenth-Century Fiction* 36.1 (1981): 47–71.

Felski, Rita. *The Gender of Modernity*. Harvard: Harvard University Press, 1995.

Fillin-Yeh, Susan. "Introduction: New Strategies for a Theory of Dandies." *Dandies: Fashion and Finesse in Art and Culture*. Ed. Susan Fillin-Yeh. New York: New York University Press, 2001. 1–34.

Fletcher, Ian Christopher, Laura E. Nym Mayhall, and Phillippa Levine, Eds. Women's Suffrage in the British Empire: Citizenship, Nation, and Race. New York: Routledge, 2000.

Foster, Gwendolyn Audrey. *Troping the Body: Gender, Etiquette, and Performance*. Carbondale: Southern Illinois University Press, 2000.

Foucault, Michel. *The History of Sexuality: An Introduction*. 1976. Trans. R. Hurley. 3 vols. New York: Vintage Books, 1990.

Franklin, J. Jeffrey. *Serious Play: The Cultural Form of the Nineteenth-Century Realist Novel*. Philadelphia: University Pennsylvania Press, 1999.

Gallagher, Catherine. *The Body Economic: Life, Death, and Sensation in Political Economy and the Victorian Novel*. Princeton: Princeton University Press, 2006.

_____. "George Eliot and *Daniel Deronda*: The Prostitute and the Jewish Question." *Sex, Politics, and Science in the Nineteenth-Century Novel*. Ed. Ruth Bernard Yeazell. Baltimore: The Johns Hopkins University Press, 1986: 39–62.

Garber, Marjorie. *Vested Interests: Cross-Dressing and Cultural Anxiety*. New York: Routledge, 1992.

Garelick, Rhonda K. *Rising Star: Dandyism, Gender, and Performance in the Fin de Siecle*. Princeton, NJ: Princeton University Press, 1998.

Gaskell, Elizabeth. *The Life of Charlotte Brontë*. 1st ed. New York: D'Appleton & Co., 1858.

Gaughan, Richard T. "Mr. Hyde and Mr. Seek: Utterson's Antidote." *Journal of Narrative Technique* 17.2 (Spring 1987): 184–97.

Gettelman, Debra. "Reading Ahead in George Eliot." *Novel* 39 (2005): 25–47.

Gilbert, Pamela K. *Disease, Desire, and the Body in Victorian Women's Popular Novels*. Cambridge, UK: Cambridge University Press, 1997.

_____. "Madness and Civilization: Generic Opposition in Mary Elizabeth Braddon's *Lady Audley's Secret*." *Essays in Literature* 23.2 (Fall 1996): 218–33.

Gill, Rebecca. "The Imperial Anxieties of a Nineteenth-Century Bigamy Case." *History Workshop Journal* 57 (2004): 59–78.

Gilmour, Robin. *The Idea of the Gentleman in the Victorian Novel*. London: George Allen & Unwin, 1981.

Glick, Elisa. "The Dialectics of Dandyism." *Cultural Critique* 48 (Spring 2001): 129–159.

Habermas, Jürgen. *The Structural Transformation of the Public Sphere: An Inquiry into a Category of Bourgeois Society*. 1962. Trans. Thomas Burger. Cambridge, MA: The MIT Press, 1989.

# Bibliography

Haggerty, George E. *Men in Love: Masculinity and Sexuality in the Eighteenth Century.* New York: Columbia University Press, 1999.

_____. *Queer Gothic.* Urbana: University of Illinois Press, 2006.

_____. *Unnatural Affections: Women and Fiction in the Later 18th-Century.* Bloomington: Indiana University Press, 1998.

Haight, Gordon S. *George Eliot: A Biography.* Oxford: Clarendon Press, 1968.

_____. ed. *The George Eliot Letters.* Vol. 6. New Haven: Yale University Press, 1955.

Hammerton, A. James. "Pooterism or Partnership? Marriage and Masculine Identity in the Lower Middle Class, 1870–1920." *Journal of British Studies* 38.3 (July 1999): 291–321.

_____. "Victorian Marriage and the Law of Matrimonial Cruelty." *Victorian Studies* 33 (1990): 269–92.

Hardy, Barbara. *George Eliot: A Critic's Biography.* London: Continuum, 2006.

Harris, Ruth. *Murders and Madness: Medicine, Law and Society in the Fin de Siècle.* Oxford: Clarendon Press, 1989.

Hart, Lynda. "The Victorian Villainess and the Patriarchal Unconscious." *Literature and Psychology* 40.3 (1994): 1–25.

Heath, Stephen. "Psychopathia Sexualis: Stevenson's *Strange Case.*" *Critical Quarterly* 28.1/2 (1986): 93- 108.

Hekma, Gert. "'A Female Soul in a Male Body': Sexual Inversion as Gender Inversion in Nineteenth-Century Sexology." Ed. Gilbert Herdt. *Third Sex, Third Gender: Beyond Sexual Dimorphism in Culture and History.* New York: Zone Books, 1994. 213–39.

Herzog, Annabel. "Tale of Two Secrets: A Rereading of Daniel Deronda." *Differences: A Journal of Feminist Cultural Studies* 16:2 (2005): 37–60.

Hoeveler, Diane Long. *Gothic Feminism.* Philadelphia: Pennsylvania State University Press, 1998.

Hoeveler, Diane Long, and Lisa Jadwin. *Charlotte Brontë.* New York: Twayne Publishers, 1997.

Hollander, Rachel. "Daniel Deronda and the Ethics of Alterity." *Literature Interpretation Theory* 16 (2005): 75–99.

Holmstrom, John, and Laurence Lerner, eds. *George Eliot and Her Readers: A Selection of Contemporary Reviews.* London: The Bodley Head, 1966.

Hook, Andrew, and Judith Hook. Introduction. *Shirley.* By Charlotte Brontë. London: Penguin Books,1985. 7–32.

Hopkins, Lisa. *Giants of the Past: Popular Fictions and the Idea of Evolution.* Lewisburg: Bucknell University Press, 2004.

Huggins, Mike, and J. A. Mangan. *Disreputable Pleasures: Less Virtuous Victorians at Play.* New York: Frank Cass, 2004.

Hughes, Winifred. *The Maniac in the Cellar: Sensation Novels of the 1860s.* Princeton, NJ: Princeton University Press, 1980.

Hurd, Madeleine. "Class, Masculinity, Manners, and Mores: Public Space and Public Sphere in Nineteenth-Century Europe." *Social Science History* 24.1 (2000): 75–110.

Irving, Washington. *The Sketch Book of Geoffrey Crayon, Gent.* 1820. New York: Modern Library, 2001.

Jagger, Gill. *Judith Butler: Sexual Politics, Social Change and the Power of the Performative.* London: Routledge, 2008.

James, Henry. "*Daniel Deronda*: A Conversation." 1876. *The Great Tradition: George Eliot, Henry James, Joseph Conrad.* Ed. F.R. Leavis. New York: George W. Stewart, 1948. 249–66.

# Bibliography

_____. *Henry James: Literary Criticism*. Ed. Leon Edel. New York: Library of America, 1984.

Johnson, Claudia L. "F. R. Leavis: The 'Great Tradition' of the English Novel and the Jewish Part." *Nineteenth-Century Literature* 56:2 (2001): 199–227.

Judd, Catherine. *Bedside Seductions: Nursing and the Victorian Imagination, 1830–1880*. New York: St. Martin's Press, 1998.

Kane, Michael. *Modern Men: Mapping Masculinity in English and German Literature, 1880–1930*. New York: Cassell, 1999.

Kanzer, Mark. "The Self-Analytic Literature of Robert Louis Stevenson." *Psychoanalysis and Culture*. Eds. George B. Wilbur and Warner Muensterberger. New York: International Universities Press, 1951. 425–435.

Kerber, Linda K., Nancy F. Cott, Robert Gross, Lynn Hunt, Carroll Smith-Rosenber, and Christine M. Stansell. "Beyond Roles, Beyond Spheres: Thinking about Gender in the Early Republic." *William and Mary Quarterly* 46 (July 1989): 565–85.

King, Andrew. *The London Journal, 1845–83: Periodicals, Production and Gender*. Aldershot, Hampshire: Ashgate, 2004.

Klein, Lawrence E. "Gender and the Public/Private Distinction in the Eighteenth Century: Some Questions about Evidence and Analytic Procedure." *Eighteenth-Century Studies* 19.1 (Autumn 1995): 97–109.

Kucich, John. *Repression in Victorian Fiction: Charlotte Brontë, George Eliot, and Charles Dickens*. Berkeley, LA: University California Press, 1987.

"The Ladies' Column." *The Penny Illustrated Paper* 24 (October 1868): 11.

"Lady Audley's Secret." *The Times* 24406 Nov. 18, 1862: 4C.

Landes, Joan B. *Women and the Public Sphere in the Age of the French Revolution*. Ithaca, NY: Cornell University Press, 1988.

Lane, Christopher. *The Burdens of Intimacy: Psychoanalysis and Victorian Masculinity*. Chicago: University of Chicago Press, 1999.

Lang, Andrew. "Review of *The Strange Case of Dr. Jekyll and Mr. Hyde*, by Robert Louis Stevenson." *Saturday Review* 61 (9 January 1886): 55–56.

Langland, Elizabeth. "Nobody's Angels: Domestic Ideology and Middle-Class Women in the Victorian Novel." *PMLA* 107.2 (1992): 290–304.

_____. *Telling Tales: Gender and Narrative Form in Victorian Literature and Culture*. Columbus: The Ohio State University Press, 2002.

Laqueur, Thomas W. *Solitary Sex: A Cultural History of Masturbation*. New York, Zone Books, 2003.

Leavis, F. R. *The Great Tradition: George Eliot, Henry James, Joseph Conrad*. New York: George W. Stewart, 1948.

Lesjak, Carolyn. *Working Fictions: A Genealogy of the Victorian Novel*. Durham: Duke University Press, 2006.

Lewes, G.H. "Currer Bell's *Shirley*." *Edinburgh Review* 91.183 (1850): 153–73.

Lieber, Francis. *The Character of the Gentleman*. Philadelphia: J.P. Lippincott & Co., 1864.

Lindemann, Ruth Burridge. "Dramatic Disappearances: Mary Elizabeth Braddon and the Staging of Theatrical Character." *Victorian Literature and Culture* 25.2 (1997): 279–91.

Linehan, Katherine Bailey. "'Closer Than a Wife': The Strange Case of Dr. Jekyll's Significant Other." *Robert Louis Stevenson Reconsidered: New Critical Perspectives*. Ed. William B. Jones, Jr. London: McFarland & Co., 2003. 85–99.

Linton, Eliza Lynn. "The Girl of the Period." 1868. *'Criminals, Idiots, Women, and*

# Bibliography

*Minors': Victorian Writing By Women On Women.* Ed. Susan Hamilton. Peterborough, Canada: Broadview P, 1996. 172–6.

Lipvak, Joseph. *Caught in the Act: Theatricality in the Nineteenth-Century English Novel.* Berkely: University of California Press, 1992.

Loesberg, Jonathan. "The Ideology of Narrative Form in Sensation Fiction." *Representations* 13 (1986): 115–138.

Logan, Thad. *The Victorian Parlour.* Cambridge, UK: Cambridge University Press, 2001.

"London Bachelors and Their Mode of Living." *Leisure Hour* 35 (1886): 239–42, 349–53, 413–16, 486–89.

Lovesey, Oliver. "The Other Woman in *Daniel Deronda.*" *Studies in the Novel* 30.4 (Winter 1998): 505–520.

Mainardi, Patricia. *Husbands, Wives, and Lovers: Marriage and Its Discontents in Nineteenth-Century France.* New Haven: Yale University Press, 2003.

Malane, Rachel. *Sex in Mind: The Gendered Brain in Nineteenth-Century Literature and Mental Sciences.* New York: Peter Lang, 2005.

"Marriage Versus Celibacy." *Belgravia* 6 (1868): 291–7.

Marshall, David. *The Figure of the Theater: Shaftesbury, Defoe, Adam Smith, and George Eliot.* New York: Columbia University Press, 1986.

Mason, Diane. *The Secret Vice: Masturbation in Victorian Fiction and Medical Culture.* Manchester: Manchester University Press, 2008.

Matus, Jill L. "Disclosure as 'Cover-up': The Discourse of Madness in *Lady Audley's Secret.*" *University of Toronto Quarterly* 62.3 (1993): 334–55.

_____. *Unstable Bodies: Victorian Representations of Sexuality and Maternity.* Manchester: Manchester University Press, 1995.

Maynard, John. *Charlotte Brontë and Sexuality.* Cambridge, UK: Cambridge University Press, 1984.

McCracken, Scott. "Embodying the New Woman: Dorothy Richardson, Work and the London Café." *Body Matters: Feminism, Textuality, Corporeality.* Eds. Avril Horner and Angela Keane. Manchester: Manchester University Press, 2000. 58–71.

McKee, Patricia. *Public and Private: Gender, Class, and the British Novel (1764–1878).* Minneapolis: University of Minnesota Press, 1997.

McMullen, Lorraine. *An Introduction to the Aesthetic Movement in English Literature.* Ottawa: Bytown Press, 1971.

Melling, Joseph, and Bill Forsythe eds. *Insanity, Institutions and Society, 1800–1914: A Social History of Madness in Comparative Perspective.* New York: Routledge, 1999.

Mellor, Anne K. "Interracial Sexual Desire in Charlotte Dacre's *Zofloya.*" *European Romantic Review* 13 (2002): 169–173.

Miles, Robert. "Avatars of Matthew Lewis' *The Monk*: Ann Radcliffe's *The Italian* and Charlotte Dacre's *Zofloya: Or, The Moor.*" *Gothic Writing 1750–1820.* New York: Routledge, 1993. 160–188.

Miller, D.A. *The Novel and the Police.* Berkeley: University of California Press, 1988.

Miller, Elizabeth Carolyn. *Framed: The New Woman Criminal in British Culture at the Fin de Siècle.* Ann Arbor: University Press of Michigan Press & Library, 2008.

Miller, Karl. *Doubles: Studies in Literary History.* London: Oxford University Press, 1987.

Mitchell, Donald G. *Reveries of a Bachelor.* New York: Charles Scribner's Sons, 1889.

Moore, Grace. "Something to Hyde: The 'Strange Preference' of Henry Jekyll." *Victorian Crime, Madness and Sensation.* Eds. Andrew Maunder and Grace Moore. Aldershot, England: Ashgate, 2004. 147–61.

# Bibliography

Morgan, Thais. "Victorian Effeminacies." *Victorian Sexual Dissidence.* Ed. Richard Dellamora. Chicago: University of Chicago Press, 1999. 109–126.

Morris, Virginia B. *Double Jeopardy: Women Who Kill in Victorian Fiction.* Kentucky: University Press of Kentucky, 1990.

Mort, Frank. *Dangerous Sexualities: Medico-Moral Politic in England Since 1830.* 2nd ed. London and New York: Routledge, 2000.

Murphy, Margueritte. "The Ethic of the Gift in George Eliot's *Daniel Deronda.*" *Victorian Literature and Culture* 34 (2006):189–207.

Nabokov, Vladimir. "*The Strange Case of Dr. Jekyll and Mr. Hyde.*" *Lectures on Literature.* Ed. Fredson Bowers. London: Weidenfeld & Nicolson, 1980. 179–204.

Nelson, Carolyn Christensen, ed. *A New Woman Reader: Fiction, Articles, and Drama of the 1890s.* Peterborough, Canada: Broadview Press, 2001.

Nemesvari, Richard. "Robert Audley's Secret: Male Homosocial Desire in *Lady Audley's Secret.*" *Studies in the Novel* 27.4 (1995): 515–28.

Nicholson, Linda J. *Gender and History: The Limits of Social Theory in the Age of the Family.* New York: Columbia University Press, 1986.

Nordau, Max. *Degeneration.* New York: D. Appleton & Co., 1902.

Norton, Rictor. *Mother Clap's Molly House: The Gay Subculture in England 1700–1830.* Gloucestershire, UK: Chalford Press, 2006.

Nunokawa, Jeff. *The Afterlife of Property: Domestic Security and the Victorian Novel.* Princeton, NJ: Princeton University Press, 1994.

_____. "Homosexual Desire and the Effacement of the Self in *The Picture of Dorian Gray.*" *American Imago* 49.3 (1992): 311–321.

O'Connell, Lisa. "Marriage Acts: Stages in the Transformation of Modern Nuptial Culture." *A Journal of Feminist Cultural Studies* 11.1 (1999): 68–111.

Orel, Harold, ed. *The Brontës: Interviews and Recollections.* Iowa City: University of Iowa Press, 1997.

Pallo, Vicki A. "From Do-Nothing to Detective: The Transformation of Robert Audley in Lady Audley's Secret." Journal of Popular Culture 39.3 (June 2006): 466–78.

Pankhurst, Sylvia. *The Suffragette Movement: An Intimate Account of Persons and Ideals.* New York: Longmans, Green & Co., 1931.

Parkins, Wendy. "'Transparent Allegory' and Charlotte Brontë's *Shirley.*" *Brontë Society Transactions* 20.3 (1991): 127–132.

Pateman, Carole. *The Sexual Contract.* Palo Alto: Stanford University Press, 1988.

Patmore, Coventry. *The Angel in the House.* Eds. Thomas J. Collins and Vivienne J. Rundle. *The Broadview Anthology of Victorian Poetry and Poetic Theory.* Peterborough, Canada: Broadview Press, 1999. 739–760.

Paxton, Nancy L. *George Eliot and Herbert Spencer: Feminism, Evolutionism, and the Reconstruction of Gender.* Princeton, NJ: Princeton University Press, 1991.

Peschier, Diana. *Nineteenth-Century Anti-Catholic Discourses: The Case of Charlotte Brontë.* New York: Palgrave Macmillan, 2005.

Petch, Simon. "Robert Audley's Profession." *Studies in the Novel* 32.1 (2000): 1–13.

Phillips, Roderick. *Putting Asunder: A History of Divorce in Western Society.* Cambridge, UK: Cambridge University Press, 1988.

Picker, John M. "George Eliot and the Sequel Question." *New Literary History* 37 (2006): 361–388.

Plotz, John. *Portable Property: Victorian Culture on the Move.* Princeton, NJ: Princeton University Press, 2008.

Poovey, Mary. *Uneven Developments: The Ideological Work of Gender in Mid-*

# Bibliography

*Victorian England.* Women in Culture and Society. Chicago: University of Chicago Press, 1988.

Powell, Kerry. *Women and the Victorian Theatre.* Cambridge, UK: Cambridge University Press, 1998.

Press, Jacob. "Same-Sex Unions in Modern Europe: *Daniel Deronda, Altneuland,* and the Homoerotics of Jewish Nationalism." *Novel Gazing: Queer Readings in Fiction.* Ed. Eve Kosofsky Sedgwick. Durham: Duke University Press, 1997: 299–329.

Ramelson, Marian. *The Petticoat Rebellion: A Century of Struggle for Women's Rights.* London: Lawrence & Wishart, 1967.

Riquelme, John Paul. "Oscar Wilde's Aesthetic Gothic: Walter Pater, Dark Enlightenment, and *The Picture of Dorian Gray.*" *Modern Fiction Studies* 46.3 (2000): 609–631.

Robinson, Daniel N. *Wild Beast and Idle Humours: The Insanity Defense from Antiquity to the Present.* Cambridge, MA: Harvard University Press, 1996.

Robinson, Solveig C. ed. *A Serious Occupation: Literary Criticism by Victorian Women Writers.* Peterborough, Canada: Broadview Press, 2003.

Roper, Michael, and John Tosh, eds. *Manful Assertions: Masculinities in Britain Since 1800.* New York: Routledge, 1991.

Rosenberg, Rosalind. *Beyond Separate Spheres: Intellectual Roots of Modern Feminism.* New Haven, CT: Yale University Press, 1982.

Rosenberg, Sheila. "Encounters in the *Westminster Review*: Dialogues on Marriage and Divorce." Eds. Laurel Brake and Julie F. Codell. *Encounters in the Victorian Press: Editors, Authors, Readers.* New York: Palgrave Macmillan, 2005.

Rosenman, Ellen Bayuk. "'Mimic Sorrows': Masochism and the Gendering of Pain in Victorian Melodrama." *Studies in the Novel* 35.1 (2003): 22–43.

Rover, Constance. *Women's Suffrage and Party Politics in Britian, 1866–1914.* Toronto: University of Toronto Press, 1967.

Ruskin, John. *Sesame and Lilies.* 1865. New Haven, CT: Yale University Press, 2002.

Russo, Mary. *The Female Grotesque: Risk, Excess and Modernity.* New York: Routledge. 1995.

Schmid, Susanne. "Byron and Wilde: The Dandy and the Public Sphere." *The Importance of Reinventing Oscar: Versions of Wilde during the Last 100 Years.* Eds. Boker, Uwe, Richard Corballis and Julie A. Hibbard. Amsterdam: Rodopi, 2002. 81–89.

Sedgwick, Eve Kosofsky. *Between Men: English Literature and Male Homosocial Desire.* New York: Columbia University Press, 1985.

_____. "The Character in the Veil: Imagery of the Surfaces in the Gothic Novel." *Publications of the Modern Language Association* 96 (1981): 255–270.

Showalter, Elaine. "Family Secrets and Domestic Subversion: Rebellion in the Novels of the 1860s." *The Victorian Family.* Ed. Anthony S. Wohl. London: Croom Helm, 1978.

_____. *The Female Malady: Women, Madness, and English Culture, 1830–1980.* New York: Penguin Books, 1987.

_____. *A Literature of Their Own: British Women Novelists from Brontë to Lessing.* 1977. Princeton: Princeton University Press, 1999.

_____. *Sexual Anarchy: Gender and Culture at the Fin de Siècle.* New York: Penguin Books, 1990.

Shuttleworth, Sally. *Charlotte Brontë and Victorian Psychology.* Cambridge, UK: Cambridge University Press, 1996.

Sinfield, Alan. *The Wilde Century: Effeminacy, Oscar Wilde and the Queer Moment.* New York: Columbia University Press, 1994.

# Bibliography

Skultans, Vieda. *Madness and Morals: Ideas on Insanity in the Nineteenth Century.* London: Routledge; Boston: Kegan Paul, 1975.

Smith, Adam. *The Theory of Moral Sentiments.* Ed. Knud Haakonssen. Cambridge, UK: Cambridge University Press, 2002.

Smith, Andrew. *Victorian Demons: Medicine, Masculinity and the Gothic at the Fin de Siècle.* Manchester: Manchester University Press, 2004.

Snyder, Katherine V. *Bachelors, Manhood, and the Novel 1850–1925.* Cambridge, UK: Cambridge University Press, 1999.

Spark, Muriel, ed. *The Letters of The Brontës: A Selection.* Norman: University of Oklahoma Press, 1954.

Stephens, Elizabeth. "Pathologizing Leaky Male Bodies: Spermatorrhea in Nineteenth-Century British Medicine and Popular Anatomical Museums." *Journal of the History of Sexuality.* 17.3 (September 2008): 420–38.

Stevenson, John Allen. "'Heathcliff is Me!': *Wuthering Heights* and the Question of Likeness." *Nineteenth-Century Literature* 43.1 (1988): 60–81.

Stevenson, Robert Louis. *The Letters of Robert Louis Stevenson.* Ed. Bradford A. Booth and Ernest Mehew. Vol. 5. New Haven, CT: Yale University Press, 1995.

_____. *The Strange Case of Dr. Jekyll and Mr. Hyde.* 1886. Ed. Martin A. Danahay. Peterborough, Canada: Broadview Press, 1999.

Storer, Richard. "Leavis and 'Gwendolen Harleth.'" *F. R. Leavis: Essays and Documents.* Eds. Ian MacKillop and Richard Storer. London: Continuum, 2005 (1995): 40–9.

Sturrock, June. "Murder, Gender, and Popular Fiction by Women in the 1860s: Braddon, Oliphant, Yonge." *Victorian Crime, Madness and Sensation.* Eds. Andrew Maunder and Grace Moore. Hampshire, UK: Ashgate, 2004. 73–88.

Sussman, Herbert. *Victorian Masculinities: Manhood and Masculine Poetics in Early Victorian Literature and Art.* Cambridge, UK: Cambridge University Press, 1995.

Symonds, John Addington. *Male Love: A Problem in Greek Ethics and Other Writings.* New York: Pagan Press, 1983.

Sypher, Eileen. "Resisting Gwendolen's 'Subjection': *Daniel Deronda*'s Proto-feminism." *Studies in the Novel* 28.4 (Winter 1996): 506–24.

Tatar, Maria M. *Spellbound: Studies on Mesmerism and Literature.* Princeton, NJ: Princeton University Press, 1978.

Thomas, Ronald R. *Dreams of Authority: Freud and the Fictions of the Unconscious.* Ithaca, NY: Cornell University Press, 1990.

Thormählen, Marianne. *The Brontës and Religion.* Cambridge, UK: Cambridge University Press, 1999.

Tilley, Elizabeth. "Gender and Role-Playing in Lady Audley's Secret." *Studies in Literature* 16 (1995): 197–204.

Toker, Leona. "Vocation and Sympathy in *Daniel Deronda*: The Self and the Larger Whole." *Victorian Literature and Culture* 32.2 (2004): 565–74.

Torgerson, Beth. *Reading the Brontë Body: Disease, Desire, and the Constraints of Culture.* New York: Palgrave Macmillan, 2005.

Tosh, John. *Manliness and Masculinities in Nineteenth-Century Britain: Essays on Gender, Family, and Empire.* New York: Pearson Longman, 2005.

Tromp, Marlene. "Gwendolen's Madness." *Victorian Literature and Culture* 28.2 (2000): 451–67.

Tromp, Marlene, Pamela K. Gilbert, and Aeron Haynie, eds. *Beyond Sensation: Mary Elizabeth Braddon in Context.* Albany: State University of New York Press, 2000.

# Bibliography

Trumbach, Randolph. *Sex and the Gender Revolution: Heterosexuality and the Third Gender in Enlightenment London.* Vol.1. Chicago: University of Chicago Press, 1998.

Uglow, Jennifer. Introduction. *Lady Audley's Secret.* By Mary Elizabeth Braddon. London: Virago, 1985. i–xix.

Veeder, William. "Children of the Night: Stevenson and Patriarchy." *Dr. Jekyll and Mr. Hyde after One Hundred Years.* Eds. William Veeder and Gordon Hirsch. Chicago: University of Chicago Press, 1988. 107–55.

Vickery, Amanda. "Golden Age to Separate Spheres?: A Review of the Categories and Chronology of English Women's History." *Historical Journal* 36.2 (1993): 383–414.

Voskuil, Lynn M. "Acts of Madness: Lady Audley and the Meanings of Victorian Femininity." *Feminist Studies* 27.3 (2001): 611–39.

_____. "Feeling Public: Sensation Theater, Commodity Culture, and the Victorian Public Sphere." *Victorian Studies* 44.2 (2002): 245–74.

Vrettos, Athena. *Somatic Fictions: Imagining Illness in Victorian Culture.* Stanford, CA: Stanford University Press, 1995.

Wagner, Tamara S. "'Overpowering Vitality': Nostalgia and Men of Sensibility in the Fiction of Wilkie Collins." *Modern Language Quarterly* 63.4 (2002): 471–500.

Ward, Ian. "The Case of Helen Huntington." *Criticism* 49.2 (2007): 151–182.

Warren, Joyce W. *Women, Money, and the Law: Nineteenth-Century Fiction, Gender, and the Courts.* Iowa City: University of Iowa Press, 2005.

Waters, Karen Volland. *The Perfect Gentleman: Masculine Control in Victorian Men's Fiction 1870–1901.* New York: Peter Lang, 1997.

Weed, David M. "Sexual Positions: Men of Pleasure, Economy, and Dignity in Boswell's London Journal." Eighteenth-Century Studies 31.2 (1997–98): 215–234.

Weeks, Jeffrey. *Sex, Politics & Society: The Regulation of Sexuality Since 1800.* 2nd ed. London: Longman, 1989.

Welsh, Alexander. *George Eliot and Blackmail.* Cambridge, MA: Harvard University Press, 1985.

Wilde, Oscar. *The Picture of Dorian Gray.* 1891. Ed. Isobel Murray. Oxford: Oxford University Press, 1994.

Willburn, Sarah. "Possessed Individualism in George Eliot's *Daniel Deronda.*" *Victorian Literature and Culture* 34 (2006): 271–89.

Williams, M. Kellen. "'Down with the Door, Poole'": Designating Deviance in Stevenson's *Strange Case of Dr. Jekyll and Mr. Hyde.*" *English Literature in Transition (1880–1920)* 39.4 (1996): 412–29.

Willy. *The Third Sex.* Trans. Lawrence R. Schehr. Urbana: University of Illinois Press, 2007.

Wingerden, Sophia A. van. *The Women's Suffrage Movement in Britain, 1866–1928.* New York: St. Martin's Press, 1999.

Winter, Kari.J. "Sexual/Textual Politics of Terror: Writing and Rewriting the Gothic Genre in the 1790s." *Misogyny in Literature: An Essay Collection.* Ed. Katherine Anne Ackley. New York: Garland, 1992. 89–103.

Wise, Thomas J. and Alexander Symington. *The Brontës: Their Lives, Friendships and Correspondence.* 4 vols. Oxford: Blackwell, 1980.

Wollstonecraft, Mary. *A Vindication of the Rights of Woman.* 1792. New York: Dover Publications, 1996.

Womack, Kenneth. "'Withered, Wrinkled, and Loathsome of Visage': Reading the Ethics of the Soul and the Late-Victorian Gothic in *The Picture of Dorian Gray.*" *Victorian Gothic.* Eds. Ruth Robbins and Julian Wolfreys. New York: Palgrave Publishing, 2000. 168–181.

# Bibliography

Wright, Daniel L. "'The Prisonhouse of My Disposition': A Study in the Psychology of Addiction in *Dr. Jekyll and Mr. Hyde.*" *Studies in the Novel* 26.3 (Fall 1994): 254–267.

Yaeger, Patricia. "Violence in the Sitting Room: *Wuthering Heights* and the Woman's Novel." *Genre* 21.2 (1998). 203–229.

# Index

# Index